Tarnished Memories

Jennifer Harrison

Visit www.jenniferharrisonwrites.com

Cover Design: Seyi Paul

Amazon: https://www.amazon.com/author/jennifer_harrison

Goodreads: https://www.goodreads.com/jenniferharrison

Instagram: https://www.instagram.com/jennifer.harrison.writes/

Facebook: https://www.facebook.com/jennifer.harrison.writes

TikTok: https://www.tiktok.com/@jennifer..harrison

Playlist

Miss Me More - Kelsey Ballerini

Whatever it Takes - Imagine Dragons

Body Like a Back Road - Sam Hunt

God Gave Me You - Blake Shelton

H.O.L.Y - Florida Georgia Line

Alone Together - Fall Out Boy

Like I'll Never Love You Again - Carrie Underwood

Marry Me - Thomas Rhett

House of Memories - Panic at the Disco

Better Man - Little Big Town

Rockstar - Nickelback

Hey Look Ma, I Made It - Panic at the Disco

All-American Girl - Carrie Underwood

Author Note

Hello readers,

Thank you so much for picking up my book. Before you get started, I wanted to give you a quick warning. This story contains mention of, and later a flashback to, an attempted suicide. This scene can, understandably, be upsetting from some readers. If you feel this may impact you negatively, you have a couple of options. You can skip the second half of Chapter 31 or skip the book entirely. Only you know what's best for you.

I hope you enjoy Ember and Wes' story.

To the girls who were always told they had to have it all figured out.

I see you.

Ember

Wesley Barrett was my everything. Things were perfect, we were making plans for the future, I just had to finish High School.

But then he cheated on me.

My parents turned on me.

And I ran as far away as I could get with zero intention of ever returning.

Seven years later a phone call from my brother had me heading back to the small town I grew up in.

Everything was exactly the same as I remembered it. And the man who wrecked me still made my heart flutter.

Wes

A broken heart sent me a thousand miles from home. I thought I knew what love was. And then I met her. Ember Davis was everything I never knew I needed.

She saw me in a way no one ever had, and I was ready to give her the world. Then one mistake destroyed everything.

She ran, and I had no choice but to face my new reality. A reality without her.

It's been seven years, and she's back. Things aren't what they appear to be and it's my chance to explain, if only she would let me.

CHAPTER ONE

Coyote Ridge

PRESENT

Ember

I blew out a frustrated sigh. I could pull every hanger from my closet, and it wouldn't change the fact that I only owned a single dress. And if that wasn't bad enough, it still had the tags on it from when I bought it - two years ago.

My pajamas sat folded on top of my dresser, taunting me. "I'm just gonna cancel," I mumbled into my phone, crossing the small space to plop down on my bed.

"No. You're not," My best friend's voice was laced with humor.

"I can't do this, Tatum!" I threw my hand up in the air. "I don't even know what I was thinking, saying yes."

She chuckled, "You were thinking that he's a fine as hell man and you haven't gotten laid in seven years."

My face flushed pink. "It's not like that."

"Look, Em. Do you like him?"

I bit my lip. It wasn't a matter of liking him or not. Brent was a genuinely nice guy. Smart, driven, so damn hot, and he was interested in me, as evidenced by the months he spent asking me out, not fazed when I politely declined. Then the way his face lit up when I finally agreed to dinner. "I... Yeah."

"Then what's the problem?"

I fell backward with a bounce when my head hit the mattress. "It's just... I don't know! It's complicated."

She sighed; all humor gone. "Babe. I know you're scared, but you've gotta get back out there."

A dull ache in my chest reminded me why "getting back out there" was never on my list of things to do. Getting back out there meant moving on. Moving on meant closing the door on a monumental part of my life. While I'd happily give up the pain of the past, it wasn't that easy. I rubbed over my heart with the heel of my hand, trying to soothe the pain. "But what if..."

"Don't do that, Em. You've been in this holding pattern since..."

"Don't say it," I cut her off.

"I wasn't gonna mention he who shan't be named," she chuckled. "Girl code, right?"

I squeezed my eyes shut and took a deep breath, blowing it out slowly. "It's been seven years," I murmured, as though that made a difference. There was no statute of limitations on heartbreak.

"That's what I'm sayin'!"

I sat up, looked at my open closet door and swallowed thickly, "Do you think I'm ready?"

"Only you know for sure, babe. But you'll never know unless you try."

"I guess."

"When is he picking you up?"

I glanced at the time. "In an hour?"

"You better stop stalling and get ready."

"I hate you," I growled into the phone.

She barked out a laugh. "Call me when you get home. I want to hear all about it."

"I'm scared," I whispered.

"I know, but it's just dinner. Worst case scenario, you don't have to cook tonight."

I blew out a heavy breath. I went back to my closet and pulled out the navy-blue wrap dress. "Yeah, okay. Love you."

"Love you too. And don't forget - I want details."

"Yeah, yeah. Call you later."

I set my phone on my dresser and held the dress up in front of the mirror. I caught my cat's eye in the reflection. "I can do this. It's only a date, right Mr. Jangles?" The orange tabby cat just stared back at me.

I reluctantly clipped the tags off and slipped it on, smoothing the skirt down over my hips until it stopped several inches above my knees.

Flutters filled my chest as I looked at my reflection in the mirror. The dress looked better than I expected. The sweetheart neckline overlapped, wrapping down around the bodice leading to a low cut in the back. The skirt flowed loosely, flaring just a little when I twisted from side to side.

I turned so I could see the back, gathering my long honey-blonde hair in my hand and held it up. A shiver rolled through me; the dress showed a lot of skin.

"You can do this, Ember. It's just a date," I told myself. *It's just a date.*

I took my time curling the ends of my hair, so it flowed in loose waves down my back. At least it would cover what the dress didn't. I leaned in close to the mirror and ran my fingers over the light smattering of freckles that decorated my cheeks and nose. I pretty much never wore makeup, but this was a special occasion, so I grabbed my mascara and ran the wand over my lashes a few times, making my blue eyes pop.

My mouth was suddenly dry and the ache in my chest was back. Seven years later and his voice, even in my head, sounded exactly the same. *"...your cornflower blue eyes... I could disappear into their depths and be perfectly at peace"*

I replaced the wand back inside the tube of mascara and flicked off the light. That was enough primping for one night.

Soft lighting and candles gave the restaurant that gentle, romantic ambiance. It was nice; easily the nicest restaurant I've ever been to.

"You look beautiful tonight." Brent pulled my chair out for me.

"Thank you." I caught a hint of his cologne, warm and musky. He smelled really good, yet it did nothing for me. *Shouldn't I feel something? Want or desire or... something?*

When he took his seat across from me, he looked nervous, which oddly put me a little more at ease. "Thank you for bringing me here."

"You're welcome." He lifted his menu, and I did the same, studying him over the top of it. He was clean shaven, his sandy brown hair carefully styled. He was well built; his burgundy button-down shirt had the top two buttons undone revealing smooth tan skin. He had the sleeves cuffed up, exposing his strong forearms.

Brent was the epitome of man-candy. Unfortunately, he didn't give me butterflies.

"Where are you from?" I asked, realizing I didn't really know anything about him. Maybe the butterflies would come later...

"From here. I've lived in Coyote Ridge all my life."

"I'd ask how you like it, but since you're still here, I imagine that's a good thing."

He chuckled. "When I was younger, all I wanted was to leave. Then I did, and I realized just how much I love it here. How about you? Where are you from?"

I cleared my throat, "Um," I took a sip of my water, debating how much I wanted to share. I generally pretended my life before didn't exist. That my life began the day I crested the top of the mountain. "I'm from Nebraska," I finally offered.

"Corn..." He mused, his lips tipping up into a smile.

I laughed, "It's not all corn!"

"So, what brings you all the way out here?"

I thought about it for a moment, again debating just how much I wanted to share. Home was a black hole of feelings I preferred to shove down and ignore. The closest to home I ever wanted to get was a phone call to my brother or my best friend. "One day I woke up and decided to head west, check out California," I got straight to the point. "Then my car had other plans and broke down just outside of town. I never quite realized how much car repairs cost, so instead of continuing on to Cali, I spent my last dime getting her fixed. Thankfully they needed help at the diner, so I was able to get a job while I handled things."

"Why didn't you leave when you had your car fixed?"

I shrugged. "It just didn't seem as important anymore." I took another long sip of water and changed the subject. "So, tell me about you? Have you always wanted to work in real estate?"

I was surprised at just how easy he was to talk to. The waiter brought our orders as we continued to chat about his job, his family, things he enjoyed. Every time he tried to steer the conversation to me and my life, I kept it light, and he never pushed for more. It was refreshing.

Belly full, I pushed my plate away and leaned back casually in my chair, wine glass in hand.

"Do you want any dessert?" He asked, still working through his steak.

Something about Brent felt effortless, comfortable, and while I should have felt awkward, waiting for him to finish eating, I didn't. "No, I'm good," I said, smiling over the top of my glass.

He took another bite and pushed his plate aside. "Sorry I'm taking so long," he laughed uncomfortably. "I can take the rest of this to go."

I sat up and reached across the table, placing my hand over his. "No, it's fine. Really. I'm enjoying your company."

"You are?"

My cheeks heated with embarrassment and the realization that I was having a good time. Then his russet brown eyes met mine and I had to look away. "I am. I'm…" I pulled my hand back and held it in my lap. "I'm sorry it took me so long to come around."

"Hey," he reached over, lightly grazing his fingers over my cheek. "We're here now. Nothing else matters."

For the first time since he picked me up, I felt a nervous flutter in my stomach. He looked like he wanted to kiss me, and honestly it wouldn't take much for him to lean in and press his lips to mine. The idea made my breath stall in my lungs, and a nervous sweat broke out between my shoulder blades.

I took a deep breath and leaned into his hand, hoping he would just do it and get me out of my head. My heart raced as he leaned closer, pausing just inches from me as if asking permission. I swallowed thickly, gave a small nod and closed my eyes just as my phone started to ring.

I jumped back; the moment was broken.

"I'm so sorry, I..." I reached into my purse, which was draped over the back of my chair. My phone was set to Do Not Disturb, so it had to be important. I only had one person setup as allowed, and I had mixed feelings about seeing his face lighting up my screen.

I swiped to answer. "Hold on a sec," I whispered in greeting. I covered the mouthpiece. "It's my brother. I... I need to take this. I'll be right back."

Brent's smile was warm and genuine. "No worries."

I held the phone to my ear as I hurried to the bathroom near the back of the restaurant. "Miles? What's up?" I finally asked once I was inside and confirmed the stalls were empty.

"Hey, Em. Is everything okay? You sound weird."

I leaned back against the sink. "I'm..." I blew out a heavy breath. "I'm on a date."

"Oh, shit. Um..." His voice was strained, sending my imagination into hyperdrive.

"What is it? You don't normally call me on Saturdays, especially at this time of night." I sucked in a sharp breath. "Is it Lainey? Did something happen?"

His shallow breaths filled the line, sending my anxiety through the roof. "Miles?" I prompted.

"It's mom. She..." His voice cracked and my stomach sank.

"What? Talk to me, Miles. Is she okay?"

"I don't know," he whispered. "She... she's in surgery now."

"What happened?"

"Some sort of accident at work. I don't have all the details, just... God, Em. There was so much blood."

I gripped my phone tighter, my knuckles turning white. "She's gonna be fine though, right?"

"You need to come home."

I pressed my fingers to my forehead and squeezed my eyes shut.

"Em? I need you."

"I..." my chest felt like it was being squeezed by a vice. "I-I can't," I whispered.

"Please, Em? I can't do this on my own."

"Where's dad? And..." I clenched my jaw, memories of the last time I saw my parents flooded my senses, knocking me off balance. I took a deep breath and blew it out slowly as I fought to control my emotions.

"They're here... well, dad is. Ken..."

"Don't," I cut him off sharply. I had a hard enough time *thinking* her name, I couldn't stand to hear it.

"You know I wouldn't ask you to come back here unless it was important, right? I wouldn't do that to you."

"I know," I managed. My brother was the strongest person I knew. He never asked for anything. I turned around and gripped the sink as worst-case scenarios played out in high definition in my mind.

"So, you'll come?"

I squeezed my eyes shut and nodded. "I'll be there tomorrow."

"Thank you!"

The relief in his voice told me I was doing the right thing, but it didn't change the sick feeling in my stomach or the tremor that ran through my body. My breath came out in short pants as I fought to keep the panic at bay. "I-I need..."

"I know. I'll keep them away. I promise."

Brent pulled into the empty space beside my car and killed the engine. "Is there anything I can do?" he asked.

"Thank you, but no."

I pulled the handle and before I was all the way out of the car, he was right there, taking my hand in his. "Are you going to be okay?"

I lifted one shoulder in a half shrug, honestly not knowing. Going home was never an option. Nothing, and I mean *nothing* could make me go back... except Miles. And my mom too, apparently. For some reason I still cared...

He walked me to my door and waited until I was just inside before asking, "Will you call me?"

The concern in his eyes made everything so much harder. On a normal day, he was hot. Seeing this side of him, sensitive and vulnerable made me want to give him anything. "Brent..." I looked down and with shaky hands smoothed the length of my dress as conflicting emotions warred in my chest.

"It's okay," he took a step back, his hand rubbing the back of his neck nervously. "Just... Let me know when you're back in town."

I released a shaky breath and nodded. I turned to close the door at the same time he stopped it with his foot. "I had a good time tonight. I didn't want to leave without telling you."

I brought my eyes back up to his and that little flutter I felt at dinner was back. I sucked in a ragged breath and licked my lips. If I was going home, I wanted to do it knowing the taste and feel of another man's lips. I needed to.

I stood up on my toes and brought my mouth to his in a gentle kiss. His hands cupped my cheeks as my lips parted and our tongues touched. His lips were soft, his mouth tasted sweet, but it was all wrong.

I pulled away as pain lanced through my heart. I had finally kissed another man, and all I could think about was *him*. A tear rolled down my cheek and I quickly swiped it away. "Thank you for tonight," I whispered. "I had a really nice time."

His strong hands held my face, his thumbs brushing the tears away. "I really like you, Ember. Let me know when you get there so I know you're safe."

"Goodnight."

I closed the door and fell back into it, unable to make myself move. I touched my fingers to my lips, as though I could still feel him. I sucked in a ragged breath as a sob broke free. I couldn't do it, yet I knew I had to.

I pulled my phone out and called Tatum.

She answered on the first ring. "It's only nine! Was he that bad?"

I choked on a sob as my body slid down the length of the door until I was little more than a heap on the floor. Of course the first thing she would think of was how my date went. "It was okay," I managed.

"Just okay? A man should never be *just okay*, Em."

"Tatum!"

"Well, I'm gonna need more information. It's early, so either the sex was bad, or the date was. Which is it?"

I resisted the urge to laugh. "No, we barely kissed," I sniffled, swiping at my nose with the back of my hand.

"That bad, huh? Damn, girl..."

"Tatum," I groaned, desperately needing for her to stop thinking about Brent and sex. "Have you heard about my mom?"

"Your mom? No, why? Did something happen?"

I pulled my knees to my chest, suddenly remembering I was wearing a dress. I blew out a shaky breath and managed to get to my feet.

"Wait..." Tatum said, followed by whispered voices and then the snick of a door closing. "Was your mom at work tonight?"

I stared at my closet, knowing I had a suitcase stuffed in the back. I held my phone to my ear with my shoulder as I grabbed the handle, yanking it over yet another box of stuff I could never look at or bring myself to get rid of. "I don't know! Yeah, maybe?" I snapped when my suitcase snagged the top of the box, knocking it over and spilling its contents.

"Hon, there was an accident at the factory tonight."

"What?"

"I don't know much, just that something happened that shut it down. There were police cars and an ambulance out front when I drove past. I didn't even think about it because your mom doesn't usually work weekends."

The corner of a picture frame caught the light and I quickly turned away, ignoring the spilled box, and tossed the suitcase on my bed. I started throwing clothes in it, not even bothering to fold them, as I forced myself to focus on the task at hand. "Miles called, said she was in surgery, but that was it." I groaned, "I didn't really give him much of a chance to talk."

"Why?" she asked, not an ounce of judgment in her voice.

I plopped down on the bed and buried my face in my hands. "You know why."

"Babe, it's been seven years..."

"I know! Don't you think I know?" I shoved my half-full suitcase off the bed, not even flinching when it spilled over. My hands shook and sweat beaded on my forehead. It felt like the world was caving in on me, like if I moved, I'd be crushed. My breaths came out in short gasps, "I can't do it, Tatum. I have to tell Miles I can't do it."

"Breathe, babe. Take a deep breath." I could hear her inhaling, then blowing it out, trying to calm me like she always did when we were younger. I followed her lead, repeating the process two more times until my racing heart slowed and the pressure on my chest eased up a little.

"Thank you."

"I got you. Always. Now, when will you be here?"

Bile rose in my throat at the thought of returning. "Is he... I mean... Are they...?"

"Don't," her voice was commanding, instantly shutting down that line of questioning. "You're coming home, and you don't have to think about any of that."

"How can I not?"

"Just..." I could hear her warring with herself on the other end of line. "Look, Em. I made you a promise that I would never talk about it. *Any* of it, and I'm not gonna start now."

"Thank you." I bent to pick up my suitcase only to find my cat curled up inside. I lifted him out and held him close to my chest, tucking his head under my chin. He immediately began to purr, easing some of my anxiety. I'd have to ask someone to take care of him while I was gone.

"But if you're coming home," she continued, cutting off anything else I might have said, "You're staying with me. Most of town is safe, but I'll feel better if you're here. This is a one hundred percent asshole free zone."

"What about Brandon?" I countered with a light chuckle.

"Yeah, that asshole doesn't count. Not with the things he can do with his..."

"Tatum! I do not need to know about that!"

She laughed, and I couldn't help joining in, the air instantly feeling lighter. Tatum made everything better.

I flopped back on my bed, looking up at the rotating blades of my ceiling fan. "Tell me one thing?"

"What's that?" she asked, before amending, "I reserve the right to deny you an answer."

I sighed, "Nevermind."

"Good choice."

Chapter Two

Linford

Present

Ember

The hospital loomed ahead of me, the large building looking out of place surrounded by fields of green and gold.

My car grumbled as I pulled into a spot on the far side of the cracked asphalt lot. I rubbed her dash as I apologized profusely to the older car. "I'm sorry, baby. You did so good, I just need you to stay strong a little longer. I promise to have Frank give you some lovin' as soon as we get home." I kissed the steering wheel needing, more than anything, for Carrie to play nice.

Yes, Carrie. I may have named the 2010 Subaru after the queen, Carrie Underwood. After all, they were both strong, independent, reliable women. Plus, they both looked great in silver.

I sat tall, checking my hair in the rearview mirror. I drove straight through the night, stopping only to pee or get gas, and it still took nearly nine hours to get here. Freaking Linford Nebraska, population 4,623 and a place I was hoping that I'd never see again.

Deciding I looked about as good as I was gonna get, I pushed my door open and climbed out on shaky legs, groaning as a blast of cold air hit me. It was May, and according to my phone, fifty-five degrees, but it certainly didn't feel like it. I ran my hands up and down my arms, reaching into the back of the car for a hoodie and tugged it over my head.

The little bit of work I did trying to make myself presentable was pointless - as soon as my hoodie was on, static sent my hair flying in every direction. Grumbling, I pulled the elastic from my wrist and tied my hair up. If people wanted me here, they'd have to settle for whatever I felt like giving - which wasn't much.

I pulled the hood over my head as I scanned the area nervously, looking for anyone I might know. I breathed my first sigh of relief when I found the area practically deserted; only a handful of cars were parked in the lot. Maybe I could do this. Check on my mom, visit with Tatum, then haul ass back to Coyote Ridge.

Nervous energy filled me as the hospital doors opened with a whoosh. I pulled out my cell and called Miles as soon as I reached the lobby. I had absolutely no idea where to go, and I refused to talk to anyone I didn't absolutely have to. The last thing I needed was to spark the small-town gossip mill.

"Em?"

"Hey, I don't know where I'm going," I said quietly, trying to hide the quiver in my voice.

"I'll be right down."

I carefully surveyed the lobby, thankful no one was in sight. It had been years since I set foot in Linford General Hospital, not since the last time my sister...

I let the thought die and kept my head down as I stood just outside the elevator doors. I clenched my hands in my hoodie pocket as my heart threatened to beat out of my chest.

I startled at the ding of the elevator and the second those doors slid open, it was like I was eighteen again, looking up into the proud face of my big brother. "Miles," I exhaled a breath I didn't realize I was holding.

Miles looked so much different than he had the last time I saw him. He was tall, but gone was the lanky 20-year-old, and in his place was a man who filled out his clothes. His hair, still the ruddy brown I remembered, was clean-cut, no longer hanging down into his face, and his brown eyes held a spark I hadn't seen before.

"Hey, Em." He stepped out and pulled me in for a hug. I melted into his warmth and familiar smell, "God, I've missed you."

He started to let me go, but I held on tighter, "Not yet," I whispered, the only thing I could manage as a knot of emotion clogged my throat.

"Shh," he soothed. "She's going to be okay." He gently rubbed my back up and down and when a cry broke free he kissed the top of my head.

I pulled back, just enough so my voice wouldn't be muffled by his chest. "It's not that."

He wiped the tears from my cheek as he looked down at me, his brows pulled together, "What is it?"

"I..." I shook my head and tried again. "I've missed you."

He chuckled, "We talk all the time."

My shoulders relaxed and I punched him in the shoulder. "It's not the same, and you know it."

"Yeah, yeah." He grabbed a strand of hair that had managed to escape its confines and gave it a tug before stepping back into the elevator. "You could always come back home. You know we'd all love to have you."

My heart stuttered in my chest and my skin itched to leave. "No," I shook my head.

He ran his hands up and down my arms, "Come on, Em. It's been *years*."

I squeezed my eyes shut and took a deep breath, blowing it out slowly. "Just forget about it."

The ride to the second floor was filled with awkward silence. I always thought he understood, but maybe that was just me being naive again. My dad always said I was...

I kept my head down as I followed him out of the elevator and down a sterile hallway until we came to a door that was cracked a few inches. Miles didn't hesitate, he pushed the door open and went in like it was nothing. When I didn't immediately follow, he took a step back and placed his hand on my shoulder with an encouraging squeeze. "They're not here," he whispered.

I took a deep breath, my chest expanding with the effort, and blew it out, steeling my nerves. I gave him a nod and followed him inside.

The room was bright and without personality. White walls, white floor... Gray chairs and couch. At least that was something.

"Ember?"

My eyes snapped up to the one thing, or rather person, I was avoiding. "Mom," I rasped, taking in the woman I hadn't seen in years. She looked small, fragile, which wasn't right. My mom was a warrior, not the wisp of a woman looking at me with tears in her eyes.

"Oh my god," she cried. "You're here!"

I swallowed around a lump in my throat. "I'm here."

"Well, don't just stand there. Get over here, let me get a look at you!"

I cautiously took the few short steps to reach her bed and Miles slid a chair over, so I could sit. My nose crinkled as I took in the antiseptic, chemical smell that permeated all hospitals, but seemed especially strong in her room.

The rich long auburn hair I remembered my mom having was gone, and in its place was short, limp strands of what looked like box dyed burgundy, grown out a little at the roots. Her brown eyes held so many questions and I shifted uncomfortably under her scrutiny. When her hand reached out for mine, I took it, shocked at how cold her skin felt, how small it felt in mine. I looked up at my brother and he gave a small shake of his head, and I knew I wasn't the only one who noticed.

"My babies are all grown," a tear streamed down her cheek as she continued to study my face.

"Mom..."

"Ember Rose," she scolded. "I haven't seen you in seven years, the least you can do is let me admire the woman you've become."

Miles snorted and I just caught his smirking face. "Don't look at me, I'm not the one who ran away."

I scowled at him and he just laughed. "I'm gonna go, I told Lainey I'd meet her for lunch."

"Tell her I said hello," my mom said, a content grin on her face.

Once the door snicked shut, she turned her attention back to me. "I'm so glad you're here," she adjusted herself on the bed, and tried to hide a wince when she moved to her side. But I saw it.

"Mom, do I need to go get..."

"No, baby. You need to sit and tell me about yourself."

I swallowed thickly, not convinced she was okay, but let it go. She knew herself better than I did. Who was I to tell her anything? "What do you want to know?" I asked, realizing I hadn't spoken to my mom in easily a year, probably more. Even then, our conversations were short and superficial at best.

"Are you still living in that town?"

I nodded, "I love it there. I can't imagine living anywhere else."

She cringed at that, and part of me felt a tinge of remorse. "Sorry."

She brushed over my apology with another question. "Are you seeing anyone?"

"Mom," I sighed. "Why do you always have to ask that?"

"Does that mean yes?"

I sat taller and squared my shoulders. After everything that happened, she had no business in my personal life, especially my dating life. "No, that does not mean yes. That means I don't want to talk about it." My voice came out stronger than I felt.

She gave me that look, the one that said she knew I was being an ass but was going to let it go - for now. Well, mostly. "I just want you to be happy."

"I am, mom. I don't need to be seeing anyone to be happy, you know."

"I know. It's just the thought of you all the way out there, by yourself."

"I'm not by myself. I have my friends."

"You still working at that diner?" Judgement laced her words, instantly setting me on edge.

I took a deep breath and held it, reeling my temper back in. I was a calm person, a patient person. It took a lot to get me riled up, and with just two questions, my mom was pushing my last button. I knew better than anyone that my life wasn't what it could have or even should have been. I let my breath go slowly and plastered a fake smile on my face. "I am. It's a great place. I think you'd like it."

"I'm sure I would, but..."

"Don't. Please, mom."

She adjusted on the bed again, and this time there was no denying the pain. "You okay?" I asked, hoping she'd be honest with me this time.

"I'm fine, baby. But maybe you could go get the nurse for me?"

I slipped out of the room and looked both ways down the hall, not sure which way to go. I decided to head back the direction we came from. I didn't make it far before I ran into someone I used to know. "Stacy?"

The stout woman stopped dead in her tracks, her eyes snapping to mine. "Ember? What are you doing here?"

I arched my brow, "Um... my mom?"

"Oh, right." She had the decency to at least look embarrassed. "I'm sorry, I just..."

Her sentence trailed off, but she didn't stop staring, and I found myself fidgeting, uncomfortable with the attention. Another nice thing about Coyote Ridge; it was a small town too, probably smaller than Linford, but since I didn't grow up there, people didn't act like they knew anything about me. I was a mystery, and mysteries didn't get scrutinized, not like this anyway.

Despite being gone for years, it was evident people still thought they knew me...

While she was busy staring with her jaw unhinged, I stared right back, taking in the shorter woman, with her bright pink scrubs and dark hair pulled up in a tidy ponytail. She used to be slim and curvy. The popular girl that everyone wanted to be friends with. Everyone but me.

Annoyed with her scrutiny, I snapped my fingers in front of her face, something I wouldn't have been caught dead doing before I left town. "Hey. My mom needs a nurse. She's in pain."

Her head jerked back a moment before fixing me with a scowl. "I was just heading that way."

"Good. Let's go."

I followed her back to my mom's room. "Stacy! I didn't know you were on shift today!"

I rolled my eyes but couldn't ignore the hurt I felt as my mom spoke to someone with such familiarity, while I, her own daughter, was practically a stranger. "Mom, I've gotta..." I gestured over my shoulder, needing to get out of there before I said or did something I'd regret. "Will you be okay without me?"

She waved me off. "Yeah, yeah. Go on. Tell Miles to check in on your dad, will ya?"

I left without answering. Miles didn't need me to tell him anything, and it wasn't worth the fight.

My car was a welcome sight. I fell inside and leaned my head against the steering wheel. "Hey, girl. Whaddya say we go see Tatum?"

I pulled out my cell and dialed. It barely rang once before my best friend was practically squealing on the other end. "Where are you?"

I chuckled, looking out the windshield for the first time since I climbed into the car. The all-too-familiar anxiety made a comeback as a couple of women I knew stood by the hospital entrance, staring across the lot right at me. I groaned, "Is it okay if I head over?"

"Only if you explain that noise you just made. You can't possibly mean that for me, so what is it?"

I stuck the key in the ignition and turned it. Carrie purred and I patted her dash in thanks. "I've been spotted."

"What do you mean?"

I backed out of the spot, phone held to my ear with my shoulder. "It would appear word of my return has traveled, because there's a growing crowd standing in front of the hospital staring at me."

"I didn't tell anyone except Brandon."

I laughed at her serious tone. "I know. It's probably Stacy. I ran into her inside."

Tatum groaned. "God, I hate that bitch."

Leave it to my bestie to make me laugh while in the midst of an uncomfortable situation. "Tell me more."

"Not 'til you get your hot ass over here. You have the address?"

"Yeah. I'll see you in five."

CHAPTER THREE

Linford

PRESENT

Ember

T he sage green bungalow butted up against one of the main roads through town, even though it was on the outskirts. Two steps led up to a wide porch which housed a slew of potted plants. A large ash tree provided shade over the yard, and from one of its larger branches, hung a yellow rope with a tire tied to the end. A plastic slide was knocked over on its side, and beside it was a mess of toys.

I pulled up along the curb and barely had the car in park before Tatum was yanking my door open and dragging me out. "I can't believe you're here!" she practically squealed.

I wrapped my arms around the one person who knew me better than anyone in the world. Tatum and I had been friends since we were two. As my mom told it, she and Tatum's mom set us in the sandbox at the elementary school and we were instant friends.

I inhaled the coconut scented oil she used in her gorgeous black hair mixed with the cherry blossom lotion she used on her dark skin. It reminded me of better days, sitting outside in the sun, her trying to teach me how to braid; me failing miserably. Gossiping about boys and dreaming of extravagant vacations in exotic places. I sucked in a deep breath and held it, already feeling the waterworks trying to make their great escape. I had already cried enough for one day, I didn't need another round of tears.

"You okay girl?"

I nodded into her shoulder. "Yeah. I will be."

She chuckled, "Well, as much as I love your hugs, I think we may want to relocate this reunion."

I pulled away just in time to catch one of her neighbors taking a picture on her cell phone. "Seriously?"

"I've got this. You go on in."

I started up the porch steps, but couldn't resist watching my best friend storm across two lawns to get to the busy body hanging over her porch railing. "Edie!" She shouted.

Edie quickly tucked her phone in her pocket as Tatum approached.

"Delete it," Tatum snapped. "Have a little respect."

"It's a free country. People deserve to know." Edie looked over Tatum's shoulder, catching me watching them. She turned her attention back to my friend and shook her head. "I don't want any trouble, that's all."

Tatum held out her hand, "Then don't make trouble. Delete the photos. Now."

Edie pulled out her phone and made a show of deleting the pictures. Once Tatum was satisfied, she marched down the steps and back across the lawns. Just as she reached her porch steps, Edie shouted, "Thought I should mention, I sent them to Lou before I deleted them!"

Tatum growled and looked like she wanted to attack. I grabbed her shoulders and held her back.

"You should probably run along now, Edie!" I shouted. "I'm not gonna hold her forever!"

It took less than two seconds for the nosy woman to disappear back inside her house. I nudged Tatum up the steps, pulled open the screen door then followed her in. "I'm gonna kill that woman," she fumed.

"Everyone was going to find out eventually."

"Yeah, but not like that."

I shrugged. One thing I was all too familiar with was small town living, where everyone knew everyone, and God save you if you ended up fodder for the gossip mill. I became a feast when I left town, so I guess in a way it made sense that returning would stir up even more.

The entire encounter wasn't wholly unexpected, however Edie's words stuck with me. I made a mental note to ask Tatum what she meant by, *"people deserve to know."*

I looked around the home my best friend shared with her husband and two boys. It was quaint and comfortable. Rich mahogany floors stretched out from one end to the other, covered with stylish rugs and the occasional hot wheels car. The living room had an overstuffed sofa with an afghan folded neatly across the top, and an armchair that looked lived in, for lack of a better word. Family photos lined the walls, her and Brandon from homecoming our senior year, their wedding photo, and then each of their boys, together and individually. "I like your home."

"Thank you." Her chest swelled with pride. "Come on, let me give you the tour."

I followed as she pointed out the kitchen, bathrooms, and finally the bedrooms. "This is mine and Brandon's." she pushed open the door to the room at the end of a narrow hallway. It was bright and sunny, just like her personality. A full-size bed made up with lavender bedding and pillows. The curtains were open, letting in a stream of light, through which I could see the vast fields that took up much of the town.

In Linford, you either worked in town, at the factory, or one of the nearby farms. Maybe it was a good thing I left.

Not picking up on my melancholy mood, Tatum crossed the hall and pushed open a white door with a nameplate attached. "This here is Caleb's room."

I peered inside and couldn't help but smile at the little bed covered with a blue bedspread full of red, yellow, and green cars. The room was surprisingly tidy for a little boy, though there was an overflowing toy box in the far corner right beside a rug that was laid out with roads, no doubt to play with his cars on. The walls had various posters, Lightning McQueen, of course, but a couple others of characters I didn't recognize. "He's four?" I asked, hoping my memory was serving me right. Instant regret hit me at missing such a huge part of my friend's life.

"Yeah, he's my baby," she beamed.

She closed the door and moved on to the third and final room, this one also had a nameplate. "Jadon?" I asked, though there was no reason to.

She pushed the door open and stepped inside. "Yeah, my little man."

This room was a bit different from Caleb's, though the boy wasn't that much older. The bed was the same as the one in Caleb's room, except this one had a red bedspread covered with the different Marvel characters. His walls were also adorned with posters; Iron Man, Spiderman, and... "Who's that?" I asked, pointing to a picture of a little tree-man.

"That's Groot," she shook her head. "You know... Guardians of the Galaxy."

I arched my brow and shook my head. "Yeah, sure..."

"Girl, that movie came out before you even left town. Don't tell me you don't remember it. Chris Pratt. Need I say more?"

I nodded and smiled, fanning myself like it was suddenly one hundred degrees. "Oh, I know Chris Pratt. The rest - nope, nothing."

"You mean he..." She stopped herself, her lips pressed into a thin line as if it pained her not to finish that sentence. She shook her head in annoyance then let it go. It didn't take a genius to guess what she was going to say... "This is your room while you're here."

"What?" I held up my hands and backed out of the room. "No, I can't. This is Jadon's room. I don't want to be in the way. I'll take the couch, or better yet, I'll book a room at the Golden Lodge."

"First of all, don't be ridiculous," she said, ticking up one finger. "Second, that place closed down a couple years ago."

"What? Why?" I masked my relief with genuine curiosity; I didn't have the money to pay for a room, and missing work was definitely not helping my financial situation.

"Margaret passed away, and Freddy went shortly after. Said he couldn't live without her."

My hand shot to my mouth. "Did he?"

She threw her arm over my shoulder and chuckled. "No. Everyone said it was a broken heart."

"You can't die from a broken heart," I argued, feeling that all too familiar ache of mine. "I think I'd know."

"Oh, babe. I'm sorry." She pulled me into a full hug, and I squeezed my eyes shut, willing away memories of those last days...

I soaked in her comfort and yawned; exhaustion finally caught up with me. "Can I just lay down?"

She gave me one final squeeze. "Of course. I assume your bag is in Carrie?"

I cracked a smile at her remembering the name I gave my car. "Yeah."

She gave me a push toward the bed. "Stay here, I'll grab it and be right back."

"I can..."

She fixed me with a glare and I held up my hands in surrender. "Okay, mamma bear."

"That's right, don't cross me."

"God, I've missed you."

"Me too, babe."

I was asleep the moment my head hit the pillow. Not only had I been awake for more than twenty-four hours, but more than half of that was emotionally draining.

My dreams were wonderful; so wonderful my heart physically ached as soon as I opened my eyes.

"Hello," a small voice greeted me immediately, and I had to blink a few times before I could see clearly.

"Hey, there." A pair of golden-brown eyes stared at me curiously, and I felt horrible that I didn't know which one of Tatum's boys this was.

"Do you like my room?" He asked, and I couldn't help grinning. This little man had to be Jadon.

"I do. It's very cool." His eyes, so much like his mothers, lit up, and a gap-toothed smile warmed my heart. "Maybe you could tell me about the guys on your walls?" I suggested.

Jadon hopped up on the foot of the bed with a little bounce, just missing my feet. I laughed quietly to myself and pushed up into a sitting position. He pointed to the picture of the little tree-man first. "That's Groot. He's not my favorite, but he's really cool."

"What about that one?"

He sat up on his knees. "That's Iron Man," he practically shouted. "His real name is Tony Stark, but he's a superhero and has this really cool suit."

"I see." I grinned. "Does he have any superpowers?"

He gave me an odd look, probably wondering how I didn't know about Iron Man. He didn't need to know that I've seen almost all the movies; I was enjoying hearing him talk.

"He's just a man," he said, his finger pressed to his chin in thought. "But he made his suit, and it can do all sorts of really cool things."

"So, he's really smart?" I asked.

"Yup."

I looked at the next poster on the wall and decided to throw the kid a bone. "Do you like Spiderman?"

His jaw dropped when he looked at me, "You know Spiderman?"

"I do." I leaned closer to him, "Do you want to know a secret?"

He nodded excitedly. "He's my favorite," I whispered.

"Mine too!"

I leaned back and held up my fist and he bumped his against it without hesitation. "I think we're gonna be good friends."

"My mom told me she knew you since she was my age."

I nodded, thinking back to those early days. "Actually, we've been friends even longer than that."

"How come I've never seen you before?" he asked, just as the door swung open and a not too happy looking Tatum stood with a little boy on one hip, and her hand on the other.

"Jadon Alexander! What did I tell you?"

He slid off the bed, looking thoroughly scolded, even though he only got first and middle named. "Sorry mom."

"It's okay," I cut in, not wanting him to get in trouble for coming into his own room.

Tatum sighed and lowered the boy who must be Caleb to the floor. "Did he wake you?"

I shook my head, "No." I glanced around the room, noticing the dimming light. "What time is it?"

"Close to seven." She held my phone out to me. "It went off a few times," she added as I closed my hand around it. "I didn't want it to wake you."

"Thanks."

I unlocked it and did a quick sweep of my messages. I had a couple missed calls from Miles, but other than that, only a couple of texts. One from Miles, one from my friend who was watching my cat, and then there was Brent. My cheeks heated as I opened his first.

> **Brent:** I never heard from you, just wanted to make sure you got there okay. Talk soon.

"Who's the guy?" Tatum asked, her face clearly stating she already knew everything, but needed me to fess up anyway. Sure, she knew about Brent, except in our conversations he was always "The hottie." Talking about a hot guy was fine; talking about Brent made it real, and I couldn't do real.

"What guy?" Jadon asked, not so subtly trying to check out my phone.

"A new friend," I said, giving Tatum a look that said, "leave it alone."

I typed a quick text back and was about to say something else, when it started ringing. "Hey, Miles."

"Hey, you okay? You didn't answer when I called or respond to my text."

Tatum looked like she wanted to stay and protect me, but the boys were looking restless, so I waved her away, mouthing "Thank you."

"I was asleep," I stretched as I stood. "I drove through the night, remember?"

"Sorry," he sighed. "Mom was just asking about you and I didn't know what to tell her. She was worried you'd left."

I rolled my eyes. "I'll let you know before I leave."

"You didn't last time," he replied all too quickly, and I felt it like a punch to the gut.

"Things are different this time."

"Look, I get it, okay, and I'm not here to judge. We just... we miss you, Em."

"I've missed you too."

"I didn't call to give you a hard time." He sounded almost apologetic, and I appreciated it. Out of everyone, Miles was the only person who had nothing to apologize for. "I just thought you'd like to come by one more time before visiting hours are over."

"Yeah. Let me get myself together and I'll be right over."

The hospital looked even more depressing with the sun low in the sky. I rode the elevator up and when I reached my mom's room, I knocked lightly on the door before pushing it open. "Hey, mo…" I stopped dead in my tracks as I locked onto a pair of eyes that I saw every time I looked in the mirror.

My dad rose from his chair beside the bed. Aged from years of working construction, and what I imagine were a rough seven years, his once strong build had gotten softer. His belly pushed just over his waistband and his dark hair was strewn with gray as was his beard.

He never wore a beard before.

He took a step toward me, and I automatically took a step back. "Ember…" His jaw was clenched, and his hands curled into fists by his side. I took another step back and then another. He narrowed his eyes and his lips curled up in a sneer, looking more and more like he did the last time I saw him. He was saying something, but I couldn't hear anything over the buzzing in my ears. I took another step, and then I slammed into something hard.

Warm hands gripped my upper arms, and I spun, ready to run, to attack.

"Em. Em!" Miles shouted as my fist hit him in the chest. "Stop!"

"You promised!" I screamed. "You promised me!"

He wrapped his arms around me and backed us out of the room as I buried my face in his chest, perfectly happy hiding in my brother's arms. "I didn't know he was here," he whispered into my hair. "I stepped out for a few minutes to call Lainey. He must've shown up while I was away. If I knew…"

"Can we go?"

He hesitated, and I knew he was staring down the man at my back. Though I couldn't see him, I could still feel his presence, the anger rippling off him in waves. "Come on," he said, not speaking loudly enough for anyone to hear. "I'll take you out."

CHAPTER FOUR

Linford

PRESENT

Ember

Miles parked in a spot right in front of Paula's, the diner I waitressed at all through high school. I turned in my seat as he killed the engine. "I can't go in there."

"Come on, Em. It's just Paula's. I promise they're not here."

"How can you be sure?" I stared into my brother's earnest face, willing him to understand that it was too much. The memories were too much. "This was... We..."

"I know," he pushed his hands through his hair in frustration. "But you can't avoid everything."

I laughed, though there was no humor in it. "I've done a pretty good job of it so far. Up until today things were great."

"Damn it, Em!" he snapped.

This was a mistake. Miles was the most level-headed guy I knew; he never lost his temper, especially not with me. *He said he understood!* I threw open the door to his 2018 Ford F150 and hopped out. If he was this irate now, what was going to happen when shit inevitably hit the fan?

I took off toward the street. Tatum didn't live too far away, maybe a mile. I could walk that easily, and then I could get out of town.

Miles' large hand wrapped around my bicep, jerking me to a stop. "Don't do this!" He pleaded, a look I didn't recognize flashed across his face. "You're letting them win, don't you see?"

I shook him off and stabbed a finger in his chest as angry tears rolled down my cheeks. "What do you think is gonna happen when word gets out that I'm back, huh? You think everything is going to be all sunshine and rainbows? That we'll all just look at each other and realize that it was all some sort of *misunderstanding?*" I couldn't hide the tremble in my voice.

"I didn't say that!"

I swiped at my face, hating that they were getting more of my tears. "I can't Miles. Don't you understand? You know what they did! What they demanded of me!"

He stared at me in that way only a big brother looked at his little sister. Like he knew better; like I was being childish. He inhaled sharply and the stern look on his face shifted until all I saw was pity. I hated that one almost as much.

He pulled me into his chest and pushed my hair out of my face. "How about this? You go sit in the truck, and I'll grab us some burgers to go. We can drive out to old man Miller's back lot and watch the sun set."

"Okay," I mumbled into his hard chest.

We got back to the truck just as a couple came strolling out of the diner. They stopped dead in their tracks as soon as they saw me. "Ember? Is that you? Oh, shit, what're you doing back here?" The woman pulled out her phone and lifted it like she was going to take my picture.

Miles opened the passenger door and urged me inside. "I've got this," he whispered, shutting the door and hitting the lock from his key fob.

I lay the seat back as far as it would go, convincing myself that if I couldn't see them, then they couldn't see me. But even I knew that was juvenile - especially since they already *had* seen me.

I couldn't hear everything they were saying, but it was clear Miles wasn't happy. "Leave it alone," he practically growled. "She's been through enough."

"Why's she even here?" The woman asked, her voice not hiding any of her disdain for me.

"I swear to God, Julie..." Miles snapped.

"Does Ken..."

"Don't," Miles held up his hand, halting her mid sentence.

I sank lower in my seat and pulled my phone from my pocket. I opened the Spotify app and hit play on my favorite playlist. Kelsey Ballerini drowned out their voices as she sang about the man who tried to squash her spirit, but she came back stronger. I wished, not for the first time, that I was that strong.

I typed out a quick text to Tatum.

Me: I don't think I can do this

Tatum: What's going on? What did she/they/who do?

Me: My dad was there

Tatum: Oh shit. Did he say anything

Me: I didn't give him a chance

Tatum: Good for you. Screw him. Where you at now?

Me: Paula's. Miles wanted to grab some burgers…

I watched the three little dots bounce across the screen, indicating she was typing for what seemed like forever. Either she was writing a paragraph, or…

Tatum: Miles means well

Me: I know

Tatum: So what's going on? If you're at Paula's, and you're texting me…?

Me: Julie Watson is here with Luke

It wasn't until Miles said her name that I even recognized them. Luke wasn't so bad, but Julie was as big of a gossip as anyone.

Tatum: Oh shit

Me: What is going on? I know everyone likes to gossip, but this feels like more. What does everyone know that I don't?

Tatum: It's not that bad

Me: Tell me

Tatum: You're better off not knowing

Me: Tatum Marie!

Tatum: Fine. When you get back we'll talk

The click of the truck doors unlocking got my attention, and a second later Miles was at the drivers' side door, bag and drink carrier in hand. I peeked out the window then raised my seat up and pushed his door open.

"Thanks."

He held out the bag of food and drinks and I took them so he could climb in. I forgot just how good Paula's food smelled. Freshly baked buns, grilled beef, and then those fries... I set the bag next to my feet. I couldn't think while my stomach rumbled. "What does everybody know that I don't?"

He backed out of the lot and took a right, heading out of town. "I grabbed you a strawberry shake. That still your favorite?"

"Miles..."

"I had them put everything on the side, I don't know what you like anymore."

"What aren't you telling me?"

His lips thinned while he kept his focus purely on the road. "I'm not a little kid anymore!" I grumbled, folding my arms over my chest and turning to look out the window. "Whatever it is, don't I deserve to know?"

"Em…"

"No, Miles. You, Tatum… You're both treating me with kid gloves. I'm a grown woman!"

He sighed and pulled off the side of the road, the truck kicking up dust and gravel as he hit the brakes. He pushed both his hands through his dark hair and blew out a heavy breath before turning to face me. "Look, Em. You left. You left without telling anyone."

"I know I did!" I threw my hands in the air. "What does that even matter? It was better that way. *For everyone.*"

"Fuck," he breathed out, turning his head to look out the window. "Do you remember when you were eleven? You and dad got into an argument, and you took off?"

I swallowed thickly, already knowing where this was going. "Yeah."

"Nobody knew where you were, search parties were formed, the whole town was scared somebody kidnapped you."

I rolled my eyes and huffed out a laugh, "What a joke, nothing ever happens around here. I was fine."

"I knew that. You knew that. Even Tatum knew that. But everyone else?"

"I was a kid, that makes sense…"

"Do you know how hard it was keeping my mouth shut when I knew damn well where you were?"

"I'm sorry, okay?" The pain in his voice sent a wave of guilt through me and I dropped my eyes to my hands. "I said I was sorry!"

"It was hard when you were little, and I knew where you were. But when I wasn't here, when I was in school a couple of hours away and Tatum called me..."

"She did?"

He turned to face me and took my hand. "Em, do you even know how much people love you?"

"They sure have a funny way of showing it," I choked out a laugh, trying to ease the tension. I know I asked him to stop treating me like a kid, but suddenly his conversation felt too heavy.

"It was so much worse," he whispered. "I drove home as fast as I could. We... we checked out all the usual places, everywhere we could think of that you'd hide - despite the fact that they already looked. I called hospitals in all the surrounding cities, while Tatum spoke with the police."

He inhaled sharply, looking like he was about to cry and was fighting it back. "Miss Barrett tried forming a search party, but..."

"She did?" I choked out and for the first time I felt guilty about how I left things. "I didn't know," I managed.

Miles leaned over and kissed the top of my head. "I love you, Em. You say I don't understand, and maybe I don't fully, but... I just want to protect you."

When I didn't respond, he put the truck in drive and continued down the road, turning off at some point onto a gravel road, only stopping when we reached the edge of a barren field. "Come on, let's eat."

He grabbed something from the back seat and hopped out of the truck. I used the hem of my shirt to wipe my tear-stained cheeks, then got out, following him around the back, where he had the tailgate dropped and a blanket spread across the cold surface. I passed him the food and drinks before climbing up next to him, my legs hanging off the end.

We sat in near silence, only the sound of the crickets and cicadas keeping us company as we watched the last remnants of light disappear over the horizon.

Belly full, I lay back and gazed longingly at the night sky, trying to pick out the different constellations. "I love looking up at the stars," I said quietly.

Miles crumpled the last of his trash and tossed in the paper bag before laying back beside me. "It's peaceful," he admitted, folding his arms behind his head. "Do you have a good view where you live?"

"I do," I turned to look at him, and decided it was time I was honest with someone. I never told anyone where I ended up. All they knew was that I lived in a small town, several hours away. I never wanted to risk anyone coming after me. With everything he just told me, and how hard he was fighting to protect me, I knew I could trust him. I cleared my throat, keeping my focus on the dark night sky. "I live in this little mountain town in Colorado. Coyote Ridge. Sometimes, at night, I drive out along one of the backroads until I'm away from the city lights and lay out on the hood of my car and gaze at the stars."

"I know."

"You what?" I sat up on my elbows and took in his relaxed posture.

"I know." He scrubbed a hand over his face and sat up, not bothering to look at me. "I paid a guy to track you down about a month after you left. It took him a little time... Thanks for changing your number by the way, that did not help at all," he chuckled.

I was too shocked to laugh. "That was the point," I whispered.

"I only ever told Tatum and Miss Barrett."

I sat the rest of the way up, a wave of panic crawling up my chest. "You told Miss Barrett?"

He nodded. "You didn't see her, Em. She... She needed to know you were okay. She promised she'd never say a word to anyone, and as far as I know, she hasn't."

"No one ever reached out," I admitted. "Not until I called you and Tatum."

"Come on," he said, hopping down off the truck, effectively ending our conversation. "I should probably get back. I imagine Lainey will be worried."

I pulled my phone out of my pocket and was shocked to see that it was getting close to eleven. And there was no phone service all the way out here. "Oh, god. Tell her I'm sorry. I never meant..."

He wrapped an arm around my shoulder and gave me a squeeze. "It's okay, she'll understand. I'll take you to get your car."

As soon as we were near city limits, both of our phones started pinging with messages. Tatum for me, and I imagine Lainey for him.

When I made it back to Tatum's house, she was sitting on the porch, a blanket wrapped around her shoulders. She didn't get up when I approached, just opened her blanket in invitation. I sat down and put my head on her shoulder as the blanket closed around me.

"I'm sorry I disappeared," I whispered.

"It's okay. I knew you were with Miles."

"Not tonight." I took her hand and laced my fingers with hers. "Seven years ago. I didn't realize how that impacted you."

"Old news, babe."

"You're a good friend."

She laughed, and it was light and immediately lifted my spirits. "Duh." She gave my hand a squeeze. "Still want to know what happened after you left?"

"I do, but not tonight." I yawned. "Come on, we should get some sleep."

CHAPTER FIVE

L'inford

PRESENT

Ember

I felt a renewed sense of duty when I reached the hospital the next morning. I knocked on my mom's door and peeked inside, despite knowing she was alone, before pushing it all the way open. According to Miles, our dad was at work and though I didn't want to hear her name, Kennedy wouldn't be back in town for at least a few more days. I almost asked where she was, then the sudden tightness in my chest reminded me why I didn't ask questions.

My mom looked peaceful as she lay sleeping. With her like this, it was easy to forget the betrayal that tore us all apart. I tried to convince myself, not for the first time, that she had no choice, only to be reminded that she's a grown woman, and at that time I was still a kid, and the child she was supposed to protect.

I pulled up a chair and forced down the bitterness that, for years, was all-consuming and took her hand in mine. "I love you, mom." I whispered.

"Love you too, baby."

I startled at the sound of her voice and she chuckled. "I thought you were asleep."

"I was, but then I felt this angel enter the room, and I knew I had to wake up. I don't know how long she'll be around, so I need to soak up as much time as I can." She squeezed my hand, and I almost felt bad for leaving. Almost.

"Sorry."

"Don't be. Believe it or not, I understand. I don't blame you."

I opened my mouth and closed it a couple of times before I managed, "You don't?"

"No."

I squirmed in my seat, not sure how to take this new information. "But... You said..."

"I know. And I meant it, I still do. But after all these years, I can understand why you left."

Knowing she understood why I ran almost made me feel better, then she had to ruin it by saying she *meant* it. I forced a smile, despite the mixed emotions swirling inside. My anger was justified, she deserved to hear all the things I've bottled up inside me for the past seven years. Except this trip wasn't about me, it was about her.

Miles made it sound like she wasn't gonna make it, but she seemed fine. "What happened?"

"Oh, you know..." she turned away from me, picking at a loose thread on her blanket. "Accident at the factory."

"I heard that, but... how?"

"I don't know, I was just on the floor one minute, and the next... I wasn't."

"Since when do you go down on the floor? I thought you were done with that."

"Damn it, Ember," she snapped. "You don't live here anymore. You don't know how things work."

It was like someone flipped a switch on her mood and her words felt like a slap to the face. I sucked in a deep breath and blew it out slowly, counting to three, and when that didn't work, I tried again, this time counting to five. "You're right, I know nothing, I never did." The words tasted foul as I said them. So much for getting answers.

I stood up and gave her a kiss on the forehead. "I'm gonna let you get some rest." I didn't bother waiting for a response.

Back in the parking lot, I sat in Carrie, my head resting against the overheated steering wheel. I really needed to get a sun visor if I was going to be here for long, yet the idea of staying made my skin itch.

I turned the key in the ignition and pulled out of the lot. Knowing Kennedy was away, town felt a little safer. I drove down Main Street with my windows down, enjoying the light breeze that brushed over my heated skin. I pulled into a space just off the road in front of my favorite coffee shop. If there was any place I missed, it was this. "Deja Brew" was one of two coffee shops in town, but the only one that served food.

The second I pulled the door open and took that first deep inhale, savoring the rich aroma of coffee and baked goods, I felt like I was home. I stepped up to the counter and placed my order, a vanilla latte with caramel and cinnamon and an apple cinnamon crumble muffin. I paid and moved to the end of the counter to wait for my order. The place looked the same as it had all those years ago; wood-paneled walls painted over so many times the paint was peeling, and eclectic artwork gave it a homey feel. Even the tables and chairs were the same, all mismatched and...

I sucked in a sharp breath as I locked eyes with a pair that were the most unusual shade of gunmetal blue and my world came crashing down around me.

CHAPTER SIX

Linford

8 YEARS AGO

Ember

"Is it quittin' time yet?" I asked, squatting down behind the counter. Paula's was the best restaurant in town and nothing said that more than the steady stream of customers that came through the door all evening. It didn't help that it was a Friday night, and I was on my sixth shift in a row. My best friend, Tatum, needed the night off; her boyfriend Brandon was about to ship off for basic training. The man was a year older than us and joined the US Army right after graduation.

I couldn't blame her for wanting the night off. If I had a boyfriend who was about to leave for lord knows how long, I'd want to spend my last night with him too. I could, however, blame her for her lack of forethought. She knew this day was coming for well over a month. She could have requested the night off in advance. But then she wouldn't be the wild and impulsive girl I called my best friend.

"What time is it?"

"Ten til, but don't get too excited. We had a last minute order called in."

"Ugh, you're kidding me!"

Linny, my manager, chuckled. "You're young. You'll survive."

The sound of the jingling bell over the door was like music to my ears. *Please let this be the pick-up order.* I stood up, wiping my hands on the back of my jeans. My breath caught when I took in the man who crossed the dining area with cool confidence.

He was, for lack of a better word, beautiful. He was easily six feet tall, taller than my brother, who was 6'1, and where Miles was tall and lanky, this guy was built. His clothes looked like a second skin, hugging his broad chest and straining around his biceps. His chocolate hair, cropped close on the sides and longer on top, looked so soft my fingers twitched with the need to run through it, and his strong jawline was peppered with at least a days' worth of stubble.

"Hey, I'm here to pick up an order for Barrett?"

His words barely registered as my eyes locked in on his, which were the most unusual shade of gunmetal blue.

Linny set a bag on the counter just in front of me, "Here ya go, sweetie."

The sound of her laugh snapped me back to reality and my cheeks blazed with embarrassment for having been caught staring. "Um..." I took the bag and lifted the receipt she set just underneath it. "That'll be $23.75."

He pulled a couple twenties from his pocket. His rough fingers brushed mine as he handed them to me, sending a spark of electricity through my body and I pulled away quickly.

Our hands touched again when I passed him his change, though it looked like he did it on purpose this time. My eyes shot up the second I felt that spark. His lips curled up on the sides in a knowing grin and it was the sexiest thing I think I've ever seen.

I smiled back and dipped my head low, unable to take my eyes off of him, as heat rose in my cheeks. I didn't even have to look to know they were pink.

He stuffed the change in his pocket but set the $10 back on the counter before taking the bag. "Thanks ladies," he said with a nod looking over my shoulder, no doubt at a grinning Linny. "Thanks Ember." He winked and left just as quickly as he came.

Butterflies swarmed my stomach as I just stood there staring.

"Pick your jaw up off the floor and let's get this place closed up." Linny laughed, giving me a little shove.

"He knew my name," I mumbled, feeling more than a little dazed.

"What's that?"

I turned to face the woman who found this all too amusing. "He knew my name," I said again.

She arched an eyebrow. "Honey, for a smart girl, you sure are dumb when it comes to men." She pointed to my chest, at my nametag.

I covered my face with both my hands. "Oh my god, I'm such an idiot!" I groaned.

"Maybe a little."

"Linny, you're supposed to make me feel better! He probably thinks I'm some weirdo creep with the way I was staring."

She laughed, "Don't stress it. We all know you have zero experience with the opposite sex."

"Linny!"

"Relax, it wasn't that bad."

"Really?"

She barked out a laugh as she locked the front door. "No, it was bad. But it was cute. Besides, I think he's a little old for you."

I covered my face with my hands. *Was it possible to die of embarrassment?*

CHAPTER SEVEN

Linford

PRESENT

Ember

I blinked a couple of times, praying I was seeing things, but I most definitely was not. Wes was sitting at *our* table, looking better than the last time I saw him. Dark hair hung over his forehead, the line of his jaw even more defined. His black shirt fit to perfection; the sleeves strained against the muscles in his arms. I swallowed thickly as my eyes dropped to his lips. I should have noticed him the second I entered the shop. I should have...

My thoughts were interrupted when I took in his company. Across from him sat a little girl with long blonde hair. She was up on her knees, picking at a muffin - an apple cinnamon crumble muffin. "Daddy?"

My breath caught as pain lanced through my chest. Anger, and devastation threatened to swallow me whole if I didn't get out of there. I spun on my heel and ran out the door. I jumped in my car and reversed out of my space, not even checking to see if the road was clear.

He was supposed to be gone...

CHAPTER EIGHT

Linford

8 YEARS AGO

Wes

Cornflower blue. There was no other way to describe them. Her eyes were cornflower blue. You'd think with a name like Ember, they'd be some fiery shade of brown, but no… They were cornflower blue.

I pulled up outside my aunt's house and threw my truck in park, taking a moment to just breathe. Ember… The moment I laid eyes on her, my stomach filled with butterflies. *God she was beautiful.* For the first time in months, I felt something. Suddenly life felt bearable.

"Wesley?"

My head snapped up at the sound of my aunt's voice calling my name. *How long had I been sitting here?* "Coming!"

I grabbed our bag of takeout, thankful it was still hot, and headed inside. "You okay, hun?"

"Yeah, why wouldn't I be?" I asked, taking the food to the table and setting it out. "Where do you want to eat?"

"The table is fine," she said, slowly rolling her wheelchair over.

"Stop," I grumbled. "I'll help you."

"I'm fine," she swatted at me as soon as I was within swinging distance.

I ignored her protests and rolled her over to the table, locking her wheels as I placed a to-go box in front of her. "Drink?"

"I've got a glass of Coke in the living room, if you'd be so kind," she snarked.

I rolled my eyes at her attitude, knowing how hard it was for my aunt to accept help from anyone. Angie Barrett was the queen of independence, leaving home at sixteen and heading west with little more than the clothes on her back. She somehow ended up in podunk USA and found her forever home. She got a job, and before long she had her own house and a whole new set of friends.

I grabbed her drink and set it beside her on the table. "Do you know how much sugar is in a glass of Coke?"

It was her turn to roll her eyes. "Don't start in on me. You've always been my favorite nephew, but that can change real quick."

"I'm your only nephew," I laughed.

"I can fix that," she said, holding up a plastic butter knife, aimed at me.

I arched an eyebrow at her and shook my head. "Don't worry, Ang. I don't care how much sugar is in that Coke. My dad on the other hand…"

"That man doesn't know how to live."

I knew better than to touch that statement, choosing instead to take a bite of the giant burger. I groaned as my eyes rolled back in my head.

"Good, huh?"

"So good."

She took a long drink, watching me over the rim of her glass.

"What?"

"Care to tell me what's got that look on your face?"

I wiped my hands on a napkin, "What look?"

"Oh, I don't know. The one where you're smiling?"

"I smile."

She huffed out a laugh. "Boy, you haven't smiled once since you got here."

"First of all," I held up a finger, "I haven't been here that long. Second... you ever think that maybe it's your charming personality?"

She cocked her head to the side and blew out a heavy breath. "Your dad told me about Andy..."

I flinched and just like that, my good mood was gone. Hearing her name felt like a punch to the gut.

"Now there's the face I've gotten used to." She gave me an apologetic smile. "Sorry, hun."

"Old news, Ang."

"It's okay to be not okay, you know."

"I'm fine, really."

Thankfully she dropped the topic of my ex. Unfortunately, that's all she dropped. "So, why the smile?"

I rolled my eyes. "I'm not smiling."

"You were when you were sittin' in that truck of yours..."

I shoved my food away and moved to get up, but she held out a hand to stop me. "Sorry, it's just... You've looked so lost, that I figured something must've happened. Did something happen?"

I blew out a heavy breath and pushed my hair back away from my face. "Not really, I just..." Heat rose to my cheeks and embarrassment rolled over me at how ridiculous this felt. I was a twenty-year-old man. Getting all googly-eyed over some girl felt immature. But whatever. This was my aunt... "Do you know a girl named Ember?"

Her eyebrows shot up and she shook her head. "No."

"No you don't know her, or no...? Cuz you look like you know her."

"Wesley, I love you, but no. Ember is a good girl. She's going places."

"What's that supposed to mean?" I snapped. I was getting sick of everyone telling me I was no good, that I had no future. I got up to leave and her hand wrapped around my wrist as I passed her.

"Wesley, wait."

I stopped, keeping my back to her. "Ember is special. She can't be your rebound... She deserves more than that, that's all."

"Yeah, well..." I shook my head. *Well, what?* I blew out a heavy breath. "I'll stay away," I offered. Her arched brow told me she didn't believe me. Hell, I didn't even believe me.

CHAPTER NINE

Linford

PRESENT

Wes

"I got this book all about otters. Did you know that mama otters swim on their backs with their babies on their tummy?"

"I did not know that," I grinned at my little girl. She was so damn smart. "What else does your book say?"

"Well, they use rocks to..."

A familiar voice caught my attention and when I looked up it was like all the air had been sucked out of the room. I swear my heart stopped the moment our eyes met. Cornflower blue. Her eyes were cornflower blue. The most beautiful eyes I had ever seen were staring back at me. Eyes I never thought I'd see again.

"Daddy?"

Ellie's voice broke the spell and I blinked. That's all it took for Ember to turn on her heel and run out the door.

"Ember?" The barista called out, holding a to-go cup and a brown paper bag. *She didn't even wait for her drink.*

I started to get up, but the second I did, I caught sight of her car peeling out and racing down the street. "Shit," I cursed under my breath, and of course my daughter heard it.

"That's a bad word," she scolded.

"I know, baby. I'm sorry."

"Who was that?" she asked, twisting her body to look out the window.

I scrubbed a hand over my face as my heart raced a million miles a minute. "Nobody, baby." I knew she was back in town; Miles warned me, told me to stay away. I started to cuss him out, I had as much right to see her as anyone else; maybe even more. Then I saw the look on his face and gave up. I had only seen it once before, seven years ago when he beat the shit out of me for hurting his sister. I deserved it, every punch, every kick, the black eye and bruised ribs.

"Eat your muffin." An apple cinnamon crumble muffin, Ember's favorite.

Ember

I sped through two stop signs and one red light before I hit the open road. I called Tatum, distracted driving be damned.

"Hey, girl," my best friend answered.

"Did you know?" I demanded, trying to slow my racing heart.

"Know what?"

"About Wes? About Deja Brew..."

"I'm sorry, you're going to have to be a little more specific." There was a moment of silence before I heard a door click shut. "It's Monday."

"Way to state the obvious," I snapped.

"Wes takes Ellie to Deja Brew for tea and muffins on Monday's after kids camp at the library."

I groaned, "I thought he was out of town!"

"Who told you that?"

I could kick my own ass for making assumptions. "Doesn't matter. Why's he going to *my* coffee shop!?"

"I hate to break it to you babe, but you left."

"Can everyone stop saying that?" I practically screamed. I took a deep breath, counted to three, and blew it out. "Sorry. It's just... I saw him. I saw *her*."

"She's adorable, right?"

"Tatum," I practically growled.

"Oh, come on, Ember." Her voice was a strange mix of pleading and exasperation.

Betrayal was a feeling I knew all too well; I just never expected it to come from my best friend. She was familiar with her, with Ellie. She called her *adorable*.

"I can't." I hung up and turned off my phone. A lead weight settled in my stomach as I realized I couldn't trust her. I couldn't trust anyone from my old life. I spun my car around, not even slowing as the back end caught on some gravel and slid off the road. It was time to go home.

About an hour out of town, in the middle of a deserted highway, Carrie started to grumble. "No, baby. Please don't do this to me. Just..."

Steam billowed out from under the hood. I pulled off to the side of the road and killed the engine. I threw my door open and got out, pacing back and forth the length of the car. I clenched and unclenched my hands, trying to cool the rage burning inside me, but it was useless.

I threw my head back and screamed as loud as I could. It helped a little but wasn't nearly enough. I stormed over to the side of the road and kicked up a few good-sized rocks with the toe of my sneaker. Taking aim at a tree a short ways away, I threw the rocks as hard as I could.

Of course I missed.

One look back at Carrie and my stomach sank. She's done this before, a couple of times. Frank always did what he could, within the limits of my budget. That meant shortcuts and partial fixes. I climbed back into the car and rubbed the dash, "Please, baby. Just start, get us home and I'll make sure you get everything you need. Even if it means I don't eat for a month."

I turned the key and winced at the pitiful sputtering of the engine. "Please!"

I let go of the key and sat back in my seat as I mentally tallied up how much money I had in the bank, minus my upcoming rent, and the wages I was already losing by being all the way out here in my own circle of hell. *Why did I agree to come?* A pang of guilt shot through me as I remembered my mother's frail body in that hospital bed. But other than that, she looked fine, she was going to be fine. I never even saw where she had been hurt.

I turned my phone back on, surprised there were no missed calls or texts. I started to search for a tow company, one that could get Carrie and I to a garage, somewhere far from Linford. I waited and watched the little blue status bar at the top of the browser... It wasn't budging. I looked at the top right of the screen. No service, I had zero fucking service. "FUCKING COUNTRY!" I screamed, throwing my phone on the passenger side floor.

After a few more minutes of self-pity, I popped the hood in the universal sign for distress. Someone would drive by and offer to help, even if it was just driving on to the next town and sending someone back.

One hour passed, then two. When I spotted a car off in the distance, I got out and waved my arms to get their attention.

They sped right past.

I got back in the car and rested my head against the steering wheel, letting the first tears fall. I never should have come.

Another hour passed, along with three more cars - none of which stopped or even slowed down. My head ached and my stomach rumbled; I never did get my coffee or my muffin.

The sun was sitting low in the sky, and it didn't look like any help was coming. I closed the hood and got back in. I gave my steering wheel a kiss and turned the key. She sputtered, then stopped. The next time I turned the key, I got nothing.

Carrie was officially dead and I was stranded in the middle of nowhere.

I turned on my hazard lights, still holding out hope someone would see me. In hindsight, I probably could have walked to the next town. It was likely several miles away - in either direction, and without water it would have been a disaster, but would it have been any worse than being stranded out here all night?

Another hour later I spotted a pair of headlights in my side mirror fully expecting them to speed past, but when the vehicle slowed and stopped behind me, I threw my door open and ran out to meet them. "Thank you for stopping!"

"I swear to God Ember!" Miles slammed his truck door. "I have been looking for you for hours! Were you even gonna tell me?"

I deflated, my arms falling limply to my sides. "I'm sorry," I managed, feeling like a little kid again. It was like no matter what I did, I was screwing something up. It was becoming more and more obvious that I didn't belong here. "As soon as I get Carrie fixed, I'll be out of your hair and you won't have to worry about me any more."

"Damn it, just stop!" He blew out a heavy breath and closed the distance between us. He wrapped his arms around me, hugging me tight. "You know it's not like that."

He pressed a kiss to my forehead, and I cracked. "Do I?" I choked out a sob and buried my face in his chest. "I never should have come back."

"Shh," he whispered, smoothing a hand over my hair. "Don't do that."

"He was there, Miles. He was there..." I wrapped my arms around his waist, needing something to hold onto.

"I know. I'm sorry. I should have told you."

"It was my coffee shop first..." I hugged him tighter. "She was eating my muffin..."

"What?" He leaned back and pushed my hair away from my face. "Who was what?"

"Their daughter... She had my muffin." It sounded so ridiculous when I said it out loud. Thankfully he let it go, not asking any questions.

"What's wrong with Carrie?"

I turned to look at my traitorous car. "She just sputtered, then stopped. I'm afraid she's dead." I inhaled sharply. "Oh, god. What if she's dead?"

Miles hugged me tighter before leading me to the passenger side of his truck. "Get in. I'll get someone to take a look at her."

CHAPTER TEN

Linford

8 Years Ago

Ember

Warm summer nights are the best. When the stifling heat is replaced with a cool breeze and the sounds of nature all around. And then there was the smell. I stood just outside McCook's, the only grocery store in town, and inhaled deeply, appreciating the smell of summer. I couldn't explain it, it was just… summer.

The bell over the door jingled as I went inside. I grabbed a basket and hurried through the store, picking up everything from the list my mom sent me while I was at work. I didn't understand why she never had Kennedy run errands. It's not like she had a job…

I shook my head, pushing that thought away. It was pointless. Kennedy was her baby, but if you asked me, she was a brat.

"You got it?" the cashier asked once I had everything loaded into two bags.

"Yeah, I'm good."

I was almost to the door when she called out, "Tell your mom I said hi!"

I turned and continued walking backward, giving her my friendliest smile. "I will." Then I slammed into a wall. A warm, good smelling wall.

"Whoa," rough hands grabbed me before I fell, though the bags didn't fare as well.

All the air was sucked from my lungs the second my eyes met his. Gunmetal blue...

His dark hair was shaggier today, hanging down over his forehead into his eyes like he had been running his hands through it. My arms warmed where he held me, and I found myself leaning in to him. Butterflies swarmed in my belly as his scent washed over me. Woodsy with a hint of spice and... engine oil?

I didn't even know his name.

"You good?" He asked, breaking the spell.

"Shoot," I groaned, my face heating with embarrassment. Not only was I caught staring, again, but my groceries had scattered all over the ground beside us.

He let me go and I knelt to collect my stuff, and of course he knelt down at the same time. "Ember, right?"

I nodded and kept my head down, unable to speak when he was this close. *What was wrong with me?* I never got like this - around anyone. Not even when Jonah asked me out back in the sixth grade. I could never get over the fact that he used to eat his boogers when we were in kindergarten.

"Here, let me help." He made quick work of gathering everything up, passing me the carrots and peppers before finally taking hold of a runaway onion...

Once everything was stuffed carefully back in the bags, he took my hand and helped me to my feet, still watching me like I was some sort of puzzle he couldn't figure out. "Thanks," I managed. My hand tingled where he still held it and flutters filled my chest. "I better get home before it starts getting dark."

He looked outside, the sun was only just starting to set so I had a little time. "Let me walk you to your car," he offered, finally letting me go and following me outside. I missed his touch immediately.

"Oh no, that's okay." I adjusted the bags in my hand as I stepped off the curb.

"Where are you parked?"

I looked over my shoulder; he was right behind me. "I..." I took a deep breath and blew it out slowly. *God this man was gorgeous.* I mean, I've seen hot guys before, but they were *guys*. And to be fair, I grew up with all of them. This one though... he wasn't just a guy. He was a *man*. With strong man hands, and a man's body, and a man's... needs.

Heat flared up my chest and into my cheeks as my belly did somersaults. What would he think when I told him I don't have a car? Would he think I'm just some silly little girl? More importantly, why did I care?

I had two options. One - I could lie. Tell him I left it at home and walked to the store. Or, two, I could tell the truth and risk the embarrassment. And really, what did it matter? I didn't even know his name, or what he's doing in town... I doubt he'll go to my school come fall; there's no way he's still in high school. "I don't have one," I admitted with as much confidence as I could muster. It could work, a dash of humiliation mixed with an ounce of confidence hopefully equaled a strong woman.

"Huh," he said, hands on his hips. Lord help me, the way his biceps strained the sleeves of his shirt...

"I don't live that far," I shrugged resuming my walk, needing to get out of there before I said or did something stupid.

"I can give you a ride," he offered.

"Thanks, but I think I can make it." I gave him one last smile over my shoulder before leaving him standing alone in the middle of the grocery store parking lot. My cheeks flushed when I saw the grin spread across his face. What I wouldn't give to see that every day.

Chapter Eleven

Linford

Present

Ember

The first thing I noticed was the smell of bacon. The next was that I wasn't in my bed. Or even Jadon's. My head was pounding and my mouth tasted horrible. I sat up and rubbed my eyes, trying to remember what happened last night.

I groaned as images of the coffee shop played in my mind. I flopped back and threw my arm over my eyes when I remembered my tantrum and speeding out of town.

Then there was Carrie... She had the worst timing, though I couldn't say the same for my brother. Miles found me and dragged me back to town. He stopped by T's Liquor and grabbed a six-pack of beer and a bottle of peach schnapps for me. He drove us back to his place, where I finally got to meet his girlfriend, Lainey, and had way too much to drink.

The latter wasn't difficult, I never drank…

"Em?"

The door creaked open, and I flinched at the light that streamed through. "Light," I croaked. "Too bright."

He chuckled. "That'll teach you to try to keep up with Lain…"

He sat at the foot of the bed looking a little sheepish. I couldn't figure out why, until a memory surfaced… "Have a good time?" I asked, aiming for a straight face, but failing miserably. I may or may not have gone to the kitchen for a glass of water and walked in on some "nocturnal activity" on the kitchen table.

"Piss off."

"Nah, I'm good."

He swatted at me, and it was almost like old times. "I've missed you," I admitted.

"Miss you too. Now, Lain made breakfast. Pancakes, bacon, hash browns…"

"Tell me you're gonna marry her."

He chuckled, rubbing a hand over the back of his neck. "Maybe one day." He stood and smacked my leg. "Come on, we've got things to do."

"Like what?"

"We gotta go see mom. And then there's the small matter of your car…"

"Do you think she's gonna make it?"

"Mom?"

I furrowed my brow and shook my head. "No, Carrie."

He rolled his eyes. "I don't know, on both counts."

I climbed out of the bed, thankful I had the forethought to sleep in my clothes. "What do you mean? Why do I feel like you're keeping something from me?"

"Come on," he called over his shoulder. "This breakfast ain't gonna eat itself, and Lainey is a great cook."

After a quick stop by the bathroom, where I managed to tame my mess of hair, I sat at the table across from one of the most beautiful women I've ever seen. Miles met Lainey when they were both at school in Omaha. For reasons unknown to me, she agreed to leave the big city to be with my brother. If I ignored the fact that he was my brother, I could admit that Miles was a catch.

"So, what's the plan for today?" she asked, blowing the steam from her coffee.

Miles kissed her cheek and stole a piece of bacon from her plate. "I need to run by the hospital and check in at work."

He turned to me just as I stuffed a forkful of pancakes in my mouth. "Am I taking you to the hospital? Or to Tatum's?"

"Mmm," I held up a finger while I finished chewing. "I need to get Carrie. Find a tow company, maybe get her to the next town over."

Miles rolled his eyes. "I already called Bob. He owes me a favor."

I shook my head. "But... Bob's here."

"Great deductive skills there, Em."

"But I need..."

"You need to be with your family," he interrupted.

I opened my mouth to say something, but he raised his hand, stopping me before I could utter a sound. "Even if it's just me and mom. You need to be here."

"But..."

He raked his hand through his hair, pushing it away from his face. "As much as I wish you could, you can't avoid it forever."

"You don't understand," I argued.

He pulled out the chair beside me and tried to take my hand, but I yanked it away. "I do. And I also know how things have been since you've been gone. She..."

"No," I cut him off. "Don't."

"Fine. How about this..."

I slapped my hand over his mouth before he could utter another word. "No."

He lifted his hands in surrender, and thankfully when I let my hand fall away, he let it go.

He sighed, and I watched the silent conversation he had with Lainey before his shoulders slumped and he grabbed his phone. He pressed it to his ear and stepped out of the room. I only caught part of the conversation before Lainey reached over and touched my arm. "He means well."

"I know. It's just..."

"I can't imagine," she consoled, giving my arm an affirming squeeze. "But you might want to hear him out. If not today... then sometime."

Miles returned, a defeated look on his face. "Bob's already got a guy out there hooking your car up to tow back."

I slumped down in my chair, "Looks like I'm staying."

I wasn't in the mood to deal with anyone, so Miles reluctantly agreed to drive me to Tatum's. I stared out the window trying to figure out what I was going to do. My car was on her way to Bob's Auto. There was no way I could get out of town until she was fixed, and I didn't even know if I had enough in my bank account to cover the cost of repairs. The last thing I wanted to do was be indebted to anyone - especially here.

Miles stopped at a red light, one of only three in town, and I caught a glimpse of a cherry red mustang convertible parked by the library. "Who's car?"

All the color drained from his face. He licked his lips, then hit the gas, despite the light still being red.

I twisted in my seat to get another look at the car. "Who's car?" I demanded.

"Em... Just forget you saw it, okay?"

"Miles! Who's car!?"

He shook his head. "It's Kennedy's, okay?" He shouted, hitting the steering wheel. "It's Kennedy's."

Chapter Twelve

Linford

8 Years Ago

Ember

Tatum, Kennedy, and I sat on the tailgate of Brandon's truck just outside of Paula's diner. He was currently living the dream in Fort Leonard Wood, Missouri. Actually, from what I heard, he was quite miserable. Apparently, army basic training was grueling. Fortunately for us, he didn't need his truck, and he said Tatum could use it while he was away.

"There's too many options, and I don't like any of them," I groaned, dropping my phone in my lap.

"Give me that," Tatum snatched my phone and started scrolling. "What about this?"

"Ugh," I cringed. "I'm not driving that." It was an olive green Ford Pinto.

"Okay, let's try this. If you could get any car, if money wasn't an issue, what would you get?"

"Easy," A smile spread across my face as I snatched my phone from her hands. I typed what I wanted and held it out. "This. A cherry red, Ford Mustang convertible."

"Give me that," Kennedy grabbed my phone before Tatum could. "That car is lame."

I shoved her. "It is not."

Kennedy flipped her dark auburn hair over her shoulder and hopped off the tailgate. She passed my phone to Tatum, who hadn't even seen the car yet. "The car is lame, the color is tacky, and you'll look ridiculous driving it."

"Kennedy!" Tatum snapped. "You're such a little bitch."

"You can't call me that," she pouted.

Tatum hopped down and stood toe to toe with her. My bestie was fierce.

Kennedy, though two years younger than us, stood at least two inches taller than Tatum. Tatum refused to be intimidated. She got right up in my sister's face. "Kennedy Davis, you are a royal bitch." She half bowed, then spat on her brand new shoes, a pair of white leather Nike's with a pink swoosh.

I laughed; I couldn't help it. Then Kennedy turned her glare on me, and the smile fell off my face. "I'm telling mom." She folded her arms over her chest, popped her hip out, and arched a brow at me.

"Go ahead," Tatum taunted. "See, this is why nobody likes you." She booped my sister on the nose.

Kennedy got right in her face, mere inches separated them. "That's where you're wrong, gutter trash." Her lips tipped up in a cruel smirk. "*Everyone* likes me. Just ask your boyfriend." Kennedy shoved Tatum, knocking her off balance before slamming into her with her shoulder.

"Yeah, right! He wouldn't touch you with a ten foot pole!"

Kennedy brushed her hair over her shoulder with a smirk as she walked away. My jaw hit the floor.

Tatum turned back to me, tears threatening at the corners of her eyes. "What's that mean?"

I hopped down and pulled her into a tight hug. "It means that Kennedy doesn't like hearing the truth and is lashing out the only way she knows how."

"Do... do you think Brandon...?"

I shook my head. "No. I don't."

"I should call him."

I let her go and closed the tailgate of Brandon's truck. "Yeah, but I really don't think you have anything to worry about. He's crazy about you." I knew Brandon would never cheat on Tatum, but that didn't mean other men hadn't cheated on their girlfriends with Kennedy. She was easier than tripping over a rock; which is reportedly how she fell into bed with the captain of the football team.

"You sure?"

I looped my arm through hers. "I am. Now come on, before we're late."

No sooner were we inside then one of the other waitresses came rushing over. "Thank God you're here."

"Nice to see you too," I laughed. "What's up?"

"Something happened and my sitter needs me to pick up my baby early. I hate to do this, but do you think you could cover my tables?"

"Yeah, I got you. Take off, I'll see you later."

"Oh my God, Ember, you're a life saver."

I laughed, "I'll remember you said that."

The diner wasn't that busy. Just a handful of tables, and between Tatum and I we had it covered easily. I made my rounds, checking in at each table, making small talk with several of our regulars. Honestly, in a town this size, I knew just about everyone. Well, maybe.

I started to head back to the counter when I saw someone seated at one of the tables in the back corner. We never sat anyone there unless the restaurant was packed, which it clearly wasn't. "Hey, how you doin tonight," I asked before I even reached the table.

My mysterious stranger looked up and an easy smile spread across his face. "Pretty good now," he chuckled and the sound was music to my ears.

My steps faltered, but thankfully I managed to get to the table without falling on my ass, or freezing up like an idiot. "Hey," I greeted, fighting the blush that wanted to light up my cheeks. "We just keep running into each other, don't we?"

He nodded. "It's bound to happen a time or two in a town this small."

"I suppose that's true." I looked at the table in front of him, noting his plate was near empty, and his glass was empty. "Can I get you anything? Another drink? Some dessert?"

"Actually, yeah. I placed an order to go, would you be able to see if it's ready?"

For some reason, the thought of him leaving made me a little sad. It wasn't like I thought about him every day since the first time I saw him. Okay, maybe I did. Or, maybe it was because I was finally able to talk to him without making a fool of myself - though even that was a close call. "I'll be right back."

I spun on my heel and hurried back to the kitchen. When I rounded the corner, I nearly ran face first into Tatum. "Whoa, girl. What's the rush?"

"He's here!" I whisper shouted, glancing back over my shoulder.

"Who's here?"

I gave her a look, the sort of look you could give your best friend and she'd understand without question. But Tatum was a brat. I could tell by the smirk on her face, the quirk in her eyebrow, that she was going to make me say it. I grabbed her by the shoulders and walked her over to the corner. "Table twelve," I whispered.

"There's no one there."

"What?" I peeked around her, and sure enough, the table was empty.

"Are you sure he's not a figment of your imagination," she chuckled.

"Whatever," I rolled my eyes and went into the kitchen. "Hey, you have a to-go order for table twelve?"

"Sure do!"

A second later I had a bag in hand and was on my way back to his table, and once again, I ran right into him. "We've got to stop meeting this way," he laughed, holding me steady.

Butterflies took flight in my belly, and I found myself stammering again. "I... uh..." I held up the bag, unable to form a complete sentence while his rough hands were touching me.

He took a step back, and that wasn't much better; his scent remained. That same woodsy, spicy scent, that haunted my dreams. "That for me?"

His fingers grazed mine as he took the bag, and my cheeks heated. I had to remind myself that he was just a guy. A *really hot* guy, but still, just a guy. "Did you already pay?" I asked. If I were smart, I'd have checked the receipt on the bag. But when it came to this man, all intelligence flew out the window.

He gestured toward the register at the front counter. "I have not."

I rang him up, and this time he passed me a credit card. I snuck a peek at his name as I ran it through the machine. Wesley. Wesley

Barrett. I don't know why that name didn't register before. The first time I saw him he was picking up an order for "Barrett." He had to be related to Miss Barrett.

As soon as the machine printed the receipt, I had him sign and passed him back his card. This was usually the time I said something clever, said I'd see them later, but none of that really worked with this guy. With *Wesley...* "Thanks for coming in," was all I could manage.

He turned to leave, but then came right back. "Something wrong?"

"Would you like to go out with me sometime?"

My eyebrows shot up. "Me?"

For the first time since I laid eyes on him, he looked nervous. His Adams apple bobbed as he swallowed and nodded. "Yeah."

"I, uh," I cleared my throat. Was it hot in here? "Yeah, uh, I'd like that."

He let out a breath and pushed his hair out of his face. *Was that relief I saw on his face?*

"Can I..."

"She's free tomorrow!" Tatum shouted from wherever she was hiding.

I laughed nervously, tucking a strand of hair behind my ear. "I'm free tomorrow. Want to meet at Deja Brew? Around six?"

"It's a date." He winked and the second his back was to me I spun on my heel to go yell at my bestie.

"Tatum!" I whisper-shouted.

"What?" She fanned herself. "He's hot."

"Don't try to change the subject," I shook my head, trying to hold onto my indignation, when I was actually thankful. "You were eavesdropping!"

She shrugged. "Looks to me like I helped."

"Well, yeah."

She looped her arm through mine and pulled me back around the counter. We still had tables to cover, guests to take care of. "You're new to this whole dating thing. I just wanted to help."

"Thanks," I smiled, unable to stay mad at her.

I paced back and forth in front of Deja Brew. I got there early, mostly because I was early to everything, but also because being late gave me anxiety. I was second guessing that decision though. What if he got here, took one look at me and changed his mind? What if I'm too simple? I've read that guys from the city always think small town girls are simple... Is he from the city? He had that city boy look, didn't he?

I paused my pacing to check my reflection in the window. I wore my favorite pair of skinny jeans, a pale blue off the shoulder top and my knock-off converse sneakers. My hair hung in loose waves, nearly reaching my waist, and I went for minimal makeup. Maybe I should have worn more. Maybe I should have done something with my hair. Maybe...

Too nervous to stay, I turned to leave, stopping just before I slammed into Wesley. "Hey!" A nervous laugh broke free. "We have got to stop meeting like this."

"I don't know," he shrugged, his hands tucked in his pockets. "It's not so bad."

Heat flared in my cheeks, and he laughed. It was almost like making me blush was a sport. "Come on," he gestured to the door that was propped open. "I'm dying to try out this coffee shop my aunt keeps raving about."

"Your aunt?" I asked, feigning ignorance. There was only one Barrett in town that I knew of.

"Yeah. I'm staying with her while she heals from back surgery."

"Oh, I didn't know," I admitted, suddenly feeling bad for not checking on her. I've been so focused on myself, I didn't even realize she hadn't been by the diner lately.

We went to the counter, and even though it was six in the evening, I still ordered my usual - a vanilla latte with caramel and a cinnamon apple streusel muffin. Wesley stared at the menu for a couple minutes before asking me what I recommended.

We got our drinks, and my muffin, and took a seat at the table near the door. I smiled to myself, already learning something about my new friend. Wesley didn't know his way around a coffee shop, which in today's world was rare.

I popped the top off my cup and blew to cool it down while waiting for him to take his first sip.

"What?" he laughed.

"I'm dying to know what you think."

He took a deep breath and brought the cup to his lips. Steam was still billowing from the tiny opening in the lid, but he either didn't notice or didn't care that he was about to burn his tongue. "You might want to..."

He took a sip and made a face, but not a pained face, more like he was curious...

"Is it bad?"

He took another sip and leaned back in his chair. "No. It's... interesting."

"Interesting?"

He nodded. "Like, I can taste the coffee, but it's sweet, but not too sweet. What did you call it?"

"Just a latte with hazelnut and cream."

He took another sip then leaned forward, resting his arms on the edge of the table. "What's yours taste like?"

"It's... Vanilla and caramel. Not much to it, really."

"Can I have a taste?"

I arched an eyebrow. Were we at that stage of our relationship yet? Wait... *relationship?* I swallowed thickly before sliding my cup across the table. I swear my whole body heated the second his full lips touched the cup, right where mine just were. I looked down at my hands, folded in my lap before my imagination could run off even farther.

"Mmm." My eyes were drawn to his mouth as his tongue swept across his lips. "That's good. But you know what would make it better?"

"What's that?" I asked, taking my coffee back.

"Cinnamon."

"Cinnamon?"

He got up and went over to the counter and came back a second later with a little shaker of cinnamon. I watched reluctantly as he popped the lid off my cup. I was a very basic person, and I liked very basic things. It took Tatum forever to convince me to add caramel to my drink, so this terrified me. I watched him sprinkle the cinnamon on top and stir it with one of those plastic stir sticks. "Try that," he said, standing back, watching me carefully.

I shoved down all my reservations and brought the cup to my lips. I watched Wesley over the rim as I swallowed my first mouthful, knowing I'd say it was good whether it actually was or not. "Oh my god!"

"Good, right?"

I nodded. Thank God I didn't have to lie. "It really is. What made you think of that?"

He returned the cinnamon to the barista and dropped back into his seat across from me. "I dunno. Just... vanilla, caramel, both sweet, but you needed a little spice." he winked, and I swear, I melted a little.

Spice is good, I thought, thankful he couldn't hear my thoughts.

"Tell me about yourself," he said, reaching over and picking a piece off the top of my muffin.

I stared at him slack-mouthed before swatting his hand. He chuckled and my stomach did a somersault. I swear, this man's laugh could be bottled and sold as a cure for depression. "My aunt tells me you're a good girl."

I groaned, covering my face with my hand. "God, I wish everyone would stop saying that."

"Why?"

I shook my head, "What's the first thing you think of when you hear *'good girl'*? Wait... you talked to your aunt about me?"

His cheeks turned the cutest shade of pink. That he was nervous too made me feel better.

"I did. I asked her what she knew about you." He looked down at the table, where his hands were tearing up pieces of a napkin. "She told me to stay away from you. But..." His eyes met mine through his dark eyelashes.

"But what?"

He raked a hand through his hair. "I tried, but there's just something about you. That little voice in my head just kept telling me *I have to get to know this girl.*"

"You hear voices?" I joked, arching a brow. Little by little I found myself relaxing.

"I do, and they usually steer me in the right direction," he winked. "Did they get it right this time?"

I laughed, "Guess that's to be determined."

"I'm okay with that."

"So tell me, Wesley…"

"Ah, so you did check out my name yesterday," he laughed.

I shrugged. "You gave me little choice. You knew my name, but never gave me yours. Desperate times and all that…"

"You could have asked…"

"Yeah, but that would have required me being able to say more than one syllable words in your presence."

"You're not doing so bad right now. And everyone calls me Wes."

I took another sip of my coffee, hoping to hide the flush in my cheeks. But he wasn't fooled. "You're cute when you blush."

And of course, my cheeks flared hotter at that. Thankfully he decided to throw me a bone and changed the subject. "My aunt Ang is a stubborn woman. She had back surgery a couple of weeks ago, and I don't even know how my dad found out, but the second he did, he started packing his bags to come out here to help her out."

"What did she say about that?"

He shook his head. "She told him if he so much as showed up at her door, she'd make sure it was the last thing he ever did."

"So he sent you instead?"

He shook his head, "No. Well, sort of."

He fidgeted in his seat, and grabbed another napkin to shred. "You don't have to explain."

"No," he reached across and put his hand over mine. "It's just… Not really first date, or really any date, sort of stuff."

"That's okay, we can talk about something else." I looked down to where our hands were still touching. *Could I be any more awkward?*

He cleared his throat. "I was seeing this girl, Andy." He sat back and interlaced his fingers on the table top. "We had been together for years. We're talking all through middle and high school..." He looked up at the ceiling, took a deep breath and blew it out. "She went to college, and I stayed home, working at my dad's shop. He's a mechanic."

That explained the scent of motor oil.

"The first couple of years were normal, then this last year she started acting strange. We'd make plans and she'd show up late, or not at all. She started ignoring my calls, so I knew something was up. One Friday night we had plans to go to a movie, but she canceled at the last minute, saying she wasn't feeling well. So, I made her favorite soup and drove over to her dorm."

He glanced up at me only to drop his gaze a second later, back to his hands where he had resumed shredding the napkin. "We, ah... We never went to her dorm. I only saw it once, the day I helped her move in. When I got there, she wasn't home but her roommate was. Turns out, she's been spending a lot of time at various parties or 'events,'" he said with air quotes, "for lack of a better word."

He took a deep breath and looked across the table at me, for the first time since he started telling his story. "That wasn't a big deal. So what, she liked to party and do stuff that every college kid does. But then her roommate let it slip that Andy was telling everyone that I..."

He inhaled a shaky breath and pressed his thumb and middle finger to the corners of his eyes like he was trying to stop tears from forming. "I shouldn't be telling you all of this," he laughed. "You're going to think I'm some sort of monster..."

He wasn't kidding when he said this wasn't first date stuff. I reached over and took his hand, offering him comfort and friendship at the very least. I was a firm believer in giving people the chance to show their true colors. Plus, I had a feeling he wasn't the bad guy in this story. "You can tell me."

He looked across the table, our eyes meeting and I could feel the honesty in his next words. "Andy, uh…" His eyes dropped back down to his hands. "She claimed that I forced myself on her that I… *raped* her, and threatened her if she ever told anyone." He laughed, but there was no humor in it.

My breath caught and my mind started to race. This *definitely* wasn't the sort of thing you told someone on a first date. Or second or third. *If he actually did it, wouldn't he keep it tucked away and hope no one ever found out?* What happened to make her say that?

And why wasn't I running away?

"What did you do?" I whispered.

He looked up and our eyes met; his said everything his words couldn't convey. Fear, embarrassment, anger, and sadness. "I set the soup on her desk, thanked her roommate for talking to me, and I left. I turned off my phone and drove the hour back home. When she called later that night, I didn't answer. She sent me so many texts apologizing, asking me to forgive her. But I couldn't, you know? How do you come back from something like that?"

"I can't imagine."

He blew out a heavy breath. "I kept ignoring her calls, and when she finally showed up at my house, I officially broke it off. Told her I wasn't mad, but I was hurt. Told her we were done. She cried, and as much as I wanted to console her, to forgive and go back to how things were, I couldn't. I ended up blocking her number, but she kept coming over." He shrugged and slowly lifted his eyes. "So when Ang needed help, it was the perfect time for me to get away."

I gave his hand a squeeze. "I am so sorry that happened to you." I had so many questions, but now wasn't really the time to ask. Was it?

He cleared his throat and when our eyes met again, I could feel the weight of his pain. "So did I ruin it?"

"Ruin what?"

"This? Us?"

He sounded so genuine, and I didn't think you could fake that sort of emotion. I brushed aside the weight that had settled over us and arched an eyebrow. "Mighty presumptuous of you, already calling us an 'us'," I smirked, trying to lighten the mood. I knew better than most just how petty some girls could be. Case in point - my sister.

He laughed, "My aunt was right."

"Miss Barrett usually is," I joked. "But what about specifically?"

"You."

The night was over far too soon. We probably would have stayed longer, but the coffee shop closed, and since I was only seventeen, I had a curfew. "Can I give you a ride home?"

I shook my head. "No, it's probably best if you don't."

"So is this it then? We have a fun night, and that's it?"

"Are you asking me on a second date?" I blushed. *Where did this flirty girl come from, because it certainly wasn't me...*

"Ember, I would *love* to have a second date with you."

"Give me your phone."

He unlocked it and handed it over without question. I sent myself a text, "Now I have your number, and you have mine."

He grinned and it was everything, especially after he bared his soul. "So I can take you out again, but I can't drive you home?"

I shook my head. "I didn't exactly tell my dad where I was going. Plus," I playfully hit his shoulder. "I'm pretty sure you're a little old for me."

He rolled his eyes. "I'm only twenty, and you're what... eighteen? Nineteen?"

"I'll be eighteen at the end of September."

"I'm not that much older."

I shook my head, "No. You're not." I sighed happily, looking at all the street lights that lit up the street. "I had fun."

"Me too." He reached over and took my hand. "I'm not ready for this night to end."

"Me neither," I whispered.

He moved in closer, so our bodies were mere inches from each other. He brushed my hair over my shoulder, his fingers grazing my neck sending flutters through my chest. His eyes flicked from mine, down to my lips, and back again. He licked his lips. "I really want to kiss you right now."

"You do?"

He nodded. "Can I kiss you, Ember?"

"I've never been kissed before," I admitted, not even feeling embarrassed. Wes just had a way of making me feel safe, and free.

He smirked as he brought his lips down to mine. "Guess I better make it good then."

His kiss was tentative, his lips soft, just brushing over mine. I pressed up into him, and that was all the encouragement he needed. He parted my lips with his tongue and I lightly brushed his with mine as warmth spread through my body. With one hand behind my back and the other in my hair, he held me close as our mouths said all the things we were unable to with words. When he finally pulled away, it was too soon.

We were both breathing heavily, and it took everything in me not to go back for more. Based on the way he was looking at me, he felt the same.

He leaned his forehead against mine. "I had a great time with you tonight. I don't feel right leaving you here."

"I had a great time too, but my dad..."

He nodded in understanding. "Will you call me when you get home?"

I shook my head. "No. But I'll text you."

He pulled me back into his body and brought his lips to mine once more. "Be safe. Goodnight, Em."

"Goodnight, Wes."

CHAPTER THIRTEEN

Linford

8 YEARS AGO

Ember

I hugged the porch railing to avoid the creaky step. I had officially missed curfew for the first time ever. It was only by ten minutes, but I knew even one was too much for my dad. I turned the knob slowly and cringed when the door creaked open. I poked my head inside, it was dark, and I could just make out the faint murmur of the TV from the other side of the house. I carefully closed and locked the door and tiptoed up the stairs, unable to breathe until I was safe in my room.

My phone pinged with a new text while I was walking home, but I was in too much of a hurry to look. I pulled it out of my pocket and couldn't stop the smile that spread across my face or the way I suddenly felt like I was floating on a cloud.

> **Wes:** I don't think I told you how beautiful you are

> **Wes:** I'm going crazy over here. Tell me you're feeling this too

> **Wes:** Okay, either you're in trouble, or the date didn't go as well as I thought. Put me out of my misery

I giggled as I typed out a quick message.

> **Me:** Sorry, I just got home. I missed curfew and had to sneak in

> **Me:** I had a great time

Arms stretched wide, I fell back into my bed, grabbed my pillow and held it over my face while I half squealed into it. *He called me beautiful*. No guy ever made me feel like this.

My phone started to ring and I quickly answered it. "Hey, Tatum."

"Don't you, *hey Tatum* me. How'd it go? Dreamy or serial killer? You can never tell these days..."

"Tatum!" I squeaked. "Oh my god, I can't believe you would ask that!"

"So what is it," she pressed, without an ounce of shame.

"He's..." I took a deep breath and blew it out in a dreamy sigh. "He's better than I expected."

"I knew it!" she laughed. "So, tell me about it already! What did you do?"

"We just talked."

"You *talked?* That's it? You just talked?"

"You act like that's a bad thing."

"Girl," she giggled. "My first date with Brandon, we did a fair bit more than just talk."

"Like what?"

"I'm not sure your innocent mind can handle it."

"Tatum!" I whisper-shouted as I sat up. "You're supposed to be helping me!"

"Okay, okay!" she laughed. "Well, there was talking, and a lot of kissing."

"We kissed," I cut in quietly, worried someone would hear.

"You kissed him? Why didn't you lead with that? How was it?"

"It was... amazing," I swooned. If this were a cartoon, I'd have little hearts floating around my head. "Does it always feel like that?"

"I can't really tell you that. Some guys are horrible kissers, but you don't know until you have a basis for comparison. Maybe you should kiss Jonah, then you'll have something to compare it to."

"I am not..." I started a little too loudly. "I am not kissing Jonah!" I hissed.

"Why not? I did. He's not too bad. A little too much tongue, but he does this thing..."

"I do not need to know this!" I groaned.

"I'm just messing with you," she giggled. "I mean, Jonah is pretty good, but... I'm happy for you, Em. It's about time you get yourself a boyfriend."

"He's not my boyfriend." *Was he my boyfriend?*

"No?"

I nervously picked at a loose thread on my covers. "Well, I don't know. We didn't exactly..."

"Are you going to see him again?"

"Yeah," I blushed, feeling the heat rise in my cheeks. "He's been texting me."

"What's he saying? You can't leave me in the dark here!"

I laughed, "Hang on a sec."

"Just put me on speaker."

"I can't, someone could overhear you."

"What, it's not like they've just had their first date ever. They'll get over it. I'm actually surprised your mom isn't there grilling you."

"They don't know," I whispered.

"You didn't tell them?"

I shook my head. "No. It felt weird. Plus, he's not from around here. And..."

"And what?"

"He's older. Do you really think my dad is going to be okay with this?"

"Hold up. How much older?"

"He's twenty."

"Damn girl! You really did go and get you a man," she chuckled. "Now, what do those texts say?"

Butterflies filled my stomach and I couldn't stop smiling if I wanted to. "He wants to go out again. I'm gonna tell him I'm free tomorrow."

"NO!"

"What? I thought you'd be happy."

"Have I taught you nothing? You've got to keep them wanting. Don't seem overeager. Give him a couple of days..."

"That's ridiculous."

"That's the real world, babe. Trust me."

"Okay," I rolled my eyes and quickly typed out a message.

Me: I'm free Saturday

Wes' foot touched mine, and he grinned over his coffee cup. I arched a brow at him and he slowly reached his hand across the table, his pinky touching mine. My cheeks flushed and butterflies swarmed my belly at the tiniest contact.

"I like it when you blush. It brings out the color in your eyes," he said, his pinky hooking around mine.

"You make me nervous," I whispered.

He sat up and leaned over the table. "You don't have to be nervous around me."

I looked down at where our hands were touching and realized I had to be honest with him. He was a man, an *experienced* man, and I was, well... me. "I've never done this before."

"Hang out at a coffee shop with an incredibly handsome and sexy man?"

I laughed, shoving his hand away. "No!"

He reached over and took my hand lacing our fingers together. They fit perfectly. "Don't be nervous with me. I really like you, I think you're sweet, fun, cute..."

"Cute? Just what every girl wants to be called..." I sighed, looking down at our hands. Cute was a good thing, every girl wanted to be cute, yet for some reason cute made me feel like a little kid, not a woman who could hold his attention.

"Look at me."

Slowly I brought my eyes up to meet his. "Ember, you are beautiful." He reached over and took a strand of my hair between his fingers. "Your hair is this perfect shade of blonde, and your eyes, your corn-flower blue eyes... I could disappear into their depths and be perfectly at peace. You have curves in all the right places, but maybe the best thing," he dropped my hair and brushed his fingertips down my cheek, his thumb tracing over my lips. "Your smile lights up the room, and makes my heart stutter every time you flash it my way."

If I thought my cheeks were hot before, they were scalding now. "I don't know what to say," I whispered.

"How about this," he sat back again, picking up his coffee. "Why don't you show me around town. I've been here a few weeks, and I don't feel like I've been anywhere."

"There really isn't much to see."

"That's okay, because the only thing I really want to see is you." He winked.

I laughed, "That was so cheesy!"

"Yeah, but you're not being shy now, so it worked."

"Smooth, Wesley. Real smooth."

"Come on." He stood and took my hand. "Show me around this place you call home."

CHAPTER FOURTEEN

Linford

PRESENT

Ember

I hated taking over Jadon's room, but I had nowhere else to go. The little boy was playing with his superhero figures when I arrived, and Tatum told him to go outside so I could lay down. I buried my face in his pillow and screamed. Tears pricked at the backs of my eyes, but I refused to cry.

"Hey, babe."

I didn't bother looking up, even when I felt the bed dip with her weight.

"I'm sorry, okay? It's just..."

"Did you know about the car?" I turned my head just enough that I could see her.

Her eyebrows furrowed, "Miles told me Carrie broke down on the highway. You were leaving, weren't you?"

I nodded, though I doubt she could tell. "Not my car. Kennedy's…"

She blew out a heavy breath and readjusted her position on the bed. "Oh shit."

"That's my car," I sniffled, losing the battle as a few tears escaped, rolling down my cheek and soaking into the pillow.

"I didn't even put that together until now."

"Why is she doing this to me?"

Tatum crawled across the bed so she could lay beside me. She curled up on her side, stroking my hair in a soothing motion. "Kennedy is a bitch. She always has been. But I think there's something more there. She's…"

"Evil. She's evil."

"I wouldn't be surprised if she has devil horns hidden under her hair."

I chuckled, swiping at my nose. "Do you think she did it on purpose?"

"The car?"

I glared at her over my shoulder. "Yes, the car."

"I don't know. Maybe?"

"That was my dream car, and she said it was lame and tacky, remember?"

"Maybe she changed her mind?"

I huffed out a breath. "Yeah, maybe." I rolled over onto my back and stared up at the ceiling, covered in those plastic glow-in-the-dark stars. "What's she like?" I asked, not sure I wanted to know.

Tatum sat up and arched an eyebrow. "You made me promise never to tell you about her. Are you sure you want to know?"

I closed my eyes. "Want to? No. I don't want to. But I think maybe I need to. Since I'm going to be stuck here for a while."

"Oh yeah," she cringed. "Have you talked to Bob yet?"

"No. That's a problem for another day."

Tatum crawled off the bed and grabbed my hands, giving me a little tug. "Come on. This conversation requires tequila."

"It's barely noon!" I protested.

She dragged me from the room and deposited me at the kitchen table. She picked up her phone and next thing I know, she was packing up a bag for the boys. "Brandon will be here in a few to take these guys to the park."

"Tatum," I groaned. "I'm completely disrupting your life! I should just go..."

"Go where?"

I slouched in my chair. She had me there, my options were limited. "I could stay with Miles."

She rolled her eyes. "Yeah, and listen to him having hot sex every night?"

"I never should have told you that," I shuddered.

"Probably not," she laughed.

Less than twenty minutes later, Brandon had one boy on his hip, the other on his back, and was headed out for a "boys" day. Fatherhood looked good on him.

Tatum cracked the lid of a brand new bottle of tequila and poured a couple of shots. We tipped them back, and I cringed at the taste. She poured a couple more, only talking when I swallowed that one too.

"I don't really know where to begin, or what to say. You know your sister. She's... She's..."

"How about you tell me what she's doing these days."

Tatum poured a couple more shots and tipped hers back before answering. "She's a stay at home mom," she said with air quotes.

Hearing Kennedy and mom in the same sentence stung. I remember when we were younger - she never wanted to be a mom. She hated kids. And now... "Does she only have the one?"

Tatum nodded. "Yeah, she..." She cut herself off and gave me a sad smile. "When you left, things were bad for a while. She had half the town wrapped around her little finger, somehow managed to convince them you were the problem."

"That's why people have been whispering and pointing?"

Tatum flinched, but nodded. "Sorry. I've avoided the situation like the plague and I've tried sticking up for you, but you know how Kennedy was. People just took her word for everything, and there was nothing anyone could say or do."

"Does she have a house around here?" The fact she still lived here brought me more joy than it probably should have. She always wanted to get away, go live in New York or California. She thought she was going to be a model or star in a reality TV show. Guess her dreams were dashed at the same time mine were.

Tatum chuckled, "You're gonna love this."

"What?"

"They live with your parents."

"Wait, what?"

She nodded, unable to hide her smile. "You know your parents... There's no way they'd let their baby out of their sight. I mean, look what they tried to do to you."

I sighed and leaned forward, resting my arms on my knees. "Are they..."

"Don't." Tatum cut me off, taking my hand. "Don't ask me that."

I nodded, thankful she knew me well enough to stop me before I went down the rabbit hole. I tapped my shot glass and she filled it to the brim. "What else?"

"Well...," she started, then a twinkle lit up her eyes. "I'm pretty sure she's hooking up with some guy over in Wickett."

My eyebrows shot up at that news. The idea of her being unfaithful never crossed my mind, though it probably should have. "Wow."

"I know, right? Not terribly surprising, but still..."

I closed my eyes and sucked in a deep breath, blowing it out slowly. "I think I've heard enough."

I held out my glass for another shot and threw it back. There was one other thing I needed to know. Another forbidden subject. "Does he still work at Bob's?"

"No. I'm not sure about the details, but I do know he went to work for your dad."

I breathed out a sigh of relief. "Can I borrow your car?"

Tatum barked out a laugh. "Oh hell no!"

"Not now, dummy. Tomorrow. When I'm sober."

"Anything you need."

Tatum offered to come with me, but I didn't want to drag her from her boys again. The more time I spent with them, the more I realized how badly I wanted kids. How much I always wanted kids.

I parked on the side of Bob's Auto and took a deep breath, steeling my nerves. I hadn't seen Bob in... well, seven years. I wiped my clammy hands on the back of my jeans as I pulled open the office door. I couldn't help but smile when Bob's head snapped up, a giant grin spreading from ear to ear.

Bob was one of the nicest guys you'd ever meet. He was an older man when I met him, even more so now, with his head of thinning white hair hidden under a ball cap. He always wore blue coveralls that fit snugly over his round belly, and had permanent grease stains underneath his fingernails. "That really you kid?"

He pulled me in for a hug. I closed my eyes and breathed him in; he still smelled the same, bad cologne and motor oil. "It's me," I smiled, wiping a tear from my cheek.

"I didn't think I was ever gonna see you again. Even after Miles had me pick up your car..."

"I didn't think I'd see you either," I admitted, taking a step back, a pang of guilt settling in the back of my throat. *How did I let so many important relationships go?*

"I can't believe you still have that same car." He glanced through the small window in the door leading into the garage bay.

"Well, if you can't fix her, I may have to get a new one," I sighed. "How bad is it?"

"Not entirely sure yet," he shrugged.

I took a deep breath and blew it out noisily. "I was wondering if we could work something out. I know for a fact I don't have enough to cover repairs. I was hoping you'd let me make payments? You know I'll pay..."

He shook his head. "No can do, kiddo."

My heart sank. "Is there anything I can do? I can't stay here, Bob. I have a life in..."

He gave my arm a squeeze. "Come on." He pulled open the shop door and gestured me through.

I spotted my car instantly, and Bob already had one of his guys working on it.

"Hey Bob, you got any..."

Everything faded away. Everything except *him*. Wes just stood there frozen in place, a dirty shop rag in his hands. I couldn't move, couldn't think, could barely breathe.

"Em?"

CHAPTER FIFTEEN

Linford

8 YEARS AGO

Wes

I held out the other half of my sandwich. My girl was always hungry.

She giggled and kissed my cheek as she took it. "Thank you."

I put my arm around her shoulders and pulled her close to my body. We had only been seeing each other for about a month, but I already knew she was it for me; I would never find someone as special as her. Ember was my world. When I was with her, everything felt right. When we were apart, I counted the seconds until I could be with her again. She was so damn beautiful, I could stare at her for days and never get bored. She was funny, and smart, so fucking smart. She challenged me like no one ever had before. And more - she supported me. She cared about my thoughts, ideas, and even encouraged my dreams.

I never felt like this about anyone, not even Andy. My heart throbbed painfully, knowing our days were numbered; the idea of leaving her made me sick.

I absently ran my hand up and down her arm while our legs dangled over the tailgate of my truck. We spent so many days out here, parked down by the lake, having lunch in the bed of my truck. I started keeping a blanket and pillows with me, to make it more comfortable.

She lay her head on my shoulder and I pressed a kiss to the top of her head. "What are you thinking about?"

My lips curled up in a smile. "You."

"Be serious," she poked me and I yelped.

"I am," I laughed. "And now I'm thinking we should go swimming."

"Swimming? But we don't have…"

"Come on." I hopped down and held out my hand. She looked at me with questions burning in her eyes. I took her hand and gave her a little tug, pulling her behind me down to the water's edge.

"We're gonna get soaked!" she protested, pulling back.

I let go of her hand and yanked my shirt off over my head. I toed off my boots and my hands went to my belt buckle, all while she stood there and stared, her mouth hanging open.

"Wes!" she whisper-shouted. "What are you doing?"

I slid out of my jeans and grinned at her, wearing nothing but my boxer briefs. "Do you trust me?"

"You know I do!"

I crossed the small space between us and took her lips in a kiss. "Come on, baby. Let's go swimming." I reached down and gripped the hem of her sundress, asking permission with my eyes. When she gave me a small nod, I slowly lifted it over her head and dropped it with my discarded clothes.

She stood before me, wearing nothing but a pair of basic cotton panties and a matching bra, using her hands and arms to try to cover herself. She refused to look at me, and I worried I pushed her too far. Ember was, as my aunt put it, a good girl. Before me, she had never kissed a guy, so I imagine being seen like this was difficult for her.

"Look at me, baby." I tipped her chin up with my fingers and stared into the endless depths of her eyes. Her eyes slowly slid up to mine, but she still looked nervous. "Don't be scared," I whispered. "We're just swimming."

"But..."

"You're beautiful, Em." I cupped her face with my hands and kissed her forehead. "Just swimming. I promise."

She swallowed and gave me a small nod.

I took her hand and led her down to the water. I kept my eyes forward, not looking back until I knew she was under the water. I pulled her body up against mine, groaning at the feel of her bare skin pressed against me. I clearly wasn't thinking straight when I suggested swimming; If we stayed like that much longer I wouldn't be able to hide my erection.

I dipped under the water and swam a little ways away so I could get myself under control. As soon as I surfaced, a look of confusion crossed her face, right before I sent a splash of water her way.

"Wes!"

I chuckled. "Got ya!"

"I don't think so!" she shouted, swinging her arm through the water and sending a wave in my direction.

"Come on, Em! You can do better than that!"

For the next hour or so, we played like a couple of kids enjoying a hot summer day. And in a way, I guess we were.

Somewhere along the line her self-consciousness disappeared, and I found myself touching her in ways I hadn't expected. Her skin was so soft, and I could see myself getting carried away. I was desperate to keep myself in check.

Ember swam to me and wrapped her arms and legs around me. We were in shallow enough water that I could stand, which made holding her that much easier. "Hey, babe," I grinned, pressing a playful kiss to her lips.

Her expression turned serious and she pulled her bottom lip between her teeth, something I noticed she only did when she was nervous. A moment later I realized why when she rolled her hips. "Ember," I groaned in warning. We had kissed and touched, but never under our clothes, or below the belt.

"Wes?" she asked, looking up at me through dark lashes.

"Yeah?"

"Do you want me?" Her cheeks flushed pink as she rolled her hips again, the movement rubbing against my already semi-hard dick.

"You know I do," I breathed out, trying to find an ounce of restraint.

"How come we haven't?"

"Do we have to do this right now?" I asked, my breathing getting heavier as I slowly lost the battle, my dick growing impossibly hard against her. Sex was easy. It was only ever Andy, until we broke up, and then I found myself in bed with a different woman every night. If I wanted sex, I didn't have to try. *So why was I taking my time with Ember?*

"Tatum said…"

I shook my head. "I don't care what Tatum said," I snapped, then quickly added, "You're special. I don't want to rush things." There was more to it than that, but it wasn't time, not yet.

"But…"

"God, Ember," I groaned, gripping her ass and pressing my hardness against her. "I want you so fucking bad, but I'm trying to be a gentleman here."

She grinned, and I knew I was in trouble as my mind and heart warred with my body.

I carried her out of the water, all the way to my truck, ignoring the sting of the rocks and twigs under my bare feet. It didn't help that she was kissing my neck, my jaw, and even nipped at the lobe of my ear. My mind raced, trying to come up with a way I could make this work. I set her on the tailgate and had to pry myself away from her. "Stay here," I said, pressing a kiss to her forehead and tugging the blanket over her shoulders.

I jogged back and gathered our clothes. By the time I made it back, she was laid out on the blanket right there in the truck bed. I closed my eyes as my heart thundered so loudly I couldn't think straight.

I dropped our clothes by the wheel well and crawled over top of her when she spread her legs to make space for me. I held myself up with my arms on either side of her head as I brought my lips to hers. Ember was sweet, like honey, and I could never get enough of her.

Her hands were on my back and she hooked a leg around my ass, pulling me closer. I groaned and she moaned into my mouth as I pressed against her center. I was half tempted to take her right there; my dick was fully on board with that. My head, however, knew that she deserved so much more than impromptu sex in the bed of my truck.

Reluctantly I pulled away, putting enough space between us that I could think. Her hands slipped into my hair, and when she tried to drag me in for another kiss, I pulled away completely, sitting on my knees between her spread legs.

"What is it?" She asked, pushing up so she was resting against her elbows. "Did I do something wrong?"

"No, baby," I rasped, my dick pressing uncomfortably against my wet boxers. I scrubbed my hands over my face as I tried to figure out how to say what I needed to say without hurting her.

She reached for me again, and I took her hand, keeping her from touching me. "We can't do this."

"What? Why?" Confusion swirled in her eyes.

"Baby, I..." I shook my head. Why was this so hard? I knew no matter what I said, it was going to hurt her. Guilt swirled in my stomach. I couldn't do this, not when I was...

I reached for my clothes, pulling my shirt over my head and tugging on my jeans. She just sat there, mouth agape.

I handed her her dress and looked away, unable to stomach the pained expression on her face. We packed everything up in silence, stowing the blanket and pillows behind the seats of the truck. When I was finally brave enough to look at her, a lump formed in my throat. The hurt that radiated off of her was overwhelming. Not only that, but she looked broken.

I turned on the engine and drove away from our spot, not heading back toward town, but in the opposite direction. I had no destination in mind, I just needed to clear my head, and fix this. When I woke up this morning, I never would have imagined myself in this position. Then a single phone call had me turning down sex with the woman I love.

Love?

Fuck. When did that happen? When did I fall in love with Ember Davis?

After about twenty minutes of tense silence, I pulled off on the side of the road. I ran my hands over the steering wheel, working up the courage to face her. "Ember, let me explain."

"No, it's okay. I get it," she smiled, but it was forced. I knew all her smiles, and I hated this one, the one she pasted on when she was upset, but didn't want to make waves.

"I don't think you do." I reached over and took her hand, surprised she let me touch her. She turned in her seat so she was looking at me. The pain behind her eyes was like a knife to the gut.

"It's okay, Wes. I'm too young, too *inexperienced*. You're probably used to women who know what they're doing. I get it."

I reached out and cupped her cheek, surprised when she leaned into my touch. "It's not that at all."

"So you're saying that if I wasn't a virgin you would have slept with me by now?"

I winced, knowing there was some truth to that statement. "Baby, that's not it."

"Then what is it? Am I just that repulsive to you?"

"Damn it, Ember. You're special! You're so fucking special to me, that I don't want to hurt you!"

"Then don't!"

"It's not that easy!"

"It *is* that easy, Wes! Either you want me, or you don't. Which is it?"

I pinched the bridge of my nose and inhaled deeply. "This isn't going the way I thought it would. I'm not... I'm not saying this right. Just, please. Listen to me."

She held up her hand, "Wait. This isn't going the way *you thought it would*? What the hell does that mean? You've been planning this? For how long, Wes? How long were you going to let me pine after you like some silly little girl, just so you could humiliate me like this?"

"It's not like that!"

"Then tell me what it's like, because I'm really not getting it."

I reached out and took her hand, rubbing my thumbs over her knuckles as I recounted the words I had practiced so many times. "Never in my life have I felt what I feel for you. In a short month, you have come to mean more to me than anyone ever has. You are the light in my darkness, the warmth in my soul. When I thought I was dead inside, you breathed life into me. You gave me purpose, something to look forward to, something to live for." My heart was racing as I attempted to fill my words with everything I was feeling. "I know we haven't known each other long, and that terrifies me, that I could feel so deeply so soon. When I say you're special, I mean it."

I brushed my lips over her knuckles. "I am in love with you. I don't know when it happened. I wasn't looking for it, but here we are. I love you, Ember, and I want to treat you right. You deserve so much more than me..."

"Wes..." Her eyes brimmed with unshed tears.

"Just... let me get this out," I pleaded and she gave me a small nod. This was the hard part. "Ang is doing better. She's out of the wheelchair and getting around just fine."

"That's great, but I don't understand..." Her brows pulled together in a frown.

"She doesn't need me anymore," I deflated. "My dad called..."

"You're leaving?"

I cringed. Hearing the words out loud made it that much more real. "I don't want to, Ember. You have to believe me, but I can't just keep living off my aunt. Besides," I took a deep breath and dropped my gaze to where I held her hand in mine. "You have a future. You're going to finish school, then go to college and live your dream. You've got a plan, goals. I'll just hold you back." My heart clenched in my chest. I knew

I was breaking her heart, I just hope she realized I was breaking mine too.

"That's ridiculous!" she cried. "You won't hold me back. You *don't* hold me back."

"Oh, come on, let's be real..."

"I *am* being real!"

"What do you really see happening here?" I said more harshly than I intended. "I stay, live with my aunt while you finish high school. You'll go off to college, and then what? I follow you like a stray dog?" I shook my head, insecurity and that all too familiar ache crawling its way back in.

"It wouldn't have to be like that!"

"No? Because the way I see it, there's nothing here for me!"

"What about me?" she cried. "Am I nothing to you?"

"You're everything to me!" I shouted, wishing she could see, could feel just how much this was hurting me too.

"Then why? Why won't you try?"

"I..." I closed my eyes. "I can't."

"Please, Wes!" Tears rolled down her cheeks and I felt like such an asshole. And this is why I couldn't sleep with her. No matter how much I wanted to, no matter how much I cared, I was still leaving, and she was still going to hate me. At least this way I didn't take something from her that she could give to someone more deserving.

"You're going to go to college and discover all the world has to offer. You're going to meet so many people and have so many options. You're going to find someone better than me, and then what?" I choked out. Memories of Andy flooded my mind. As much as this was for her, it was for me too. I couldn't go through that again, not with Ember... I let everyone believe I was okay after what Andy did. That couldn't be further from the truth. If that happened with Ember - I don't think I would survive that.

"That'll never happen!" she fisted her hands in my shirt, her eyes pleading with me. "I could never do that to you!"

I covered her hands with mine, holding them to my chest, soaking up the feeling of her skin against mine. "You don't know that," I whispered.

"You're a coward." She yanked her hands away from mine and shoved me back.

My heart was breaking, and there was nothing I could do. As much as I wanted to, I couldn't change my circumstances. "Em, please. We still have a couple more days."

"What's the point, Wes?" She shook her head. "Just take me home."

I pulled up outside her house and before I could even shut the engine off, she was slamming the door and storming up the sidewalk. I caught a glimpse of who I suspected was her dad as she pushed her way past him into the house. He stood in the doorway staring at me, confusion written all over his face.

He had no idea who I was.

I don't know why it surprised me that Ember never told her parents about us, but it did. More than that, it *hurt*.

I waved awkwardly before I pulled away and drove the ten minutes it took to get back to my aunt's house. I sat in the hollow silence of my truck, hating how cold it suddenly felt, and it had nothing to do with the weather. It was unusually hot, ninety-five degrees, and I didn't have air conditioning. No, the cold wasn't the weather, it was the absence of my heart - the heart I left with the only girl I ever truly loved.

I didn't even know if she loved me back.

I rested my head against the steering wheel, trying to come to terms with the pain I felt in my chest. I knew breaking things off was going to be hard, but never in a million years had I expected it to feel like this.

I don't know how long I sat there, stewing in my pain. It wasn't until a rapping on my window snapped me out of it that I noticed it was dark out. I rolled my window down, meeting the concerned face of my aunt. "Wes, honey? What's the matter?"

I shook my head. "Nothing," My throat felt raw. I didn't even realize I had been crying. "I'll be in in a minute."

Angie was a take no shit kind of person, so it shouldn't have surprised me when she walked around my truck and climbed into the passenger seat. "What happened?"

I shook my head as tears rolled down my cheeks, dropping onto my fisted hands. I rubbed my chest with the heel of my hand. "It hurts."

"Who hurt you, honey. Did Andy…"

"I hurt her, Ang. The only girl I've ever loved and I hurt her," I choked out.

She reached out and rubbed her hand over my back. "Talk to me, honey, cuz I *know* you're not talking about Andy… What happened with Ember?"

"I told her the truth."

"Which is?"

I swiped at my cheeks, giving her a look that said, "are you kidding me?" She was there when I got my dads phone call this morning.

"You did not," she practically growled, swatting my shoulder. "I swear to God, Wes…"

"What am I supposed to do?" I complained. "I have to go home! He needs me!"

She scoffed. "Your dad is a grown-ass man who can hire some help. He needs you like I need a third arm."

I arched a brow at her and she swatted me again. "What? It's the best I could come up with on short notice!"

I huffed out a laugh. Leave it to my aunt to make me laugh during the worst moment of my life. "That's not all," admitted after a few minutes.

"What else did you do?"

"I can't talk to you about this!" I groaned. I once had a sex talk with my dad. Back then I thought nothing could be more humiliating. Something told me talking to my aunt would be worse.

"Hit me with it. There's nothing you can say that I haven't heard before."

I sighed, and rested my head against the steering wheel, looking down at the stitching holding its cover on. Unable to look at her, I mumbled, "She wanted to have sex."

"Excuse me?" Her voice held a tinge of anger, and I recoiled.

"She wanted to have sex."

"Wesley Allen Barrett. You better not have hurt that girl."

I turned my head, not taking it off the steering wheel. "I hurt her, but not in the way you think."

"You better explain."

"I wouldn't do it. I told her she was special, she deserved so much more than me, and I wouldn't take that from her." I groaned, remembering the whole conversation. "You should have seen the look on her face when she realized I was turning down sex."

Angie scooted across the seat and awkwardly wrapped her arms around me. She wasn't a hugger, which made this that much weirder. "I'm proud of you, Wes."

I huffed out a laugh. "Thanks?"

She gave me a pat before letting me go and opening the door to get out. "Come on, let's figure out how to fix this."

"Angie…"

"You're not leaving. If I have to go all the way down to Huntsville and beat some sense into that man, I will."

"Don't be ridiculous. You hate Texas."

She nodded. "I do, but I'd do it for you."

Fifteen minutes later, I sat at the kitchen table with my head in my hands as my aunt paced back and forth, phone pressed to her ear. This was going about as well as I expected.

"Don't you dare Ang me!" she shouted. "That boy deserves the chance to find his own way!" Pause. "You've never given him the freedom to!" Pause. "For fuck's sake, Drew. You filled that boys' head with nothing but engines from the moment he could hold a wrench. He never knew anything else!"

She stopped her pacing and looked at me, a wicked gleam in her eyes. "He has a woman here. She's good for him, Drew."

I smacked my head against the table. *Why did she have to bring Ember into this?*

"Andy was no good for him, you and I both know that. That girl was nothing but a soul-sucking leech." Pause. "I've known Ember her entire life. There is no one more suited for Wes than her."

She threw her hands up in the air and I could only guess what my dad was spouting off now. Part of me felt guilty. My dad really did need me, and I was leaving him in a lurch by not going back. Except I needed Ember. I'm not sure I could live without her. It's only been a few hours and already I felt dead inside.

"No she's not some small town, small minded girl looking for a meal ticket. This girl is going places. She has plans, and a big future. She's good for him, and believe it or not, he's good for *her*." She rolled her eyes, but gave me a grin. "I don't expect anything from you. I just want Wes to be happy. *She* makes him happy." Pause. "Drew, I love you, but I'm not letting him leave. You'll just have to be an adult and hire some help instead of leaning on your son to do it for you."

I don't think he got another word in before she hung up and dropped down into the chair across from me. "So?"

She cringed. "He wants you home. He doesn't think staying here for a girl is a valuable use of your time."

I nodded and stood up, the chair making an awful screech as it slid away from the table. "I'm already packed, I'll be on the road first thing in the morning."

"Sit your ass back down, I'm not done talking to you."

I reluctantly obeyed, I just wanted to sleep. At least there I could pretend life was going to be okay.

"Your dad wants you home, but over my dead body." She arched an eyebrow, daring me to argue. "Ever since your mamma ran off, he's been clinging to you, terrified of being alone." She reached out and placed her hand on my arm. I hadn't thought about my mom in years. "He's a grown man, Wes. And so are you. You deserve to find your own way."

"But..."

She held up a hand, cutting me off. "I know I told you to stay away from her, but I was wrong. I have never seen that girl look so happy. It's like you ignited a fire in her that we've never seen before. I want this for her as much as I want it for you."

"What am I supposed to do? I've looked around, nobody is hiring. I can't just sit here and live off of you and your generosity..."

"Don't you worry about that. I've got a couple ideas."

"What about..."

"Stop building roadblocks! Do you want her?"

I swallowed thickly and nodded. "I love her, Ang."

My aunt got this dreamy look in her eye and it made me wonder how much of her story I actually knew. "If you love her, you'll fight for her." She stood up and pushed away from the table. "Now, it's late and we've got a busy day ahead of us. Go get some sleep, your new life begins tomorrow."

CHAPTER SIXTEEN

L'inford

8 YEARS AGO

Wes

The lot was overrun with weeds, popping up through the cracks in the pavement. The rollup garage doors were shut up tight, and a closed sign hung over the window in the door. I half expected to see a stray tumbleweed blow past.

"Are you sure about this?"

Ang pushed her car door open. "Come on. Bob's great, you're gonna love him."

I took one more look at the dilapidated garage, the sun faded sign reading "Bob's Auto," and got out. I stayed close to my aunt as she knocked on the door. Much to my surprise, it swung open only a moment later and an old man stepped out and wrapped her in a giant bear hug.

"Miss Barrett, same as always. Only call when you want something," he chuckled. He took a step back and held her at arm's length. "You look like you're doing well. Surgery was good?"

She nodded. "Sure was. And then my nephew showed up unexpectedly to help me out."

He looked over her shoulder at me and I gave him a nod. "And now he wants to stay?"

Angie looked back at me with a shit-eating grin plastered across her face. "He may or may not have fallen in love."

Bob looked me up and down. "Who's the lucky lady?"

"Ember Davis, sir," I answered, feeling awkward being talked about like I wasn't even there.

His eyebrows shot up. "The Davis girl? What's Mitch think about that?"

I looked to Ang for help, having never heard the name before. She mouthed, "her father" and I swallowed past a lump in my throat. "He doesn't know, sir."

Bob barked out a laugh and shook his head. He waved us into the office behind him. It looked slightly better than I expected; clean considering it looked like it was right out of the 1980's with dark wood paneling and a red tile floor. The desk, made of solid oak, was obnoxiously big, with a monstrosity of a computer setup on the far side. The monitor alone took up over half the surface area. A couple of uncomfortable looking brown plastic chairs sat against one wall and an old TV tray was tucked away in the corner with a coffee pot sitting on top. *How could anyone manage a business like this?*

He plopped down in an oversized chair behind the desk and gestured for us to pull up the plastic chairs and sit across from him. "Miss Barrett tells me you're a mechanic," he said, hands folded under his chin.

I nodded. "Yes sir."

"Where did you study?"

I sat up a little taller and looked at my aunt. "I, uh..." I cleared my throat when she gave me a half shrug. "I didn't." I stuttered. "What I mean is, my dad owns a shop and he taught me everything I know."

He rubbed his chin, as though contemplating my worth. "Tell me why I should hire you."

I took a deep breath and thought carefully about my answer. Truthfully, it didn't look like he did enough business to warrant the help, but if he was willing to hire me, then I'd take it. I'd do anything to stay. "I know cars; new ones and older ones. I can rebuild a carburetor just as easily as I can track down an issue with the computer system. I work hard, and am always looking for ways to improve."

He nodded. "This shop hasn't been open or running for a while. I haven't been able to keep up with the newer cars. Think you could help me with that?"

That didn't surprise me, given the state of the office. "Yes sir. I could even set you up with a better system," I pointed to the ancient machine on his desk.

Bob chuckled and shook his head. "Yeah, that thing hasn't worked in ages. I could never get the internet setup and then one day it just turned on to a black screen with a white cursor... I've been doing everything by hand ever since."

My eyes nearly popped out of my head. Doing things by hand would be a nightmare. My mind swam with possibilities, ways to fix this place up and bring in more business. "It wouldn't be too hard to set up wifi, a laptop with the software you need. Get everything digital..."

"Let me stop you there, son," he held up a hand. "I can't pay that much, and you'll only be part time."

My stomach dropped. It was something, but no way would it be enough. "I understand." Ang put her hand on my arm when I started to get up, urging me to sit back down.

"When can he start?" she asked.

He looked me up and down, as though he were still considering whether or not I was worth his time. Finally he stood up and reached out a hand. "How about Saturday?"

I took his hand and nodded, looking from him to my aunt. She was determined and I found myself both grateful and reluctant to trust her. "Yes sir. I'll be here."

I left Angie inside, chatting away and sat down heavily in her car. I pulled out my phone and for the hundredth time, checked my messages. My texts to Ember were all left on read, and she was ignoring my calls. I pressed the call button next to her name and held the phone to my ear. It rang once and went to voicemail. Either she blocked my number, or was rejecting my calls. I sighed and typed out another text that I knew she wouldn't respond to instead of leaving one more message she probably wouldn't listen to.

> **Me:** Please, Em. I need to talk to you

I watched it go from delivered to read, and then nothing.

By the time Angie got back in the car, I just wanted to go home. And by home, I meant back to Texas, where I could wallow without the memory of the girl I loved everywhere I looked. "This isn't going to work," I said quietly.

"What do you mean, *this isn't going to work*? Wes, you've got to give this a chance."

"Part time. Low pay. I can't live off of that, and I don't know anyone else who's hiring."

"Don't worry about that right now. You have a job, that's a start. It's not like you really have that many expenses."

I rolled my eyes. "I'm not living off of you, or my dad. If I'm staying with you, I'm going to start paying you rent."

She rolled her eyes, but didn't deny me. She understood, probably better than anyone, how important it was to be independent and pay your own way. "Fine. We'll work out an agreement. But I'm going to insist we start small. As circumstances change, so can our agreement. Deal?"

I nodded. "Yeah, deal. But that's not the only problem."

She backed out of the lot and steered us toward Paula's. "What else?"

"Ember won't take my calls or respond to my texts."

"Do you blame her?"

"No, but..."

"Give it time. Don't y'all have that bonfire tomorrow night?"

Tomorrow was the fourth of July. Ember and I were planning on attending the bonfire they had every year to celebrate out on Old Man Miller's back lot. Apparently bonfires were something they did around here once a week or so all summer long and even into the fall. This was supposed to be my first, but now... "I don't know."

She pulled up outside the diner and although I knew Ember wasn't working today, I still felt sick at the idea of going inside without her. "Come on."

I followed her inside, my hands stuffed in my pockets. Angie didn't wait to be seated, she just marched over to one of the booths and slid in, gesturing for me to do the same. Not even two minutes later, a familiar voice said, "Hey, Miss Barrett. What can I...?" Tatum's words dropped off, and a second later, I was being hit in the head by a hard, laminated menu. "What. The. Hell. Are. You. Doing. Here?" Each word was punctuated by another hit.

"What the hell?" I snapped, throwing my hands up to protect my head as she swung at me again.

"You don't belong here," she practically growled. "You need to leave."

"I'm not going anywhere."

"Aren't you supposed to be going back to Texas?" she sneered. "Or was that some bullshit excuse to break my best friend's heart."

"It wasn't an excuse!" I looked to my aunt for help. Frustration flared inside me as she just sat there, arms crossed over her chest, lips curled up at the edges like she was trying not to laugh. The hard menu smacked me in the back of the head again.

"Then what the hell are you still doing here? Go. Be gone. We don't want you here anymore."

"I'm not leaving! Not unless Ember tells me herself that she wants me gone. That she doesn't care about me anymore."

"Yeah, that's not gonna happen." She tucked the menu under her arm and put her hand on her hip, popping it out. "She doesn't want to talk to you."

"I've noticed."

"Then take a hint. You broke her heart, Wesley." She almost sounded sad as she turned to my aunt and pasted on a fake smile. "I'm sorry, Miss Barrett, but Wesley is no longer welcome at this establishment."

My aunt's features softened as she reached out and touched Tatum's arm. "I was kind of hoping we could have a word."

"I have nothing more to say to *him.*"

"Then talk to me, sweetie."

Tatum reluctantly gave me her back and focused all her attention on my aunt. "I'm not gonna sit here and defend Wes' actions. I told the boy he was being an idiot, but in his defense, he didn't really see any other way."

"Well, his way sucks, and my best friend is devastated."

She didn't say anything I didn't already know, yet her words dug the knife a little deeper. The thought that I could cause pain to the woman I loved with all my heart made me sick. I didn't deserve her, and if she never forgave me, it would be no less than I deserved.

"Believe it or not, Wes is too."

Tatum glanced back at me, her expression giving away everything her words didn't. She was hurting too, because Ember's pain was her pain. They were that close. "What do you want from me?" she finally asked, cutting to the chase.

"Tatum, you know Ember better than anyone. Do you think she could be persuaded to give Wes another chance? Or at the very least let him explain?"

Tatum sighed, her shoulders slumping with the action. "I don't know. Maybe? But... How do we know he's not going to do it again? I can't stand seeing her like this."

"I can't guarantee he won't be an idiot again. Mostly because all men are idiots," Tatum chuckled at that. "What I can say is that I won't allow this particular circumstance to get in their way. He's not going back to Texas, he's staying right here."

Tatum looked at me, studying my face for any signs of deceit. She must not have found any because the next thing I knew, my aunt was scooting over, and Tatum was sliding in next to her. "What's the plan?"

CHAPTER SEVENTEEN

Linford

8 YEARS AGO

Wes

If I were home, I'd be hanging out with my friends, out on the water on one of their boats. We'd have a stash of fireworks ready to launch at a moment's notice, and a cooler full of cheap beer. We'd drink, joke around, and blow shit up like we did every year.

When everything happened with Ember they were the first to know, after Ang. I told them I was coming home. Then this morning came around and they wanted to know where I was. "Shit." I quickly typed out a text in our group chat, hoping they wouldn't be too pissed.

Me: Change of plans. Staying in Nebraska. Gotta get my girl back

Penn: You're joking. Tell me you're joking

Penn: Julie's coming and she's bringing Andy. She said she'd only come if you did

Me: Fuck you. I told you I wouldn't touch Andy with a ten foot pole

Penn: You two used to go at it like rabbits! Come on, take one for the team

Jazz: You do realize Texas pussy is as good as Nebraska pussy. Probably better

Me: Fuck off

Jazz: So you won't mind if I fuck Andy?

Me: Be my guest. Make sure you wrap it up though - who knows where she's been

My phone pinged with a few more messages, but I didn't bother to read them. They would just be more of the same. My friends were certified jackasses, but that didn't mean I loved them any less.

I checked myself in the mirror again, straightening my shirt, buttoning and then unbuttoning the top two buttons. I ran a hand through my hair, it was a wreck, but I had time. I had to remind myself that I had time.

Tatum graciously informed me that Ember would be working today. Apparently, she wasn't doing well with idle time, so when it came to today, a day we made plans to spend together, she practically begged for the extra shift.

It worked for me. As far as I could tell, she had no idea I was still in town. If I had somewhere to go, I took my aunt's car. Tatum helped too, keeping me informed when it came to Ember's schedule. I just needed time for a grand gesture, to set things right.

I grabbed my wallet and keys. "I'm heading out!" I shouted. I had a few things to pick up in Wickett, which was an hour's drive each way, and I wanted to be back before dark. I wasn't familiar with Old Man Miller's back lot, though Tatum had driven me out there to scout it out ahead of time. I just wasn't confident in my ability to find it by myself in the dark.

"Don't forget the flowers! And maybe grab some chocolates too? Girls love that shit."

I laughed, smiling at just how invested my aunt was. "I think I can handle this."

"Don't be so sure," she goaded me. "Look what happened last time you were left to your own devices."

"That's different and you know it."

"Go, before it's too late," she shooed me out the door."

With my windows down, I cranked the radio up as I hit the highway. Ember was always going on and on about how music has meaning. Give her any mood or situation and she could give you a country song that fit. To me, music was always something to drown out the noise in my head, to fill the silence. Go figure now, when I'm fighting to get back the one thing that makes sense to me, "Whatever it Takes" by Imagine Dragons would come on...

"Yeah, I hear you, bro." I'll do whatever it takes to get a second chance and do things right.

It was close to five when I got to town. Wickett was a metropolis compared to Linford, yet it was still considerably smaller than where I grew up. I stopped by a couple shops first. I knew what I wanted, and it had to be perfect. Fortunately, the third place I went in had exactly what I needed. With that taken care of, I followed my aunt's advice and grabbed some chocolates from a little boutique store, and then finally, stopped at the florist.

Ember loved flowers, but she wasn't the kind of girl you could just buy a bouquet of roses for and call it a day. Roses meant little to her. Same goes for carnations, mums, and any sort of lily. Thankfully this place had what I was looking for. I called in advance and was assured it would be ready.

They were more perfect than I could have imagined. I didn't know much about flowers, so I only had two requests. There had to be daisies and there had to be cornflowers.

My shirt clung to my back as I raced back home. The July heat and lack of air conditioning combined with my anxiety meant I was sweating my ass off. If I didn't hurry, I wouldn't have time to clean up.

Angie met me at the door, holding it open so I could zip past and hop in the shower. "Tatum called about an hour ago. Said Ember was getting off early, and they were going to head straight to the bonfire!" she shouted through the bathroom door.

"How much time do I have?"

She chuckled. "Oh, negative twenty, give or take..."

I banged my head against the tiled wall as hot water rolled over my shoulders. "Can you make sure everything is ready? Please? It's all in my truck."

By the time I was ready, I had three texts from Tatum, and a whole slew from my friends back home. I ignored the ones from my friends and went straight for Tatum's.

> **Tatum:** Sorry, I tried to hold her off. Hurry!

> **Tatum:** Man, I'm doing my best here, but my girl is determined to get smashed

The next text came with a picture. I leaned against the wall and zoomed in. Ember looked stunning. Her long blonde hair hung in loose waves down her back. She had on a white, off the shoulder sundress that hugged her breasts, then flared out at her waist reaching about halfway down her thighs. Her favorite pair of cowboy boots completed her outfit.

She had a beer in her hand raised high over her head and a huge smile on her face. If I didn't know her as well as I do, seeing her smile would have made me second guess my decision to stay and fight for her. But I knew that smile. That's the one she wore when she was hurting and didn't want anyone to know.

> **Tatum:** Please tell me you're here!

I turned the corner to run out the door, "Ang!" I shouted, nearly crashing into her.

"Slow down, boy."

"I can't. She's getting wasted, and I can't do this if she's drunk. I need her sober."

Angie handed me my keys and practically shoved me out the door. "Don't come back until you have good news!"

"Wish me luck!"

Finding the place was surprisingly easy, thanks to the giant fire in the middle of the field. I hopped out of my truck, grabbing everything except the chocolate. I checked myself in the side mirror before I pulled out my phone and sent a quick message to Tatum.

Me: I'm here

Tatum: About damn time. Get into position. I'll bring her to you

Me: Thank you

I skirted the outer edges of the party, shocked at just how many people were there. I didn't realize this many people even lived around here. When I found the spot we agreed on, I tucked myself behind a large tree and waited. The blaring music and laughter were all drowned out by the thundering beat of my heart.

Scuffling feet approached, followed by Tatum's frustrated whispers. I couldn't make out what she was saying, except that she wasn't happy. I swallowed thickly as I held my position, waiting until the girls were mere feet away from me.

"What, Tatum?" Ember grumbled. "It's a freaking party. Just let me have this."

"Em, come on. This isn't you."

"Whatever." She pushed past her friend, stomping back the way she came.

Tatum caught my eye and though it wasn't ideal, this was the only chance I was going to get. I stepped out from behind the tree, just in time to catch Ember as she tripped over a tree root. "Shit," she giggled. "Who put that there?"

It took her a moment to register my hand around her arm as she regained her footing. She gasped when her eyes met mine and her body went rigid. I watched her change from the happy, giggly, drunk girl, to confused, to hurt, and finally pissed. "Let me go," she snapped, jerking her arm free.

"You got this?" Tatum asked, hands in the air and ready to retreat.

Ember spun around and almost fell again. "You're in on this?" I caught her around the waist, only for her to jerk free and face down her best friend. "Why would you do this?" she asked, with a tremor in her voice.

Tatum looked at me over Ember's shoulder, then back to her friend. "Just listen to him. Hear what he has to say, and if you still hate him, I'll help you cut his dick off."

I flinched back, unable to suppress the need to cover myself. Tatum smirked, "I'm gonna go talk to some of the guys. I won't be far."

Ember had a hard time letting go, but eventually Tatum freed herself from her grasp and I was finally alone, in the dark, with my girl. "Em," I whispered, slowly approaching her from behind.

"No, Wes. I can't do this," she sneered.

I set the flowers down by the tree and ducked my head low so I could see into her eyes. Those beautiful cornflower blue eyes that looked so sad. "I'm so sorry, baby. I never meant to hurt you. I just... I didn't see another way. But now..."

"But now you have?" she snapped. "What changed, Wes? Huh?" She took a step back and looked me up and down. "Did you realize that what we had here was good?" She took another step back and I reached for her. She swatted my hand away. "Or did you decide fucking a virgin wasn't such a bad idea after all?"

Her words felt like a slap to the face. "Em, come on. You know me better than that."

"Do I?" She arched an eyebrow at me, hurt radiated from her in waves. "I thought I did, but the Wes I knew would never throw me away like that." She took another step back and crossed her arms over her chest.

Throw her away? "Baby, let me explain."

"Don't *baby* me, Wes. I am not a baby."

I couldn't help it, my lips curled up at the side. Drunk Ember was kind of funny. Her pain wasn't though. "No. You're not a baby. You're the sun, the moon, and all the stars in the sky. You're the air in my lungs, the beating of my heart."

She shook her head as her anger faded only to be replaced with a look of utter despair. I reached out and this time she didn't avoid me. I cupped her cheeks, swiping away the tears that escaped her beautiful eyes with the pad of my thumb. "I thought I didn't have a choice. The last thing I wanted to do was hurt you. I thought I was doing the right thing, but I was wrong." I took a step closer to her until we were only inches apart. "I have spent so much of my life taking care of everything by myself that I never considered asking for help. I told you I don't want to hold you back, and I meant it. I still mean it, but maybe…" I licked my lips as my heart hammered in my chest. She looked up at me with so much love and I couldn't believe I almost gave her up. "Maybe I can be there for you, find a way to support you."

"Wes?"

I leaned my forehead against hers, "Leaving you that day at your house was the hardest thing I've ever done. Leaving Linford would have meant leaving my heart behind. I could do it, but it would kill me."

I pulled back enough to look into her sad eyes. Black streaks ran down her cheeks from her mascara. I ran my thumbs through them, brushing her tears away. "Don't cry, baby."

She wrapped her slim fingers around my wrists and pulled my hands away from her face. "You hurt me."

My hands fell to my sides. "I know I did, and if I could take it back, I would."

She crossed one arm over her stomach, gripping her elbow and dug the toe of her boot into the dirt. "I can't do this, Wes. It hurts too much."

My stomach sank with the realization she might not forgive me. "I'm so sorry, Ember. I'm so, so sorry."

She looked up through watery eyes. "I understand, and I'm going to miss you. But... I can't do this. What do you even want? Forgiveness?" She tried to smile, but the wobble of her chin made it impossible. "You're forgiven, okay?"

I shook my head and reached out for her again. I wrapped an arm around her waist and pulled her body close to mine. I brushed the hair away from her face. "I don't think you understand. I'm not giving you up. I'm yours and you're mine."

"What?"

"Can you give me another chance?"

"But..." She furrowed her brow, "you're leaving."

I shook my head. "No, baby. I'm not going anywhere. Not without you."

"But your dad..."

I took a risk and pressed a kiss to the corner of her mouth. "My dad will get over it. But you..." I leaned my forehead against hers again. "You're everything to me; wherever you are, that's where I want to be."

I trailed my fingers down the smooth skin of her arm until our hands met. Her smaller hand fit so perfectly in mine, like she was made for me.

"You're staying?" she asked, lacing our fingers together.

I grinned, "Yeah, baby. As long as you'll have me." I pulled back so I could see her face and was so thankful I did. The blush that crept up her cheeks as she bit her lip was sexy as hell.

Her nod was so subtle, and it was all I needed. I didn't hesitate; I wrapped my arms around her and lifted her up, smashing my lips against hers. Her legs wrapped around my waist, and I walked us back toward the tree where I had been hiding. She felt so good in my arms and for the first time in almost a week, I could breathe. I couldn't believe I almost gave her up.

I slowly lowered us to the ground so I was sitting with my back against the tree and she was straddling my lap. I slid my hands up her back, sending a shiver down her spine and couldn't control the moan that slipped out when she ground against me. I could lose myself in her and it took everything in me to break our kiss.

I leaned my forehead against hers as we struggled to catch our breath. I blindly reached over to where I left her flowers. "I got these for you."

"They're beautiful," she murmured, bringing them to her nose.

"Nowhere near as beautiful as you are." I brushed my lips over hers as I dug in my pocket for the gift I bought her. Her eyes grew wide when I held out the little blue velvet pouch. "I got you this," I whispered as she took it from my hand.

With nimble fingers, she carefully pulled the bag open and emptied it onto her hand. Her breath caught as she took in the simple silver bracelet, with three charms already linked on it. "This is for me?" She asked, disbelief written all over her face.

I nodded, lifting the bracelet and pointing out each charm. "The sun, because you light up my life, you keep me warm, and I forever want to be in your orbit."

She laughed, just like I hoped she would. "And this one?" she asked, pointing to the coffee cup.

"That one's pretty obvious. It's for our first date." I pointed to the last charm, a little truck.

"Is that because we always go everywhere in your truck?" she asked, laughing. The sound was music to my ears.

"The truck is for all the truck bed picnics we've shared. And a memory of how badly I wanted to take you in the bed of my truck not so long ago."

Her face flushed pink, and I quickly brushed my lips against hers. That day was hard for both of us, but mostly her. "Here," I took the bracelet and clasped it around her wrist. It fit perfectly, just like I knew it would. "We can add more charms for every adventure we have together."

"You mean it?"

"I do." I leaned in and pressed my mouth to hers, moaning when our tongues met, relishing her sweet honey taste, even if it was over-powered by cheap beer. When I pulled away this time, we were both smiling. It hit me then that I wanted to make her smile for the rest of my life. Whatever it takes.

CHAPTER EIGHTEEN

Linford

PRESENT

Wes

Her jaw clenched and her breathing picked up, but at least she wasn't running. I wanted to go to her, wrap my arms around her and explain everything. Tell her how sorry I was. But she was like a skittish animal, sure to bolt at the first sign of danger.

I don't know how long we just stood there, staring at each other until Bob finally broke the silence.

"Wes offered to work on your car," he said, placing a hand on her shoulder. I've never been so jealous of a hand in my life.

Ember startled, and almost seemed to relax. Then, as if someone opened the dam, all her anger and pain flooded back in, and she was closed off once again; the walls she built slamming firmly into place. She took a step back and as much as I wanted to take a step forward, I held my ground. Her eyes dropped as she wrung her hands nervously. "How much?"

"How much what?" Bob asked.

She took a deep breath and held it when her eyes met mine again. She blew it out, and with it, some of the tension. "How much do I owe you?"

I shook my head. "Nothing."

"No. I don't take charity. How much?"

"Ember…"

She held her hand up, cutting me off and turned back to Bob. "I want the bill."

He looked from her, to me, then back to her. "I…" His shoulders slumped as he nodded. "I'll make sure you get it."

"Thank you." Without giving me another look, she turned on her heel and stormed through the door.

Before I even realized what I was doing, I took off after her, catching up to her just as she reached Tatum's car. "Ember, wait!"

Her steps faltered, then she straightened her spine, standing taller with her shoulders back. She walked just a little faster, then yanked the door open and slid into the drivers' seat. I got there just before she could pull the door shut, blocking it with my body. "Let me explain," I pleaded, unable to take my eyes off of her, the way her breath hitched and her teeth bit into her bottom lip. She was just as beautiful today as she was the day I met her. My heart raced and my palms began to sweat.

I prayed for this moment so many times over the past seven years. I rehearsed what I'd say in my head thousands of times, and now that we were here, my mind was blank.

She sighed, "I can't do this, Wes."

"Can we just get coffee or something? Sit down and talk about it?"

The edge of the car door scraped my arm as she yanked on it in frustration. "I think we've talked enough, don't you?"

"Baby…"

"Wes, I haven't been your *baby* in years," she bit out, her lip curling up in disgust.

"Please," My heart hammered in my chest as I inched forward, ready to get on my hands and knees and grovel. I'd do anything if she'd only hear me out. "Ten minutes. Give me ten minutes and if you still hate me, I'll let you go," I lied.

Fury burned in her eyes as she glared up at me. "Tell me this… Are you still with her?"

I stumbled back a step, smacking into the car door; the question was like a fist to the gut. I swallowed past a lump in my throat and searched her eyes as though they contained the answer I needed. I wanted to say no and in my heart, that was the truth. We weren't together in the ways that mattered, but that was semantics, and would never be enough. As I looked into the depths of her cornflower blue eyes, I realized nothing I could say would ever matter as long as my situation stayed the same. Not even the truth.

I sucked in a ragged breath and took a step back. Ember slumped back into her seat and her face fell with the movement. The tears that welled in her eyes broke a piece of me I didn't realize was still intact. "It's not what you think," I whispered.

She sucked in a ragged breath and sat up taller. "You know what I think, Wes? I think… No. I know you broke my heart. You ruined everything!" she growled. "I *loved* you! I would have done *anything* for you, but then you… you…" Her chin wobbled as a tear rolled down her cheek. She quickly swiped it away.

"It's not what you think!" I cried, falling to my knees. "Just let me explain!"

"I've heard enough."

My chest felt tight; I couldn't get enough air. "Ember, please!"

Her lips pressed into a thin line, eyebrows drawn together. She was closing herself off. I moved closer to her, my knees digging into the gravel. I wasn't ready to give up, I couldn't give up. I didn't want to do it like this, but... "I never cheated on you!" I cried.

She huffed as she yanked the car door shut, not even flinching when the door slammed into my shoulder. I sucked in a sharp breath and tears welled in my eyes as she started the engine. I pressed the heels of my hands to my eyes, unable to watch her drive away with whatever was left of my heart.

"Tell me this, *Wes*," she sneered. I looked up through watery eyes to see her staring down at me from the rolled down window. "Do you still have a daughter?"

I nodded.

"Then that's all I need to know."

The squeal of tires assaulted me as she slammed on the gas. I swept up a handful of gravel and threw it as hard as I could at the red blur of taillights speeding away from me. "FUUUUCK!"

Whoever said grown men don't cry, never had their soul ripped from their body and shredded beyond repair. I felt hollow, unable to move as I sat there on my knees, head hung low while tears streamed down my face. I cried until I couldn't cry any more, and still I couldn't drag myself from this spot.

A hand gripped my shoulder, and I knew without looking that it was Bob. Besides my aunt, and Ellie's mother, he was the only one who knew the truth. I looked up into his kind eyes hating the pity reflected back at me. "Your aunt called, Ellie's crying for you."

I went to wipe my cheeks on the sleeve of my jumpsuit, only to find that my face was dry. Bob wordlessly helped me to my feet, and walked me to my truck. There was nothing he could say to make me feel better. My throat was raw. I had to clear it a few times before any words would come out. "I'll be back tomorrow."

He shook his head. "Take a day or two. We'll fix this."

"Nothing can fix this. I fucked up and this is my punishment."

"Excuse my language, but what you call fucking up, I call being a good guy."

"You saw her, Bob. Anyone who makes that girl that sad is not a good guy." A sob broke free, it hurt so bad. "I should've just ended it when I had the chance," I rasped.

"You don't mean that."

I could still remember the bitter taste of metal as the gun touched my tongue. As much as I wished I could pull the trigger that night, I'm grateful my aunt found me first.

I took a deep breath and blew it out slowly, thinking of the girl who had become my world. Her long blonde hair and bright smile. Big green eyes that saw the wonder in everything.

As if on queue, my phone lit up my aunt's number on the screen. "Hey, Ang."

Bob gave me a nod and took a step back, giving me room to back out of the lot. I held the phone to my ear with my shoulder as I pulled out onto the main road. "Have you been crying?" her voice held that note of pity that I hated.

"What's up? I'm on my way," I said, not wanting to get into it with her again. She was torn between me leaving Ember alone, and wanting me to fix it. Only, it just became very clear - there was no fixing this.

"I don't know what happened, but Ellie's crying. Nothing I say or do is making it better, she just wants her daddy."

My heart broke, knowing exactly what my little girl needed. "I'll be there in five."

I barely had the truck in park before Ellie came charging out of the house. "Daddy!"

I got out in time to catch her, her little arms wrapped around me, her head pressed into my neck. "Hey, baby girl." I held her tight, pressing a kiss to the top of her head.

I carried her back into the house and sat on the couch, holding her in my lap. She pulled back, her tear streaked face matching my own. "What's wrong, daddy?" she asked, touching my cheeks.

"Nothing, baby." I kissed her nose. "Want to tell me what you've been up to today?"

She scurried off my lap and ran into the kitchen, returning a minute later with a few sheets of paper she'd been coloring. She handed them to me then climbed up beside me to point out what they were. The first was a...

"That's an otter, like in my book," she said matter of factly. "It's a momma, and that," she pointed to a red mess of color on the animal's stomach. "That's the baby."

"Wow, you did such a good job." I shuffled to the next page.

"That's me and my friend Jadon on the playground," she pointed to two stick figures, one yellow and the other brown. It still shocked me the day Tatum finally let her son play with Ellie. They've been best friends since. It's been hard keeping them apart this week, though she and I both knew if Ember found out our kids were friends, she'd lose it.

I desperately wanted to tell Tatum the truth about Ellie, but both Ang and Bob said it would only cause more problems. I sighed, flipping to the next sheet. And there it was, the reason for my girl's tears.

"That's momma and me," she whispered.

I pressed a kiss to her cheek. "That's a very good drawing, baby girl." I ran my fingers over the crayon lines, the two stick figures, one tall with long brown hair, the other shorter with long yellow hair. The little one had a big smile and was holding a bunch of flowers. The taller one had a scowl on her face, much like the real woman.

"Daddy?"

"Yeah, baby?"

"Why doesn't momma love me?"

The question hit me right in the gut. Everything I did was for this girl. I gave up everything for her, *everything,* while her mother was hardly ever around, and when she was she wanted nothing to do with her. She was supposed to be gone this week, on a trip with her "friend," though rumor had it she was seeing someone else. Apparently word got back to her that Ember was in town, and of course she was here to stir up trouble.

She was in town, and couldn't be bothered to visit with her own daughter. If it wasn't for Ellie, I'd have left this place a long time ago.

"Your momma loves you, she's just not very good at showing it."

"But..." she climbed back onto my lap.

I kissed her forehead. "You wanna stay here tonight?" I asked, knowing there was no way I could take her home while her mother was in one of her petty moods. I wasn't particularly excited to see her either.

She wrapped her arms around my neck and held on tight. "No, daddy, I want to stay with you."

I chuckled. "I meant we could both stay. I bet Aunt Angie would like that."

Her eyes got really big, and I knew I made the right decision. "You mean that?"

"Hey, Ang!" I called out, knowing for a fact she was just around the corner eavesdropping.

"Hey, guys. You feeling better, sweet girl?"

Ellie nodded and I kissed her cheek and tickled her belly until she squealed. "Would you mind if we stayed here tonight?" I asked, pleading with my eyes. I hadn't stayed here in years. My old room was still made up, only instead of being mine, it was Ellie's for when she stayed over.

"Yeah, I think that would be fine."

I got Ellie in the bath, and then into her favorite princess night-gown. She read me a book while I combed the tangles out of her hair, then french braided it to keep it out of her face.

"Are zebras white with black stripes, or black with white stripes," she asked as soon as I finished, a very serious look on her face.

"That is a very good question," I said, picking her up from where she sat at the foot of the bed and tucking her under the covers. "I'm not sure. What does your book say?"

She closed it with a sigh. "It doesn't."

"Maybe we should get you another book?" I offered, but she just shook her head.

"The library doesn't have any good zebra books."

I took the book from her and set it on the nightstand. "I have an idea. Why don't you and I take a trip to Wickett tomorrow and see what their bookstore has?"

Her face lit up. "You mean it?"

I chuckled, "Yeah."

She settled down into her pillow, a big smile spread across her cheeks. "I can't wait until I'm bigger and can take care of real animals," she said as her eyelids started to droop.

CHAPTER NINETEEN

Linford

8 YEARS AGO

Wes

Ember's hands tugged playfully on my hair as I whispered kisses over her shoulder and up her neck. I was comfortably nestled between her legs, my arms holding most of my weight on either side of her head. I buried my face in her hair and inhaled deeply. God, she smelled amazing; like honeysuckle and oranges. She rocked her hips up into mine, grinding against my hardness, and I chuckled. We still hadn't slept together. She was getting impatient and I insisted it had to be special.

"Wes," she groaned. "Stop teasing me."

"Sorry, baby." I nipped at her earlobe, laughing when she swatted me. I rolled off her and grabbed my phone, checking the time. "What time do we need to leave?"

"4:30 at the latest," she leaned up on her elbows. "What time is it?"

I sighed, throwing my arm over my eyes as though hiding would slow down time. "4:15."

She jumped out of bed and quickly righted her clothes and smoothed down her hair. Just because we hadn't slept together didn't mean we didn't do other things. "We have to go!"

"Are you sure we can't just stay here? I can think of a few animalistic traits you can learn right here in bed," I waggled my eyebrows at her.

"Wes!" she laughed. "While I'm not opposed to that," her cheeks flamed red, "I need the community service hours."

"That's dumb." I reached out and grabbed her by the waist, pulling until she fell back into bed with a squeak. "I need you more than they do."

The smile that spread across her face could melt even the coldest man's heart. She pressed her lips to mine, and when she pulled away, it was too soon. "Didn't you have to do community service for school?"

I let her go and sat up, scanning the room for my shoes. "No, and even if I had to, I don't know that I would have."

"Wes!" she swatted at me, and I caught her hand.

I brought my mouth to hers, loving that I could kiss this woman whenever I wanted. "I wasn't a good guy before I met you," I bit her bottom lip then licked it better. "You've changed me."

"You can't do that to me," she groaned. "When are you going to give in and let me have what I want?"

"Soon, baby." I let her go and swatted her ass. "Now get ready. We have a long drive ahead of us."

She scowled at me and all I could do was laugh. I adjusted myself, my dick straining uncomfortably against my jeans. Me being twenty and her seventeen made me nervous. I looked it up, the age of consent in Nebraska was sixteen so she was legal, but I still wanted to wait. It was torture, but she'd be eighteen in a week.

Ember sat beside me in my truck, feet pressed against the dash and her face buried in a book about animal anatomy or something like that. She hummed quietly along with the radio. I learned pretty quickly that she hated silence while she studied, and she studied a lot. If she wasn't at school, she was at work, and if she wasn't at work, she was with me, and when she was with me, she studied. My aunt told me she was smart, but I never considered that she was valedictorian smart. She was top of her class, and I refused to let that change because of me.

My thumbs tapped the steering wheel to the beat of Sam Hunt's "Body Like a Back Road." It was a far cry from the music I typically listened to. Ember was turning me into a country fan and I wasn't even mad about it.

I pulled up outside the Wickett animal shelter just before six. The nondescript building was brick painted a light gray. There weren't any windows, aside from the one on the large metal door just under a sign reading "Wickett Animal Shelter." She stared out through the windshield, her knee bouncing with anxiety. "Relax." I squeezed her hand and kissed her temple. "It's going to be good."

"I don't know if I can do this," she swallowed thickly.

"What's got you scared?"

She leaned back and shook her head. "What if I'm not cut out for this sort of work?" Her eyebrows pulled together, her bottom lip pinched between her teeth.

"Come on," I pushed my door open and took her hand. I slid out and pulled her with me out the driver's side door. "How long have you wanted to work with animals?"

"Since I was a little girl."

I squeezed her hand. "Exactly. You're passionate about it. And," I gave her a little tug, encouraging her to follow me to the door. "This is the perfect opportunity to find out if it's really something you want and can do. You're just volunteering. They're not going to ask you to do anything you're not qualified or willing to do."

She held my hand in her vice-like grip as I led her through the door and up to the front desk. The inside was far more welcoming than the exterior. Cream walls covered in photos of various animals. Wooden display racks held everything from pet food, to toys. The place didn't smell that great, but then again, what animal facility did? Even pet shops had a distinct smell.

The tension in her shoulders eased when an older woman stood up behind the counter wearing pink scrubs covered in bunnies. Her red hair was short and curly and she wore glasses with one of those straps so when she took them off, she could just let them hang like a necklace. "Good afternoon, how may I help you today?"

"Hi. I-I'm Ember Davis. I'm here to volunteer."

The woman's head dropped back, eyes to the ceiling. "Thank you Lord Jesus." She turned her attention back to Ember. "We have been in desperate need of help. The last person to sign up to volunteer never showed, so I was a little concerned you'd be the same."

Ember finally eased her grip on my hand and her smile lit up her whole face. "I've been dreaming of this for forever," she admitted. "I've always wanted to work with animals."

"I have a feeling we're gonna get along just fine." She looked past Ember to me, "And you?" she arched an eyebrow.

"Oh, I'm just the ride…" I held my hands up and took a step back.

"Bummer, we could really use some extra muscle. But that's okay. Thanks for bringing this beauty in."

Ember turned around, her hands settling on my waist. I knew what she was going to ask before she even opened her mouth and I mentally cursed myself. She had me wrapped around her little finger and she knew it. "Wes?"

I kissed her forehead. "Yeah, baby." I looked up at the woman who was waiting expectantly and sighed. "Where do you need me?"

After that, my time with Ember became a little more limited. If she wasn't at school, she was at work, if she wasn't at work, she was studying, and if she wasn't studying, she was volunteering. That meant I was volunteering too, but at least I got to spend time with her.

On her eighteenth birthday, she was scheduled at the shelter. I checked with her family, they didn't have any plans which really grated on my nerves. I called the shelter and asked if there was any way she could get the day off. They were shocked to hear it was her birthday too, and told me that, under no circumstances, did they want to see her. Which worked out perfectly for me.

Just like every other Saturday, Ember was up and ready to go by eleven. I picked her up and made the drive to Wickett. When I didn't turn down the street that led to the shelter, she turned to me confused. "Wes, you missed our turn."

I shook my head. "No, I didn't."

"Yes. You did."

I reached over and took her hand, lacing our fingers together. "No, baby. I didn't. I'm taking you out." I brought our hands up and brushed my lips over her knuckles.

Her eyebrows pulled together, "But I'm scheduled..."

"No, you're not," I chuckled at how flustered she was getting.

"Yes. I am. I'm scheduled every Saturday. They need me."

"*I* need you. Besides, I spoke with them last night. They made me promise you wouldn't show up today."

"Why would you do that?"

I stopped at a red light and looked at her beautiful face. Even makeup free, she was gorgeous. I tucked a loose strand of hair behind her ear. "It's your birthday, and I've made plans."

When the light turned green, I continued down the road until I saw the "Now Leaving Wickett" signs. "Where are we going?" she finally asked once we were back on the highway.

"Columbus," I said, tapping my fingers against the steering wheel to the beat of whatever song was playing. I didn't recognize this one.

"What's in Columbus?"

I grinned. "You'll see."

About twenty minutes later, I pulled up at "Best Auto Sales." Not the greatest name for a used car dealership, but that didn't matter. What did matter was that they had a few cars in Ember's price range that actually looked decent.

I hopped out and walked around the front and opened her door. She took my offered hand, "What are we here for?"

I chuckled. "Isn't it obvious?"

"Well, yeah, sort of. Are you trading in your truck?"

"No, baby."

"Then what?"

A salesman came out to greet us, interrupting her line of questioning. "What can I do for you folks today?"

I put my arm around Ember's shoulder and pressed a kiss to the top of her head. "My girl here is in need of a car."

Ember's head jerked up and I just winked.

The man showed us several cars, an old Volkswagen that looked like it had seen better days, a Chevy that was just a bit out of her price range...

Finally, after about an hour of walking the lot, Ember made a couple of laps around a Silver 2010 Subaru Outback, running her fingers along the hood before finally coming to a stop at the window, where a sheet was taped with all the car's information. Mileage, customizations, and the price. She cringed when she hit that part and her face fell.

"What is it, baby?" I stood behind her, looking down the sheet. Everything looked good, until you got to the price. It was a couple grand more than she had budgeted for. I did some quick thinking, rubbing my hands up and down her arms. "Can we take this one for a drive?"

The salesman gave me a quick nod and hurried inside to grab the keys.

"What are you doing, Wes? I can't afford this?"

I shrugged. "Let's see how she drives."

She sighed, but didn't argue. The salesman handed me the keys, and I passed them to Ember. "You sure?"

"Yeah, baby. If she's gonna be your car, you have to make sure you like how she drives."

She looked good sitting behind the wheel. The salesman had her take it around the small town, and even had her jump on the highway for a minute or two so she could get a feel for how it handled at speed. From where I sat, the car was worth the price. I just had to figure out how to make it happen.

We returned to the lot, and the salesman immediately asked, "What do we think?"

Ember chewed her lip, looking at me in the rearview mirror. I asked her what she wanted with my eyes, and she gave me a tiny nod.

I pushed my door open. "Mind if I check out the engine?"

"Be my guest," the salesman said, climbing out after me.

Ember popped the hood, and I immediately saw a couple of things that were concerning, but they weren't enough to talk down the price that much. The salesman scratched the back of his head as I pointed things out. "Let me go see what I can do."

I pulled Ember into my body, her back to my front and rested my chin on her head. "How much do you think he'll drop the price?"

I kissed the top of her head. "A grand at most."

She twisted in my arms to look up at me. "That's still not enough."

As expected, the salesman came back, with an offer to drop the price by $800, which was honestly more than I expected. "We'll take it," I said before Ember could protest.

We followed the salesman inside, keeping a little space between him and us. "I don't have that much money," she protested quietly.

"Don't worry about it, I've got it." I gave her hand a squeeze while I tried to guess what Ang was going to say when I didn't pay rent next month.

Ember quietly signed the papers where she was told and when it came time to pay, she gave him her bank information and I gave him mine. Before he could step away, I handed him a post-it note telling him how much to take from each account. Thirty minutes later, she was the proud owner of a 2010 Subaru Outback.

She climbed behind the wheel of her new car with a faraway look in her eyes. I knew why, but that didn't make me worry any less. She was used to taking care of things on her own, just like I was. Everything she needed, she paid for herself - that included basic necessities from notebooks and pencils for school to the type of shampoo and lotion she liked. Having someone step in and help was outside of her comfort zone. While her parents seemed like good people, they didn't contribute to her needs outside of food and shelter, and that didn't sit right with me. Though I wasn't in the best financial situation, I would do everything in my power to take care of her.

I squatted down beside her. "Follow me?"

She nodded and I kissed her cheek, closing her door. I waited for her to start the engine before climbing into my truck and heading out of the lot. I led us back to Wickett, where there was a restaurant that I've been wanting to try for a while. Ember parked beside me but didn't move to get out of her car.

I pulled her door open and reached in to take her hand. "Come on, let's get some dinner."

She followed me quietly, and when we got to our table, I did that annoying thing where couples sit on the same side of their booth. I slid in beside her and pulled her into my arms. "What's the matter?"

"It's too much, Wes."

"What is?"

She pinched my side and I laughed. "The car!"

I took a deep breath and blew it out slowly. "Em, you needed a car. You love that car, I could see it all over your face."

"But..."

I kissed her, cutting her off. "That is a good car. It's safe, and Subaru's are notoriously reliable. I can work on it, I'll fix the issues it has."

"But you don't have the money to pay for it," she complained. "And I can't... I don't know when I'll be able to pay you back."

"Baby, look at me." She turned in my arms and looked up. I hated that she worried about me like that. I leaned my forehead against hers, "Let me worry about the money, okay? I had it in my account, and it went to a good place. Trust me, okay?"

"But what about...?"

"Happy birthday, baby." I pressed my lips to hers, ending all arguments.

After a quiet dinner, Ember followed me home to my aunt's house. I climbed into her car so she could drive us down to our spot by the lake.

"Did you come up with a name for her?" I asked, laying beside her on the hood, looking up at the stars.

"I was thinking Carrie."

I sat up on my elbows. "Carrie? Like prom queen killing everyone Carrie?" She swatted me, "Ow!"

"Carrie, like Carrie Underwood."

I nodded, "Ah... that makes sense."

"It does?"

I chuckled, "Yeah, baby. She's a strong, independent woman, not afraid to kick anyone's ass. Makes sense you'd want your car to be the same."

"I love you, Wes."

"I love you too, Em."

She rolled onto her side and cupped my cheek. "Thank you for the best birthday ever." She pressed a soft kiss to my lips, and my heart swelled with love.

"My pleasure."

Ember pulled up right outside the garage bay like I told her to. She jumped out and ran straight into my arms, not even caring that I was covered in grease. "Hey, baby," I laughed. "Miss me?"

She brought her lips to mine. I cupped her cheeks as I tasted the sweet cherry of her lip gloss. I could get lost in her kisses. "I missed you so much."

"How is that even possible?" I wiped a smudge of grease from her cheek, "I just saw you this morning?" We had a set morning date, coffee in the school parking lot before her first class.

"That was *hours* ago!"

I laughed and shook my head, returning to the car I was working on. "How was school?"

She shrugged, "It was school."

I arched a brow at her. Ember loved school. I watched her curiously as she folded her hands behind her back, crossed her ankles, and twisted her body slowly from side to side. "What's up?" I asked, wiping my hands on a rag.

"Well," her cheeks blazed pink and I grinned. "Next week is homecoming, and I was wondering if... maybe..."

"I'd love to."

"Wait. You don't even know what I was gonna ask!"

I grinned and crossed my arms over my chest. "Sorry. What were you wondering?"

She sighed, "I was wondering if you'd be my date. But it's a dumb high school dance, so..."

"Oh, baby." I cupped her cheeks, bringing my mouth to hers. "Dumb high school dance or not, if you're there, so am I," I whispered over her lips before closing the space with a slow kiss.

"You mean it," she panted when we broke apart.

"I do."

"God, I love you, Wesley Barrett."

"And I love you, Ember Davis."

CHAPTER TWENTY

Linford

8 YEARS AGO

Wes

I paced back and forth in my aunt's living room, fighting the urge to loosen my tie. I don't know why I was nervous. I've been to homecoming dances before. Hell, I was homecoming king my senior year. But this was different. This was *Ember*.

Angie stepped in front of me and smoothed down the lapels of my suit. She was surprisingly chill, considering I told her I wouldn't be able to pay her rent for the next couple of months. She readily agreed that Ember's car was a much better place for my money to go. "Cut that out, you're making me nervous."

"I'm making *you* nervous? *I'm* nervous!" I gave in and tugged at my tie and Ang smacked my hand away.

"What are you nervous about? It's just a dance. You two have done way more than dancing before..." she rolled her eyes.

"No. We haven't," I blew out a heavy breath.

"Don't lie to me," she poked me in the chest. "I've heard that girl moan your name more times than I can count. You should be thankful I'm not a gossip."

"Oh my god, Ang!" I groaned. "What I do with my hands and tongue is none of your business!"

"Wait. You're telling me you've never..."

I looked up to the ceiling as though not looking at her would make this less awkward. "Not that I want to have this conversation with you, but no. We haven't."

"Huh," she took a step back, putting her hand on her hip.

"What?"

She laughed, shaking her head. "You must have one talented tongue for the sounds that come out of your room."

"Ang!"

She shrugged. "You asked."

I sighed and raked my hand through my hair. "Can we stop talking about my sex life?"

"Well, we could, if you had one." She winked and dropped down onto the couch, turning the TV on.

"Oh my god, I cannot believe you."

"You still nervous?" she asked, one eyebrow arched.

I paused, thinking about it. "No, I guess I'm not."

"Then my work here is done."

I had only met Ember's dad once. The man was scary. He wasn't quite as tall as me, but he was built, easily outweighing me by thirty pounds. He owned a construction company and it was obvious he wasn't afraid to get his hands dirty. His dark hair was always neatly styled, and though his eyes were the same color as Ember's, his held a darkness. I swallowed thickly when he answered the door. "Good evening, Mr. Davis."

"Wes," he grumbled.

"I'm here to pick up Ember for the dance."

He grudgingly stepped aside, allowing me to squeeze past him just in time to see the most beautiful woman I had ever laid eyes on gracefully descend the stairs. She wore a long, emerald green dress with a slit halfway up her thigh and the tiniest straps. Her hair was pulled up with a few curls trailing down, leaving her neck exposed. My mouth watered just thinking about how her skin tasted.

Movement to my left reminded me that we weren't alone and I shifted uncomfortably as I reigned in my thoughts.

"Hey, Wes." she said when she reached that final step.

"Hey baby. You look incredible."

She dipped in a small curtsy, "Thank you."

I carefully fastened the corsage I bought, made of white orchids, to her wrist. I kissed her cheek and couldn't help my grin when her cheeks flamed pink.

"Come on, let's go." She looped her arm through mine.

"Wait, don't you want a picture?" I looked to her mom and dad who stood nearby, arms crossed over their chests. "I, uh…" I pulled my phone from my pocket and unlocked it. "Mrs. Davis, would you take a picture of Ember and I?"

She took my phone and snapped a couple of photos before handing it back. "Thanks."

She nodded, "No problem. I never thought my daughter would find herself a boyfriend."

I blinked down at her, offended that she would say something like that about her daughter. I gave Ember's hand a squeeze and she just smiled up at me, so maybe I was being sensitive. I let it go with a shake of my head and a promise to have Ember home before eleven.

The dance was held in the school gym. I guess it made sense, considering the size of the student body. Back in Texas, they rented out a ballroom at one of the local hotels - granted my school had thousands of students. I parked at the back of the lot and blew out a heavy breath. I still wasn't able to completely shake my nerves. *It's just a dance...*

Except it was more than that.

Ember looped her arm through mine as she led the way around the side and in through the open gym doors. The lights were dim, and silver stars hung from the ceiling from what I assumed was fishing line. A few tables with white tablecloths were set up around the perimeter, and music thumped through the speakers. I laughed; it was music I actually knew.

"What's so funny?" Ember asked.

"This," I said, pointing up.

She cocked her head to the side. "The decorations?"

I laughed, "No, baby. The music. For some reason I assumed everyone in this town listened to country. I actually know this."

She rolled her eyes, "Come on, brat. Let's find Tatum."

I brought her hand to my lips. "You know I love you."

"I do. And I love you too."

Finding Tatum wasn't difficult. Just look for the brightest dress in the room and there she was. Her dress was yellow. Like sunflower yellow, and her long black hair hung in a smooth sheet down her back. I don't think I'd ever seen her hair without her braids.

The girls threw themselves at each other, leaving me, and Tatum's date, standing awkwardly. He shook his head and held out his hand. "Hey, I'm Brandon."

"Wes," I said. I nodded toward the girls who held each other in a hug while dancing around in a small circle. "You look like you've done this before."

He laughed, rubbing his hand over the back of his buzzed hair. "You could say that. I've known these girls since forever."

"Ah, so you grew up here too?"

"Yeah, up until recently. I just got back from basic. What about you, what's your story?"

I looked at the girls who were talking in hushed whispers about a hundred miles an hour. You'd think they hadn't seen each other for ages. I knew better though - they got ready together, over a facetime call. "I'm from Texas, came out to help my aunt for a while, and that's when I met Ember." I grinned, I couldn't help it. "Now you couldn't pay me to leave."

He chuckled. "She's a good one."

Something about the way he said it bothered me and I found myself clenching my teeth. "Yeah. She's the best."

Brandon stole his girl away a couple minutes later, and the tension in my shoulders eased. I told myself I wasn't a jealous guy, and with Andy I never was, yet something about Brandon knowing Ember for so long left me feeling like an outsider, like I didn't belong. Then she tucked her hand in mine and everything felt right once again.

"Dance with me?" I whispered, leading her onto the dance floor.

We swayed to the music, and I found myself dreaming of the day I could do this in front of all our friends and family, only she would be wearing white, and my ring.

The thought caught me off guard, it was completely out of left field. The odd part was, it didn't scare me. Growing up with just my dad after my mom walked out on us, marriage was never on my radar.

Sure, Andy had mentioned it once or twice over the years, but I always brushed it off.

Warmth spread through my belly as I realized that I wanted it all. The big wedding, the house, dog, kids... God, Ember's and my kids... Would they have blonde hair or brown? Her eyes or mine? Would they have freckles dotting their noses and the most amazing smiles just like their mother?

"I can hear you thinking," she whispered into my neck.

Her breath against my skin sent a shiver down my spine. "I was thinking about you, me, the future," I answered honestly.

"Good things?"

"The best." I brought my mouth to hers.

"Wanna get out of here?" she asked, a mischievous twinkle in her eyes.

I took her hand without a second thought and led her away from the dance floor and back out the door we came in. We didn't stop until I had her pressed up against my truck. I cupped her face and brought my mouth to hers, savoring the taste of her cherry lip gloss. "Don't you want to stay and see who will be named the homecoming queen?" I whispered against her lips.

"Nah. It'll probably just be Stacy or one of her minions."

I arched an eyebrow. "What about your sister?"

She shook her head, "She's a sophomore, so she's just part of the court." She pulled back and looked up at me, "Let's just go."

I drove us down to our spot by the lake and stopped under the tree where we always parked. Butterflies fluttered in my stomach when I reached over into the glovebox and pulled out a dark, silk blindfold. "Come here," I whispered.

"What... What's that for?"

I grinned, "Trust me?"

She nodded, "Yes."

"Good." I carefully tied the blindfold behind her head and instructed her to stay put until I had everything set. I went around the back of the tree and grabbed the basket I left there earlier in the day, filled with everything I needed.

I covered the truck bed with thick, fluffy blankets, and a few pillows. I had a small generator that I flicked on, powering the strings of twinkle lights I strung up overhead. They cast a soft yellow light over the area, giving it that intimate ambiance. I set up my portable speaker, pressing play on a custom made playlist of all Ember's favorite romantic songs. Finally, I pulled out a bottle of wine and a couple of glasses.

My pulse raced as I opened her door and took her hand. "Would you like to join me?"

She took my hand and blindly followed me around the back of the truck. "Wes?"

I carefully untied the blindfold and when it dropped her hands flew to her mouth as she took it all in. I pulled her into my arms and carefully removed the pins from her hair, letting it fall in long waves down her back. "God Gave Me You," by Blake Shelton played through the speaker as I brought my mouth to her ear, softly singing along with the words I felt deep in my soul.

I kissed her neck, trailing my lips across her smooth skin down to her shoulder. Her breath hitched when I slipped my fingers under the straps of her dress and slowly slid them down. I kissed my way back up her neck until I met her lips again. Her hands moved under my suit jacket and pushed until it fell down my arms, landing in the dirt at my feet.

I found the zipper at the back of her dress and looked to her for permission. Her small nod was all the invitation I needed. The sound of the zipper set my heart racing, and when the dress fell into a pool at her feet, my breath caught. She was so beautiful standing before me wearing a black, lacy, strapless bra and matching thong. Her skin pebbled with the cool breeze that blew past and I wasted no time wrapping my arms around her, pulling her against my body. My lips found hers as she worked to remove my clothes, button by button. I was uncomfortably hard when she finally pushed my pants down my hips; I didn't know how much longer I could wait.

I toed off my shoes and stepped out of my pants. I pressed my nose to her neck, breathing in her sweet honeysuckle orange scent just before I lifted her onto the bed of the truck. I climbed up right after her and settled over her body, between her legs.

I explored her naked flesh, fingers gliding across the smooth planes of her stomach, and over her ribs. I brought my face down to her breasts, kissing the exposed skin and when she arched up, I deftly unclasped her bra and pulled it away to reveal the most perfect set of breasts I had ever had my hands on. Her nipples were the prettiest shade of pink and pebbled when I ran my fingers over them. I sucked one into my mouth and groaned when her hands fisted in my hair, pulling me closer. I let go of one nipple and moved to the other, giving it the same treatment.

She moaned loudly, the isolation of the lake giving her the freedom to let go. I released her nipple with a pop and trailed my lips down her body until she was squirming and crying out my name.

I ran my knuckles down the front of her panties; they were soaked. "What do you want, baby?" I pressed a kiss to her pelvic bone.

"You," she panted. "I don't want to wait anymore."

I grabbed the condom I had tucked away and shoved my boxer briefs down, freeing my hard cock. I rolled on the condom, not taking my eyes off of her. "Are you sure? We don't have to…"

"Please," she pleaded. "I need you, Wes."

"I love you, Ember." I slid her panties off and settled between her legs.

"I love you, too."

I kissed her while I tenderly made sure she was ready. The last thing I wanted to do was hurt her. I slid my fingers between her folds and pressed one inside. God, she was tight.

I pumped my finger in and out, then added a second. My cock throbbed to be inside her. I pulled my fingers out and slid them between my lips; my eyes rolled back in my head as her taste exploded on my tongue.

"Wes…"

"I got you, baby." I lined myself up and stared into the depths of her cornflower blue eyes, so full of love and trust. I gently pushed inside, watching her face as her warm heat welcomed me, stopping every time she winced. "You okay?"

"Yeah. It hurts, but it's okay." She lifted her hips, forcing me further inside and I groaned. "Don't stop, Wes."

I glanced down to where our bodies were connected and a ragged breath escaped me. It never felt like this before. It was everything and more; so much more. I nuzzled her neck, pressing a kiss to her pulse point until my cock was fully seated. I held my breath, afraid to move. She was so tight, felt so good, I had to fight to keep from blowing early. I dropped my head to her chest, catching my breath, when she lifted her hips again. "Oh god, baby. Don't move."

"Wes, please," she begged.

"I don't want to hurt you." I brushed her hair away from her face and pressed my mouth to hers, our tongues meeting in soft, languid strokes.

Her hands slid slowly over my back, sending a shiver down my spine. "It doesn't hurt... well, it does, but it feels better than it hurts."

I pulled out painfully slowly before sliding back in, over and over. "Are you okay?"

Her hands cupped my ass, "More," she whimpered.

My eyes rolled back in my head as I thrust into her harder, "God, you feel so good, baby."

"Wes..." She lifted her hips, meeting me thrust for thrust.

I gripped her leg and hitched it up, driving deeper as she cried out for more. I crashed my mouth to hers, our kiss frantic as our tongues tangled together.

The pressure continued to build up inside me and when I felt her wet heat squeezing me tighter, I reached between us and rubbed her clit until her eyes rolled back in her head. "Come on, baby," I whispered in her ear. I pulled back just enough to see her face, her flushed cheeks, her lips parted as she panted. "You are so fucking beautiful. Come for me."

"Oh, god! Wes!" she cried out as her body clamped down around me. It only took me two more pumps before I exploded in her, her name a prayer on my lips.

I buried my face in her neck as I fought to catch my breath. "I love you so much."

She wrapped her arms around my neck and giggled, "I love you too."

I grinned against her skin, then carefully pulled out of her. I took off the condom, cringing at the blood that covered it. "Em, are you okay?" I hadn't even thought about that. I mean, I heard that virgins were supposed to bleed, but... Andy and I had been each other's first, and she didn't.

"Mmmhmm."

I turned around and she was curled up on her side, a goofy grin on her face. I pulled on my boxers and climbed in next to her, pulling a blanket over her body so she wouldn't get cold. "Are you sure? Are you in any pain?" I cupped her cheek and pressed a kiss to her forehead.

Beneath the glow of the twinkle lights, her skin appeared to be glowing. She grinned up at me, "I'm a little sore, but I'm great."

She shivered as a cool breeze blew through. As much as I would have loved staying naked with her in the back of my truck, it wasn't the best idea. We climbed out and she reached for her dress at the same time I grabbed my shirt. Before she could slip into her gown, I pulled my shirt around her body and buttoned it up. It hung down to her knees and the sleeves were too long, but damn if it didn't make me hard all over again, seeing her in my clothes.

I grabbed the bottle of wine when we climbed back up into the truck, and popped the cork. I poured two glasses, handing one to her. I clinked my glass against hers, "Cheers, baby."

"Cheers."

"Was it everything you hoped it would be?"

"More," she whispered. She reached up and cupped my cheek, her soft fingers grazing over my rough stubble. "Was it... I mean, was I... okay?"

I put my arm around her and pulled her into me until her head rested against my shoulder. "You were amazing."

"Are you sure? Because I know you've been with other women before. I can..."

"Shh," I pressed a kiss to her forehead. "You make me sound like a whore."

She swatted my chest. "You know what I mean."

I chuckled, "Yeah, baby, I know. And it was perfect. You were perfect." I brought my mouth to hers and grinned against her lips. "It's probably a good thing we did this out here, and not at your house or mine."

She groaned, "Oh my god. What would your aunt think?"

I chuckled as our conversation came back to me, "Oh baby, she already thinks we've been having sex like crazy."

She pulled away and stared up at me, opening and closing her mouth until she finally managed to squeak out, "What?"

I brushed my knuckles over her cheek. "Apparently you're very vocal."

She buried her face in her hands. I didn't even have to look to know her cheeks were flushed red. "Oh my god, Wes!"

I kissed her again. "Don't worry about it. I set her straight. Told her I just have a very talented tongue."

She swatted me and jumped out of my arms. "You can't say stuff like that! What's she going to think of me now?"

I grabbed my shirt and pulled her back until she was sitting in my lap. "She thinks you're getting it good," I whispered in her ear, unable to contain my grin. "And she's happy for us."

A shiver rocked through her and I couldn't help but smile. "She is?"

I nodded. "Yeah, baby."

CHAPTER TWENTY-ONE

Linford

PRESENT

Wes

The breeze that swept through the garage was a welcome relief. I wiped my forehead on my arm, having dropped the top half of my coveralls down hours ago, tying them around my waist. Whoever's been working on Ember's car really didn't know what the hell they were doing.

"We need to talk!"

My head jerked up so fast at the sound of Miles' pissed off tone, it slammed into the hood of the car. "Damn it!" I cursed, throwing my wrench across the garage. Rubbing my head, I turned to face the man who had made it clear, in no uncertain terms, that I was to stay away from his sister. "What do you want, Miles?"

"What the hell are you doing?"

"What does it look like? I'm fixing her car!"

Miles stepped right up into my space, which would be comical if he didn't have the power to ruin my life completely. I had at least forty pounds and a couple of inches on him. We may both work for his dad, but he stayed in the office while I did the heavy lifting. He jabbed his finger into my chest knowing I would stand there and take it. "You know what I mean. Why?"

My nostrils flared and I threw my head back, needing a moment to quell my frustration. I focused on the chain hanging to the side of the rolled up garage door and took a deep breath. The pressure in my chest eased as I blew it out; it wasn't Miles' fault. He was just protecting her, and I couldn't be more grateful for that. Except he didn't need to protect her from me. The last thing I ever wanted to do was hurt Ember.

I rubbed the back of my neck, trying to squeeze away the tension that was slowly building up as I stared one of my many obstacles in the face. "Bob said you called in a favor. He asked me to pick it up."

"Why would he do that? You don't work here anymore."

"Because it's Ember, that's why."

Miles took a step back, shaking his head. "And what are you looking to get out of this?"

I held my hands up, offended he would even think that of me. "Nothing, man. I just want to help."

He grabbed one of the stools we kept in the empty bay, and sat with his body slumped forward, arms pressed into his knees. "I like you, Wes, god help me I do. But my sister... You hurt her. You hurt her so bad she left without saying a word and as far as I can tell, never had any intention of coming back."

I returned to Ember's car, glancing under the hood where hoses were held together with electrical tape and what I believe was once a coat hanger. "I never wanted to hurt her," I said, leaning my hip against the car. "I was just trying to do the right thing."

"And by right thing, you mean owning up to fathering a child with a woman who wasn't your girlfriend?"

I pressed my lips into a thin line as his words hit home. That is exactly what I did, and I would never regret that decision. Much like Ember, Ellie deserved so much more than me, more than I could ever give her.

Miles lifted his chin at me. "She said you told her you never cheated. What game are you playing?"

I never should have said that, but I was tired of being the bad guy. I wanted her to know I'd never betray her like that, even though at the time I wasn't completely sure. I studied him carefully, debating whether or not I could trust him. Miles was a good guy... I pulled a rag out of my pocket, needing to do something with my hands. "I never cheated on her," I admitted, my voice low. "I would never do that to her."

"Then how?" He stood and got right back in my face, the heat of his anger rolling off of him in waves. "How can you have a daughter if you never cheated?"

"She's not mine."

"What?"

My shoulders slumped, as I confessed the biggest secret I'd ever kept. The secret only my aunt and Bob knew. Of course, Ellie's mom knew, though she wasn't aware that I found out the truth. "Ellie's not mine."

"What do you mean, she's not yours?"

I stepped around him and grabbed a stool, "Sit." I rolled over another and sat across from him. "You ever look at her?"

"At Ellie?"

I rolled my eyes. "Yeah, at Ellie. You ever look at her? Like *really* look at her?"

"She's a cute kid, of course I have."

"Tell me. What color is her hair, her eyes?"

Miles looked at me, eyebrows pulled together in confusion. "She's a blonde, with... green eyes?"

"Exactly. Blonde hair, green eyes. Now, look at me. Brown hair, blue eyes. Her mom - Brown hair, brown eyes... It didn't exactly add up to me."

"Yeah, but that doesn't necessarily mean..."

"I had a paternity test done."

It was like time stood still as Miles processed what I just said. He didn't move, didn't blink. I don't even think he was breathing. "Why?" he finally managed.

"At first, I didn't know what was true. I was drunk the night it supposedly happened. I didn't think I could ever do something like that, but she had the test and her story..." I shook my head. "I suddenly felt like I couldn't trust my memory, and if, on the off chance the baby was mine... I'm not the kind of guy who would abandon my child."

"But why? Once you knew, why didn't you say anything?"

I looked down at my hands; rough, calloused with the stain of grease under my nails. This is who I was, but everything changed that day. "The second I laid eyes on that little girl, I fell in love. She was so tiny and helpless, and as soon as I held her I never wanted to let her go."

I swallowed thickly and looked up into Miles' wrecked face. "Every day I fell a little more. When she smiled at me for the first time, when she gripped my finger. When she cried at night, I was the only one who could soothe her."

A single tear rolled down my cheek as I remembered all the little moments. "When she rolled over for the first time and started to crawl. When she said her first word…"

Miles choked out a laugh, and I could tell without even looking that he was crying too. "Her first word was dad."

I nodded, "Yeah. Every day I brush her hair - I even learned to braid to keep it tame. We read stories and she wants me to teach her things…"

He swiped at his cheeks when he looked up at me. "But why didn't you say anything? We could have fixed this!"

I shook my head. "How? Miles, *she's not mine*! What am I supposed to do? The second I admit the truth, her mom is going to make sure I never see her again. She'll take her and run, and there's nothing I can do about it."

"You don't know that."

I gave him a look that clearly said, "are you kidding me?"

"Your name is on the birth certificate," he argued.

"Yeah, that doesn't mean a whole lot in the eyes of the law," I chuckled, though there was no humor in it. "I'll have to take her to court and fight, and it's an uphill battle. You and I both know I can't afford something like that. We're barely scraping by as it is."

"Fuck, man. Why couldn't you just be an asshole? This would be so much easier."

I shrugged. "I don't know. I'm pretty sure if you asked Ember, she'd tell you I'm the biggest asshole."

Miles sighed and stood up, ready to leave. "Do you love her?"

"Ellie? Yeah, I think we just established that."

"No you idiot. Ember… Do you love her?"

"With everything that I am."

He nodded and walked out of the garage without saying another word. I picked up my discarded wrench and returned to the car, but I couldn't focus. I pulled out my phone and dialed the only person who would understand.

"Everything okay?"

"I love how when I call, you immediately jump into problem solving mode."

"So this is a friendly call, nothing's wrong?"

I sighed, "I didn't say that... I messed up, Ang."

"What happened?"

"Miles came by. It all just came out..."

"When you say all..."

"I mean all. Everything. He knows Ellie's not mine. What if he goes to the cops?"

There was a long pause, then, "Maybe it's not a bad thing."

"But you said..."

"I know what I said. But that was before. Miles is a good guy, he only wants his sister to be happy. He wants what's best for her and I think he knows that's you. Now he knows why you haven't been able to fix things."

"Yeah, but what if..."

"Give him credit, Wes. We all know you're the only parent that girl has. He won't jeopardize that."

"Fuck, Ang. I'm scared."

"Relax. You at the garage?"

"Yeah."

"Stay put. I'll be there in a few minutes with a little ray of sunshine."

I laughed, "Thanks, Ang. Make sure she's wearing clothes she can get dirty."

"Yeah, yeah."

Ember

I held the pillow over my head as tight as I could, but it did nothing to drown out Miles' voice. "Go away!" I screamed into Jadon's Iron Man sheets.

"I'm not gonna tell you again. Get your ass out of this bed, we're going to see mom."

I rolled over, pushing my mussed hair out of my face. "I'm not going."

"Damn it, Ember! What was the point of coming all the way out here if you're not even gonna see her?"

"I should have just stayed home. This was pointless."

He grabbed me by the ankle and yanked until I was half hanging off the bed. "I'm done playing nice. It's not like it makes any difference. As soon as this is all over, you're going to leave and we'll be lucky if we ever see you again anyway."

He dropped my leg and stormed out of the room.

"Miles!" I scrambled to my feet and chased him out the door. "I'm sorry, okay?"

He stood with his hands on his hips, shaking his head. "No. You're not. I don't know what happened to you, but you've become almost as selfish as Kennedy. And that's saying something."

"Take it back." I demanded.

"No. I'm not gonna lie to you to make you feel better. I called you out here for a reason, and so far you've done nothing but make this about yourself." He stormed out the door, letting it slam behind him.

I wanted to chase him down, to argue with him, but he was right. I was supposed to be here for our mom, for *him*, and so far I've thrown a fit over seeing my dad, spotting Kennedy's new car, and of course - Wes.

God, Wes.

I still couldn't get those words out of my head, *I never cheated on you!*

I rolled my eyes. If he didn't cheat, then the sky wasn't blue. You don't have a kid without sex. That's basic biology, and he most definitely has a kid. He even admitted it.

I blew out a heavy breath. Miles was right, it was time for me to grow up and stop acting like a brat. I went to the front door and pushed it open, only to find Miles leaning against the hood of his car, arms folded over his chest. "You done throwing a fit?"

"I'm sorry."

He nodded. "Go get dressed. We only have an hour or so before dad gets there, so if you want to avoid him, we need to get going."

The TV was on when I stepped into her room. She didn't seem to notice me at first, but then, without taking her eyes off the screen, she said, "I didn't think I'd ever see you again."

"What makes you think that?" The look on her face was answer enough. "Sorry."

"Come sit."

I dragged a chair over to her bedside and did as I was told. "Tell me about your life. How's work?"

I fought the urge to roll my eyes. "Work is fine. It's a diner, nothing different from working at Paula's."

"You were always meant for more."

"Yeah, well things change."

Her pained expression said more than her words ever could. She changed the subject. "How about your friends? What are they like?"

I smiled, thinking of my only friends back home. "They're great. Ned and Nancy - they're twins, and they both work with me. Nancy and I hang out sometimes. Ned's always trying to get us to go hiking or fishing, or anything outside."

"Is he cute?" she asked, waggling her eyebrows.

I barked out a laugh, "Oh my god. I don't know. I've never thought about it. He's just... he's Ned."

"Well, is there someone? You can't stay single forever."

"Who says I am?"

She arched her brow, daring me to lie to her. "I'm not really seeing anyone, no. I did go on a date recently. He's a good guy."

She winced as she pushed into a sitting position and was quickly overcome with a bout of coughing. "Go on," she encouraged once the coughing settled.

"I don't know. He's a guy. He comes into the diner a lot. He works in real estate."

"So he's rich?"

"Mom!"

"What? Tell me he's not..."

"I don't know. I never asked, and besides, it doesn't matter!"

"Why not?"

I shrugged. "I'm not sure I'm gonna see him again."

"Does that mean you're staying?" her voice was full of hope and I hated dashing it, but I couldn't lie.

"No. I can't."

She started coughing again. She had a tissue clenched in her hand and when she pulled it away it was spotted with red.

"Is that blood?" I leaned forward and reached for her.

"I'm fine," she waved me away. "It's nothing."

My heart thumped wildly in my chest. "No, that's definitely not fine. What's wrong, mom?"

"I'm fine, it's just a cough." Before I could argue, she waved me off and changed the subject. "Your dad misses you, you know."

I studied her face; she seemed fine aside from that cough. I let it go. "Doubtful."

"He does. He regrets what happened. So do I."

"Oh? So if given the chance, you'd take it back?"

She shook her head. "No, I never said that. I just regret how you took it."

And just like that, my worry was gone. "How was I supposed to take it?" I folded my arms over my chest and sat back in my chair, putting some space between us.

"Ember, just... You need to talk to your father. And to Kennedy."

"No."

The coughing started up again, only this time it didn't look like it was going to stop. I pressed the button to call the nurse, and when she got there she told me I should go and come back later.

As soon as my hand wrapped around the door handle, my mom made one last request of me. "Please go see her. She's lost. She's always looked up to you."

I didn't answer, I didn't want to disappoint her, but there was no way I was going to see my sister.

CHAPTER TWENTY-TWO

Linford

8 Years Ago

Ember

The steady dum-dum of Wes' heartbeat threatened to lull me to sleep. I closed my eyes as I absently traced the lines of his abs. Since he started working for Bob his muscles were becoming more prominent and defined. I wasn't about to complain.

I sighed as I snuggled into him, relishing the feel of his calloused fingers brushing up and down my back. "You getting sleepy, baby?" he asked, pressing a kiss to my forehead.

"Maybe a little," I yawned.

I protested when he moved, and his chest rumbled with laughter. "It's already almost nine, we should probably get you home."

"Nooo," I whined, holding him tighter.

"Trust me, the last thing I want is for you to leave my bed. But if you miss curfew again, your dad is going to castrate me."

I sat up, hugging the sheet to my chest. "This is ridiculous. It's winter break!"

Wes gripped the side of the sheet and tugged it down, revealing my naked body. "Wes!" I covered myself with my arms; it didn't matter how many times he saw me naked, I don't think I'd ever get used to being fully exposed.

He grinned, not even trying to hide the fact that he was staring at my chest as he folded his hands behind his head. "What? I needed one more look before you leave me alone in this cold bed."

"I don't want to go," I protested.

He pulled me into his arms. "I know, baby, but it's only a few more months. Then Omaha."

"Then Omaha." I grinned and kissed the corner of his mouth. "And then I can sleep with you every night."

He chuckled. "I'd love nothing more."

"I can't believe Miles convinced our parents to let me move in with him instead of staying in the dorms."

"Honestly. Me too."

"He likes you, you know?"

He brushed kisses down my neck, I could feel the curve of his smile against my skin. "What's not to like?"

My breath hitched and my eyes rolled back in my head as the throb between my legs begged for attention. "Wes, you have to stop if I'm ever going to get out of this bed..."

He groaned, falling back into the soft mattress, throwing an arm over his eyes. "Get dressed, I want to talk to you about something before you leave."

"What?"

"Get dressed so I can look at you," he chuckled, giving me a little shove.

I laughed as I gathered my clothes, quickly tugging on my jeans and oversized sweater. "I thought you liked looking at me without my clothes on."

"You have no idea. But if I get one more look at those perfect tits, I'll just drag you back into bed and never let you go."

I swatted at his bare chest. "It's safe, I'm dressed."

He peeked out from under his arm before removing it altogether. He sat up and leaned against the headboard, the sheets pooling at his waist. He ran his hand through his hair, pushing it back away from his face. "I know I didn't give you much for Christmas..."

"Wes, don't." I sat next to him, pressing a finger over his lips. I twisted my wrist, the three new charms he gave me for my bracelet tinkling together; a letter E, two linked hearts, and the third was a snowman, marking the first time he saw snow, and the snowman I made him build with me. It was perfect.

He licked my fingers and I yanked my hand away with a squeal.

"I didn't give you much for Christmas," he chuckled, daring me to shush him, "but that's because I was waiting on something."

"What were you waiting for?"

His eyes lit up as he pulled me into his lap. "There's this concert next month in Kansas City I'd like to take you to."

I furrowed my brows as I traced my finger over the stubble on his jaw. "A concert? Like Imagine Dragons or Fall Out Boy?"

He chuckled, "Nah. That would be for me. This is for you..."

"Who...?"

"Florida Georgia Line."

My fingers stopped their movement and my eyes snapped to his as my jaw hit the floor.

He took my hand and pressed a kiss to my palm. "I was wondering if, one, you want to go, and two, if you think your parents will let you. It's about a four hour drive each way, so we'd want to spend the night there..."

I searched his eyes, "You're serious?"

"Yeah, baby."

I threw my arms around his neck. "I really, *really*, want to go."

"Good." He gave me a quick kiss and climbed out of bed next to me, not at all ashamed of his nakedness or his semi-hard dick. "Now you just have to convince your parents to let you."

I got up and grabbed my purse. "I will."

He swatted my ass with a grin, "Now go, so you don't miss curfew, because that will make getting permission even harder."

"Speaking of hard," I licked my lips, looking down his impressive body.

"Stop ogling me and go," he laughed. "I love you."

I put a little extra sway into my hips as I left his room. "Love you too."

Despite the heavy snow, I made it home with three minutes to spare. I hung up my coat and kicked out of my boots. I ran different arguments through my head the whole drive home. The, "I've been a good girl, I've never done anything out of line," argument. The "It's one night, we'll get separate rooms," argument. The "I'll call you every hour to check in," argument. Then finally, the most ridiculous but might actually work argument, "I'll wear a chastity belt and you'll hold the only key." They didn't need to know Wes and I were already sleeping together.

I stepped quietly into the living room where they were sitting comfortably, watching a movie. I cleared my throat and ignored the sudden dryness of my mouth. "Mom? Dad?"

"Hmm?" My mom asked, not looking up from the TV.

"Can I talk to you guys about something real quick?"

My dad picked up the remote and paused the movie. "What's up?"

The second both their eyes were on me all my arguments flew out the window. "I... uh..." I stammered. I took a deep breath and reminded myself it would be okay. I've never asked for anything like this before. Hell, I never really asked for anything at all. "Wes wants to take me to a concert in Kansas City next month, and I'd like to know if I can go."

My dad's eyebrow arched as he looked from me to my mother, who turned in her seat to do the same. "What's the concert?"

"Florida Georgia Line."

"And what time would it be?"

"I'm not sure, probably late. Wes said we'd have to stay the night since it's a long drive."

My dad shook his head. "No."

"No?"

"No. You're not spending the night with that boy."

"We'd get separate hotel rooms," I responded quickly. "I'll check in regularly."

"Not happening." His tone brooked no argument.

I knew asking was a long-shot, an uphill battle, but I didn't expect him to shut me down completely right from the start. "But daddy!"

"I said no!"

"Mom?"

The front door opened and slammed shut. I cringed, knowing how much my parents hated slamming doors. I checked my phone, it was a quarter to ten. Curfew was 9 for Kennedy. I only got an extra thirty minutes.

She came strolling into the living room, still wearing her boots, tracking snow the whole way. "Hey, I'm home."

"Hey, sweetie," my dad said, giving her a big smile and patting the arm of his chair for her to sit with him.

I ground my teeth. This was typical. Kennedy could do pretty much anything, and she was still "daddy's little girl." Slamming doors, tracking snow through the house... missing curfew. Three things tonight alone, and it was "Hey sweetie." If I stepped out of line the tiniest bit, I was grounded.

I tried to bring the conversation back to the concert. "Mom?"

"Yeah?"

"The concert?"

"Concert? What concert?" Kennedy asked, sitting a little taller.

"Wes wants to take your sister to a concert," my mom supplied.

"What concert?"

"Florida Georgia Line."

"Ooh, I wanna go."

I narrowed my eyes at her. "You don't even like country music."

"Yes I do."

I folded my arms across my chest. "Name one song."

She smirked, "Cruise. That's even a Florida Georgia Line song."

"Well, if Kennedy wants to go..." my dad started, smiling up at her.

"I do!"

"Then I guess you can go. But," he held up a finger, "you will get two rooms, one for you girls, and one for him. And don't you even *think* about going into his room at any time. Understand?"

I nodded, "Yes sir."

He dismissed me with a nod and wrapped an arm around Kennedy, pressing play on their movie. I stepped in a puddle of melted snow on my way back down the hall and blew out a frustrated sigh as I peeled off my soggy socks. I climbed the stairs and when I made it to my room, every last bit of excitement I felt when I left Wes' house was gone.

I pulled out my phone and typed a quick message.

Me: I have news

Wes: Good news?

Me: Depends on your definition of good

Wes: Uh oh

Me: So I can go to the concert…

Wes: That's good news :)

Me: Only if we take Kennedy with us

Wes: And not so good news

Me: I'm sorry. Just forget it. We can go to a concert another time

Wes: Nah. I want to take you to this. So what if Kennedy comes. It'll be fine

Me: She's gonna ruin it. She doesn't even like country!

Wes: Then why does she want to come?

Me: Because she likes making me miserable

Wes: I'd say you're overreacting, except I've seen your sister. Don't worry, baby. We'll have fun, even if she's there

Me: I love you

Wes: I love you too. Get some sleep, tomorrow I'm teaching you how to change your oil

Me: I'm still not convinced that's a valuable use of our time, but if you insist

Wes: I do

Me: Whatever you want. Goodnight

Four hours in a car with your boyfriend and bratty kid sister is never a good idea. Wes and I put together a road trip playlist with all my favorite Florida Georgia Line songs, and Kennedy threw a fit. She complained about the music the whole time, saying it was crap. Like I said, she doesn't like country music. The only reason she knew the one was because Nelly did a remix with them.

I eventually gave up and put on whatever she wanted, so long as she shut her mouth. It worked for a minute, and then she decided to sing along - off key at the top of her lungs. Wes was great, he held my hand, lacing our fingers together, for most of the drive, occasionally pressing a kiss to my knuckles.

We checked in at the hotel first so we could drop off our bags and freshen up before the show. I took my time getting ready, curling my hair and putting on some makeup. I slipped on a cute pair of skinny jeans paired with a cream colored, off the shoulder blouse, and of course my favorite boots.

Kennedy, on the other hand, wore a black leather skirt, and a red sequined top, knee-high, high heeled boots, and enough makeup to make a hooker jealous. I shook my head; she was going to stand out like a sore thumb.

We met Wes in the hall just outside of our rooms, which were conveniently right next to each other. He looked incredible in jeans and a black button-down, his hair styled just the way I liked it. He took my hand and pressed his mouth to mine. "Hey, baby," he grinned against my lips. "You're so fucking sexy."

"Get a room," Kennedy groaned, making a gagging sound and shoved past us.

I spun around, ready to tear into her when Wes pulled me into his chest. "Let it go. Don't let her ruin our night."

As soon as we were in the venue, Wes immediately took me to the merchandise booth and bought me a concert tee. Kennedy just disappeared.

There were so many people, I couldn't see over or through them. "Did you see where she went?"

Wes stood behind me, hands massaging my shoulders. "No. But she has her phone, and she knows where our seats are."

"I can't stand this," I complained, turning in his arms, burying my face in his chest and inhaling his comforting scent.

"Me neither, but if this is the only way I could bring you, then I'd do it again."

"You can't be serious? I swear she's possessed by Satan, and our parents don't even notice."

He chuckled. "Come on, baby. Let's get in there."

The second Brian Kelley and Tyler Hubbard stepped out on that stage, all thoughts of my bratty sister disappeared. I sang along, cheered, and during the slow songs, swayed side to side in Wes' strong arms. I grinned when he sang along, whispering the words in my ear about a man who was lost, and the woman who broke through his defenses and saved him. My man was everything.

Not for the first time I asked myself, "how did I get so lucky?"

We remained in our seats long after the concert ended. Long enough we were still there when the crew started dismantling the stage. The seat beside me had remained empty for the duration of the show, but Wes refused to let me dwell on it. Kennedy was sixteen. She was grown enough to be responsible. Sort of.

I sent her a text, telling her to meet us by the merchandise booth, but when we got there, she was nowhere to be found. "Wes, I'm worried."

He pressed a kiss to my forehead. "Try calling her."

I pressed the call button and held the phone to my ear. It rang several times before going to voicemail. I called again, and then once more.

"What?" Kennedy snapped, sounding a little breathless.

I let out a sigh of relief. "Where are you? Wes and I are..."

"I got bored. Came back to the hotel."

"Are you kidding me?" I rubbed my temple with my free hand, my head starting to ache.

"Chill out, *mom*. It's fine."

I hung up without saying goodbye. "She's at the hotel."

Wes' brow furrowed. "How did she get there?"

I shook my head. "No idea."

Wes took my hand and gave it a squeeze. "Come on. Let's go make sure she's okay."

I didn't want to go back to the hotel, that meant saying goodnight to Wes, and I wasn't ready for that. We didn't really have any other options though. It was late, and despite not wanting to, we had to make sure my sister was safe. I could only imagine what my parents would do if something happened to their *baby*.

It took forever to get back to the hotel. There were so many people trying to leave the venue at the same time, that it was almost pointless to even try until some of the traffic cleared out. I was so thankful for Wes, having grown up in a big city, he was familiar with how to navigate this sort of traffic.

It was nearly one when we made it back to the hotel. Wes stood beside me as I pushed the door to my room open to find Kennedy passed out on one of the beds, the TV blaring loud. I pulled the door shut, "I don't want to go in there."

Wes put his arm around my shoulders and pulled me into his side. "Come on. I brought us a little something on the off chance we'd have some alone time."

I bit my lip, looking from my room to his next door. I promised my dad I wouldn't go into Wes' room, but how would he find out? "What is it?"

He unlocked his door and held it open while I went inside. This room was the same as mine, just in reverse. He toed off his shoes by the door then dropped his phone, keys, and wallet on the dresser. His duffel bag sat neatly on the far bed, and he unzipped it, pulling out a couple of t-shirts, then finally what he was looking for. "Where did you get that?"

"Teddy's a buddy of mine."

I laughed, reaching for the bottle of whiskey. Teddy owned the only liquor store in town, aptly named "T's Liquor." "He knows you're not twenty-one, right?"

"Yeah, but we both agreed that I'm mature for my age."

I shook my head, twisted the cap, brought the bottle to my nose and immediately choked on the air.

"Whoa there," Wes laughed, taking the bottle from me. "I don't know how they do it where you come from, but where I'm from we drink our liquor, not snort it."

I swatted him, snatching the bottle back. I brought it to my lips and took a long gulp. The amber liquid burned all the way down my throat, and I broke out in a coughing fit.

Wes took the bottle and rubbed my back. "Didn't anybody teach you how to drink?" His tone was light and teasing.

I shook my head. "No. Tatum tried to get me to try tequila a couple of times. But I never wanted to get into trouble."

"First of all, gross. Second, you're not worried about getting into trouble now?"

I lifted one shoulder in a half shrug. Being the perfect daughter was wearing on me. It didn't really seem to matter, I was never good enough anyway. "Not really. Like you said, I've only got a few more months, and then we're moving to Omaha. I've already gotten my college acceptance letter, all that's left is finishing high school."

Wes brought the bottle to his lips and took a long drink. I stared at him with my mouth open. "How do you do that?"

"Practice," he winked at me. "Unlike you, my incredibly sexy, incredibly smart and talented woman, I was a hooligan. Late nights partying. Staying out all night drinking with my buddies. I may or may not have raised a little hell and smoked a bit of weed."

"Wes!"

He laughed, "I told you, I wasn't a good guy before I met you." He kissed my forehead, "You make me better and make me want to *be* better."

"Tell me about it?"

He pulled his shirt off, unbuttoned his jeans and slid them off then climbed onto the bed so he was leaning against the headboard. "About what?"

I followed his lead, unsnapping my jeans and peeled them off. I went to his duffel and grabbed one of his t-shirts. I yanked off my blouse, unclasped my bra and pulled his shirt on. I gripped the front collar of the shirt and brought it up to my nose. It smelled like him, like safety. Like home.

I crawled up onto the bed and sat beside him so our legs touched. "Tell me what it was like living in a big city, going to parties. Staying out all night…"

He took another long drink before passing the bottle back to me. "Tell you what. I'll tell you anything you want to know, if you tell me why your parents let Kennedy get away with murder."

I closed my eyes and leaned my head back against the headboard. I passed the bottle back to him. "Honestly? I think it's because she almost died when she was a baby. The doctors didn't expect her to live, so when she did, my parents decided they'd give her everything."

"What was wrong?" He took a long drink and held the bottle out to me, but I shook my head.

"There were a couple of things. I don't know all the details, I'm only two years older than her, so I was pretty much a baby then too." I took a deep breath and blew it out, watching his throat as he swallowed another mouthful. "She had a heart condition. They had to do a transplant. And then something happened. There were complications..."

"That sounds rough."

"Yeah. I don't really remember much about it."

"So now they just let her do whatever she wants?"

"Pretty much. It's probably not as bad as it seems, but it's annoying going around wearing ratty shoes when she gets a pair of brand new shoes costing more than $160 every few months. I wear thrifted clothes, and my mom takes her to the city to buy brand new ones. I have a job to get what I want or need and my parents buy her everything she wants..."

He wrapped his arm around my shoulder, pulling me closer and I laid my head on his shoulder. "That sounds frustrating."

"It is."

"What about Miles?"

"Eh, he's a guy. And the oldest, so it's a little different. But I can say, with confidence, that he doesn't like it."

He nodded. "I like him."

I smiled and took the bottle for another sip. "Me too."

Wes and I laid in his bed for hours, talking, laughing, dreaming of the future.

"What do you want for your life?" I asked. We were laying on our sides facing each other, our fingers intertwined.

"I never gave it much thought. I guess I want a family, a good job. Stability."

"Me too." I brought my hand that wasn't tangled with his up to his brow, smoothing his hair away from his face. "I want a family, kids, a dog or a cat."

"And your own vet practice?" Wes asked, arching an eyebrow.

"Yeah, my own vet practice."

He brought his mouth to mine in a soft kiss. "Tell me about these kids..."

My cheeks heated. "I'm thinking a little brown haired, blue eyed boy. He'd like fishing and playing in the mud. And he wouldn't be too embarrassed to hold his mama's hand."

"And the other?"

His nose nuzzled my cheek and it was getting harder to focus on the conversation. "Eleanor, that's what I'd call her. Long blonde hair she'd let me braid. We'd have tea parties with her stuffed animals and dance in the rain."

"Mmmm. That sounds perfect."

I woke up in my own room the next morning, my head more than a little fuzzy. I sat up, checking the other bed, but it was empty. "Kennedy?"

The room was silent, the only light coming through a crack in the curtains. I slipped out of bed, still wearing only Wes' shirt, and fumbled through my bag until my hand wrapped around a pair of leggings. I pulled them on and cracked the room door open. I spotted her instantly, her hand on the handle to Wes' room. "What are you doing?"

"I was gonna wake him up, see if he wanted a coffee."

"Don't you think waking me up would've been nice?"

She rolled her eyes. "No. He's nice to me, you're a bitch."

She'd said it to me so many times, you'd think the words wouldn't hurt anymore, but they did. "Four more months," I told myself. "Just four more months."

CHAPTER TWENTY-THREE

Linford

PRESENT

Ember

Begging for a ride or borrowing someone's car was more than frustrating. I hated it. It's not like getting around Linford on foot was any sort of inconvenience, but many people still weren't thrilled with me being back in town. Tatum filled me in on the rumors my sister spread when I left town. *God, I hated her.* And my mother wanted us to "play nice." Screw that.

I kept my head down as I walked along the fenced area next to the elementary school. I could hear the screams and giggles from an ongoing game of tag, and it reminded me of so many worry-free days spent with my friends. Part of me wanted to look. The other part warned me to keep on walking. I didn't know if their kid was one of the ones playing.

I stepped off the curb when I saw a crunched-up soda can. I kicked it as I walked, keeping myself entertained, while also keeping my focus down. Bob's Auto Garage was about another ten minutes down the road. To say I was grateful to get Bob's call this afternoon was an understatement.

I kicked the can all the way to the garage, picking it up when I reached the front door so I could throw it away.

The office was empty when I walked in, and I noticed the garage bay doors were closed as well. Either Bob was in the shop, or he had to step out for a bit and forgot to lock up. I stepped around the desk and peered through the window in the shop door. I groaned; Bob was in there, but he wasn't alone.

For someone who doesn't work at the garage, he sure is here enough.

The way I saw it, I had three options. One - turn around and head back to Tatum's and come back later. Two - sit in the office and wait until Wes leaves. Three - suck it up and go in there.

I closed my eyes and counted to ten. It was time to take Miles' advice and stop acting like a little kid.

I knocked first, then pushed the heavy wood door open enough to peek my head through. "Hey, Bob. I'm here for my car?"

Wes stopped whatever he was saying mid-sentence and stared at me. My breath caught and my heart rate spiked. I used to love being on the receiving end of that stare. Now it just felt like a knife to the chest.

"Hey, kiddo," Bob smiled. "Come on in, Wes and I were just talking about your car."

I swallowed past the lump in my throat and pushed the door the rest of the way open. My hands fisted at my sides as I crossed the garage, stepping around a car in the first bay, to where they stood in the second. "What's the verdict? She gonna live to sing another day?" I joked, trying to keep my emotions light.

The corner of Wes' mouth tugged like he wanted to smile, but he held back.

Bob stuffed his hands in his pockets, swaying front to back on the balls of his feet. "I'm gonna let Wes fill you in…"

"But…" he was already on his way out of the shop. I forced a smile on my face, thinking of Miles the whole time. *You're a grown woman. Don't be a brat.*

"So, uh…" His voice quavered with nerves as he rubbed the back of his neck with his hand. "It's fixed and ready to go, just…"

The ringing of my phone cut him off and I pulled it out of my back pocket. I was still a little worried about my mom and was waiting on a call from Miles. But this was neither the hospital nor my brother. "Nancy?"

I turned away from Wes, my stomach knotting up with a whole new set of worries. What was wrong? Did something happen to Mr. Jangles? Did my apartment burn down…?

"When are you coming home?" My friend whined.

"Well, hello to you too." I stole a peek over my shoulder; Wes stood, leaning against the bumper of my car, ankles and arms crossed. "I'm not sure yet. Is everything okay?"

"Define everything."

"The diner? My apartment? Mr. Jangles?"

I heard a snort behind me and turned to glare at Wes. His eyebrow was arched, and he mouthed, "Mr. Jangles?" at me. I flipped him off. My stomach flipped when he smiled. Looking at Wes was like looking into the sun. Beautiful and dangerous.

"Yeah, yeah. It's all fine. The diner is getting slammed though, so we could really use you. And…"

"And?"

"Oh my God, Em. Brent has been in here every day asking about you! What do I tell him?"

My cheeks flushed pink with embarrassment. "He has?"

"He told me you went on a date?! Why am I only just now hearing this, and from *him*? I thought we were friends!"

I sighed, "Everything happened so fast," I stole a look at Wes, smiling internally at the tension in his stance and the way his jaw clenched. "He sent me a few texts, I just haven't had time to get back to him."

"So, you're going to?"

I had mixed feelings about seeing Brent again. He was great, and we actually had a good time, but... he wasn't Wes. The problem was, Wes wasn't mine, hasn't been for a long time.

"Yeah, I think so. He's just so sweet, and smart, and..." I took sick pleasure from driving the knife a little deeper into Wes's heart. "He's driven and successful."

"Tell me something I don't know."

I laughed, though it felt forced. The triumph I felt just moments before died quickly when I chanced another look at Wes. His back was now to me, shoulders slumped. If I didn't know any better, I'd say someone kicked his puppy.

"Hey, Nance? I gotta go, but I'll talk to you soon."

"Yeah, okay. Let me know when you're coming home. We miss you!"

"Miss you too."

I ended the call and stuffed the phone in my back pocket.

I cleared my throat, "Um. You were saying? About my car?"

He turned around and pulled a set of keys out of his pocket. "Drive safe," he whispered, dropping them into my outstretched hand so our fingers wouldn't touch.

I stood frozen as he stepped around me and out the shop door. Seconds later, I heard the sound of an engine, then tires squealing out of the lot. Guilt wrapped itself around me. I shouldn't feel guilty, he hurt me first! But that didn't make what I did any more right. Especially since I had no intention of going out with Brent again.

CHAPTER TWENTY-FOUR

Linford

PRESENT

Wes

My fist slammed into the steering wheel, once, twice, three times, but it did nothing to quell the pain in my chest. If I didn't know any better, I'd say I was having a heart attack. But I knew this pain; it was the pain I felt the morning I woke up and she was gone. The day she left and I had no way of finding her.

I slammed my foot on the brakes as soon as I pulled into my aunt's driveway. My breathing was ragged, my vision blurred with unshed tears. Fire burned through my veins, and there was nothing I could do; this was all my fault.

I raked my hands through my hair and took a deep breath, in through my nose, and blew it out slowly. I did it again, and again, until the shaking in my hands had calmed. There was only one thing that could make me feel better, and she was about four feet tall with long blonde hair.

I knocked just before I let myself into the house. Hushed voices floated from the kitchen, followed a second later by the screeching of a chair across the floor.

"Daddy!" Ellie screamed, running out of the kitchen, arms held out wide.

I knelt down and hugged her tight when she slammed into me, bringing my hand to the back of her head, holding her close and smoothing down the tangled strands of her wild hair. I breathed in her strawberry shampoo and kissed the top of her head. "Hey, baby girl. What have you been up to?"

"We was makin cookies!" She pulled away and her smile slipped. Her little hand cupped my cheek, "You cryin?"

I shook my head, "No, I'm not crying." And then a tear rolled down my cheek, making me a liar.

She arched her eyebrows, then wrapped her arms around my neck. "It's okay, daddy," she whispered in my ear. "Are you sad?"

I nodded, "Yeah, baby, I'm sad," I rasped. In my peripheral, I could see Angie leaning against the doorway, wiping her hands on a towel.

"Want me to kiss it better?" Ellie asked.

She was so sweet, so innocent. I had to remind myself that everything I did was for her; Ellie was all that mattered. I tapped my cheek. "How about right here?"

She smacked her lips against my cheek, "Better?"

"Thank you, baby girl. I'm much better now."

She gave me the biggest smile before taking off, back into the kitchen. Angie swatted her with the towel as she ran past. "Slow down!"

"Sorry auntie," she called out just before we heard the screeching of a chair.

"She's decorating cookies," Angie answered my silent question. "Did you talk to her?"

I stood up and stuffed my hands in my pockets. "Yeah."

"And? Did Miles talk to her? What did she say?"

I lifted one shoulder in a half shrug. "I don't know, but none of it matters anyway. She's seeing someone."

"No, she's not."

"His name is *Brent,* and apparently he's everything I'm not," I managed, speaking around a lump in my throat. I squeezed my eyes shut and shook my head.

"Oh, honey," Angie pulled me in for a hug and I immediately wrapped my arms around her, holding on like she was my life raft.

I tried to be strong, tried to keep it all together, but it was too much. A sob tore through me. "It's over," I choked out. "It's all over, Ang. She doesn't want me!"

She rubbed slow circles over my back, much like she had so many times over the past year. "Don't give up hope, not yet."

Hope. Hope was all I held onto for the past seven years. "I'm not sure how much longer I can take it." I took a deep breath and blew it out slowly, pulling away from her and wiping my cheeks with the backs of my hands. "Ember was it for me, and if she doesn't want me, then it's over. I... I can't, Ang. I can't do it."

"Wes..."

I sucked in a deep breath and shook my head. "I can't..." I wiped my nose with the back of my hand. "Ellie's enough. That little girl loves with her whole heart. She's my everything, that's just how it has to be." I don't know who I was trying to convince, her or myself, not that it mattered.

My phone started ringing, but I ignored it. The only people I cared about were in this house. Everyone else could wait. It started ringing again, but I silenced it, not even looking at who was calling. Angie arched a brow at me, "Aren't you gonna get that?"

I shook my head, and a moment later, her phone started to ring.

"It's Miles. He's probably looking for you." A knowing grin crossed her face as she answered. "Hey, Miles."

All humor vanished the second he started talking.

"What is it?" I whispered, unable to make out his side of the conversation. She just shook her head at me.

"How's Ember?" She dropped down onto the couch, fisting her shirt at the hem. "What do you need?"

Questions flooded my mind. Did something happen to her? To her car? Is she okay? Did she skip town already? I didn't want to care, but I did. I squatted down in front of my aunt, setting my hands on her knees. "What happened?" I mouthed.

"I'll tell him. Thanks for letting me know."

She ended the call and dropped the phone onto the cushion beside her. Her hand went to her mouth just before a sob broke free. I moved to sit beside her, pulling her into my arms. My throat was suddenly dry; my aunt was a warrior; it took a lot to make her cry. Worst case scenarios flooded my mind, and I was terrified to know what it was.

"Shh, what is it?" I asked, holding her as tears streamed down her face. I'd only seen her cry like this once before, after Ember disappeared without saying a word to anyone. "What happened?" I swallowed thickly, unable to ask the question I really needed to know. "Whatever it is, I'm here," I whispered, the words as much for her as they were for me.

Finally, as her sobs eased into sniffles and ragged breaths, she said two words I never expected to hear.

"It's Leanne."

Ember

I sat in uncomfortable silence as my mother glared at me. The part of me that cared what she thought died seven years ago, so it didn't bother me too much when I told her no.

"You *will* go see your sister. You *will* go see your father!"

I shook my head. "I'll compromise. I'll *call* dad, but Kennedy is a no-go."

"Damn it, Ember! Why can't you just do what you're told?"

I folded my arms over my chest. "Oh, I don't know. It's not like I spent my entire childhood doing exactly what I was told. And look what good that did…"

She started coughing, her entire body rocking with the force. "You," she forced out between fits. "You didn't have to run away!"

I sighed, "Mom, just let it go."

The coughing got worse, her hand flew to her chest, her tissue covered in red. I jumped up, "Mom?" The coughing didn't ease and I began frantically looking for the call button that she kept by her side. "Where's the button, mom?" I cried. Her hand fell from her mouth as another cough broke free, a spray of red hitting me and her white covers.

I swiped at my face and ran out the door. "Help! Someone!" I screamed, racing toward the nurse's station.

"What is it?" Stacy stepped out from behind the desk, her voice oozed annoyance.

"My mom, she's coughing blood. It won't stop, I don't know what to do."

Stacy shouted for someone to get the doctor, and everything became a flurry of movement and sounds. It was like I was watching my life from the outside looking in. My heart pounded in my chest and all I could do was stand there and watch.

At some point, someone redirected me so I was standing against the wall, instead of the center of the room, making everyone walk around me. I was so checked out, I didn't even register their hands on me or the movement. Not until things seemed to calm down.

I watched from a distance as her coughing stopped and she let out a long wheeze before she was laid back in the bed, looking peaceful, like the energy had been drained from her body. It made sense, in a way. It seemed like every time I came to visit, she looked a little more tired - yet no one would tell me what was wrong.

I startled when a hand came down on my shoulder, and I looked up just as the doctor moved on, heading out the door. I returned my focus to my mom and the nurses who remained standing at her side.

"Should I go?" I asked, feeling a little guilty for getting her riled up.

Stacy glared at me from the other side of the bed. "You never should have come back."

Her words were like a slap to the face, and yet I couldn't bring myself to disagree with her. "Can you let her know I'll be back later?"

She barked out a laugh, but there was no humor in it. The other nurse, the one who had her back to me this whole time, turned sad eyes on me. "Look, I'm sorry. I won't fight with her anymore."

She shook her head, her mouth opening and closing as though she wanted to say something, but the words wouldn't come out.

"Go home, Ember. We don't want you here," Stacy snarled. She practically stomped across the room, slamming her shoulder into mine as she passed. "Don't worry. I'll call your dad and Miles and see what they want to do with her body."

"What?" I spun on her. "What do you mean?" A loud sob came from the other nurse as my eyes slowly tracked from her to the woman lying quietly in the bed. "She's... she was fine," I argued; the words didn't make sense, yet I could feel the truth in them.

Stacy huffed. "You know, if you actually gave a damn about your family, you would have known Leanne had cancer. It was just a matter of time..."

"No," I shook my head, my voice hoarse from speaking through the lump in my throat. "You must be mistaken. There was an accident at the factory," I repeated the words that had brought me back to the town I loathed. I raised my voice, "he said there was an accident at the factory."

"Yeah, an accident after your mom collapsed."

"But that doesn't mean..."

"She collapsed because she couldn't breathe, Ember! Because of the cancer you fucking idiot."

I shook my head. "That's not possible. She would have told me." *Wouldn't she?*

I crossed the room on unsteady feet and reached out taking my mom's hand in mine; it was already cold. I stared at her chest, willing it to move. "Mom?" I choked out as a tear rolled down my cheek. "Mom, wake up..." I pressed my hand to her shoulder, giving her a little shake. "Please," I whispered as I remembered the last thing I said to her. *Was this why she wanted me to make peace?*

The chair I had been sitting in earlier was suddenly behind me again and I sat down, not letting go of her hand. *She's sleeping. She's just sleeping.* She was too young to die, this was just a misunderstanding...

The longer I sat there, staring at the stillness of her body, the truth became harder to ignore.

"Em," a hand gripped my shoulder and I shrugged it off.

"This isn't funny," I wrapped my arms around my stomach. "You can give it up now."

"Em, I'm sorry. I wanted to tell you, but she swore me to secrecy."

I shook my head, "I get it, I've been selfish. Lesson learned, now stop screwing around. This isn't funny."

Miles squatted down beside me, "You're not selfish. I was being an ass before."

He carefully pulled our mom's hand from my grip and took both of mine in his. He was so warm... so *alive*. "Oh, god!" I sputtered," dragging my eyes away from her lifeless form, to the comfort of my brother. "What did I do?" I cried. "What did I do, Miles?"

He pulled me into his arms, holding me while I broke down. "Shh, you didn't do anything. It was just time..."

"No," I argued, shaking my head frantically. "I was fighting with her. I yelled at her!"

He laughed, but even I could hear the emotion break through. "She was pretty set on setting things right."

"I yelled at her, Miles!" I choked out. "The last things I said to her were... Oh god!"

I felt his jagged intake of air and I buried my face in his neck. "I'm sorry. I didn't know or I never would have... I didn't know, I didn't know, I didn't know..."

"It's okay, stop blaming yourself." My guilt ratcheted up, instead of mourning our mom, he was stuck comforting me. I really was a selfish person.

"I can't," I whispered. "I'm sorry, I'll go. I just... I ruin everything." I tried to get up, but he held firm.

"You and I both know that there is no amount of time or distance that could repair what was broken. I don't blame you for leaving, and I don't blame you for staying away." He sucked in a deep lungful of air, his chest expanding with the effort. "They made a huge mistake, and you paid the price. The worst part is that they still believe it was the right decision."

"You don't?"

He shook his head, "I think there were mistakes made, conclusions jumped to without evidence... There's a lot you don't know."

"Like what?" I asked, sucking in a ragged breath and swiping at my wet cheeks.

His lips pressed into a thin line and he broke eye contact as a tear rolled down his cheek. "You should go, dad is going to be here any minute."

"What aren't you telling me?"

He shook his head. "It's none of my business and not my place to say."

"Whose is it?" I demanded, getting to my feet.

My dad chose that moment to stumble into the room. His grief slammed into me, and guilt bubbled back up in my stomach. I gave my dad a wide berth as I retreated. All my hurt, anger, and frustration didn't matter right now. He just lost his wife...

Miles' eyes tracked my movement and he gave me a tiny nod as I walked out the door.

I fumbled with my phone, my hands shaking as I tried several times to unlock it. I hit the call button and held it to my ear.

"What's up, girl? You get your car okay? That asshole didn't..."

"My mom's dead," I whispered, cutting her off.

"What?"

"She's dead, Tatum. My mom is dead." I choked out.

CHAPTER TWENTY-FIVE

L'inford

PRESENT

Ember

The wood planks bowed under our weight as we sat side by side on Tatum's porch steps. I lay my head on her shoulder as she poured us both a glass of wine.

"Wine? I thought you'd have tequila ready for an occasion such as this," I half joked. I never knew my bestie to drink wine. It showed just how much I had missed over the years.

"We have tequila for our gossip and problem solving sessions. Wine is for mourning."

I took the glass with a sigh. "I can't believe this."

She looked thoughtful for a moment as she sipped the deep red wine. "What happened, babe?"

I shook my head, "Apparently she had cancer."

"You're kidding? And nobody thought to tell you?"

"Miles said he was sworn to secrecy. I guess one of her last wishes was for me to make amends with my family."

She snorted. "Sorry, I know this isn't the time to laugh, but you do hear how ridiculous that sounds, don't you?"

"Oh, I do. But apparently it was reasonable to her." I took a slow sip, wishing I could go back and change how I reacted to her. "It was so bad, Tatum. We were fighting, she was yelling at me, and I yelled back... Then she started coughing." I squeezed my eyes shut, remembering the look on her face. "It was like she couldn't get enough air and with every cough, blood was coming up..." I looked down at my shirt that still had a fine mist of red covering it. "I got Stacy, and then the doctor rushed in..." I shook my head. "I don't know how long it was between when the doctor arrived, and she was pronounced dead. I just kind of stood there, like it wasn't my life. It was like I was seeing it through someone else's eyes."

"That sounds horrible, I'm so sorry you had to go through that."

I pressed the chilled glass to my forehead, hoping to cool the ache in my head. "I think the worst part is when Stacy informed me I wasn't wanted..."

Tatum flinched. "She's such a bitch."

I huffed out a laugh and brought my glass to my lips, swallowing half the wine in one go. "It's no wonder she and Kennedy were always thick as thieves..." It didn't matter that Stacy was a couple of years older. In a town this size, everyone knew everyone.

"Am I obligated to make up with my dad? With Kennedy?"

Tatum stared at me slack-mouthed. "Are you kidding me right now? No. Hell no."

I nodded and a comfortable silence swept over us, punctuated by the sound of the wind blowing through, rustling leaves, and the tiniest hint of children's voices, no doubt playing on the school playground.

"What now?" Tatum asked.

"I guess... I guess there's gonna be a funeral, and then I'll go home."

"I don't want you to go," she whined, laying her head on my shoulder.

I patted her cheek. "Believe it or not, part of me doesn't want to leave."

She lifted her head, eyebrows arched so high they met her hairline. "Say more..."

I smiled. "I've missed this, *you*. And... it's kind of nice knowing everything about the place you're living."

"And you don't have that where you are?"

I shrugged. "It's different."

"So move back."

I rubbed the heel of my hand over the constant ache in my chest. "I can't. It hurts too much."

"Have you met Ellie?"

I shook my head. "I saw her once, from behind. I ran away so fast..." I'd probably be embarrassed if I didn't feel so numb, so hollow.

"I'm gonna say something you may not like, but just hear me out."

I nodded slowly. The day was bad enough, one more thing wasn't going to make it worse. I swallowed the last of my glass, knowing I wasn't going to like where this was going.

"Actually, I have a couple of things, but I'll start with the most innocent first. Ellie is the sweetest little girl you will ever meet. She's smart and funny, and such a good friend."

I scoffed, I couldn't help myself. "You know this from experience?"

"Kind of. She and Jadon are friends. The way their birthdays lined up with the school calendar means they were in the same class."

"Why didn't you tell me before?"

"Would you have listened? You want nothing to do with anything that involves that kid. She ruined your life, if you recall..."

"She didn't ruin my life. Her parent's did."

"Yeah, but you can't get one without the other."

I kept my face forward, staring at the empty street in front of us. "Why haven't I seen her around?"

"Wes and I agreed it would be best to keep them apart while you were in town."

"So you and Wes are, what... friends now?" I felt like I should be mad about it, but I just didn't have the energy.

"Don't. It's not like that."

I lifted one shoulder in a half-shrug. "It's okay. I guess if there's kids involved it doesn't really go against girl code." I held my empty wine glass out, tapping the bottle for a refill. She filled it almost to the brim, and I immediately brought it to my lips, needing a little more liquid fortification if we were going to talk about things that we always vowed to keep in the dark. "What's the other thing you wanted to say that I'm not gonna like?"

She studied my face, as though assessing whether or not I would be able to handle whatever she had to say. "He's not happy. The only time I have ever seen him smile is when it comes to that little girl. He's a really good dad."

I squeezed my eyes shut as a sharp pain ripped through me. "I always knew he would be," I whispered. "But they were supposed to be *our* kids, Tatum."

"I know. I just think…" she swallowed down the last of her glass, clearly needing a little of her own liquid courage. "I think you should talk to him before you leave."

"I'm not sure that's a good idea. Plus…" I let the word hang, questioning if what I thought I saw actually happened, and if it had, did I want to admit it?

"Plus what?"

I sighed, "I think I hurt him this morning. At that moment, it felt good to see the pain on his face. But then… I felt so guilty. I *still* feel guilty."

"What happened?"

"Remember when I told you about Brent? The hottie?"

She nodded. "The real estate stalker guy."

I swatted her. "He's not a stalker!"

"Yeah, yeah. So what about him?"

"Well, you know we went out…"

"Yeah," she arched an eyebrow, "did you sleep with him?"

I rolled my eyes, "Focus."

Her lips tipped up in a grin. "Sorry. I'm listening."

I swallowed the last of my wine and set the glass behind me. "I was about to talk to Wes, I…" I blew out a heavy breath. "My friend Nancy called, interrupting us and…"

"And?" she prompted when I let the word hang.

"And apparently Brent's been asking about me since I haven't responded to his texts. Nancy asked what to tell him, and I…" I looked down at my hands as shame washed over me. "I looked at Wes and it seemed like he was getting upset, so I laid it on thick. I told her how I was so lucky because he was all these things that I knew Wes was always so insecure about, like being wealthy and successful."

She raised her eyebrows while her mouth gaped open. "You didn't."

I nodded, her reaction made me feel even worse. "I went on to say we were going to go out when I get home and..."

"What did Wes say?"

"He didn't say anything, Tatum." I turned and gave her my full attention. "He's been trying to talk to me since I got back, and when I hung up, he just handed me my keys and told me to drive safe." I covered my face with my hands. "You should have seen the look on his face..."

"Oh, babe. When are you two gonna stop hurting each other?"

"I'm not sure we ever will. Even when I'm gone, it hurts."

"But at least you're moving on, right?"

I shook my head. "No. I like Brent, don't get me wrong. There just isn't that spark... Not like there was with Wes."

The smell of gardenias was almost overpowering as I stepped through the church doors. I had never heard of gardenias being a funerary flower, but they were always my mom's favorite so it made sense. The chapel looked almost exactly the same as it had the last time I was there - reddish-orange carpet, rich wooden pews on either side of a center aisle, and a pulpit at the front, though it wasn't front and center today.

Today, that position belonged to Leanne Davis.

The moment I saw the deep maple casket, I felt compelled to see her. I needed to apologize, to tell her how much I loved her. "Miles," I called out quietly, when I saw him talking to the pastor. Unfortunately, instead of catching his attention, I caught my dad's.

"Ember."

"Hi, dad."

He folded his arms over his chest, his cold eyes felt like knives to my heart. "You don't belong here."

"E-excuse me?"

He shook his head. "You should go back to wherever it is you're living. You've been here for what, two weeks? And look at the damage you've caused."

"I-I."

Miles approached and I looked to him for help, but he just shook his head. He placed his hand on our dad's shoulder and gave it a squeeze. "Why don't you go take a seat, the pastor is about to get started."

He patted Miles' hand and gave him a nod. "Thank you, son."

I started to follow him, to sit in the area designated for family, but Miles cut me off. "I'm sorry, Em. I fought for you, I really did, but…"

I looked around the church, all the pews filling up with her friends. I sucked in a deep breath and held it for as long as I could, wishing it would be enough to stop the hurt. I blew it out when I saw Kennedy sitting beside our dad, staring at me with the biggest grin on her face. She looked good, really good with her dark auburn hair and tan skin, and I hated her even more for it.

I swallowed thickly as I stepped around Miles, closing the gap between him and our mother. If I was going to leave, I would at least say goodbye. The casket was closed, and I ran my fingers over the smooth wood. "Help," I whispered to Miles who was right behind me. "I need to see her, to tell her I'm sorry."

He gripped my shoulder and ushered me away from the coffin. "She's already been cremated," he whispered in my ear.

"What?"

He shook his head. "We can talk later. For now, you have to go." It hurt being banished from my own mother's funeral.

I spun around, ready to leave only to be caught in Wes' gaze. My heart clenched, it was too much. I lost my boyfriend, my family… I had to leave my home and my friends, and they what… got to go on with their lives like nothing ever happened? What was the point?

A sob caught in my throat; every eye in the room was on me, and only a couple were friendly. I was done giving them what they wanted. What about what I wanted? I squared my shoulders, held my head high and walked away, but I didn't leave. I had just as much right as anyone to be here.

The pastor must have talked for nearly an hour, about how death isn't the end, and what matters is that we hold onto the memories. Several people gave eulogies; Miles told the story of when we were little and she took us to our first rodeo. That trip was just the three of us, our dad stayed home with Kennedy who was recovering from something, though I don't remember what.

It was one of my favorite memories. The cowboys were larger than life, and when we watched the bull riders, I was in awe. If you asked Miles, he'd tell you that was when I decided I wanted to be a bull rider. It was more than that though. It wasn't that I wanted to ride the bull, I wanted to take care of him when the cowboy had finished his eight second ride. The bull looked so agitated, I wanted to make him feel better. That's when I knew I wanted to be a vet.

My dad told stories about when he and my mom met, and the wonderful life they shared with their two children. Yeah, *two* children - Miles and Kennedy.

So many stories I never heard before were shared and there was so much about my mom that I didn't know, and never would. When it was over, everyone took their turn, stepping up to the casket to say their goodbye. *But if she was cremated, why would she need a casket?*

Whether she was in there or not, I needed to say my piece. I waited until my dad was out of sight, and the crowd had thinned dramatically before leaving the safety of my corner. I ran my fingers along the smooth wood and cold silver handles. I reminded myself that she wasn't in there, that if I wanted to talk to her, it didn't matter if I was here or at home. Yet I still felt compelled to speak to the ornamental box.

"I'm so sorry, mom. I'm sorry for fighting with you, and sorry for not talking to you more. I never should have cut you out like that. You were a good mom," I sniffled, wiping my nose with the back of my hand. "It may not make any sense, but I miss you."

I bowed my head as I said a quick prayer for her. I wasn't a religious person, but it felt right.

A few stragglers remained, caught up in their own conversations, when I turned to leave. I mentally wished them all well, knowing this would be the last time I saw any of them. I was leaving, and I would never come back; not to Linford.

I stepped outside into the blinding sun. I had to shade my eyes so I could see to get around those who congregated on the lawn. About halfway to my car, I heard my name and I froze in place. I knew that voice, knew I should keep walking, but if this was going to be the last time I saw him, then I was going to say what I needed to say and leave with a clear conscience.

"Hey, Wes," I turned to face the only man I had ever loved.

He looked taken aback that I wasn't yelling at him or running. I slowly took in the sweet face of the little girl he held on his hip. He looked exactly how Tatum described him - like a good dad. "Ember, I... I'm..."

"Daddy," she cut him off, tapping on his shoulder. I couldn't help but smile at how his focus turned immediately to her. She cupped her hand over her mouth and whispered, "She looks like mommy with yellow hair."

Except it wasn't really a whisper.

CHAPTER TWENTY-SIX

Linford

7 YEARS AGO

Ember

My suitcase lay open in the middle of my bed, just waiting to be filled. Excitement bubbled in my chest; Wes was taking me to Texas to meet his dad.

Spring break was never a big deal to me, especially living in Nebraska, where spring break still meant crappy weather. But Texas... I jumped up and down, squealing like a little girl. I couldn't believe my parents actually said yes!

I already had outfits for the entire week planned out, all I had to do was pack. I pulled open my dresser drawers, grabbing everything on my checklist. Socks, bras and underwear - the good ones I bought special for this trip. My cutoff jean shorts that Wes said made my butt look good, and a couple other pairs. From my bottom drawer, I pulled out my red bikini; also bought special for this trip.

Jeans, a couple of sweaters, t-shirts, and a few blouses. I even pulled out a couple of sundresses that would be nice to wear to a cafe or...

A loud thud followed by near hysterical crying snapped me from my thoughts. I pulled my door open to find Kennedy sitting on the floor, back pressed against the wall and head buried in her hands. Her body wracked with the force of her sobs.

"Hey, what's wrong?" I knelt down beside her, laying my hand on her knee. I may not have liked her ninety percent of the time, but she was still my sister, and if I thought hard enough we still had some good memories together.

"I... I..."

I put an arm around her shoulders, "Shh. What is it?" I whispered. "You can tell me, we'll figure it out together, okay?"

She looked up, her eyes red and puffy and black trails ran down her cheeks from her makeup. "I'm sorry, Em."

"What for?"

Her shoulders were tight, eyes squeezed shut as she whispered two words that would forever change her life. "I'm pregnant."

I fell back on my butt and pressed my hand to my mouth. So many thoughts ran through my mind it was hard to settle on just one. Part of me wanted to console her while another part wanted her to suffer the consequences of her actions. Then there was the fact that she was only sixteen. Sure, she'd be seventeen in a couple of months, but still, a baby? How was she going to take care of a baby?

I took a deep breath and blew it out slowly as the next dilemma came to mind. "Whose is it?" Kennedy didn't have a boyfriend, at least not that I knew of, though that never stopped her from spreading her legs.

She shook her head. *Does she even know?*

"I need mom," her chin wobbled as another sob broke free.

I pulled out my phone and checked the time. They would be home soon, and then Wes would be here to pick me up. My heart soared at the thought of a whole week with him. A whole week without telling my parents my every move. A whole week where I wouldn't have to go home at the end of the night. A whole week that would serve as a preview for our lives to come.

I turned and looked back toward my bedroom where my suitcase sat open on my bed. With Kennedy's news, spring break couldn't have come at a better time.

When our parents got home, Kennedy ran straight into our mother's arms. "What is it, sweetheart?"

My dad turned accusing eyes on me. "What did you do?"

"I didn't do anything!"

"What's wrong, Ken?" mom asked, brushing her hair away from her face.

She looked at me, as though she needed help, and I gave her a smile and nod of encouragement.

She wiped her nose with the back of her hand and took a shaky breath. "I made a mistake," she started, looking at each of our parents in turn.

"Whatever you did, we can fix it," my dad encouraged her to go on.

"I'm pregnant."

Dad took a step back, as though he had been physically assaulted by the words. His face turned this ugly shade of red as his jaw clenched. "You're what?"

"I'm sorry, daddy!"

Mom wrapped her arms around her, holding her head to her chest, and pressed a kiss to her temple. "It's gonna be okay."

"Who's the father?" dad demanded, asking the question I was desperate to know. The only guy who came to mind was Frankie Greer. She was fond of him, or at least it seemed that way since I caught them together more than once.

My dad watched her closely, as her eyes snapped up to me, then back to him. She shook her head and pressed the tips of her fingers to her lips. "I can't..."

He turned his angry eyes on me. "Ember? Do you have something you need to tell us?"

I shook my head and held my hands up. "No. I have no idea, she wouldn't tell me either."

"Come on, honey. It takes two to make a baby, and it takes two to take care of it," mom encouraged, smoothing her hair and pressing kisses to the top of her head.

Kennedy's eyes met mine, and I swear the corner of her mouth tipped up into a smile. "It's Wes."

I cocked my head to the side, wondering if I heard her right. There was only one Wes in town, so unless... I had to have misheard her. "Who?"

This time I know her mouth curled up. "Wes," she said as a tear rolled down her cheek. "It's Wes' baby."

My mom gasped and my dad practically growled as his hands curled into fists at his side. I just shook my head. I couldn't speak, could barely breathe. *It's not my Wes, not my Wes,* I told myself over and over. Kennedy was just being a bitch, trying to get under my skin like she always did to Tatum. It wouldn't surprise me if this whole thing was an act; just another way for her to get our parent's attention.

My mom watched me with sympathy in her eyes, but it wasn't true. There was no way it was true. My heart thundered in my chest. "You're lying."

"I'm not, I swear." She looked at each of our parents in turn. "He's the only man I've ever been with."

I barked out a laugh, "Yeah, okay. So I guess half the boys at school don't count?"

"Ember!" my mom snapped.

"Oh, I'm sorry," I threw my hands up in the air. "It's more like eighty percent of the boys in town..." I huffed out a laugh and when I caught my dad's glare I rolled my eyes. I was leaving soon and he wasn't going to stop me, not this time. Besides, they knew she wasn't innocent, they just preferred living in denial. "Ask anyone! Kennedy gets passed around more than a football in a Huskers game!"

"That's enough!" my dad exploded, swiping his hand through the air.

"I'm sorry, daddy!" Kennedy cried, pulling away from our mother's embrace and stepping into his open arms.

He pressed a kiss to the top of her head and smoothed her hair back. "Shhh, it's okay," he murmured to her.

"You can't be serious?"

"Ember, you will stop this, right now." The disappointment written all over my mom's face only added to my fury.

I shook my head. "No," I took a step toward Kennedy, getting close enough that I could feel the anger rolling off my dad in waves. I was beyond caring though, I was done with her trying to ruin things for me. "Wes would never!" I snarled.

She smirked then sniffled. Like everything else, this was just a game to her, and our parents were eating it up. I wanted to punch that look right off her face.

"When did this supposedly happen then?" I demanded, folding my arms over my chest. Wes was always with me, when would he have the chance, and... *why?*

She didn't hesitate. "In Kansas City."

I shook my head. "Don't be ridiculous! I was with him the whole night!" I didn't care if my parents got mad at me for staying with him.

"It was the next morning," she turned to look up at our dad's face. "I went to his room to see if he wanted a coffee. He pulled me into bed with him and we had sex."

I took a step back, disgusted with the lengths she'd go to ruin the only good thing I had. "No," I argued. "No." I ran the events of that day through my head and my breath caught when I came up a little short. That morning when I went looking for her, I found her in the hall with her hand on his door. I tried to remember how she looked, was her clothing mussed? *Had they just had sex?* No.

"This is ridiculous!"

I jumped then breathed out a sigh of relief when the doorbell rang. Wes was here and he'd set everything straight. Kennedy was wrong, she was lying. He wouldn't.

My mom invited him inside, and asked him to take a seat at the table. He looked at me expectantly, like I could give him any indication of what this was about. I offered him a half smile, that's all I was capable of. I knew in my heart Kennedy was full of shit, but I needed to hear it from him. I needed him to tell my parents that she was making shit up, that he would never touch her.

My dad glared at him, his arms folded over his chest. "Want to tell me what you're doing sleeping with my daughter?" he growled.

Wes' head snapped around to look at me, and I gave him the best smile I could muster, which wasn't much. He cleared his throat and directed his words to my father. "Ember and I are always safe and we waited until she was eighteen. I love her, sir."

"Cut the bullshit!" my dad snapped, and I flinched.

Wes looked sufficiently scared, looking from me, to my dad, and back. My heart ached for him, for me, *for us.* He started to stand, he didn't need to sit there and take this from them. My dad's hand snapped out and gripped his shoulder, pushing him back into the chair. "Sit."

Wes looked back at me, his brows pulled together. "Ember, are you okay? Are you...?"

"Come on, baby," Kennedy cut in. "Just tell them already."

My stomach clenched, her words causing bile to rise up in my throat.

"Tell them what?" He shook his head, clearly confused, confirming what I already knew. She was lying.

"That we had sex in Kansas City!"

"No. I don't know what you're talking about Kennedy, but I never touched you. I'm in love with your sister, I would never do that to her." He tried to stand up and again my dad held him down, his fingers digging into Wes' shoulder.

"Give it up, Kennedy," I fumed. "He said he didn't touch you."

She dropped to her knees beside him, a fresh wave of tears rolling down her cheeks. "Tell them," she pleaded, sliding her hands up his thighs. He flinched away from her, but she didn't stop and he couldn't move. Not with my dad's hand on his shoulder. "I'm pregnant, Wes. I'm pregnant and it's yours."

"That's not possible!" He protested, pushing her away then trying and failing to stand once again. "Ember, that's not possible. I never touched her! I would never touch her!"

Though I didn't need them, his words were like a balm to my soul. I inhaled a shaky breath. "Do you have any proof?" I asked Kennedy, knowing this was the quickest way to catch her in one of her lies.

She stood up and pulled a folded piece of paper from her back pocket, along with one of those little plastic sticks. The plastic stick landed in Wes' hands when she tossed it. The tick in his jaw told me the test was positive.

"That doesn't mean anything," I argued. "For all I know, you bought that off eBay."

She rolled her eyes. "That's disgusting. But I also have this." She held out the sheet of paper to my dad. He scanned the sheet quickly before passing it to Wes.

All the color drained from his face as he read whatever was on it.

I stumbled back a step as all the air left my body. I didn't need to see the paper to know what it said, his reaction was enough. *It's not true, it's not true, it's not true...*

It's not true, I just needed him to say it. I managed to suck in a ragged breath. "Wes?"

The subtle shake of his head combined with the fact he wouldn't even look at me might as well have been an admission of guilt. I spun on my heel and ran up the stairs as fast as my legs would carry me. I slammed and locked my bedroom door expecting him to, no, *needing* him to come after me. I held my breath and pressed my ear to the door. Silence. He didn't follow me. He didn't...

My stomach roiled and I grabbed my trash can, emptying my stomach. *Wes didn't come after me.*

I breathed in as deep as I could through my nose, then out through my mouth. I did it again and again until the shaking in my body eased. It didn't make sense, Wes wouldn't cheat on me. *He wouldn't.* Why would he, and with my *sister?* He knew how much I hated her, we even talked about it that night...

Bile burned up my throat and I heaved into the trash again. People didn't cheat for no reason, so what was his? Did he want to see if she was better than me? She was better than me at everything else, or so everyone thought.

I had to know what was going on. Was he in shock? Is that why he didn't come after me? I crawled to my door and pressed my ear against it. I could make out shouting, mostly my father. Everything was muffled though, so with a deep breath I unlocked my door and tiptoed down the hall to stand at the top of the stairs. From there I could just see into the kitchen, could see Wes sitting at the table, head in his hands.

"What are you going to do, son?"

Kennedy came into view and wrapped her arms around him. Pain lanced through me when he didn't push her off.

Was I just a joke this whole time? What did I do wrong?

"I'm going to take care of my baby," Wes finally said, his voice gravelly.

I didn't need to hear another word. I went back to my room, locked the door and crawled into bed, burrowing into my covers. I held my breath, fighting back tears. Pressure built in my chest and throat and when I couldn't hold back any longer, a sob tore through me. I hugged my knees to my chest as my body shook, tears soaking into my pillow.

I cried until my throat was raw and my eyes were swollen. I picked up the framed picture of Wes and I from my nightstand. It was taken on New Years. We were so happy, we were making plans for the future. Except I couldn't have a future with a man I had to share. Especially with my sister.

A knock at my door startled me, but I didn't make a noise. If I was quiet, whoever it was would just go away and leave me alone. I needed to think.

"Em?" Wes' rough voice cracked and I ached to go to him, to make him feel better. But who was going to make me feel better?

"Em, please talk to me…"

I pulled my pillow over my head. If I couldn't hear his voice, I wouldn't feel drawn to him.

Soon my phone started to ring, and when I didn't answer it started to ping with texts. I turned it off. I didn't want to hear anything, unless it was him telling me it was a prank, or that he had irrefutable proof that he wasn't about to be a father…

Maybe he didn't do it and was just scared. But then why would he agree to take care of *his baby*? Memories of our first date and the story he told me about his ex, Andy came to mind. She claimed he raped her. I never thought him capable, but what if… What if he took advantage of my sister? What if…?

I must have fallen asleep, because the next time I opened my eyes, it was pitch black out. I turned on my phone, convinced it was all a bad dream until it blew up with about a million notifications. My head ached and my eyes burned as I opened my texts, clicking on one from Kennedy first. It was a photo of the sheet of paper they had all been passing around. It confirmed she was about six weeks pregnant. The timing lined up perfectly. A selfie of her and Wes popped up next. They were in bed; she was curled up next to him and he was on his stomach, no shirt on, his arm slung over her stomach. Tears burned my eyes and bile rose in my throat… I knew that bed, it was the one in his room in Kansas City.

There were so many texts from Wes, but I couldn't bear to open them. It was like he ripped my heart out with his bare hand and stomped it into the mud, then picked it up and ran it through a wood chipper.

Then there was Tatum.

> **Tatum:** Brandon's home!!!

> **Tatum:** You're supposed to be excited for me…

> **Tatum:** Text me later, I know you're probably on the road already. If I don't reply, it's because I'm busy with my man

I wanted to laugh; I tried to laugh, but the weight on my chest made it impossible. It was real, all of it. Kennedy is going to have my boyfriends' baby.

My boyfriend…

My ex-boyfriend…

I looked at my suitcase; I could still go. I didn't have to go to Texas. I could go wherever I wanted.

I looked at the corkboard above my desk, where I had my college acceptance letter pinned up. I could go to Omaha and see Miles. He would let me stay with him for a little while, I know it.

I picked up the picture of me and Wes again and ran my fingers over his smiling face. It was all a lie. I set it facedown on my nightstand, unable to look at it anymore. I turned off my phone and burrowed under the covers feeling a little more settled now that I had a plan. I'd call Miles in the morning.

My head ached and my stomach growled painfully when I woke up, reminding me that I hardly ate yesterday, and what I did eat I threw up. I cracked my door open then tiptoed down the hall when I didn't see anyone. The living room TV drowned out all sound once I reached the bottom of the stairs. It was a brand new day in the Davis house, where life went on like clockwork, even when my world was falling apart.

I went to the kitchen to make myself something to eat.

"Ember? Is that you?" my mom called out.

I sighed, "Yeah."

"Can you come in here a sec?"

I took a deep breath and blew it out slowly, counting to ten before making my way to the living room. "What's up?" I asked, standing in the doorway holding an empty bowl and spoon.

"We've been talking," she started.

"I know what happened yesterday wasn't exactly expected," my dad continued. "Your mother and I think it would be best if you break things off with Wes."

I arched an eyebrow. "You think?"

"Don't get smart with me, young lady."

"Sorry," I mumbled, not feeling sorry in the slightest.

"I want you to be supportive of your sister," my mom said, rising to her feet.

I bit my lip, unable to say anything one way or the other. Support Kennedy? Yeah fucking right...

"We also decided it's best if you finish up school then stay home and help Wes and Kennedy with the baby."

My jaw hit the floor. She had to be joking... "Excuse me?"

"She's still a teenager, Ember. She's going to need your help."

Okay, not joking... I shook my head. "I have college."

"It can wait," my dad said flippantly. "There's gonna come a time when Kennedy can't go to school, and she's going to need someone to help her. She's not going to quit school just because your boyfriend couldn't keep his dick to himself."

Heat flared up my chest and neck. I was livid. If we were in a cartoon you'd see smoke billowing out from my nose and ears. "What about me and *my* future? What about the fact that it was *my* boyfriend she stole? What about…"

"ENOUGH!" my dad stood, shaking a finger at me. "You will show some respect in my house."

I suddenly felt like I was in a bad episode of Black Mirror. I always knew they cared more for Kennedy than me, but it was never more obvious than now, in this moment when they were asking, no, telling me to put my life on hold to take care of her mistakes.

I arched an eyebrow and my nostrils flared. "Let me make sure I have this right," I could barely contain the venom in my voice. "I'm going to graduate in a couple of months. Instead of going to college, I'm going to stay home and tutor Kennedy, then play nanny when she goes back to school."

My mom nodded, but my dad glared. "Don't get smart, Ember. You know what we're telling you to do. She's going to need support, and you're her sister."

I studied his face, the deep grooves between his brows that were always so pronounced whenever he looked at me, the dark glint in his eyes. I nodded, "Yes, sir. May I be excused now?" I held up the empty bowl and spoon.

"We'll talk more later," my mom said, waving me off like nothing about that entire exchange was unusual.

I mechanically returned to the kitchen and put the bowl and spoon in the sink. I lost my appetite. I lost more than that, I lost my life and all it took was one night and two words from my sister.

I returned to my room and opened my suitcase. If I rearranged it I could stuff some more things inside. Clothes, shoes, my laptop... I repacked my toiletries and found a large tote bag in the back of my closet that I stuffed with books, notebooks, and a few stuffed toys I cherished. I pulled all the pictures I had posted to my corkboard down and stuffed them inside the pages of a book and put it in the bag. Finally I returned to my nightstand and picked up the framed photo of Wes and I. After debating it for what felt like forever, I stuffed it in my bag too.

I listened out my bedroom door and was greeted with silence.

I hefted my bag over my shoulder and carried my suitcase down the stairs. I slipped my keys from the hook then stepped outside, careful not to slam the door. I loaded everything into Carrie and climbed behind the wheel.

I must have sat outside of my childhood home for a full minute before driving away. I passed Tatum's and considered stopping, but I knew she was busy with Brandon. She didn't need me.

I came to a stop just outside of town. I pushed my car door open, stepped out and closed my eyes. I took a deep breath and blew it out slowly. Where to?

A gust of wind whipped my hair around my face and the decision was made. I climbed back into my car, hit the gas and took a left out of Linford. It was time to go where the wind blows.

CHAPTER TWENTY-SEVEN

Linford

PRESENT

Wes

I flinched the second the words left Ellie's mouth. My eyes shot back to Ember, and if I didn't know her so well, I would have missed the flicker of pain that flashed in her eyes. She couldn't disguise the vulnerability that enveloped her like a cloak.

She looked exhausted, and more than that, she looked sad. I never meant to ruin her life. I was just trying to do the right thing, and if she would have just waited…

I kissed my daughter's cheek without taking my eyes off of her, afraid if I so much as blinked, she would disappear. "Ellie, this is your aunt, Ember."

"Ember…" she whispered, her voice full of awe. My cheeks heated as a wave of embarrassment washed over me. Ellie once asked me about princes and princesses. She told me I was a prince because I was handsome, unlike the other dads. Then she wanted to know if her mom was my princess. God help me, I couldn't lie to her. I told her my princess was a girl named Ember. She was the prettiest girl I had ever seen. Once I started, I couldn't stop. I told her about how smart Ember was, how funny and kind. I told her about how much Ember loved animals, and the animal shelter we volunteered at. I told her Ember was going to be an animal doctor.

She decided right then and there that she was going to be an animal doctor too, and I've been buying her every kind of animal book we could find ever since.

When Ellie asked what happened to the princess, I had to tell her the truth, at least a truth a child could understand. I admitted that I hurt my princess and she ran away. Ellie gave me the dirtiest look I have ever seen and told me I needed to say I was sorry. If I said I was sorry, then maybe the princess would come back and she could be her mommy. My heart broke a little more that day. Ember was always supposed to be my princess; the mother to my children. Instead I found myself stuck with a girl who was so vindictive and full of hate, it was a wonder she didn't have red horns and a tail.

"You know my name?" Ember asked, looking from Ellie to me.

"I…"

"You're his princess," she whispered. "He needs to say he's sorry for being mean."

Ember's brows pulled together when she looked at me, questions written across her face. I cleared my throat, "I'm not sure saying sorry is going to make it better."

Ellie gripped my cheeks, "Sure it will. Jadon's mama says to always say sorry when you do something bad."

Ember smirked. I didn't know if she knew Ellie was friends with Tatum's boy. Honestly, *I* was shocked Tatum allowed it. "Jadon's mom is a pretty smart lady."

Ellie nodded. "My daddy said you're gonna be a animal doctor."

Her smile slipped, and she shook her head. "I was going to, but it didn't work out."

Ellie's face scrunched up. "But why?"

Ember shrugged. "I don't know."

"Can you teach me about zebras?" Ellie asked, twisting in my arms and reaching for Ember.

My heart clenched when Ember reached out to take her, and then the worst thing that could happen, happened. Kennedy stepped in between them and took Ellie from me. She situated her on her hip and pressed a red-lipped kiss to her cheek. She snaked her other arm around my back, teasing the hem of my shirt. Her long nails scraped across my skin when I started to pull away.

And then I saw Ellie's face.

I couldn't remember the last time Kennedy held her, let alone paid her any attention that wasn't yelling at her. My shoulders slumped in resignation as I was forced to choose between the two halves of my heart. Ember was a grown woman and as much as I hated it, she didn't need me, not like Ellie did. And when it comes to Ellie, I can't rock the boat; I can't lose my daughter.

"Hey, baby!" Kennedy cooed obnoxiously loud. She was putting on a show.

"Hey, mama! Look, it's a princess!"

Kennedy shook her head. "No, that's not a princess. If anything, she's the wicked stepsister."

Ellie turned back to me, her face scrunched up in confusion.

Ember blew out a heavy breath and smiled. I knew that smile, it was the one she pasted on when she was keeping the peace. A smile reserved for when she was hurt and refused to show it. "It was very nice to meet you, Ellie," she said as she reached her hand out to my daughter, her voice carrying the pain she so clearly felt.

"It's Eleanor," Kennedy snapped, jerking Ellie out of her reach.

Ember froze, her arm slowly dropping to her side. She looked from Kennedy, to Ellie, and finally to me. She arched an eyebrow and her voice cracked when she asked, "Eleanor?"

I swallowed thickly but couldn't respond because I knew what she was thinking, and while she was wrong, she wasn't *wrong*. Eleanor was the name she wanted to give her daughter, *our* daughter, and that was something else that was taken from her. I tried everything to change Kennedy's mind, from compromising on names to offering her money. Her vendetta was worth more than every cent in my bank account.

It didn't take a genius to see that Kennedy was doing all of this to hurt Ember. It was all intentional, and for a while I found myself wondering what she did to get me to sleep with her. In my right mind, I never would have touched her. My mind raced as it searched for an answer; was I that drunk? Did she trick me? *Was I drugged?*

I doubted myself until I got the results of the paternity test, which confirmed what I already knew. Kennedy was using me to hurt her sister. The question was why.

"No," Ellie whined, her voice showing the first signs that she was about to lose it. "My name is ELLIE!" she screamed.

Ember took a step back and then another, and then she was gone. I jerked away from Kennedy, ready to go after her, but Ellie's continued screams held me back. The moment Ember was out of sight, Kennedy passed Ellie back to me and walked away, like she hadn't just caused a major scene at her mother's funeral.

Ellie stopped screaming the second she was in my arms, but the tears weren't as easy to shut off. With her arms around my neck, she rested her head on my shoulder, her little body shaking with the force of her sobs. I rubbed her back in soothing circles. "Shh, it's okay, baby girl. I've got you."

"Sh-sh-she made the p-p-princess leave," she wailed.

"It's gonna be okay," I whispered, pressing a kiss to her forehead as a tear rolled down my cheek. I went back inside where the air conditioning would keep us cool until I was sure Kennedy was gone. Ellie's fingers wrapped themselves in the collar of my shirt, and soon her cries became hiccups, and her eyes were getting droopy.

I swayed side to side, the motion always seemed to relax her, and before long, her hand went slack and I knew she was out. And yet, I couldn't bring myself to leave. *How did this become my life?*

"Hey, man."

I turned my head, catching Miles in my peripheral.

"They're about ready to lock up," he whispered, brushing his hand over Ellie's cheek.

I gave him a small nod, not trusting my voice to not break. I followed him out of the church, but that was as far as I went. I couldn't go home. The idea of seeing Kennedy made me want to hit something. The sheer pleasure she took in ruining her sister's life made me ill.

The problem was, I didn't know how much longer my aunt would put up with me, us, staying at her house. And it was just a matter of time before Kennedy threw a fit.

Miles held out his hands. "Give her to me."

I shook my head, "No, it's okay."

He kept his hands outstretched. "I may not know exactly what happened, but I know enough. Ember took off like a bat outta hell. I've never seen her move so fast."

"Where did she go?"

He shrugged, "Only two places I can think of, and one of them doesn't give you much time to catch up."

"You think she went home?" I carefully passed my daughter to her uncle.

"She doesn't exactly have much reason to stay," he sighed.

"So what do I do?"

"Go after her. Talk to her. Tell her the truth."

"But what about..."

"Don't worry about Ellie. Lainey and I haven't spent enough time with our niece lately."

"And Kennedy?"

His shoulders slumped at the sound of her name, the reason we were all in this mess in the first place. "I've never seen her look so proud of herself as she did today. She's probably halfway to Wickett by now."

"That's fine for now, but..."

Ellie started to stir and I reached out to take her but the look on MIles' face stopped me dead. "Go find Ember. I've got Ellie. And as for that other *problem*? Lainey has a friend who has a friend who's been dating a lawyer. He's young, just out of school, but we've been talking with him, gathering all the information we can."

"You have?"

"Kennedy may be my sister, but she's a horrible person and an even worse mother. I love this little girl and I'm prepared to do whatever it takes to ensure you get full custody of her, one way or another."

I swallowed past a lump in my throat. My aunt, Bob, and I scoured the internet looking for anything we could use to make me her legal guardian. The only thing we could come up with was me adopting her. Except if we went that route then Kennedy would know that I knew and she'd do everything in her power to keep me from being happy - especially since she knew Ember and Ellie were all I cared about. "Do you think I have a chance?"

He nodded. "With enough character statements, I think you do. Plus the way Ellie reacts to Kennedy has to account for something."

"Thank you," I whispered, finally glimpsing a sliver of light at the end of the tunnel.

"You're welcome. Now get the hel... heck out of here and go find my sister."

I grinned at his personal censorship. Ellie had called him out on cussing numerous times. I ran my hand over her head and pressed a kiss to her cheek. "I'll be back soon, sweet girl." I hopped in my truck and sped down the road toward my first, and least likely, destination.

Chapter Twenty-Eight

L'inford

7 Years Ago

Wes

I paced back and forth in the living room of my aunt's house. I didn't tell her yet; I *couldn't* tell her. But she'd know something was wrong when I didn't leave for Texas. She'd know and then she'd be pissed at me for not being straight with her.

"What the hell are you doing, wearing a path in my carpet?" Angie griped as she dropped her purse and keys on the entryway table. "Why are you here?"

"Love you too, Ang," I muttered, continuing my back-and-forth movement. If I stood still my mind would have a chance to catch up with the reality of my situation. A reality I couldn't really wrap my mind around.

"What's wrong," she stepped in front of me, halting my forward progress.

I turned around and resumed pacing, just on a shorter path. "I messed up." The words felt like acid on my tongue. I wanted to scream, "I didn't do it!" I didn't do it, and yet...

"What did you do this time?" My steps faltered at the tone in her voice, and she grabbed my shoulders, forcing me to stop.

"I didn't... I mean, I don't think..." I pushed my hands through my hair.

"Just spit it out. Whatever it is, we can fix it, okay?" She gripped my chin, forcing me to look at her.

I swallowed past the lump in my throat. "Ember is going to break up with me. Or she already has... I don't know." I turned around and fell into the couch.

"What do you mean you *don't know?*" She cocked her head to the side, "Weren't you two supposed to be on your way to Texas right about now?"

I leaned forward resting my arms on my knees and let my head hang low. "Yeah, but... It's so fucked up."

"It must be for you to unapologetically drop that sort of language. What happened?" She sat down beside me, her hand on my back. "You can tell me."

I turned my head just enough to see her and cleared my throat, "Kennedy's pregnant."

"And we care about Kennedy, why?"

I dropped my head to my hands, "She's claiming it's mine."

My aunt barked out a laugh. "What is that girl *on?*"

"She said we had sex when we were in Kansas City."

"You didn't though."

I looked at her, head still in my hands. "I don't know," I whispered, the increasing tightness in my chest making it hard to breathe. "I don't think so, but..."

"But what?" She didn't sound so relaxed anymore and I cringed away from it.

"Ember and I may or may not have been drinking after the concert. And..."

"And you decided that was the perfect time to dip your wick in her kid sister?"

I glared at her. "No, Ang," I bit out. "I would *never* do that."

"Then why does she think you did?"

"I don't know. Maybe because she's a psycho?"

Angie scrubbed a hand down her face. "Can you just... Start at the beginning."

I sighed, "I went to pick up Ember, and when I got there it sort of felt like an ambush." Thinking back, the look on her mom's face when she answered the door made me feel sick. It was almost like she was excited, which made me excited, until... I shook off the thought and told Angie everything from the plastic stick and confirmation from the doctor, to the way her parents grilled me about my future plans and how I was going to provide for their daughter and our child. Surprisingly, she listened to the whole story without interrupting.

"What did Ember have to say about all of this?"

I shrugged. "She disappeared at some point; I didn't even see her leave. I tried to talk to her, I knocked on her door. She was there, but she refused to answer. I've tried calling her, but it goes straight to voicemail. She won't talk to me." I pushed my hands through my hair gripping it by the roots as I fought to keep my thoughts grounded. "What if I've already lost her?" my voice cracked.

"Ember loves you, even a blind man could see that. But this... this is the ultimate betrayal."

"Don't you think I know that!?" I shouted, and immediately regretted it. "I'm sorry, Ang."

She put her arm around me and pulled me closer, forcing my head to rest on her shoulder. "Put yourself in her shoes. You know her better than anyone. What do you think she's doing? What do you think it will take for her to listen to you?"

"I don't know. She's so levelheaded and reasonable, until her heart gets involved. Then she shuts everyone and everything out."

"Maybe she just needs a little time to process. Call her, text her, do whatever you need to show her that you're still in this. Remind her how much she means to you."

"I can do that," I rasped.

"Then we need to focus on the other end of this problem; arguably the bigger problem here..." She reached up and slapped my cheek, "A baby, Wes?"

I closed my eyes and blew out a heavy breath. "I didn't do it. I *know* I didn't do it. We may have been drinking, but I was coherent enough to take Em back to her room after she fell asleep in mine. I *remember* that. But..."

"But what? Why are you doubting yourself?"

"Kennedy is... I'm convinced the girl is evil personified."

Angie barked out a laugh. "I'm not sure I'd go that far. She's just a girl."

"No, you don't understand. She does everything she can to hurt Ember. And she gets away with it every time."

Angie shook her head. "Stop deflecting... Why are you doubting yourself?"

I took in a ragged breath. "Kennedy had access to my room key. What if..." I studied my hands, flexing my fingers as I thought about how to express my worst fear. "What if she let herself into my room, and I mistook her for Ember in the dark? What if I was half asleep?"

She arched an eyebrow. "You can have sex in your sleep?"

I threw my head back on a groan. "Can you please be serious, Ang? This is my *life*!"

"If that is the only way this baby could be yours, then I think it's safe to say you're not the father. *But* since we can't rule it out, here's what we need to do. You need to talk to Ember, tell her the truth, tell her what has you scared. Then you need to demand a paternity test."

"I can do that. But what if she won't listen?"

"Then you'll just have to bide your time until that paternity test is done."

"How soon can I do that? Doesn't the baby have to be born first? By then, Ember will already be gone. She'll move on." I squeezed my eyes shut, the thought of another man touching her had bile rising up in my throat.

Angie typed away on her phone, then held it up. "Looks like you have a couple months to wait. But that should be enough time. There's still two months until graduation."

Pain flared in my chest. Two months. We had so much planned for those two months and Kennedy was stealing it from us. Our spring break in Texas, her prom and graduation. Maybe she'd stand by me until we have the results in hand. Maybe... It wasn't ideal, but it was better than all the scenarios my mind cooked up. "Could you call her?" I asked after a few minutes. "Tell her the plan?"

Angie shook her head. "It should really come from you."

I blew out a shaky breath as I pushed to my feet. "Thank you. Thank you for helping me figure this out."

She stood up and pressed a kiss to my cheek. "I love you, Wes. I thought I'd hate having you around all the time, but... I can't imagine life without you now. And that includes Ember. She's the best thing to happen to you."

The sun was still shining when I lay down in bed that night. I swiped through my phone, looking at picture after picture of the two of us. She was so damn beautiful, but it was more than that. She was smart, funny, caring... She held my heart, and I didn't want it back.

I opened my texts, discouraged that she hadn't opened them yet. I quickly typed out another, in case the eleven I already sent weren't enough.

> **Me:** Remember the first time I drove through the ice and snow? That deer ran out in front of us and I couldn't stop the truck and we did a full 360, smacking that damn animal with the back of the truck? I was scared half to death, but you were able to talk me down, calm my racing heart until I could breathe. This is worse than that. I am terrified that you're going to leave me. I'm terrified that when you do, there won't be anything left for me to live for.

I hit send, then immediately regretted it. I hit the call button, praying she would just answer. Just talk to me.

The phone rang once and went to voicemail. I called again, with the same result. Either her phone was off, or she was rejecting my calls. When the voicemail picked up, I left her a message. "Em, please talk to me. I swear I never touched her. I'm only worried because... Can we just talk? I want to do this in person. Then, if you're going to break my heart, I'll at least have seen it in person."

I hung up and threw my phone across the room. I rolled onto my stomach and punched the pillow until my frustration bled away and I was left a sobbing mess.

My dad would tell me to man up. I wondered, not for the first time, what he would think of me now. We rarely spoke since I officially moved to Linford. We were trying to get our relationship back on track and he was supposed to meet Ember this week. Now I'd have to call and explain why that wasn't happening; give him yet another reason to be disappointed in me.

I closed my eyes, needing to sleep, needing enough time to pass that Ember would at least take my call or respond to my messages. My mind worked on overdrive, running through endless scenarios. What if the baby is mine? What if it's not? What if Ember forgives me and the baby is mine? Would she stay with me?

Then there was the pressure from her parents. I can still remember her father's booming voice. If I thought my dad was tough on me, then Ember's dad was a prison warden by comparison.

I couldn't get the look on his face out of my head. The firm set of his jaw, the fire in his eyes as he told me I would be moving into their house and making an honest woman of their daughter. I would be fine with that if he was talking about Ember. But no, the man actually expected me to put a ring on it and settle down - with his sixteen-year-old, crazy-ass daughter, Kennedy.

There was no way in hell. If this baby did end up being mine, then I'd do my part. I'd be a good dad. But I wouldn't do it with Kennedy on my arm. I would never share a bed with her, and she would never wear my ring.

Exhaustion won sometime before dawn, and when I finally managed to pry my tear swollen eyes open, the sun was already high in the sky.

Anticipation pounded in my veins as I grabbed for my phone, followed by bitter disappointment. No missed calls, and my texts were still unread.

I only gave myself a minute to wallow. I could be patient - after Ember knew the plan. I needed her to know that I never cheated on her, we just had to wait a little longer and I'd have proof. I jumped out of bed and took the fastest shower known to man, brushed my teeth, and threw on the jeans and sweater she loved me in. "Ang!" I called out as I stuffed my wallet in my pocket. "I'm heading to Ember's!"

"Be gentle with her heart, Wes. As soon as you have more information, call me. And tell her I love her."

"I will!"

It was frigid out; I don't think I'd ever get used to springtime in Nebraska. Spring was supposed to be this perfect mix of 75-degree days and cool evenings. Not 42 degrees with a negative 20 windchill. That was probably an exaggeration, but it certainly felt that way.

My truck hadn't even warmed up by the time I parked in front of Ember's house. The first thing I noticed was the absence of her car... I picked up my phone, with its cracked screen, thanks to my tantrum, and checked our texts. They were all still unread.

I considered knocking on the door, asking if they knew where she went. I swallowed thickly as I remembered her dad's words. *"You're going to marry Kennedy and be a father to your child."*

A shudder rolled through me. *Over my dead body.* I pulled up Tatum's contact and pressed the call button.

"Wes?" she answered, a hint of mild panic in her voice.

"Hey, have you heard from Ember?"

"No. Isn't she with you?"

I leaned forward, pressing my forehead against the cold leather steering wheel. "She didn't tell you?"

"Tell me what? I haven't spoken to her since Friday after school, and she hasn't been replying to my texts. I assumed it was because you were keeping her busy."

Her insinuation would typically make me laugh. Today it made my stomach clench painfully. "Fuck. I really don't want to get into what's going on, but I need to find her. Like *really* need to find her."

"Did you check all her favorite spots?"

"Not yet. I just got to her house and her car is gone; called you first."

I could hear movement in the background followed by the slam of a door. "You take the east side, I'll take the west. Call me if you find her."

"Thanks, Tatum."

For the next three hours I scoured the east side of town and all the little places we liked to go outside of town. I checked the lake, the abandoned drive-in theater, the farm a couple of towns over where she once helped a cow give birth. That was a sight I never wanted to see again. I even went up to Wickett and checked in at the animal shelter. They hadn't seen or heard from her. And because I knew she'd never ignore a call from them, I asked if they'd try her.

The call went straight to voicemail.

I sat behind the wheel of my truck, cursing myself for not having any way to track her - no "find my friend" or any of that. I didn't even have Snapchat... but Tatum did...

"Did you find her?"

"No, but hey, I had a thought... Do you still have her location turned on in Snapchat?"

She sighed. "That was the first thing I checked. Wherever she is, her phone must be off."

"What about Miles? Would she go to him?"

"You know, it might be easier to help if I knew what was going on."

"Call Miles and ask if he's seen her. I'll meet you back in town at Deja Brew and explain everything."

By the time I made it to Deja Brew, the sun was already sinking down over the horizon. I ordered a coffee - vanilla latte with caramel and cinnamon so I could feel close to Ember, even though I had no idea where she was. I even went past her house again. Her car was still gone.

The bell jingled over the door and Tatum wasted no time storming over to me. "What the hell is going on, Wes?"

"Do you want a coffee or anything?"

She dropped heavily into the seat that was usually occupied by her best friend. "I want answers."

I leaned forward, elbows pressed into the table, as I considered what to say. I should have thought of something, some way to explain the nightmare I was living. I scrubbed a hand over my face then took a deep breath and blew it out. I focused on the coffee cup in front of me, running a finger over the plastic lid, unable to look her in the face. "Kennedy is pregnant."

I was met with silence and when I glanced up, Tatum's mouth gaped open. Clearly, she hadn't been lying when she said she hadn't spoken with Ember.

She shook her head a moment later, as though she was snapping out of a trance. "That's just... wow." Then her brow furrowed in confusion. "What's that got to do with Ember? Did she get in trouble for it? I bet her parents blamed it on her, even though we all know Kennedy has been sleeping her way through all the boys in town since she was twelve..."

"What?" I choked on my coffee.

She shrugged like it was no big deal. "Everybody knows. Even her parents, though I'm pretty sure they're in denial. But if she's pregnant... Guess they can't ignore that." She casually crossed her legs and leaned back in her chair, a little less worried now that she knew part of the problem. Then she asked the million-dollar question. "She know who the father is?"

I flinched, just thinking about the look on her face, how sure she was that we were together, that "if" we slept together, it was consensual - and I guarantee it was not. I cleared my throat, looking down at where my fingers gripped my coffee cup. "She claims it's mine," I mumbled.

Tatum barked out a laugh so loud, half the folks in the coffee shop stopped talking to look at her. "You're joking. Does she think we're all idiots? You wouldn't touch that girl if your life depended on it."

"Glad you're on my side." It hurt that Tatum saw what Ember obviously didn't.

"Wait," she sat forward, all humor gone. "Did you do it?"

"No, I didn't do it!" I clipped. "I would *never*!"

"Then what's going on? Where's Ember and why isn't she answering our calls."

I took a deep breath and leaned back in my chair, pushing my hair away from my face. I kept it longer than usual because Ember liked it that way, but right now it was pissing me off. "She insists it happened when we were in Kansas City, that I was drunk and made a move on her."

"And Ember believed her?"

"I guess? I don't know, she hasn't spoken to me since the second her eyes landed on that pregnancy test and Kennedy..." My lip curled up in disgust and I had to force the bile down as I remembered the look on Ember's face the second the words came out of her mouth. "Kennedy called me *baby*."

All humor gone, Tatum's face paled. "You *swear* you never touched her?"

I held up three fingers in the boy scout salute. "On my honor."

"Ember knows Kennedy is basically the spawn of Satan. Maybe she's just getting her head right?"

I shook my head. "I don't know, I don't think so. Something is wrong, I can feel it." I rubbed the heel of my hand over my heart. "I'm scared, Tatum."

She thrummed her fingers on the tabletop. "Miles hasn't heard from her either. Did you talk to her parents?"

I grimaced. "I can't go there. Not after... I just can't."

"What do you mean?"

I looked up and slowly sucked in a lungful of air and held it for a minute before blowing it out. When my eyes met Tatum's, I saw my own fear reflected back at me. "Her dad... he grilled me about what I was going to do about *my* baby. If I was going to step up and be a man, or if I was just some deadbeat dad." I took a long drink of my coffee, taking the moment to try and calm my rage. It didn't work. "I told him if it was my baby, I'd step up, because I would..."

"But it's not your baby, right?"

I shook my head. "Ember and I got drunk that night, but there's no way."

"Okay, I believe you. So, then what? You gave him the answer I'm sure he wanted. What else am I missing?"

I breathed out a sigh of relief, not even realizing how badly I needed her trust. "He told me in no uncertain circumstances, that I would be moving in with them, and making an," I air quoted, "honest woman, out of Kennedy."

"That man is delusional!" Tatum laughed

"I can't talk to them, not after that. Not while Ember is missing." I sucked in a ragged breath. "I can't live without her, Tatum."

Tatum called Miles, who called their parents. Apparently, they had gotten into an argument this morning, and the fact that Ember was gone didn't worry them. They said, "She'll be home as soon as she's done throwing a fit."

Deep down, I knew she wasn't just throwing a fit. Something was wrong, I could feel it. So could Miles. Tatum had to get back home and promised she'd let me know if she heard anything, while he hopped in his car to come and help look for her.

CHAPTER TWENTY-NINE

Linford

PRESENT

Wes

I watched Caleb and Jadon run laps around the tree, the former with a towel tied around his neck like it was a cape. I killed the engine and hopped out of the truck.

"Wes!" Jadon yelled, running to meet me on the sidewalk. "Can Ellie play?"

I shook my head and ruffled his hair. "Sorry, bud. Maybe later. She's with her uncle Miles right now."

His smile faltered a little, but he shook it off quickly enough. If he was anything like Ellie, he was missing his best friend like crazy. I knocked on the front door and waited with more patience than I felt.

Tatum opened the door and peered around me at her boys. "Wes?"

"Not to sound like a broken record, but have you seen Ember?"

She blew out a sigh and gestured to the porch steps. We sat down and watched the boys play. "She loaded up her car this morning, said she was leaving right after the funeral. I..."

"I knew it was a long shot coming here, but I had to try."

She put her hand on my knee and gave it an apologetic squeeze. "I told her to talk to you."

"She did." I sighed, "Well, she tried."

"Wesley Barrett. What did you do?"

"It was more than I ever dared to hope for," I admitted. The corner of my lips tipped up into a smile. "You should have seen it, Ellie was smitten with her in seconds, but..."

"Let me guess. Hurricane Kennedy?"

I dropped my head. "Yeah."

"What are you going to do?"

"I'm gonna get her back."

"Good."

"Good?"

She nudged me with her shoulder. "Yeah, good. I need my bestie back, and whether I like it or not, she's still in love with you."

Her words felt like a balm to my soul. "Did she tell you she still loves me?"

She took a deep breath and blew it out slowly. "No, but a best friend knows these things."

We sat in companionable silence watching her boys pretend to be Spiderman and Iron Man. Jadon informed Caleb that Spiderman didn't wear a cape, but the boy was undeterred.

"Do you need her address?" Tatum asked without taking her eyes off of the boy climbing the tree in front of us.

I grinned. "No, I've come prepared this time."

"What do you mean?"

I rubbed the back of my neck as a flush crept up my cheeks. "I may or may not have installed a GPS tracker in Carrie when I fixed her up."

The sting from Tatum's slap made me laugh. "You can't just *do* that!"

"Tell me you wouldn't have done the same thing. You remember what it was like back then! If we only knew where she was..."

She angled her body toward me and placed her hand on my arm. "We have her address this time. We know where she's going."

"Yeah," I agreed. "But I couldn't risk it. Miles only has her address because he hired a private investigator to track her down. And then he refused to give it to me. If she wanted to, she could disappear again, just like last time. I can't let that happen."

"She's not going to disappear again. She has a *life*."

"I know," I nodded, thinking back to the conversation I overheard in the garage. "Trust me I know."

Ellie's school backpack was always ridiculously big. While most of the girls in her class had kid-sized bags covered in princesses or whoever the latest cartoon trend was, my girl had to have the bag covered in horses. And not the typical kid-sized bags with horses - they weren't *real*. So here we were, with a backpack almost as big as she was covered in clydesdales.

It was coming in handy.

I emptied it out, setting her books and things on the corner of her desk, then stood staring at her closet. *How long was I going to be gone?*

I started pulling down her favorite things. Pink, purple, and of course her green and white striped leggings. I folded them and placed them in the bottom of the bag followed by a couple pairs of jeans, just in case. I grabbed a handful of t-shirts, Ellie was notoriously tidy but you never knew. I folded them and set them on top along with a couple of sweaters.

I pulled out the bottom drawer of her dresser and grabbed a stack of shorts, realizing she had more clothes that didn't fit her than did. With the money I just spent fixing Ember's car, I'd have to dip into our emergency savings.

"What are you doing?"

My head jerked up at the sound of Kennedy's voice. "Hey." My pulse raced with nervous energy and I was shocked I was able to keep my voice even; I honestly thought she was long gone by now. I ignored her question and went back to the pile of shorts, sorting sizes.

"I asked you," she stepped up behind me and wrapped her arms around my waist. "What are you doing?"

I dropped the clothes and gripped her hands, pulling them away. "I'm sorting Ellie's clothes. She grew out of these." I gestured to the pile of shorts.

Kennedy slid her arms around me again, this time slipping her fingers under the hem of my shirt, and pressed her lips to my neck. "Stop," I shook her off.

"Don't be like that, baby."

Her hands trailed down my body, dipping into the waistband of my jeans. I grabbed her hands and yanked them away. "I said, stop."

She giggled and brought her mouth to my ear. "How's it feel to have my hands all over you in my sister's room?" Her lips closed around my earlobe, nipping it with her teeth.

My stomach turned and my skin crawled. After Angie kicked me out and I moved in with the Davis', I took Ember's room for my own. Once Ellie came along, it became her room, and I was forced to move in with Kennedy. I would have happily slept on the floor in Ellie's room, as it was I spent more time sleeping in a chair than in an actual bed.

Things changed when Kennedy graduated. She was always fond of her nights out. Without having to worry about school, she'd disappear and not come back for days at a time. The problem was, as soon as I let my guard down and got comfortable, I'd wake up with her naked body pressed up against me. "Get. The fuck. Off of me," I growled, shaking her off again.

"Oh, come on, Wes. You haven't touched me in months!"

I spun on her. "First of all, I was half asleep and messed up on cold medicine. Second - I didn't touch you. Waking up with your mouth on my cock doesn't constitute me touching you."

"Sure didn't stop you from coming down my throat."

Embarrassment and disgust washed over me. Kennedy was always gone, leaving me to take care of Ellie by myself. I had been running a fever for a couple of days when Angie stepped in and took Ellie for the night. I picked up some cold medicine and went to bed. I was having the most amazing dream; Ember was back, and we were making up. It felt so good when she put her mouth on me. I wrapped my hands in her hair, guiding her mouth up and down... By the time I realized it wasn't a dream, it was too late. My eyes snapped open, locking on Kennedy's as she sucked me even harder. I couldn't have stopped it if I tried. "Haven't you figured it out by now? I don't want you!" I yelled, getting right up in her face. "Why don't you just go be with that guy you're fucking up in Wickett, and we can all go our separate ways?"

She laughed, dropping down onto Ellie's pink bed. She peered down into the backpack sitting in the middle. "Going somewhere?"

I swallowed thickly. "Jadon asked if Ellie could have a sleepover," I half lied.

She arched an eyebrow at me. "That's an awful lot of clothes for a sleepover."

"Yeah, because we're going to be staying with my aunt for a little while. I need some space."

"You gonna leave me, Wes?" She pouted her lips and batted her eyelashes at me.

I shook my head, grabbing the pile of shorts that still fit and stuffing them into the backpack. "What if I am?"

She stood up and pressed one of her perfectly manicured fingers into the center of my chest. "You don't want to do that."

"Why?" I threw my arms up in the air. "Why do you even care? You're out sleeping with half the state, out there living your best life! What the fuck do you want from me?"

"Honestly?"

I swallowed, my Adam's apple bobbing with the effort. "Yeah. Honestly."

"I want you, Wes."

"But why?"

She took a step back, but the feral look in her eyes had a new spark. "Because *she* had you! Because *she* ALWAYS got everything she wanted! It's my turn!"

I rolled my eyes. "You know that's ridiculous, right?"

"Don't talk about something you know nothing about. Our parents gave her everything. She had it all, the perfect little life. And then you came along, and just made it even more fucking perfect."

"Ken..."

"No, *Wes.* You know what I had? I had parents who looked at me every day with pity in their eyes. I had to do everything I could just to get an ounce of care, and even then, it never lasted. The only thing I've ever done that they cared about was getting knocked up."

"Say all that's true. What does that have to do with Ember?"

"You don't get it! If I brought home a good report card, they were so happy. If I brought home a bad report card, they were still happy. Ember brought home a good report card and they were happy. She brought home a bad report card and they fought with her. They told her she could do so much better..."

"I missed curfew, and they were happy when I got home. Ember missed curfew and she was grounded. They *cared* what happened to her!"

"You know they care..."

"Then you came along... My dad *hated* you. Every time my parents told Ember to jump, she'd ask how high, but when it came to you, she fought back. That made them care even more! They wouldn't even let you guys go to that dumb concert because they were worried you were going to have sex... *I* had sex with my dads' best friend when I was twelve, and guess what.. HE DIDN'T CARE!"

"None of this is Ember's fault."

She rolled her eyes. "I thought for sure the goody two shoes would tell daddy how I took off on you guys at the concert. But, no. I'm guessing I have you to thank for that..."

"You were just a kid," I argued.

"When she didn't rat me out, I knew I had to try something a little more drastic. After you brought her back to our room, I called up one of the guys I met when I bailed on you. I didn't plan on being back for a while; give you guys no excuse to not call my dad." She fanned herself with her hand, "That man had stamina, we went at it a few times while you were listening to sappy country music, so he was all too happy to come back for more. Then the damn condom broke and he freaked out. He brought me back, but not before buying me a morning after pill…"

My heart clenched, hearing the circumstances behind Ellie's conception. "When I got back to the hotel, I figured I'd set the Plan B box on the dresser and wait for Ember to freak out. Except I mistakenly grabbed your room key instead of ours…" She laughed, but there was no humor in it. "I thought for sure she would say something when she caught me leaving your room… But she *trusted* you."

My blood ran cold. "What do you mean, *she caught you leaving my room the next morning?*"

"You don't think that pregnancy test was enough to make her give up on you, do you?" She shook her head. "She had that image of me walking out of your room in the back of her mind the whole time… I'm surprised she didn't tell you."

"She trusted me," I whispered, realization dawning on me. Kennedy had already planted a seed of doubt, and then exploited it to her benefit.

Her wicked laugh filled the space, "And just to be sure I got my point across, I sent her the picture of us in bed."

"What picture?"

Kennedy grinned and pulled out her phone. "The one I took while you were passed out."

She held up her phone, showing me a photo of us. She was topless, smiling at the camera, while I was naked, at least from the waist up. I was laying on my stomach, one arm thrown over her waist. I swallowed thickly, "You… How…?"

"If I knew how easy it was to get your dick hard without waking you up, I'd have taken you for a joy ride. This was the best I could do though."

My chest squeezed, I couldn't get enough air. "You showed this to her?"

She shrugged. "Ember thought she could come back here and reclaim what was hers... but you're not hers anymore, are you?"

I sucked in a ragged breath as all the pieces fell into place. I knew that test wasn't enough to send Ember running. Whether she wanted me or not, I would always be hers. But Kennedy was unhinged...

She got up from the bed and wrapped her arms around my neck, grinding her hips against mine. I recoiled and even my dick wasn't interested. "Ever since my mom got sick, my dad stopped caring. Miles only cares for Ellie... and I'm pretty sure you do too."

"What about what's-his-name up in Wickett? I'm sure he cares."

"Joe?" She shrugged. "He's just a good time. But *you?* You care when I'm around. You pay attention. At one point, you used to beg me to be around more. Remember those days?" Her hands ran up and down my chest, playing with the buttons on my shirt. "We could be good, Wes, you just have to give us a real chance."

She started unbuttoning my shirt and I grabbed her hands, forcing her to stop. "No, Kennedy. No."

"No?"

I took a step back, holding her at arm's length. "No. I'm taking Ellie and we're..."

"You're what?" She yanked her hands from my grip and stormed back to the bed. She picked up Ellie's backpack and dumped it out. "Did you miss the part where I told you that Ellie's not yours?"

I shook my head. "No, in fact, I've known for a while."

"Then you should know that you can't take *my* daughter away from me."

"In case you forgot, my name is on her birth certificate, too. In the eyes of the law, she's just as much mine," I kept my tone strong, hoping she couldn't hear the quiver in my voice. Kennedy barely graduated high school, I was banking on the hope that she never bothered to look into child custody laws.

"I'll have a paternity test taken." Her voice faltered, but she recovered quickly. "I'll hire a lawyer and make sure you never see her again."

I swallowed past the lump in my throat as my biggest fear was laid out before me. "With what money, Ken?"

"Daddy will help. I bet Miles will too if he hears what you're trying to do."

I nodded but let those threats roll off my back. I knew for a fact Miles wouldn't do anything to help her. Her dad now? That was a possibility, though what he'd do when he found out she lied about me being the father was anybody's guess. She was right when she said he stopped caring when her mom got sick. He didn't care about anything, not even the company he worked so hard to build.

I picked up Ellie's backpack and the clothes she dumped everywhere. "You go ahead and get started on that," I said with more bravado than I actually felt. "For now, *my* daughter and I are going to get some space."

She tried grabbing the backpack from me, but I shook her off. "Don't," I snapped.

"Eleanor! Eleanor! Mommy needs you!" she called out, stepping out of the room.

"You can call for her all you want, but she's not here."

"Where is she?" she demanded, fire burning in her eyes.

"She's being taken care of by someone who loves her."

"You can't do this to me, Wes. She's *my* daughter!"

I spun on her, getting right in her face, "Oh yeah? Tell me this, *Ken*... What's her favorite color? Her favorite food? Maybe even her favorite animal?"

She rolled her eyes at me. "Pink, pizza, and kittens," she said with confidence, looking at Ellie's pink, kitten covered bedspread.

"Wrong. Purple, spaghetti made with macaroni, and right now, zebra's."

"That doesn't prove anything."

"Okay, how about this. Who was her teacher last year?"

She smirked, "Mrs. Appleberry."

I shook my head. "No. It was Mr. Schmidt."

Her forehead creased, "But he teaches first grade," she argued, her hand on her hip.

"And what grade do you think she just finished? God, Kennedy. I knew you didn't *care*," I glared at her. "But I never realized you were that checked out."

"Don't tell me I don't care about my daughter!" she shouted, stomping her foot. "I CARE!"

I took a deep breath and blew it out slowly. How had I let things get this bad? "Parents who care know where their kids are. They know how old they are and what grade they are in school. For the record, Ellie is six, and just finished first grade." I returned to the dresser, gathering up the rest of the things she would need. "Just so you know, Ellie cares about you. She cares when you don't show up for school plays or choir concerts. She cares when you don't tell her bedtime stories. She cares when you forget to pick her up from play dates. She cares when you don't come home at night. She cares, but you don't. And that's okay, but it's time for you to stop hurting her."

She looked like she wanted to say something else, but I put my hand up. "Just go, Kennedy. I've been taking care of Ellie for years without your help. I don't need it now." I zipped the bag and grabbed Ellie's stuffed wolf I bought her last summer at the Wildlife Safari Park in Ashland. I pushed past Kennedy, through the doorway and out of the house.

I took the long way to Miles' place, hoping that whoever Kennedy had watching me wouldn't realize where I was headed. I needed to keep her away from Ellie at all costs. I had a couple of calls to make, and held my phone to my ear with my shoulder while it rang.

"Everything okay?"

"Nice greeting, Tatum," I huffed out a laugh. "I screwed up, but it's fine. I just need you to cover for me a little."

"What did you do?" She sounded exasperated, like me screwing up was a common occurrence. Perhaps it was, but only when it came to the important things, and that was a problem.

"Kennedy showed up while I was packing Ellie's things. She..." I let my words hang as realization hit me. "There's something about Ellie I need to tell you."

"What is it?"

I swallowed thickly, "She's not mine."

Tatum's laugh was light and airy, and eased some of the tension in my shoulders. "Tell me something I don't know."

"You? How?"

"Come on, Wes. It's not rocket science. First, there's the fact that you would never cheat on Ember. Let's be real, drunk or not, you only have eyes for my bestie. Second... Ellie looks just like Ember, with green eyes. She wasn't getting those blonde locks from you or Kennedy, and she sure as shit didn't get those green eyes from either of you..."

"So you knew and you never said anything?"

She laughed, "Come on, you'd have to be blind to not see it."

"Ok, well now that I know *you* know... Here's the problem. Kennedy finally admitted it..."

"That sounds like a good thing."

"And she's going to try to take Ellie away from me."

"She can't do that."

I sighed, "Unfortunately, she can. Miles and Lainey are working on a lawyer for me, but... I'm scared, Tatum."

"What do you need me to do?"

"I told her Ellie was spending the night with Jadon, so I wouldn't be surprised if she shows up later to pick her up. Whatever you do, don't let her know that Ellie is with Miles. Please."

"No problem. If it were up to me, Kennedy wouldn't get to see Ellie ever again."

"Thank you."

"What are you going to do?"

I sighed as I turned onto Miles' street. "I'm going to talk to Miles and make a plan. I've got to get to Ember before it's too late, but I have to be sure Ellie's safe first."

"Whatever you need, we're here for you. I'll talk to Brandon, maybe he can help too."

"Thanks, Tatum. You're a good friend."

She chuckled, "I'll remember you said that."

CHAPTER THIRTY

Linford

PRESENT

Wes

Giggles filled the air as I pulled Ellie's favorite nightgown down over her head. "Lainey said we can watch a pony movie and have popcorn!" she bounced up and down on the bed.

"That sounds like a lot of fun, baby girl. But first we need to do something with this mess," I tried to smooth her hair back into a ponytail, but she swatted my hands away.

"Lainey said she'll put it in curls if I'm a good girl."

"She did, did she?"

"Mmm hmm."

I lifted her up in the air, high over my head as she squealed in delight. "I'm flyin like a eagle!"

"Look at you!" Lainey stepped up behind me and put a hand on my back. "I promise we'll take good care of her."

I swallowed thickly, lowering Ellie to my hip. "I know you will. It's just... I've never been away from her for more than a night."

"I'll be good, daddy."

I kissed her cheek. "I know you will."

She squirmed in my arms until I passed her to Lainey's outstretched hands. "I've got this. Miles is waiting for you in the kitchen."

"I'll come see you before I go, okay Ellie?"

"Ok daddy!"

The kitchen was dark, the only light coming from the range hood and Miles' illuminated phone. "Thanks for doing this," I broke the silence, pulling out the chair across from him.

He stopped scrolling on his phone and looked up at me. "Of course. I love that little girl, and despite her flaws, I do love Kennedy, but... she's not motherly material, you know?"

I nodded.

"I spoke with the lawyer a couple hours ago. He's going to file for temporary custody until we can get everything put together to file for full."

"How much is this gonna cost me? I don't care about the money; I just need to make sure I have it."

Miles shook his head. "Don't worry about that just yet. For now, he's going to help us out pro bono. The only costs we'll need to worry about are filing fees or court costs."

"Are you sure?"

"Yeah. He said he could use the experience, so it's a win-win."

The pressure in my chest eased a little. "And if Kennedy shows up here looking for her while I'm gone?"

"I'll handle my sister. Don't worry, Ellie isn't going anywhere with her."

I breathed out a sigh of relief. "Do you think Ember will give me a chance to explain?"

Miles lazily scratched at the stubble on his chin. "Probably not right away, but I think she will. She's still in love with you, but she's hurt."

"I know. I never meant to..."

"This isn't on you. You were just trying to do the right thing."

I dropped my head down, resting my forehead against my folded knuckles. "Do you know if she made it home safe?"

He smirked, "I was just about to call her, but I wanted you here when I did."

I looked at him quizzically, wanting to ask him *why*, but he already hit the call button, his phone on the table in front of him on speaker. Every ring felt like a hammer in my chest.

"Hello?"

All the air left my lungs at the sound of her voice.

"Hey, Em. You make it back okay?"

"Yeah, just a bit ago. I... I'm sorry for running out like that."

"That's okay, Kennedy can be..."

"A bitch?"

I had to bite back my laugh, but Miles didn't even try. "Yeah, a bitch. But I have a feeling things are going to be changing real soon."

"What do you mean?"

He looked to me, silently asking permission to tell Ember what was going on, but I shook my head. This was a conversation I needed to have with her myself - in person.

"Oh, you know... Life can't stay the way it was anymore."

"True. Hey, look. I gotta go pick up my cat. Talk soon?"

"Yeah, talk soon. Love you, Em."

"Love you too."

He ended the call, but I couldn't take my eyes off the phone. She was so close, yet so far. "You should get going."

I stood up, pushing the chair back with a low scrape. "I'm heading out first thing in the morning."

"Keep me posted."

I reached out and took his hand. "Thank you. For everything."

It felt so strange sleeping in my old bed at my aunt's house without Ellie. Everything just felt strange without her. I missed her smile, her laugh, her silly stories. I even missed her snores and feet digging into my side. How was I going to do this?

I rolled over onto my side, facing the wall I had spent countless nights staring at seven years ago, when I gave up hope that my phone would ring.

CHAPTER THIRTY-ONE

Linford

7 YEARS AGO

Wes

The white wall had a spot of blue in the texturing. It was so small you would never notice it; not unless you spent all your time staring at the same spot. Knowing it was there both drove me nuts, and brought me comfort. At least something in my life was constant.

"Wes, get out of bed," Angie snapped at me, not for the first time.

Ember had officially been gone for two weeks. Two weeks without a sound. She never answered her phone, never even opened her texts. And as far as I knew, I wasn't the only one getting the silent treatment. Miles wasn't able to reach her, nor was Tatum. Even Angie was trying. It was like she just disappeared off the face of the earth.

And if she was gone, I didn't want to be here either.

"What, Ang?" I grumbled, rolling over to my other side.

"You need to go to work."

"What's the point?"

"The point is, you have responsibilities, and just because Ember is gone, doesn't mean you can blow them off!"

"What if something happened to her? Have her parents agreed to file a report?" I held my breath waiting for her answer. I went to the police and filed a missing person's report, but when they talked to her parents, they told them she wasn't missing, she was just having a tantrum and would show up when she was finished.

She shook her head. "No."

I sat up and pushed my hands through my hair, tugging at the ends. "She should have been back by now!"

"I know, but there's not much we can do."

"What about a search party? We could try again."

Angie took a deep breath, her shoulders slumping as she blew it out. She crossed the room and sat softly next to me. "Until Mitch or Leanne admit she's missing, no one is willing to search. They maintain she's just clearing her head..."

"And meanwhile Kennedy is telling everyone Ember couldn't handle me dumping her..."

She wrapped her arm around me, resting her head against my shoulder. "We just have to keep moving, and hope she either comes back or contacts one of us."

"I don't know if I can do that," I whispered.

"You have to decide what you want for your future."

"I want *her*," my voice cracked.

Angie took my hand and gave it a small squeeze. "You have to consider that may not be an option anymore."

The smoke from the bonfire stung my eyes as I stared into the orange glow. Spring was slowly slipping away, taking the colder nights with it, though fifty degrees was hardly warm... It didn't stop the kids in Linford from celebrating the end of the school year in Old Man Miller's back lot.

Didn't stop me and my friends from sitting on my tailgate at the edge of the field having our own celebration.

Penn bumped my shoulder, "Hey, take a hit," he said, passing me the half-smoked joint.

I brought it to my lips and inhaled deep, holding it until my head felt a little fuzzy. I blew out the smoke, forming little rings that floated away over my head.

Jazz tapped my knee with a glass bottle. "Drink up."

I handed him the joint and took the bottle of fireball, tipping it back and swallowing large mouthfuls of the spiced whiskey. I wiped my mouth with the back of my hand and passed the bottle to Penn. I was officially twenty-one.

"So..." Penn started. "We were thinking maybe you'd like to come back home, just for a little while."

"Maybe some distance would do you some good," Jazz added.

Alone Together by Fall Out Boy blared through a speaker. It was one of my favorite songs, but ever since Ember left, it was all just white noise. It had been nine weeks and six days since I last saw her, last heard her voice. It had been an even ten since I held her in my arms. No one has heard from her, and her parents don't seem to care. As long as Kennedy and her baby are healthy...

I hopped off the tailgate, walking across the field to that giant ball of fire. Warmth hit me with each step, but I hardly felt it. I was numb. When I reached out to touch it, I could almost feel the burn. Maybe if I...

"What the fuck?" Penn's hand wrapped around my bicep and yanked me back.

"I just..."

"Come on," Jazz grabbed my other arm and started to drag me away, back to my truck.

"Wes! Baby!"

The sound of Kennedy's voice broke me out of whatever spell I was under. I shook off my friends and practically ran, jumping into the driver's seat of my truck. My friends slid in seconds later, and I was peeling out of the lot. I could see Kennedy waving at me from the rearview mirror, her round belly hanging over her cutoff shorts. I dropped nearly an entire paycheck on maternity clothes for her, and yet she insisted on wearing clothes that no longer fit.

"Was that the baby mama?" Jazz asked, twisting so he could watch her from the back window.

My eye twitched and I forced myself to take a deep breath and blow it out slowly. "Yeah."

"Damn. She'd be kinda cute if she didn't dress like trash."

"Was she holding a bottle of beer?" Jazz asked.

"Probably," I groaned. "She's fucking psycho."

"And you're sticking around to play daddy to her baby?"

I glared at my friend as I took a turn too sharp, the truck fishtailing over the loose dirt.

"Come on, talk to us," Penn pleaded. "I'm worried about you."

I drove down the ruddy road to the lake I visited far too often and parked so we were facing the water. I left the truck running; even though I couldn't feel the cold, I could tell my friends were struggling with temperature.

We sat in silence, waiting to see who would break it first. I reached behind my seat and pulled a bottle out of a brown paper bag and cracked the lid. Jack Daniels went down a little smoother than Fireball.

Jazz swiped the bottle from my hand, "Talk."

"What do you want me to say?"

"How about what you're still doing here? What are your plans? We're worried about you."

"I'm fine," I grumbled, taking my bottle back.

"No, you're not." Penn swiped the bottle this time, chucking it out the window. I didn't even see him roll it down.

"I don't know what to do!" I shouted. "Is that what you want to hear?"

"We want to hear what's going on up here," Jazz tapped my forehead with two fingers.

I slammed the heel of my hand against the steering wheel over, and over, and over again. "FUCK!"

I threw open my door and jumped out, slamming it behind me. I kicked a clod of dirt, then picked up a rock and threw it as far as I could. I didn't wait to see where it landed before I collapsed onto the ground, my body shaking with rage. I brought my knees up to my chest and wrapped my arms around them, resting my head against my knees. A sob broke free and as hard as I tried, I couldn't stop the tears from falling. It was too much.

Jazz's hand landed on my shoulder as he dropped down onto the ground to my left, Penn took the space to my right. "It's alright, man. We don't have to talk about it."

I don't know how long we sat like that, my friends silently offering me comfort. When my rage died down and my sobs became little more than ragged breaths, I lifted my head and stared over the water. The moon reflected off the surface, illuminating every ripple as it washed ashore.

"She won't take a paternity test," I finally managed, speaking the words that had been eating away at me for weeks now.

"Shit man, really?" Jazz grabbed a rock and threw it at a tree.

"Not to state the obvious, but that's kinda a red flag, don't you think?"

"Yeah, and when I told her that, she went to her parents and complained that I wasn't being supportive of her and *our* daughter."

"It's a girl?" Penn arched a brow.

"Yeah," my voice was rough as I remembered that day at the clinic. "I've been going with her to her checkups. We heard the heartbeat, and then the doctor told us we're having a girl."

"But you don't think she's yours..." Penn said.

I shook my head. "I'm almost positive she's not."

"So what are you gonna do?" Jazz asked, staring off into the distance.

I shrugged, inhaling a ragged breath. "I don't really have a lot of options. I'm gonna stick it out until she's born, then I'm going to demand the paternity test. She can't deny me then."

"What if she's not yours?"

I turned to Jazz, grateful he was taking me seriously for a change. "Then I'll be packing up and heading back to Texas. Tatum will let me know if she ever hears from Ember. Until then, there's nothing I can do. I..." I let my thoughts trail off, not wanting to give them a voice.

"Devil's advocate here - what if she *is* yours?"

That was my worst nightmare. That I could do something like that and not even remember it. That I could hurt the one person I cared about more than anything in the world. The answer to this was easier though because my fate will be my own fault and I will have deserved all of this pain. "If she's mine, then I'm gonna be a dad. I'll stay here and do what I have to."

"You gonna marry the baby mama?" Jazz asked.

"Hell no. If I had my way about it, I'd file for custody, take the baby and go home."

The tension was so thick you could cut it with a knife. Mitch Davis sat at the head of the table, fork in one hand, knife in the other, glaring at me. Kennedy and her mother both sat on the same side of the table, chatting away about nursery colors and god knows what else.

Jazz and Penn left this morning and a huge part of me wishes I left with them.

"When are you going to grow up?"

I bit my tongue. It was bad enough I was stuck sitting here at a "family" dinner.

"You cannot live a life without consequence, Wes!" he slammed the hand holding the knife against the table. "It's time for you to step up and take care of my baby. The doctor's bills have started coming in, and I expect you to take care of them. I also think it's time for you to move in. My granddaughter isn't going to have parents living in two separate homes. You will provide for her like a *real* father should."

I shook my head. "I'm sorry, sir, but I don't think now is a good time," I clipped, keeping my real thoughts smothered, lest I say something that would only cause more drama.

"Don't get smart with me," he waved his knife in the air. "You assured me you would be a father to this baby. Are you telling me you lied?"

"No sir. If I recall correctly, I said *if* the baby was mine, I would be a father. And I will. But as of right now, Kennedy is refusing a paternity test, so..."

"She doesn't need a paternity test! She said you're the father! Are you calling my little girl a liar?" His face burned red.

"No sir, but I also know I would never cheat on Ember."

"And yet my little girl is pregnant..."

I pushed my chair back and stood. "Thank you for dinner, Leanne. It was lovely." I ignored Mitch's shouting demands that I sit back down as I left the house. I closed the door quietly despite the overwhelming urge to slam it, and climbed into my truck.

I drove around the outskirts of town for a while, avoiding any major streets, appreciating the open fields and dirt roads. This is not how my life was supposed to turn out. When I was younger, I thought I'd grow up, marry Andy, and we'd have a couple of kids and a house off Galveston beach. I'd open my own auto shop, and she'd work for some marketing agency.

When things went south with her, I thought I'd never find my way again. I spent every day slaving away at the garage and every night balls deep in a different woman. And then I met Ember. She was everything I thought Andy was, only more. She was smart and funny; beautiful, and kind. She was the most genuine person I ever met. She made me feel like I mattered in a way no one else ever had. She listened to my dreams, wishes, thoughts and ideas without judgment.

Loving Ember was easy. Losing Ember...

I shook my head, pushing the thoughts away. Despite how much it hurt, I took the road that led to the lake, needing to feel closer to her. I parked under the tree where we made love for the first time and pulled out a bottle of Jack Daniels.

I took a long drink, eyes focused on the instrument panel in my truck. I turned on the radio and hit play on one of the playlists I made for our road trip to Texas. "Like I'll Never Love You Again" by Carrie Underwood came on and I instantly felt both closer to and farther away from her.

I was such a fucking sap, pining over a woman who could throw me away so easily. Not just me, but her entire family, her friends... I should let her go and move on - isn't that what Jazz and Penn were trying to get me to do? I could still hear their words of wisdom, *The best way to get over someone is to get under someone new.*

Is that what Ember was doing?

I clenched my fist around the bottle and took another long drink; the idea of some other man's hands on my woman made me want to hit something, or someone.

I sucked in a sharp breath, closed my eyes and leaned my head back as I let Carrie's voice wash over me, remembering the way Ember felt in my arms when we lay in the bed of my truck looking up at the stars. She would only ever be mine, right?

One song bled into the next, and the next. The first line of "H.O .L.Y." from Florida Georgia Line broke me. I was taken back to that night in Kansas City, holding her in my arms, singing the words in her ear while we swayed side to side. I capped my bottle and set it in the seat next to me. I pulled out my phone and typed out a text to the group chat, my vision blurred with unshed tears.

> **Me:** It was good seeing you guys

> **Me:** Tell my dad I'm sorry. Take care of him

Then I did something I hadn't allowed myself to do for weeks. I sent a text to Ember.

> **Me:** I will always love you, even when I'm gone. You're it for me

I turned off my phone and tossed it into the passenger seat. I opened my glovebox and pulled out the gun I stashed there a week ago when I realized my days were numbered. It was tucked away in a black plastic bag and I carefully unwrapped it, brushing my fingers over the barrel; the dark metal was smooth and cool to the touch. I gripped it, sliding my finger over the trigger and back again. I released the magazine, and set the gun aside.

I ran my thumb over each bullet; each one was an opportunity, but I only needed one. I picked the gun back up and slid the magazine back in until it clicked. I set it aside, unscrewed the lid to my bottle and took another long drink. The more I drank, the less it burned going down, and the less I felt - or maybe the more I felt. I couldn't tell anymore.

I picked up the gun again, getting an idea of how best to grip it. I pressed the barrel against my temple. The metal was cold, but I welcomed the feel of it. I brought my index finger to the trigger and gave it a small squeeze. I let out a soft sigh, it didn't feel right...

I dropped the gun back to my lap and took another long drink. I once owned a BB Gun, and it looked like a real gun, but it didn't feel anything like this. Was that because of the mechanics of it all, or was it just in my head.

I picked up the gun again and brought the barrel up to the underside of my chin. The metal dug in painfully. I held it there for a couple of minutes, but ultimately set it back down. The grip just didn't feel natural. *Was it even supposed to?*

I lifted the bottle of Jack to my lips, but only a drop came out. *How long had I been sitting here?*

I looked out the window, the sun had set and the moon was high in the sky. The music was still playing, this time "Marry Me" by Thomas Rhett. My heart ached as he sang about the woman he wanted to marry, but she didn't know... I wanted Ember to know.

I took a deep breath and brought the gun to my lips. I opened my mouth, and slid the barrel inside. It scraped against my teeth, sending a chill down my spine. The metal tasted bitter and I leaned my head back, finger hovering over the trigger. All I had to do was flick off the safety and squeeze.

A bang on my window jolted me and I dropped the gun. Pissed, I looked out the window and came face to face with my aunt.

I stared at the door and for some reason couldn't figure out how to roll the window down. I grabbed the handle and pushed it open. "Hey, Ang," I slurred.

"What in the hell do you think you're doing?" she snapped at me, grabbing my chin and holding my face steady.

"I'm... I'm..." I sucked in a ragged breath, looking down at the weapon sitting in my lap. "I don't know, Ang," I whispered. Seconds ticked by, her fingers digging into my cheeks. The gun slid off my lap and landed at my feet.

"I know you're hurting, Wes, but this?" She shook her head. "I love you, kid, but I can't stand by and watch you kill yourself."

"I'm not, I won't..." Beads of sweat dotted my forehead and a chill ran down my spine. My heart rate kicked up and I leaned my forehead against the steering wheel. "I'm sorry, I didn't mean... I just..."

She reached in and unbuckled my seat belt and dragged me out of the truck. I was so wasted it took her almost no effort. I fell to my knees at her feet, "I... I-I miss her, Ang!" Out of nowhere, tears came streaming down my face. "I-I don't know what to do! What do I do, Ang?" I folded in half, gripping my hair angrily. "I can't do this anymore!" I punched the dirt, "It hurts, Ang! I can't do this!"

She squatted down in front of me and ran her hand over my back. "Come on, let's get you home."

I wanted to fight her, I didn't want to go back there, back where I still had memories of her, her smile, her laugh. Her sweater that she left on the floor the last time she was over. The one that I kept tucked beneath my pillow that still smelled like her, if only faintly.

Realistically, I had nowhere else to go, even in my drunken state I knew that. I let her help me to my feet and lead me to her car. She got me settled in her passenger seat and a few minutes later I found myself staring out the window at the trees and dirt and open fields as they rushed past. I leaned against the door, my head pressed to the glass and before long my eyes were too heavy to keep open.

A rapping startled me awake. At first, I was disoriented, the sun beating down on me through the windshield. I was still in Angie's car. I turned to look out the window, where the sound had come from. The movement set off a chain reaction in my stomach. I pushed the door open and leaned out just in time to throw up, narrowly missing my aunt's feet.

I wiped my mouth with the back of my hand and sat back with a groan. "Oh, god. I'm sorry, Ang. I'm so, so, sorry. I'll clean it up."

When I didn't hear a sound, I had to force myself to look up, though the bright light wasn't doing anything for my head. Angie was there, she just wasn't saying anything, which was so out of character for her. I swallowed hard; my mouth tasted awful. When I brought my eyes back up to meet hers, I saw nothing but disappointment.

"I'm sorry," I repeated, wondering if I said it out loud the first time or if it was just in my head.

Still she didn't respond, just stood there with her hands on her hips. I unclipped my seatbelt and moved to get out. The motion made my stomach roil and I stopped, not wanting to throw up again. I took a deep breath.

"Wesley Allen Barrett," my aunt started, her voice thick, like she was speaking through tears. "If you want to kill yourself, I won't stop you, but you won't do it under my watch. Do you hear me?"

Kill myself? I furrowed my brow and climbed out of her car, pushing past the nausea that swirled in my stomach. "I don't want to kill myself," I whispered, unsteady on my feet.

"That's not what it looked like last night!" she shouted, a single tear streaked down her cheek.

"Look, Ang, I'm sorry." *What did I do last night?* "I had a lot to drink. It was my birthday weekend and Ember and I had plans and... It won't happen again. I swear."

Her head jerked in a sort of a nod, but her posture didn't change. "You're right. It won't - at least not where I can see you."

"What do you mean?"

"You're out, Wes. I won't have you living under my roof if you think for one second that people won't miss you. Do you think that's what *she* wants?"

I didn't have to ask, I knew what "she" she was referring to, and to be honest, I didn't have an answer. I tried to put myself in Ember's shoes more than once over the past couple of months. I imagined if it were her, if she were pregnant with another man's baby. Anger washed over me every time the thought crossed my mind. But I would never wish her dead.

"No," I whispered, shame spreading through my veins like a virus. I couldn't deny thinking about it. Hell, I even bought a gun...

"Good. Then get your shit together, because after what I saw last night, I'm not sure I can trust you anymore." She took a step back and turned toward the house. "Go get cleaned up and we'll go get your truck. Then you have one hour to pack your shit and get out."

"Wait! You can't be serious!" I protested, the sound of my own voice felt like a jackhammer in my head.

"Oh, I'm *very* serious."

"Where am I supposed to go?" I threw my arms out.

She shrugged and pulled open the screen door. "Figure it out. The way I see it, you have a couple of options."

"I *will not* move in with her," I snapped, storming up the steps.

"That's your prerogative."

"Come on, Ang! Please don't do this! I said I'm sorry!"

She shook her head, "You did this to yourself, Wes. Get it together and maybe you can come back. Until then, you need to figure out what you want, and you can't do that here."

"I know what I want!" I cried out.

She didn't respond, didn't even look in my direction.

I didn't pack everything, just what I considered essential. I stuffed clothes and toiletries in my duffel, and set my laptop on top. I un-pinned all the photos I had taken of Ember and I and stuffed them inside a notebook of hers that she had left on my desk. Finally, I grabbed her sweater from under my pillow.

I took everything to my truck and when I went to get in, I saw my gun sitting haphazardly under the seat. I pulled it out and stared at it. *What the hell was I thinking?*

I removed the clip and made sure the safety was on before running up the stairs and into my aunt's house one last time. "Ang!"

She stood up from the couch where she had planted herself the moment we got back. I swallowed against a lump in my throat as I held the gun and clip out to her. "Can you take these?"

"Yeah."

"For what it's worth, I'm sorry."

"Me too."

CHAPTER THIRTY-TWO

Linford

PRESENT

Wes

Energy thrummed through my veins as I pulled out onto the highway heading west. I had never been further west than Dallas, which was more north than anything. I rolled down my window and turned up the radio as the engine neared 80 miles per hour.

I sang House of Memories along with Brendon Urie, giving my mind permission to wander through the memories that I locked away since that night I tried to kill myself. Memories that were too painful to relive. But each time I stopped to fill my gas tank, with every city I passed, I found myself believing this wasn't the end of our story.

If I could have followed Ember seven years ago, I would have. I always wondered where she went, and then when I found out I wondered if she planned on going to Colorado, or if that's just where the road took her. Was she scared? Excited?

Perhaps the most torturous question was, "did she think of me?"

CHAPTER THIRTY-THREE

Coyote Ridge

7 Years Ago

Ember

I watched the meter on the gas pump, cringing with every dollar going in. I had a decent amount of savings, but I couldn't afford to be frivolous.

I wrapped my arms around my middle and inhaled deeply. I never knew air could smell so fresh; like pine and earth... I leaned against the side of Carrie and gazed up at the mountain peaks just ahead. The sky had changed from blue, to this brilliant orange, and now it was a mix of magenta and purple that reflected off the mountains. I had never seen anything quite so breathtaking.

I imagined seeing the mountains was akin to seeing the ocean for the first time; something I was *supposed* to be doing this week when we drove to see Wes' dad. Apparently his house was just about two hours from the ocean, and we were going to spend a couple of days at the beach, soaking up the sun, swimming, and even building sand castles. Wes promised we could...

Tears welled up unbidden in my eyes as the image of his smile, the way his hair fell over his forehead, his stubbled jaw, took center stage in my mind. His laugh, the way his calloused hands felt against my skin... I sucked in a ragged breath; that part of my life was over. He didn't deserve my tears and the sooner I could forget it, forget *him*, the sooner I could move on.

When the gas pump clicked, I replaced the nozzle and closed the cap. If my directions were right, the next town was about an hour away in one of the mountain valleys. I looked back up at those snowy peaks. Excitement buzzed in my veins, knowing I would be spending the night in a small mountain town. It felt exotic, and like the perfect start to my new life.

The road was quiet, and I was thankful for that. The one-lane highway that twisted and turned through the canyon had me on edge, especially after my headlights caught the eye of a mountain goat hanging out on the shoulder of the road. I slowed down enough to see there were several of them, in various places on the highway and the mountainside itself.

A couple more miles up, I spotted a pair of headlights in my rearview mirror. They were gaining on me quickly, and I immediately searched for a place to pull off, knowing I couldn't take these turns at the speed they were coming. I got off the road just as the car zipped past, kicking up dirt and rocks as it went. I jolted when a few of those rocks slammed into my car; one hit my windshield taking a good size chip out of the glass.

I groaned, the last thing I needed was to have to replace my windshield.

I gave my nerves a minute to settle before I stepped on the gas, eager to get off the highway and into town. It had been an exceptionally long day, easily the longest in my life and not only was I having trouble seeing, but the unfamiliar windy road meant I was driving slower than I normally would. According to my GPS, I'd be in town in fifteen minutes, which meant closer to twenty for me.

I breathed a sigh of relief as soon as I saw the "Welcome to Coyote Ridge" sign, and a sparsely lit valley spread out before me. For the past five minutes or so, my car was making a weird noise, and I wondered if it was as tired as I was. My first thought was to ask Wes to take a look at it, then deflated when it struck me that that was no longer an option. I'd have to find a new mechanic, new friends, new everything.

The weird noise turned into a hissing, distracting me from my spiraling thoughts. I crossed my fingers that we would make it to the hotel and Carrie would be fine after a long rest. Everything would be better after some rest. I hadn't slept in a couple of days - too excited for my trip, and then... I was running on coffee, red bull, and those 5-hour energy drinks.

I parked outside the Mountain Peaks Inn and took a lap around Carrie, kicking the tires as I went, thinking maybe that's where the hissing was coming from. But they all seemed fine. Maybe she just needed to cool off.

I checked in, spending more money for a night of rest than I antici-pated, but at least the room was cozy. I sat heavily on the bed, the mat-tress squeaking with my weight. I pulled my phone out of my pocket and for the first time since I left home, looked at my notification bar. I cringed at the number of missed calls and texts. Guilt clawed up my throat until I reminded myself that I did it for a reason. Putting my phone on Do Not Disturb was me putting myself first, something I rarely did, and I deserved it.

One at a time, I swiped notifications away. Seven missed calls from Miles; sixteen from Tatum. There were three missed calls from Miss Barrett, and my heart skipped a beat when I saw the twenty-three missed calls from Wes. There wasn't a single missed call or text from my mom, dad, or even Kennedy. The hurt I felt from their words paled in comparison to their lack of concern for my whereabouts.

They probably assume I'll be back.

Little did they know I had zero intention of returning home. Screw them, screw school, and most of all, screw Wes.

I rubbed the heel of my hand over my heart, trying to soothe the all consuming pain I felt just thinking about him, as I forced myself to look over my texts. I was careful not to open any of them, just reading what I could from the message preview. Miles said he was worried and to call him; Tatum demanded to know where I was. Then there was Wes. His were the hardest to ignore.

I didn't realize I was crying until a drop hit my phone screen and I hastily wiped my wet face. I started to swipe away Wes' texts without even looking at the preview, but I was weak.

> **Wes:** I love you more than life itself. Please come home. Let me...

I was desperate to open it, to see what it said beyond the preview, what the other forty or so messages said. I dropped my phone beside me and lay back in the bed, staring up at the ceiling.

"Wes cheated," I reminded myself. "He cheated with my sister." The image of the two of them in bed made me sick. Wes wasn't who he said he was. It was all an act, a game. *What did Kennedy have that I didn't?*

I picked up my phone and stared at the words on the screen for a moment before swiping them away without opening them. If he saw that I read his messages, he'd keep calling, and I couldn't do this. I couldn't be in love with a man who was having a baby with my sister. A man who cheated on me while I was in the room next door.

I locked my phone and shoved it in my bag. Then, just to torture myself, I pulled out the picture that I kept on my nightstand at home. I was wearing the new navy-blue dress I bought myself for Christmas. It had thin spaghetti straps, and a fitted bodice that showed just a hint of cleavage. It flared out into a flowy skirt that hung about halfway down my thigh. Shorter than I would typically wear, but I wanted to look good for Wes. My hair hung over my shoulder in loose waves.

Wes stood behind me, wearing a nice pair of black slacks and a charcoal button down that he had cuffed to his elbows, exposing his muscular forearms. His chocolate brown hair was longer than it had been when I first met him, and I loved it; loved the feeling of running my fingers through it.

We were at this restaurant in Wickett, and the waitress offered to take our picture. His face was pressed into my neck and you could just see his lips tipped up into a smile. If I closed my eyes, I could still smell his aftershave...

Tears streamed down my face as I set the picture on the nightstand. I grabbed my phone and hit play on my emo-country playlist and curled up under the covers. I let the words to "Better Man" by Little Big Town lull me to sleep. Tomorrow would be a new day, and maybe it would hurt a little less.

The first thing I noticed when I woke up, aside from my crusty eyes from too much crying, was how incredibly hungry I was. Aside from a couple granola bars, I couldn't remember when exactly I had last eaten. Despite my growling stomach, the mere thought of food made me queasy.

I rolled out of bed and stumbled through getting ready for the day. I still had about fifteen more hours to drive, and if I got started early, I could make it before the end of the night.

I picked up my phone and sighed as it pinged with notification after notification. Then, just as I was about to head outside, it started to ring. I stood in the open doorway, staring at the name flashing across my screen. Wes was persistent. I should probably just answer and tell him we're done, that I spent enough of my life playing second fiddle to Kennedy, I wouldn't do it with my boyfriend too. He wanted her, he could have her.

Except I couldn't do it. If I heard his voice, I would crumple and cave. It took every ounce of resolve to silence the phone and turn Do Not Disturb back on. I should probably block his number - block everyone's number, but I wasn't ready...

I pulled up directions to The Ridge, a diner in town, and turned onto the main road. Carrie was still making that weird noise; I crossed my fingers that she'd get me just a little farther. It didn't even have to be California, just... the other side of the Rockies. I needed a mountain range between us, minimum.

I cranked up the radio. If I couldn't hear it, then it wasn't happening. Carrie was fine; everything was fine.

I reached the diner in minutes. A bell jingled over the door when I pulled it open, and the few people already seated looked up. I felt a little awkward with all their eyes on me, then I inhaled the familiar smell of pancakes, bacon, and eggs. This was just another diner, and

I was just another patron. I was a stranger, and for the first time I thought about what that meant. I was a young, single woman, on a trek across the country. I could be anyone. I could reinvent myself, not just here, but when I get to California...

Hell, maybe I'd even cut my hair and change my name. I chuckled to myself as Rockstar by Nickelback popped into my head, thank you Wes...

I sighed, why did this have to be so hard? *Because he's the one*, a little voice whispered in the back of my mind. Except he isn't. He made his choice and it suddenly made sense why he was so quick to let her do whatever when we were in Kansas City.

A woman who appeared to be about my age, bounced on the balls of her feet as she approached, her short ash-blonde hair bobbing with the movement. Her grin ran from ear to ear. "Table for one?" she asked, looking around me to see if someone would be joining me.

"I was hoping to place a to-go order. I need to get back on the road..."

"Sure." She spun on her heel and led me to a booth near the door. She handed me a menu then stood there looking at me like I was some mystery to be solved. "Where you from?"

"Nebraska," I answered, without looking up.

"You coming or going?" she asked, leaning her hip against the table.

I looked up then, taking in her curious face and her nametag. Nancy. "Just passing through. I'm heading to California, hoping I can make it tonight." I passed the menu back. "Can I get a breakfast burrito and a coffee to go?"

"Ned likes to smother our breakfast burritos with sausage gravy. I assume you're planning to eat and drive..."

I nodded. "That actually sounds really good, but yeah."

"Take anything in your coffee?"

"Cinn…" I stopped. My stomach clenched and I shook my head, I was going to have to change my coffee order now too. I took a deep breath and blew it out slowly to quell the tremor in my voice. "A vanilla latte if possible. If not, then black is fine."

She laughed. "Girl, there's a coffee shop across town that makes some of the best latte's, among other things, but here… We're as basic as it gets."

I couldn't help the laugh that broke free. Living in a small town, I knew exactly what that was like. "Black it is," I grinned.

It didn't take more than ten minutes for her to return with a bag and two coffee cups. I arched a brow at her in question. "You've got a long-ass drive ahead of you… you'll need the extra boost."

"Thank you." I paid and returned to my car with the first genuine smile I've had since this whole mess started. It was a sign; everything was going to be okay.

I pulled out of the parking lot and jumped onto the highway. The first sip of coffee was awful, and the second wasn't much better. I turned up the radio as my car continued to whine and complain, and no less than five minutes later, a mile or so outside of town, she let me know she didn't like being ignored.

I pulled off the side of the road and popped the hood. As soon as I lifted it I was hit with a huge plume of hot smoke. I didn't know anything about cars but I didn't have to, to know that this wasn't good. "No. No, no, no, no!"

My knees buckled as everything caught up to me. I fell into the dirt then crawled around until I was leaning against one of Carrie's tires. "Why!" I screamed to the sky. "What did I ever do to deserve this!"

I brought my knees to my chest and buried my face in my hands as I finally allowed the tears to flow freely. This was not my life! I was supposed to finish high school, valedictorian of my class and go to college. I had my acceptance letter, even a scholarship that would help pay. I was supposed to study animal science and open my own veterinary practice...

I was supposed to get married, have a nice house and a couple of kids. My little brown-haired blue eyed boy who would look just like his daddy. And my Eleanor...

I choked on a sob as I thought about my babies, *our* babies. I wanted to pick up my phone, to check those texts, to listen to my voice messages. I wanted to call him, to hear his voice. I wanted to go back in time and refuse to take Kennedy with us and just go, without my parent's permission. I wanted my Wes back!

"Wes!" I cried out, face to the sky. "I need you Wes! You were supposed to be mine, not hers! Please!" I coughed and swiped angrily army face. "It's not real! Please don't let this be real..."

I focused on my breathing, in for a count of three, then out for three. Several cars drove past me without even slowing down. Not even curiosity peeks. Maybe not all small towns were the same, full of busy-bodies needing to know everyone's business.

Once my breathing calmed, I pushed myself to my feet and grabbed my phone from the car. "Damn it!" I had zero bars of service. I held my phone in the air like I saw people do in the movies and walked around, trying to get a signal, but it made no difference.

I held it up as I walked back toward town. I was nearly there by the time I had enough bars to call for help. My lungs were screaming and my head felt fuzzy. I always heard people joke about thin air at higher elevations. I never expected it to feel like this...

Frank, the local, and *only* mechanic in town towed Carrie to his shop, then gave me a lift back to the Mountain Peaks Inn. I paid for another night, hoping and praying my car wouldn't cost too much to fix, and that I'd have enough money left to at least get to the other side of the mountain. I was already using the money I had stashed away to pay Wes back for what he loaned me to buy her in the first place.

He never asked or expected me to pay him back, but I wasn't one to take charity. Now... A sob lodged itself in my throat. Now he probably needed that money more than me considering he was going to be a dad. I rubbed my eyes at the thought of him with her. Thinking about his heavy breathing and moans of pleasure being made for her made me sick to my stomach.

I plugged in my phone and curled up in bed. It was still early, but the combination of stress and crying sapped all of my energy. I closed my eyes to the steady sound of my ringing phone, letting it lull me to sleep. *I really should block their numbers.*

A banging on the door jerked me from my dreams and I was instantly on my feet. My heart hammered in my chest.

They found me.

I tiptoed across the room, peeling the curtain back just a bit so I could see who was out there praying it was Miles, or even Miss Barrett. I wouldn't be able to handle it if it was Wes, or worse, my parents. Instead, my eyes landed on the woman from the diner. Nancy.

I cracked the door open, "Hey?"

She smiled and shook her head, "Girl, you are the most exciting thing around here," she laughed.

I arched an eyebrow. "I am?"

She held out a bag and I pulled the door open the rest of the way. "I brought you dinner."

"You didn't have to..."

She waved me off and stepped past me into my room without invitation. "Frank has your car, and I just figured you might be hungry..."

"What time is it?" I grabbed my phone; thirty-seven new missed calls. I swiped away Miles, Tatum, and Miss Barrett, pausing at Wes' name. I swiped his away and focused on the next one down. I quickly dialed my voicemail, instantly regretting not clearing it earlier. The second I heard the gravelly sound of Wes' voice, I hung up. It took less than a second to hear the pain he was feeling. I couldn't do it. I couldn't get to Frank's message if I had to listen to all of Wes' first...

Nancy made herself comfortable, sitting at the foot of the bed, watching me pace back and forth as I debated what to do. "What is it?" she finally asked.

I shook my head, "Nothing, I just... My voicemail box is full."

She arched an eyebrow at me. "You running away from something?"

Her words were so close to the truth it hurt. Part of me wanted to tell her I was running from *someone.* I needed a friend, but I didn't know her, and something told me the fewer people who knew my story, the better. I wouldn't be here for long anyway.

I pulled up Frank's number and dialed, hoping he was still there. "This is Frank, leave a message at the beep."

I hung up and dropped heavily onto the bed. Nancy held out the bag of food to me, and this time I took it. My burrito was still sitting on the passenger seat of my car...

As soon as I opened the take-out box, my mouth started to water. A burger and fries were just what I needed... or any food really. I pulled it out and took a bite, moaning as the flavor hit my tastebuds.

Nancy chuckled. "Better not let my brother hear you making sexy sounds while eating his food. It'll go straight to his head - and I'm not saying which one."

If my mouth wasn't full of food, my jaw would likely be on the floor. As it was, I choked on a laugh. She just grinned. "Maybe I will tell Ned."

I shook my head, "Wait until I'm gone first, save me my dignity."

"I'll see what I can do," she laughed, getting up and walking toward the nightstand. "What's this?"

I turned to see what she was looking at, and my stomach dropped. "That's... He's..."

"He the reason you're heading to California?"

I shrugged, "Something like that." She didn't need to know I was running away from him.

She started to ask another question when my phone rang. I was afraid to look, but I couldn't exactly ignore it while she was watching me. Relief flooded my veins when I saw "Frank's Auto" on the display. "Hello?"

"Hello, is this Ember?"

"Yes, sir. Do you know what's wrong with Carrie?"

"Carrie?"

I sighed, yet another reminder that I was a long way from home. "My car," I corrected. "Her name is Carrie."

He chuckled, "Well, Carrie is in a bit of trouble. You've got a bad radiator, and some engine damage. How long were you driving her like that?"

"I-I don't know. I didn't know... My boyf... I mean..." I blew out a heavy breath. "What's it gonna take to get her back on the road? I need to get to California."

He made a high pitched whistle sound. "Hard to say without really getting in there, but I'm thinking $4,700 to start..."

"You're joking."

"No ma'am. Do you want me to start working on it?"

I closed my eyes, running the numbers in my head... No matter how I added it up, I wasn't making it out of this town - not any time soon. "Yeah. How long will it take?"

"A couple of weeks, at least. I'll have to order parts, and..."

"Thanks, Frank." I hung up and threw my phone across the room, not even caring when it broke.

Nancy flinched at my outburst, but simply asked, "Bad news?"

I scrubbed my hands over my face. *Could things get any worse?* "You could say that..." I sighed. "Looks like I'm staying for a bit. Know anyone hiring?" I laughed, though the situation was far from funny. At least I was a good eight hours from home.

"Well, actually," a grin spread across her face. "One of our waitresses just quit. I could put in a word with the boss."

"Really? I've got experience. I could even start right now."

Nancy chuckled. "Yeah, I'll head over now. Want to come?"

Chapter Thirty-Four

Coyote Ridge

Present

Ember

Bacon, pancakes, coffee, and the distinctive clacking of dishes. The familiar smell and sounds of The Ridge were like a balm to my soul. After being gone for two weeks, it was nice to be home and get back to work.

I leaned against the wall beside the order window, waiting for Ned to finish up the plate for table five. Ever since I got back, Brent had been trying to pick up where we left off. He was disappointed that I never replied to any of his texts, then in the same breath told me how good it was to have me back. He asked about my trip, and my family. When I told him my mom died, he took me into his strong arms and held me when tears threatened to fall. He was so sweet and caring, kind and gentle, and he smelled really, really good.

I would be lucky to have a man like him, and all it would take was one little word. Yes.

If only I could just move on.

Ned poked his head through the window. "Table five!" he called out, snapping me from my thoughts.

I spun around and grabbed the plate. "Thanks."

"You okay?" If he wasn't my friend, the pity in his voice would grate on me. Instead, it reminded me that I was home. Maybe not where I always intended to end up, but a place that welcomed me when I was at my lowest.

"I will be."

I set the plate of chicken fried steak and mashed potatoes in front of Brent. "Can I get you anything else?"

"No, I'm good, thanks."

I sighed in relief, I wasn't in the mood to talk. Then as I turned, his hand reached out and grabbed my wrist. "Wait," there was desperation in his voice and I felt like an even shittier person.

I turned around and met one of the kindest smiles I've ever seen.

"I'm sorry," he let go of me.

"It's okay."

"Ember, I..." He shook his head. "I really like you and I'd like to take you out again..."

"Brent, I," I cut him off.

"But I know it's not the right time," he continued. "I always knew there was more to you than what everyone sees. It's part of what initially drew me in, and while I'd like to take you out again, I want you to know that it's okay if you don't feel the same."

"Brent..." I slid into the booth across from him. "I really like you, I do. It's just..."

"There's someone else."

The words, while somewhat true, bothered me. "Not really, not anymore." I lifted one shoulder and let it drop in a half shrug. "It's complicated."

He studied my face for a moment, then picked up his fork and knife. "I'm here if you need me, for anything. I like you, even if it's just as a friend."

"Thank you," I whispered as tears welled up in my eyes. "You are too good for someone like me."

He chuckled. "Meh. I don't think so, but that's just one man's opinion."

I couldn't help but laugh; he was so damn easy to talk to. "Can I get you anything else?"

He shook his head. "I'm good. Thanks for this," he gestured between us and I reached over and put my hand on his arm.

"Enjoy your dinner."

I made a quick trip around the dining room, making sure everyone had everything they needed, then returned to my place behind the counter. They say idle hands are the devil's plaything, and nothing could be more true. Quiet moments were filled with replays of my days back home. The way his muscles bulged as he worked on my car, the woodsy spice of his cologne as I stormed past him; the way he looked at his daughter...

The bell over the door jingled and when I looked up, my heart stopped. I squeezed my eyes shut, certain I was seeing things. I missed him, that was all, and my mind was playing tricks on me.

White noise filled my ears, it was a dream. I haven't been sleeping well, that was the only explanation - it had to be a dream. When the smell of his cologne hit me I opened my eyes.

"Hey, Ember," Wes stood in front of the counter, hands stuffed in his pockets.

My mouth opened and closed, but no sound came out. I couldn't think, couldn't speak... I still wasn't convinced he wasn't a figment of my imagination. He took a step closer and when his rough fingers brushed over my cheek and tucked a loose strand of hair behind my ear, I knew he was real. My heart pounded loudly in my chest and my mouth was suddenly dry. I licked my lips, "Welcome to The Ridge." I looked past him to see who else he brought. "Table for one?" I asked when I didn't see anyone else.

"Yeah, that would be great."

His smile sent flutters through my belly. *No.* I scolded myself, forcing the memory of Kennedy's arm around him to the forefront of my mind.

I grabbed a menu and led him to the only table left in my section, which just happened to be right next to where Nancy conveniently seated Brent - right at the edge of hers. As much as I didn't want him around Brent, I didn't want her anywhere near him even more. "Can I get you something to drink?"

"Water's fine."

I gave him a nod and rushed away and into the kitchen where Ned was busy preparing another plate. "Hey, what's going on?"

I shook my head. "I just need a minute."

He stepped away from the stove and put his hands on my shoulders. "Ember, you're white as a sheet. Are you feeling okay? Do I need to get Nancy?"

I shook my head. "No, I'm fine. I just need a minute." *What is he doing here? Where's Kennedy? Where's Ellie - Eleanor?*

His eyebrows pulled together as he moved around me, taking a step out of the kitchen. He came back a second later. "Is it the guy at table seven?"

I shook my head and forced a smile that was so fake there was no way he would believe it. "Everything's fine."

"Ember..."

"I need to get him his water." I spun on my heel and grabbed what I needed.

I set the glass on the table and pulled out my order pad. "What can I get you?"

He set the menu down and folded his hands on top of the table. "What do you recommend?"

"Wes." His name came out in a sigh. "What do you want? Why are you here?"

"I'm here for you."

A thrill shot through me and I had to tamp it down. Nothing good could come from this. I shook my head. "It's too late. Go home."

"Please, just hear me out."

"How did you find me? Did Miles?"

He shook his head, "No, he offered, but... Can we talk?"

I wanted to. I *really* wanted to. Then my self preservation kicked in, conjuring the image of him and Kennedy in bed. Every time my resolve started to crack, I pulled up that picture. The relaxed set of his shoulders, the way his fingers curled around her waist... The pain was no less now than it was the day she sent it to me. "You should go."

His hand trembled as he reached out for me, then just as quickly he pulled it back. "Just five minutes," he pleaded, his voice shaky with desperation. I almost felt bad for him. *Almost.*

I squared my shoulders, "Go home, Wes." My voice sounded stronger than I felt and my heart hammered in my chest as I turned to leave. Even though I had just checked on all my tables, I made another round, stopping by Nancy's tables too. She'd be back any minute now, but I needed to do something.

Wes still hadn't left by the time I made it around to Brent's table. "Hey, Brent. Still doing good?"

He nodded and leaned forward. "Is he bothering you," he whispered, tipping his head to the side toward Wes.

"No, it's fine."

"You sure? He doesn't look like he's gonna listen."

I placed my hand on his shoulder. "He's... It's a long story."

"He the guy?"

I sighed and gave him a slight nod before stealing a peek at Wes. Our eyes met and a lead weight settled in my belly. He wore his heart on his sleeve, and the look on his face said it all; he knew who Brent was and it was evident he heard us talking.

"I'm here if you need me." Brent rested his hand on top of mine in support.

"Thank you."

I returned to Wes' table and put my hand on my hip, trying to hide just how unnerved I felt. "Look, do you want something or not?"

He held the menu up, "Cheeseburger and fries."

I took the menu and ran away as fast as I could without it looking like I was running. I passed his order to Ned just as Nancy came strolling back in. "I checked in on your tables."

"Was I gone that long?"

"No. I just needed something to do."

She gave me a nod as she settled in beside me. "Who's the hottie?" She lifted her chin toward Wes.

"Off limits."

She looked me up and down. "You're calling dibs?" She eyed me skeptically. "Don't do it if you don't mean it, a man like that looks like he knows how to use his..."

I glared at her, cutting her off mid-sentence. "Off. Limits."

"What's going on? You *never* call dibs."

I sucked in a ragged breath and blew it out slowly. Nancy would be relentless if I didn't explain, even though I really didn't want to get into it. "That's the guy," I whispered.

"*The* guy? From back home?"

I nodded.

"Fuck, he's hot. Why didn't you tell me he was so hot? What's he doing here?"

My shoulders slumped forward, it was hard keeping up the "I'm over you," posture. "Don't know, don't care. I told him to leave."

"Table seven!" Ned called out and I groaned.

Nancy reached the plate before I could. "Let me take this one."

I shook my head. "No, Nance. Please don't..."

"I'm not going to do anything."

"Nance..." I pleaded as she walked past me with a wink and a sparkle in her eye.

I didn't want to watch, but I couldn't take my eyes off of them. She set the plate in front of him, then put her hand on his shoulder. I bit my thumbnail as words were exchanged. Nancy was more than blunt. Every second Wes didn't storm out, jealousy dug her claws deeper into my chest. Especially when he threw his head back in laughter. *I used to make him laugh like that...*

I ripped my apron off and stormed through the kitchen. "I'm taking my ten!" I growled as I passed Ned, and ducked out the back door.

I paced back and forth in the alley, trying to make sense of everything I was feeling. Anger I understood. Sadness I understood. But jealousy? Why was I jealous? It's not like he's mine, I have no claim to him.

I rounded the side of the building and pulled my phone out of my back pocket, ready to call the one person who I thought had my back.

The back door slamming made me jump and I quickly shoved my phone back in my pocket.

"Em?" Nancy called out.

I took a deep breath to calm my nerves and stepped around the corner. I had no right to be upset with her, it wasn't her fault Wes was here, and it certainly wasn't her fault he was so damn charming.

"Hey, you okay?"

I shrugged, letting my shoulders drop heavily. "He gone?"

"Not yet, but soon. He's staying over at the Mountain Inn."

"Did he say why?"

She held her arms out beckoning me over. I wrapped my arms around her and rested my head on her shoulder, instantly letting go of my frustration with her and soaking in her comfort. "I figured that would be obvious."

"It's not going to happen. Doesn't he get that?"

"He loves you."

I sniffled, her words hitting me harder than I thought they would. "I love him too," I whispered. "But that doesn't matter. Not when he did what he did."

"And what's that?"

Sometimes it was easy to forget that I kept my two lives separate. All Nancy knew was what I told her when I got back. That my mom died and I let it slip that I was running away from a guy. I pulled out of her arms and wiped my nose with the back of my hand. "He cheated on me. With my sister."

"Ouch. Want me to kick his ass?"

I laughed, "No. I just want him to leave me alone. Go home, back to their daughter."

She sputtered, "They have a kid together?"

I nodded, "That's how I found out."

"I'm gonna cut his nuts off."

I had to hold her tighter to keep her from charging back inside. "I love you, Nance."

Wes was gone when we returned and I felt like I could finally breathe. I finished up my shift and went home to Mr. Jangles.

"Miss me?" I asked the cat, who had been extra lovey since I picked him up. He just meowed at me and jumped into my lap the second I sat down. I scratched him behind the ears while I pulled out my phone and finally called Miles. He answered on the first ring.

"Hey, Em."

"How *dare* you," I practically growled at him.

"How dare I what?"

"You told Wes where I live? Why would you do that?"

He sighed. "Em..."

"Don't *Em* me, Miles. Why? You *know* how I feel."

"And I know how *he* feels. You have to give him a chance to explain."

"I don't have to do anything!"

He sighed, then I heard, "Uncle Miles!" in the background. My heart clenched. My brother was taking care of their "love child" while he was here...

"Hey, Ellie," his voice was muffled like he was covering the phone with his hand. "Whatcha got there?"

I listened to their conversation, curious about the little girl, but unwilling to admit it. She was adorable, and looked a lot like me when I was little. It's what I imagined my daughter would look like. *Our* daughter. "It's daddy and the princess!"

"It's really good. Are you going to put it on the fridge?"

"I made it for the princess but I don't know where she is."

Miles chuckled. "How about we put it on the fridge until your daddy gets back and I bet he can help."

"Good idea!"

"Em? You still there?"

It took me a minute to get my emotions under control enough that my voice didn't crack when I spoke. "Why do you have her?"

"It's a long story." He blew out a breath and I could hear the conflicting emotions in his voice. "I need to get going, but promise me one thing?"

"What's that?"

"Give him a chance? Let him explain?"

"I'll think about it," I lied.

Wes was one of the first customers through the door the next morning. I refused to speak to him, maybe the silent treatment would get through to him. He couldn't charm his way out of this the way he did when he broke up with me when we were kids. A grand gesture, flowers, and a charm bracelet couldn't undo what he did.

He was back for dinner, and then breakfast the next day. And the day after that, and the day after that.

I leaned back against the wall, waiting for Ned to get his dinner ready when Nancy bumped me with her shoulder. "Did you hear?"

"Hear what?"

She nodded toward Wes. "Lover boy is looking for a job."

A weight settled in my stomach. "No."

"I heard from Lucy, who heard it from her cousin Mabel, who heard it from Tommy, who, as you know, works for Frank…"

"No. No, no, no, no."

"Afraid so. Doesn't look like he's planning to go anywhere."

I shook my head. "There has to be a mistake. He wouldn't leave his daughter. My friend Tatum says she's his whole world, and I've seen the two of them together. There's no way."

"Maybe he's bringing her here?"

The thought of Wes bringing Ellie and Kennedy here gave me hives. "No. There has to be a mistake." I pulled out my phone and typed out a quick text.

> **Me:** Do you know what's going on with Wes?

Tatum responded almost instantly.

> **Tatum:** Kind of?

> **Me:** What do you mean?

> **Tatum:** Have you spoken to him yet?

> **Me:** Does everyone know?

> **Tatum:** No, and we need to keep it that way for now

> **Me:** Why? What's going on?

> **Tatum:** Talk to him. Give him a chance to explain

I stuffed my phone back in my pocket and shook my head at Nancy. "Something's up, but no one will tell me what."

"You consider talking to him?"

"No. I can't." It wouldn't take much for him to undo all the progress I made since I ran. His presence alone was already making everything unravel.

When Ned called his order, I took his plate and set it in front of him, thankful he was on the phone and couldn't try to engage me in conversation. That didn't mean I didn't linger and overhear some of what he was saying.

"You're sure?" Pause "This Thursday?" Pause "I'll be there."

I hurried away before he ended the call and settled in next to Nancy against the wall. "Sounds like he has a job interview or something on Thursday."

"So he's staying..."

Butterflies swarmed my belly, whether in anger or hope, I didn't know. "Looks that way."

On Thursday, Wes didn't show up at the diner.

CHAPTER THIRTY-FIVE

Linford

PRESENT

Wes

Purple.

The old office space had been cleared out. The desk was replaced with a white toddler bed and matching dresser and nightstand. A bookshelf was pressed against one wall, full of all Ellie's favorite books, even a few new ones I had never seen before.

And then there were the walls - purple.

I dropped to the floor, sitting on the zebra-stripe rug beside the bed. "When did you do all of this?"

"The second you left to get your girl, I called Tatum. She and her husband came over and helped clear it out. Brandon and Miles painted while us girls went shopping," Angie was practically bouncing.

"I can't believe you did all of this..."

She crossed the room and sat down beside me. "That little girl deserves the world, and that all starts with you," she nudged me with her shoulder.

I scrubbed my hand over my face, "I didn't even think... I just..."

"Mitch hired a lawyer. He's not going to let this custody thing go easy, so this home visit is really important."

"I thought this was just an interview. I was just going to show them her bedroom at the house."

She shook her head. "That's Kennedy's house, you have to have your own space for her."

"And you're letting us use your place?"

"Of course!"

"But she's not even mine," My voice broke. I couldn't wrap my mind around why so many people would drop everything to help me get custody of a child that wasn't even mine.

"She's yours in all the ways that matter."

The front door slammed open and little feet came pounding down the hall. A second later the sweetest face I had ever seen filled the doorway. "Daddy!"

I barely had enough time to wipe the tears from my cheeks before she slammed into me, hugging me as tight as a 6 year old was capable of. I cleared my throat. "Hey, baby girl. I missed you!" I kissed her cheek, taking a moment to soak up her unconditional love. Miles appeared in the doorway a second later, and Angie quietly stepped out of the room, taking him with her.

"Do you like it?" she asked, pulling away and bouncing on her feet. "I got to pick my own covers!"

I looked behind me at the little bed, with its baby-blue comforter covered with fish. "Fish?" A pang of regret washed over me for having missed her discovery of a new favorite.

"Did you know that fish still swim when they sleep?"

I kissed her again, "I did not know that."

"And they breathe with their grills!"

"You mean gills?"

"Yeah, that!"

Her energy was contagious, giving me my second wind. I drove through the night, unwilling to miss seeing Ember Wednesday night at work, but needing to be home this morning for the home visit from child services. I would fight for her all day, every day, but not at the expense of my daughter.

The lawyer Miles and Lainey found filed for temporary custody, and part of that was proving I was a fit parent. I didn't expect Kennedy to contest it, though I probably should have.

The doorbell rang, and when I checked the time, it was 9:55. They were early.

I got to my feet and took Ellie's hand. "Come on, baby girl. We have some people to meet."

She hopped behind me, still spouting her fish facts. Guess she moved on from zebras...

Angie held the door open for the woman from child services. She had a bag slung over her shoulder and set it on the coffee table when Ang invited her to sit. "Can I get you anything?" she asked while I stepped into the room.

"A glass of water would be great."

Ellie stopped talking and hid behind me the moment she saw the woman. "Good morning," I greeted her, pulling Ellie up into my arms and sat in the seat across from her. "I'm Wesley Barrett. And this is my daughter, Ellie."

"Hi Ellie," the woman smiled warmly and some of Ellie's nerves seemed to settle. "My name is Katie."

"Hi," she whispered, lifting her hand in a little wave.

"I came over to talk to your daddy and see where you live. Is that okay?"

Ellie nodded.

"How does this work," I asked, trying to ease my anxiety. I had been a nervous wreck since Miles called.

"Well, I have some questions for you both, and I'll need to do a house inspection, make sure it's suitable."

"Do you need Ellie for any of this?" I asked, looking at my little girl who was trying to hide in my side.

Angie handed her a glass of water and excused herself to her room. "If you need me, just knock."

Katie took a long drink then set the glass on the coffee table. She turned her kind eyes on my little girl. "Ellie, would you like to show me your room?"

Ellie perked up, looking to me for permission. I nodded and she hopped off my lap. She was so damn excited about her new room that her shyness disappeared almost immediately. "Come see! I got to pick out my covers and I even have a zebra rug, but I don't love them the most anymore."

Katie chuckled, following Ellie into her room. Ellie talked her ear off about anything and everything, pulling books off her shelf and showing them to her. She asked Ellie a lot of questions about how she lives, what she does for fun, what sort of things she likes to eat. When they were finished "talking" Ellie tugged on my hand. "Can I have a snack?"

I squatted down to be at eye level with her. "Yeah. I still have to talk to the nice lady, can you ask Aunt Angie if she can help you?"

"Yup!" she was out the door in a second.

Katie picked up a couple of the books Ellie left out and put them on the bookshelf. "She seems like quite the handful."

I shrugged. "Sometimes? She's just... She has so much energy and gets so excited, it's contagious."

"I bet that gets overwhelming."

We left Ellie's room and settled back in the living room. "I wouldn't call it overwhelming. Sometimes naptime is wonderful," I laughed nervously, rubbing the back of my neck. "But even then, sometimes when she's napping, I just want to wake her up so I can experience the world through her eyes."

She cocked her head to the side. "You're not what I expected."

That caught me off guard. "I'm not?"

"Your wife..."

I held up a hand, cutting her off. "Sorry, I want to make sure I'm 100% transparent here. She's not my wife, and I'm sure you're aware that Ellie..." I looked to the kitchen where Angie and Ellie were busy making peanut butter crackers. I cleared my throat and lowered my voice, "She's not mine. Biologically."

Katie frowned and pulled out her paperwork. "That's not what her mother said." She flipped through her notebook. "She said her husband was trying to steal their daughter, but she was still hoping to work things out."

My spine went rigid and my fists clenched in my lap. I inhaled a deep breath and blew it out in a sigh. "It's a long, sordid story, and if you want to hear it, I'll tell you. But I won't lie." I stood and walked back to my room and picked up the folder of papers Miles gave me. I flipped through them as I returned to my seat, until I found the one I wanted; the one I added myself. I held it out to her, "I took a paternity test that confirmed what I always knew."

She read over the paper, clearly surprised with how her eyebrows rose. "But you still want custody?"

I nodded. "The moment I laid eyes on that girl, that was it. She may not have my blood in her veins, but Ellie's mine in every way that matters. I'll do everything I can to make sure she has the best life."

She cleared her throat, handing me back the paper. "*Kennedy* led me to believe you weren't involved in the child's life, and just wanted to take her so she wouldn't have her."

I steepled my fingers under my chin. "Did you observe Ellie with Kennedy?" I asked despite already knowing the answer to the question.

She shook her head. "The girls' grandfather was there and kept her busy while we talked."

"If I may ask you to do anything before a decision is made, it's this. Please observe Ellie with Kennedy. I don't want to say anything negative about her, she is the mother of my daughter, but... She's never around and when she is, it's like she's competing with Ellie for attention."

"I'll keep that in mind."

For the next hour I answered questions about my job, about what I do with Ellie while I'm working. I answered questions about Ellie's school and extracurriculars. I gave her a list of character witnesses, and even the names of her previous teachers and friends' parents, which was a long list of Tatum and Brandon.

Apparently Kennedy didn't have any of this information handy and promised to get it to her as soon as possible.

I walked her to the door and shook her hand. "Thank you for your time."

"It was my pleasure. It's rare to see a father so involved."

I looked over my shoulder in time to watch Ellie pull apart her peanut butter cracker and lick it clean. "Hey, Ellie? Want to come say bye?"

She hopped up and ran over, peanut butter smeared across her cheek. "Bye. Thanks for coming to see my room!"

Katie chuckled. "I am so glad to have met you."

Ellie beamed at her, then just as quickly raced back to her plate of snacks.

"Do you know when I might hear something?"

"I'm going to see if I can schedule another meeting with Kennedy and Ellie, and then I'll take my findings back to the court and go from there. Since it's a temporary order, you'll probably hear something by Monday."

I breathed out a sigh of relief. "Thank you."

"You're a good dad."

I squeezed my eyes shut and took a deep breath. Tears welled up in my eyes despite my efforts to push them down. "I really needed to hear that."

She patted my arm with care. "Talk soon."

I donned my work boots and tool belt the next morning when I showed up to work, only to discover that I had been fired. It wasn't like I just stopped going or skipped town without telling anyone; I spoke with the foreman and used my vacation days. Still, it wasn't a surprise.

The problem was that Kennedy's dad owned the company, despite never being there. After talking with Ang, it was obvious I was public enemy number one.

I hopped back into my truck and pulled away from the lot we had been working on for the past month. The housing complex was coming along nicely, but it still needed a ton of work. I should be furious, but I was oddly left with a sense of peace. Once I was about a mile away, I grabbed my phone and called Miles.

His voice was relaxed when he picked up. "Hey, man. What's up?"

"Did you know your dad was going to fire me?"

"Are you serious?" His calm broke immediately.

"Yeah, I'm leaving the job site now. Based on your reaction, I think it's safe to assume you didn't know," I laughed, though this presented me with a whole new issue. I had to have a job, something stable to even have a chance of being granted custody of Ellie.

"I had no idea. Shit, man. What are you gonna do?"

"Know anyone who's hiring?"

"No. Not around there anyway. There's a place up in Wickett that could probably use some help."

I blew out a heavy breath. "Yeah, that's not gonna work. I need to be close for Ellie."

"I know."

I flicked on my blinker and turned onto Main street. "I started looking for a job in Coyote Ridge."

"Seriously?"

"Yeah, there's a couple places up there that look promising. I told them I wouldn't be relocating for at least a month, but they seemed interested."

"So you're really doing it? What's Ember think?"

I pulled into Bob's Auto and parked on the side of the garage. I could only hope he'd take me back, at least for a little while. I leaned my head back and closed my eyes. "She doesn't know. She won't talk to me."

"Don't give up on her. She's stubborn, but I'm sure we can get her to come around. Especially when she realizes Kennedy is out of the picture."

"What if she doesn't?" The image of her running away when Kennedy put her arm around me at the funeral played in my mind on repeat. Add to that the photo Kennedy showed me from Kansas City, and I didn't have much faith.

"Don't worry about that right now. First we have to make sure you get custody of Ellie. Then we can figure out the rest."

"What if she thinks I gave up on her? I saw her, I was there, but I didn't get to tell her goodbye before I came back."

Miles chuckled. "Maybe that's a good thing."

"How?"

"She knows you chased her, she knows you care, and I'm willing to bet she's freaking out because you disappeared without a word."

"I don't want to freak her out. I just want her to give me a chance."

The drain pan made a loud scraping sound as I moved it into position beneath the old Honda Civic. I loosened the drain plug and watched from my creeper as oil drained into the black container. Nothing felt more like home than being underneath a car.

The office door slammed, followed by Bob's shouting. I stayed still under the car, hoping to go unnoticed. Last week when this happened, Mrs. Macmillan was certain Bob was screwing her over. It took about an hour to calm her down, and I just didn't have the patience for it.

"You can't be in here!" Bob shouted again, a second before a foot struck mine - hard.

"What the hell?" I rolled out from under the car, my eyes trailed up a pair of long, tan legs that lead to a short black skirt, and finally landed on one very pissed off Kennedy. I pulled up into a sitting position, using a rag from my pocket to wipe the oil from my hands. "What do you want?"

She shook a sheet of paper at me. "What do you think you're doing, Wes? The bank says they're gonna take my car!"

"And?" I pushed up to my feet and walked around to the other side of the car, putting as much space between us as I could.

"What do you mean, *and*? They said they haven't received a payment in a couple months!"

"Guess you better get on that then."

"*I* better get on it? Don't you mean you'll get it taken care of?"

I shook my head. "It's your car, Kennedy. Pay the bill." A month ago this conversation would have me sweating bullets and agreeing to whatever she said. Not anymore though.

"Stop screwing around, this isn't funny!"

I laughed, "It kinda is."

She stomped over to the car and held the paper out to me under the car's hood. "Just pay the damn bill."

I held my hands up, "Nope. Your car, your responsibility."

"But I don't have that kind of money!"

"Neither do I," I sneered, "especially since your dad fired me."

"Well you're the one trying to take Eleanor away."

I rolled my eyes. "Don't act like you care."

She huffed. "I do! She's *my* daughter!"

"She's *my* daughter too!" I snapped.

It had been two weeks since child services conducted their home visit. I thought for sure I'd know something by now, but my phone's been silent. I even checked with Miles, and nobody had heard anything. Maybe they were waiting for a time to do another home visit with Kennedy, like I suggested - where she had to interact with Ellie. I just wanted it to be over.

I want to take my daughter and run...

"Just come home, baby," she trailed her fingers down the column of her neck, between the edges of her button-down blouse, pushing them aside to reveal her full breasts, held up with a push-up bra from Victoria's Secret. I only knew because I did the laundry.

I arched an eyebrow at her, silently asking if she really thought that was going to work.

"Forget about this whole custody thing and come home. We can be a family! I know daddy will give you your job back."

"I don't want my job back, and I don't want you. I want my daughter, and I want my peace."

She dropped the letter from the bank on the engine and stormed off. "Pay it or else, Wes."

"Or else what?"

She grinned, one eyebrow arched. "Oh, baby, you don't wanna know."

As soon as she was out the door, I grabbed the letter and crumpled it up, throwing it across the garage into the garbage can.

Bob came back in, rubbing the back of his neck. "Sorry about that, she wouldn't take no for an answer and pushed her way in."

I shrugged, "It's fine."

"So you won't pay for her car anymore?"

I chuckled. "I never should have started. But if I'm going to take Ellie and leave Linford, I need all the money I can get." I rolled my neck from side to side to alleviate some of the tension. "I was already a couple of months behind since I had to rebuild my transmission. Besides, Kennedy is a grown woman - she can pay for her own car."

Bob clapped me on the back. "I'm proud of you, son."

"Thanks."

Chapter Thirty-Six

Linford

Present

Wes

It was quiet. Too quiet, and my nerves were already shot. Getting a call from Miles, asking me to head over to his place to meet the lawyer nearly sent me into a panic. At least Ellie was with my aunt. She wasn't happy about me leaving her again; ever since I got back from Colorado, she had been glued to my hip. It nearly broke my heart when she'd grab my leg and refuse to let go. I even had to take her with me to the garage a couple of times, set her up in the corner with a book, crayons and paper.

Normally I could promise her a visit with Jadon and she'd relax. That wasn't an option tonight, so I had to resort to bribery. She wouldn't settle for anything less than a banana split, with three scoops of ice cream, strawberries, chocolate sauce, whipped cream and cherries on top.

I didn't know where I was going to get it, but that was a problem for later.

I sat across from Aaron, my lawyer, at Miles' table. He slid a folder full of paperwork over to me and I flipped it open, cringing as my eyes skimmed over the legal jargon. "What's our next step?" I asked, closing the folder and pushing it aside.

"It took a while, but I finally got us on the schedule to see the judge. I know it's super short notice, but can you be in court the day after tomorrow?"

"What do I need to do?"

"The judge already has everything he needs, but he'll want to talk to you and Kennedy before he makes that final decision."

I nodded, "Yeah, whatever I have to do. I'll be there."

We spent the next hour going over what to expect. The more he talked, the more my anxiety ratcheted up. Some of this I already knew, but the intricacies were making my mind race through all the possible outcomes. I tugged at the collar of my t-shirt. "What happens if I win?"

"Then we file for permanent custody. There's a bit more to that process, but I'll make sure you're fully prepared."

I couldn't stomach asking what if I lost. That wasn't an option. I cleared my throat, "Thanks. I really appreciate it."

Miles pulled out a chair beside me and squeezed my shoulder. "It's gonna be okay. There's no judge in the world who would give Kennedy custody of a cat, let alone a child."

I wanted to laugh, but all I could do was nod.

Two days later, I found myself sitting in an uncomfortable chair in a courtroom, wearing clothes borrowed from Tatum's husband. Jeans and a button down weren't going to cut it. Thankfully Brandon and

I were close to the same size, and his slacks, shirt, and tie fit me well enough.

I leaned forward and looked past my lawyer, to the table on the opposite side of the room. Two expensive looking lawyers flanked Kennedy on either side. She was dressed up nicer than I've ever seen her before; a knee length black skirt paired with a green satin blouse. Her hair was pulled back in a sleek bun, and when she turned toward me, the smirk on her face sent my pulse racing.

My palms were sweating, and it felt like my throat was closing up. She looked relaxed; too relaxed. *Why was she relaxed?*

Aaron poured a glass of water from the pitcher on the table and handed it to me. "Drink this, it'll help," he whispered.

I took a small sip and set it aside. "Tell me the truth," I whispered. "What are my chances?"

He didn't get the chance to answer as the judge chose that moment to enter.

"All rise."

I stood, carefully smoothing my tie, and then we were seated. The judge looked from Kennedy to me, and back. "I understand we're here to settle the temporary custody of Eleanor Grace Barrett, is that correct?"

Aaron stood at the same time Kennedy's lawyer did, both saying "Yes, your honor."

He lifted a sheet of paper and adjusted his glasses as he read over it. "You filed for custody?" he asked, looking over at me.

"Yes sir."

"And the mother," he looked at Kennedy, "Is contesting. Is that correct?"

"Yes, your honor." Kennedy said, her voice sweet as sugar.

We sat in silence, the only sound the shuffling of papers as he flipped from page to page. If I wasn't so scared, I'd be pissed. He should have read through everything before he even entered the room.

But maybe he didn't have a chance since this was so last minute.

"The court appointed social worker paid a visit to each of your homes, and found them both to be suitable, but noted that she was not able to witness the interaction between the child and her mother." He removed his glasses and sat back. "Why is that?"

Kennedy started to speak when her lawyer put his hand on her arm and took over. "My client was prepared for the visitation, but when Mr. Barrett brought the child home, she had not yet had her nap. When the social worker arrived, she was asleep and it was not deemed necessary to wake her."

My head snapped over to Aaron, hoping he would call him out on his blatant lie. Katie told me Ellie was there and busy with her grandpa, not napping. Plus, I was still in Colorado when she had her visit... Aaron didn't say anything though.

"She had nothing but good things to say about her visit with Mr. Barrett, even going so far as to recommend he be awarded custody."

Relief flooded my veins, until he spoke again. "However, you're not the child's father, are you?"

My knee bounced under the table, trying to expel my nervous energy. "No, sir. I was led to believe I was until I decided to take a paternity test."

He leaned forward on his elbows, his bushy eyebrows furrowed. "And why would you do that?"

I cleared my throat as I stole a glance at Aaron. He looked just as confused as I was. "I just needed to know. I love Ellie more than anything in the world. It doesn't matter what that paper says, I'm her dad and she's my little girl."

He nodded as he leaned back in his chair, but his face gave away nothing. It was quiet for a couple of minutes before he put his glasses back on, looking over another paper. "Miss Davis, can you tell me why you told Mr. Barrett that he was the father?"

She leaned forward on her chair and grabbed a tissue from the box in the middle of the table. "I thought he was," she dabbed at her eyes. "You see, he was drunk and we..." she let the words trail off as she choked on a sob.

I wanted to scream; demand she tell the truth, but she was a good actress and the judge looked down on her with sympathy. Her lawyer placed a hand on her back, and I'd be lying if I didn't question just how well they knew each other. Had she slept with him too?

"In light of everything," the judge said, stopping my spiraling thoughts, "I'm awarding temporary sole custody to Miss Davis."

His words hit like a sledgehammer to the chest, effectively knocking the air out of me. Pain shot through my chest, leaving me paralyzed. The room faded away; voices became nothing more than muffled sounds as I tried to understand what just happened.

I lost. I lost and Kennedy won. Kennedy, who could win an award for world's worst parent, won. She's going to take her. She's going to take my daughter.

Oh, God. No. She can't. She can't have her!

I stared straight ahead, unseeing and shook my head while I clenched and unclenched my fists. I can't do it. I *won't* do it. Kennedy is going to have to pry her out of my cold, dead, hands. I'm not letting her go. *Ellie is* my *daughter!*

I never should have done it. I shouldn't have rocked the boat. I should have stayed away from Ember. I should have agreed to go home. I should have made the car payment, I should have...

I jumped as a hand squeezed my shoulder and I looked up to see the worry on Aaron's face. I shook my head. "No," I choked out. "I... I can't lose her."

"You won't. I won't let you."

"But she... He... How could he? How could he do that? How could he entrust Ellie's safety to that... that... that woman?" My voice rose with each word just as my pulse sped up.

"It'll be okay," he assured me, yet it felt like nothing would ever be okay again.

CHAPTER THIRTY-SEVEN

Coyote Ridge

PRESENT

Ember

The worn carpet felt itchy under my body, but I couldn't get up. I *could* but my mind wouldn't let me. Or maybe it was my heart.

"Why don't you just call him?" Nancy's voice came through my phone that I clutched over my head.

"I don't have his number."

"Bullshit."

"I don't. I deleted it when I left town the first time."

"You can't tell me you don't have it memorized." I could practically hear her rolling her eyes.

"That's beside the point." Excuses, any excuse would do.

"Serious question for you… What do you want?"

I rolled onto my stomach and pushed up onto my elbows. "What do I want?" I wanted to rewind time, back to before Wes cheated on me. Or maybe back to before I ever met him. Once a cheater, always a cheater. Maybe the cheating was a matter of time, and not just opportunity.

Instead of saying any of that, I answered, "I don't know, I haven't thought about that since...I don't remember when."

"Well, I think you need to figure that out before you do anything else."

"And just what am I going to do? There's nothing *to* do."

"You could call him," she laughed and I wanted to slap her.

"He's with my sister and *their* daughter. I left that pain behind."

"Two things, Em. Number 1, if he's with your sister, then why was he here? And number 2, if you're over it and want to leave it all behind, why do you care that he's gone?"

"I don't know!" I whined. It's been a month since I last saw Wes and as much as I didn't want to admit it, I *missed* him. Stupid, I know, since I refused to talk to him, but still. There was just something about him being here... "Maybe... maybe someone put him up to it."

"Like who? Your dad? Your sister?"

I barked out a laugh. "My dad would sooner see me dead, and Kennedy would gladly be the one to carry it out."

"You have a really fucked up family."

I laughed, though there was no humor in it. "There's a reason I don't talk to them."

"What about your brother? He's normal, right?"

"I've already tried him, but he's not answering any of my calls. I'm pretty sure he's pissed at me."

"Then I guess that leaves you with three options."

"Oh yeah? Let me guess," I held up three fingers, ready to tick them off. "I can go back to Linford. I can shut up and forget about him. Or... what?" *I could call Wes.* But what if he didn't answer? I don't think my heart could handle that...

"You can call Brent. I know he'd love to take you out again."

"No, not happening."

"But he's such a good guy. You even said so yourself."

"I did, and that's why I can't. I won't lead him on while I'm so mixed up."

"Fine."

As soon as Nancy hung up, I opened my texts, reading over the numerous messages I had sent to Miles over the past month. It wasn't like him to ghost me, yet that's how it felt. He hadn't ignored all my messages, but on the occasion he did reply, it was short; and he *never* answered my calls.

Was this how they felt when I ran away?

I sucked in a shaky breath and closed my eyes. I was so tired, but I couldn't sleep. Something was wrong, I could feel it. I just wish I knew what.

I swiped through my last few unanswered messages, racking my brain for something to say that I hadn't already texted. Maybe if I said something absurd it would get a reaction. I typed out the only thing I could think of.

> **Me:** Did you know that flamingos taste like chicken?

I dropped my phone on the coffee table beside me where I lay squished between it and the couch. *What sort of people actually ate flamingos... Was that like eating a puffer fish? Something done for the thrill?*

I didn't get the chance to ponder it long when my phone pinged with a new message. I quickly snatched it up.

Miles: Please tell me you aren't eating any lawn ornaments

Me: Not me, but you'd be surprised

I laughed to myself, then quickly typed out a new message, hoping he wouldn't ignore me since he was already on his phone.

Me: How is everything? You haven't been responding to my messages or answering my calls

Miles: Sorry, there's just a lot going on

Me: Are you okay? Lainey?

Miles: Yeah, we're fine

Me: Then what is it? Why is everyone freezing me out?

Miles: It's not you, but I can't talk about it

Miles: I have to go. Love you

Me: Love you too

I threw my arm over my face, burying my eyes in the crook of my elbow. What could possibly be going on that would keep him so busy he couldn't spend five minutes talking to me. And not just him -

Tatum too. She barely answered my calls, and her texts were always short.

I called Tatum, the phone ringing just once before going to voice-mail. I called again, with the same result.

> **Me:** Hey, everything okay over there?

I didn't expect a response, but my phone pinged almost immediately.

> **Tatum:** Yep, all good

> **Me:** Then why didn't you answer when I called?

I waited, and waited, and waited some more. Thirty minutes went by and still no response.

Hours later, when I curled up in bed, I was still no closer to an answer. Tatum never so blatantly ignored me. I stared up at the plain white ceiling as possibilities rolled through my mind. *Were the boys okay? Did something happen to Brandon?*

She said everything was good, but was she lying? Everything couldn't be good if she was ignoring me...

Were they mad because I ran again? It's not exactly running if I just went home, but... I sat up and scrubbed my hands over my face. Was it because of how I treated Wes?

I got up and tugged my bedroom curtains open and cracked the window. The fresh air combined with the glow from the moon usually helped me relax. I crawled into bed, letting the covers hang loose over my body. I closed my eyes, willing myself to sleep.

That nagging feeling that something was wrong kept growing. But what was it, and what could I do from so far away? *Did something happen to Kennedy?*

I rolled onto my side, focusing on the clouds that floated slowly across the moon, filtering the light that streamed in. I inhaled deeply, the scent of pine filling my nose, as I tried to make sense of it all. Wes and Miles would be upset if something happened to Kennedy, but not Tatum, so it couldn't be that. *Was it Ellie?*

As childish and ridiculous as it sounds, I really wanted to hate that little girl. From my brief interaction with her, I knew that was impossible. It was evident that Wes was doing the majority of the parenting. She was smart and sweet.

She said I was his princess.

I rolled onto my other side and flipped my pillow so the cool side was up and reached for my phone. I opened my texts and typed out a quick message, needing to know if my gut feeling was right.

> **Me:** Did something happen to Ellie?

> **Miles:** Sort of

Wes

Engines I understood. They were machines, built to function in a specific manner. They didn't require any sort of interpretation. Sure, there were nuances from one to another, but the mechanics were the same. Unlike the law.

The law was very specific, written in such a detailed manner that you had to go to school for *years* just to understand it. The law, like engines, shouldn't require interpretation. Yet, that's what happened. It wasn't black and white, or about right or wrong. It catered to whoever had the bigger wallet, whoever could tell the best lies, whoever was the better actress.

Sweat rolled down my forehead, pooling at the tip of my nose, threatening to drop with each crank of the ratchet. Engines I understood...

"Come on, Wes. It's after six and I'm not paying you overtime."

"Don't want it." I pulled out the spark plug, giving it a once over before grabbing one of the new ones I had set out.

"You've been here since seven this morning. You need rest."

"Five, and I'm fine."

"Five?"

I stood up to my full height, careful not to hit my head on the hood of the car I was working on, and rolled my shoulders. "I've been here since five. And I'm fine. I need to get this done."

Bob sighed, "Come on, you're gonna burn yourself out. Go home, get some rest, and don't come back for a couple of days."

"I'm good." I ducked back down under the hood.

"Damn it, Wes. I know you're hurting, but..."

I growled, "You have no idea, Bob."

"You can't keep going on like this!" He argued, throwing his hands up in the air. "It's been two weeks!"

"SHE TOOK MY DAUGHTER!"

"Working yourself to the bone isn't going to get her back!"

Rage vibrated through my body. I threw the ratchet across the garage, hitting one of the rolling doors. "She won't even let me talk to her!" I cried out. My knees buckled until I fell against the car, sliding down until I was on the ground. My nostrils flared and my breath came in short pants. I couldn't get enough air, I couldn't...

I dropped my head in my hands; no matter how hard I tried, I couldn't wipe the image of Kennedy dragging Ellie away from me from my mind. The way she grabbed her around the waist and yanked while Ellie held on tight, her little arms wrapped around my neck. Her cries for "daddy" as she was hauled away and buckled in the back of Kennedy's car.

I didn't know what to do. I wanted to hold onto her, to not let her go and keep her safe, but Kennedy brought a police officer with her... *Who does that?*

All I could do was tell her over and over how much daddy loved her, and that I'd see her soon. *When would soon get here?* I needed Ellie as much as she needed me. Maybe more.

"Are you appealing the decision, or filing for full custody? What's your next move?"

"I can't appeal a temporary order, but Aaron is filing the paperwork for full custody."

He hummed quietly in thought before asking the million dollar question, "How are you going to win?"

I lifted one shoulder in a half-shrug. "I don't know. I tried to do things the right way, to prove I was a good dad, but it clearly wasn't enough." I raked my fingers through my hair, tugging on the ends in defeat. There were only two things I could think to do, and neither sat right with me. "I could try to pay her to back off, to let me have Ellie," I offered, knowing there was no way I'd ever have enough money. Plus, Kennedy was smart, she'd never give up custody like that. She didn't want Ellie - she wanted power, control. She wanted *me.*

I'd never give myself to her, I'd sooner hire a hitman and risk prison.

"Pretty sure I don't pay you enough for that," Bob grimaced.

"I know, and I don't even think it would work." I rubbed the back of my neck, wishing I could ease the tension. "My only other thought is to play dirty. Dig up evidence of her being a bad mom, catch her on video or get enough witnesses that wouldn't turn on me and lie..."

Bob adjusted his hat, wiping the sweat off his brow. "Problem with that is nobody has ever really seen Kennedy with Ellie. She has avoided that child like the plague, unless she knew she would bring her positive attention."

"Do you have a better idea?"

He shook his head, "No, but I'll do what I can to help."

CHAPTER THIRTY-EIGHT

Coyote Ridge

PRESENT

Ember

"Don't look at me like that," I grumbled at my cat, lifting him out of my suitcase for the millionth time. I swear, every time I went to my closet or dresser, he crawled back in. He clearly knew I was leaving again, and wasn't happy about it. "It'll only be a few days." I couldn't afford anything more. I was already on thin ice with my landlord after paying last month's rent a week late.

I clutched Wes' hoodie, wanting to bring it with and leave it at home at the same time. Leaving it at home meant I wasn't ready to let him go, but bringing it meant the same thing - except it could also mean returning it and forcing myself to move on.

Do I want to move on?

I picked it up and brought the soft material to my nose, inhaling deeply. It no longer smelled like him; hadn't for a very long time, but if I closed my eyes, I could almost remember how it felt when my hands grazed the soft material while he wore it. I could remember grabbing the hem and pulling it up and over his head, so I could touch his bare skin - then later, pulling it over my head after crawling out of his bed.

I set it in my suitcase and zipped it shut, removing the temptation to leave it behind. At least this way I had the choice.

"You ready to go?" I asked Mr. Jangles as though he could actually answer me. When he didn't budge, I scooped him up and loaded him into his carrier. He meowed in protest. "Relax. You like Nancy's house, remember?"

I loaded him and my suitcase into my car and ten minutes later we were standing on Nancy's doorstep. Her grin stretched from ear to ear. "I can't believe you're going to get your man."

I passed the cat over to her, "He's not my man. Not anymore."

"But he could be again."

My heart thumped loudly with something akin to hope, but I had to keep my wits. It's been more than a week since I last heard from Miles or Tatum, despite my efforts to find out what was going on. I was tempted to call my dad or sister but hell would sooner freeze over.

"I don't even know where I'm going to stay," I worried aloud.

"What will happen if you just show up at your friend's place?"

I shrugged, "Before I'd have said she'd welcome me with open arms. But now...? I don't know."

"At least it's still summer. You won't freeze to death if you have to sleep in your car."

I grimaced. "Let's hope it doesn't come to that."

I assumed leaving town on a Sunday would mean less traffic. Unfortunately, I didn't account for the number of tourists leaving town first thing to get home before Monday came. Heading down the mountain was slow going at best and it took everything I had not to rage. But it was more than just bad traffic wearing on me. It was everything - Miles, Tatum, *Wes.*

When I was just a couple of hours away, before my phone service started to get spotty, I called Tatum.

"Hey, you've reached Tatum. You know what to do."

I hung up without leaving a message and called Miles. When he answered, I nearly ran off the side of the road. "Hey, Em. Everything okay?"

"Well, hello to you too," I snarked.

"Sorry..."

"It's fine. I just wanted to let you know I'll be there in a couple hours."

Silence stretched between us for so long I had to make sure the call wasn't dropped. "You're coming here? Now?"

"Yeah. That a problem?"

"No. No, it's fine. Does... Does anyone else know?"

His question caught me off guard. "I tried calling Tatum... What's going on?"

He blew out a long breath, "Call me when you get to town."

"Miles. Is everything okay?"

"Yeah. Yeah, everything's fine. There's just a lot going on."

"Okay. Well, I'll see you soon then."

I pulled up to Bob's Auto a couple of hours later. I spotted Miles, standing just inside one of the open bay doors. I drove right up to the door and rolled down my window as he approached. "What's going on? Why did you ask me to meet you here?"

"I need you to pull inside and turn off your car."

"What?" I looked at the open door, confusion and self doubt swirling in my belly. "I've never parked in a garage before."

"Just pull straight in, I'll guide you."

I managed to park without issue, only worrying about pulling in far enough. Miles assured me I was fine, but I didn't believe him until I was out of the car and able to see for myself. He pulled the chain secured to the metal door and slowly lowered it and locked it in place. Only then did he give me his full attention.

"What are you doing here?" He wrapped me in a tight hug, his words and actions feeling contradictory.

"I thought you'd be happy to see me."

He chuckled, "I am, it's just..."

I rolled my eyes. "There's a lot going on, yeah, you told me."

He pulled away and took my hand, tugging me toward the office door. "Come on, we need to get out of here."

I looked over my shoulder back at Carrie, "But, my car..."

"You don't need it."

"Yes, I do!" I yanked my hand away from him. "I'm not going anywhere until you tell me what's going on."

He scrubbed a hand over his face in frustration. "Ember, can we please talk about this in the car?"

"Why can't I have *my* car?"

"BECAUSE YOU SHOULDN'T BE HERE!"

My body jerked at the force of his words, and I suddenly regretted my decision to leave home.

"Damn it, Ember," he reached for me, but I took a step back, ready to climb back in my car and drive another eight hours straight home. "I'm sorry, okay? I didn't mean it like that."

"No, it's fine," I repeated the words that he said to me when I told him I was coming. "I'll just go."

"Don't." He reached for me again, and I took another step back. "I'll explain everything, but... We can't be seen here. *You* can't be seen here."

"Here? As in Bob's? Or here as in Linford?"

"Linford." He reached for me again and this time I let him take my hand. "I promise, I'll tell you everything, but can we *please* go?"

"I don't like this secret shit," I shoved him off.

"I'm sorry, it's just... Can we go?"

I crossed an arm over my stomach, gripping my other elbow. "Let me just grab my suitcase."

As soon as I clicked my seatbelt in place, Miles gave me another of his apologetic looks. "Can you lay your seat back?"

"This is ridiculous!" I threw my hands up in the air then did as he asked, leaning back so far I couldn't see outside. "Care to start talking?"

"Em..." He raked his hands through his hair as he pulled out of the lot. "I..." He took a deep breath, and blew it out slowly, like he was trying to buy himself time, or figure out what to say.

"Just say it, whatever it is. Is it about Wes? I can take it, you know..."

Confusion and disbelief flashed across his face in the brief moment he looked over at me.

"I'm serious."

He looked like he wanted to argue, but finally nodded. "Okay, well, Kennedy took Ellie away from Wes and won't let anyone associated with him see her. I'm lucky she still thinks I hate him."

"Don't you though?"

He shook his head, "No, not since I found out a few things."

"Like what?"

"You need to talk to Wes."

I threw my hands up, "I am so sick of that bullshit line!"

"Have you ever considered just *talking* to him?"

"I tried," I huffed. "Kennedy made it clear I wasn't wanted."

"Yeah, and since when do you believe anything she says?"

"You know what? Fine! Take me to his place then."

"Can't."

"What the hell, Miles? You've been on my ass to talk to him, and when I finally agree, you won't take me?"

"It's not about you."

"Then what is it? Why won't any of you talk to me?"

"It's complicated, but... We need to get Ellie back."

"So get her back."

He shook his head as he pulled up to his house. "If only it were that simple." He killed the engine and when I moved to put the seat up, he put his hand out to stop me. "Wait." He reached into the backseat and pulled out a black zipper hoodie. "Put this on, keep the hood up."

"You're joking."

"It's just a precaution."

I rolled my eyes, "I didn't come here for some covert op." I pulled the hoodie on just like he asked. He'd never give me answers if I kept pushing him.

I kept the hood up and my head down as I followed him into the house. As soon as I was through the door, familiar arms pulled me in for a hug. "Tatum?"

"Oh my god, Ember. I can't believe you're here!"

"What are you doing here?"

"Come on, everyone's in the kitchen."

"Everyone?" She looped her arm through mine and pulled me into the kitchen. I stopped dead in the doorway. "What's going on?"

Miles shrugged, "I told everyone you were here, and we need to talk."

I looked from person to person, my mind running wild with what could possibly bring everyone together at 7:00 on a Sunday night. I was not surprised to see Brandon, since Tatum was here, but next to him was Bob, then a few guys I didn't know. When my eyes fell on Miss Barrett, a sob broke loose. Lainey was beside me a second later, her arm wrapped warmly around my shoulders. She led me over to the table and pulled out the chair beside Wes' aunt.

Before I could sit, Miss Barrett was on her feet, pulling me into the warmest hug I'd had in years. "It's so good to see you. I've missed you so much."

"You have?" I wiped my eyes with the back of my hand. "I thought you hated me."

"Never. That nephew of mine though..." she chuckled and I couldn't help the laugh that burst free.

I looked over her shoulder at the three strangers. "Who are they?" I whispered in her ear.

She pulled back and looked at the men who were now standing. "This is Penn," she pointed to the man on the far left, "and that's Jazz. They're Wes' friends from Texas."

I nodded. I'd heard their names before, though I didn't understand what they were doing here, in my brother's kitchen. "Nice to meet you," I managed.

My eyes fell on the third man who stood with his hand held out. "I'm Aaron Mason. Wes' lawyer."

I quickly turned back to Miss Barrett, then to Miles, questions burning in my eyes. "Why does he need a lawyer? Wait..." I turned my focus back to his friends. "Where is he?"

Miss Barrett took my shoulders and gave me a gentle push, guiding me into the chair that had been pulled out for me. "He's at home. It killed him, but it's for the best."

I shook my head, looking around the table again. "Can someone start explaining?"

Miles and Lainey took the last two seats at the table while Tatum sat on her husband's lap. I wanted to ask where the boys were, but I needed other answers first.

It was Miles who spoke first. "I can't tell you everything, because some of this needs to come from Wes," he eyed everyone at the table, and they all nodded. It only pissed me off more that they all knew something about him that I didn't. I bit my lip to keep from snapping at him.

He explained the custody situation, how Wes filed for temporary custody and lost. How Kennedy took Ellie and refused to let anyone see her - except Miles. Anyone close to Wes couldn't get near her.

"Isn't that illegal? To keep her from her father?" I asked, looking at the lawyer.

"It's complicated," Miles answered for him.

I gestured around the table, "So what's this clandestine meeting all about? We're not in a Harry Potter novel..."

Tatum snorted, but everyone else looked confused. I just shook my head.

"We filed for full custody of Ellie," Aaron said. "But as I'm sure you know, Kennedy is a good liar and is good at getting people to lie for her. We can't go to court without concrete evidence that she's a bad mother, and we're having a hard time getting that."

"And what makes you think she's a bad parent?" I arched my brow. I didn't know anything about what happened over the past seven years, but based on how things looked at the funeral, Kennedy appeared to be the doting mother.

Miles shook his head, and Tatum's jaw hit the floor. "Have you met her?" Penn spoke up for the first time, his voice incredulous. "She has got to be the most self centered person I have ever met."

"She's never home," Jazz spoke up next. "I can't count how many times I was on the phone with Wes while he had a screaming baby in his hands. It was always the same story, Ellie was hungry, but Kennedy was gone and spent the grocery money on god knows what…"

"We set up a regular shipment of baby formula and diapers and shit so she'd be taken care of," Penn said with a shrug. "We couldn't send money, she always found a way to take it…"

"So, she's irresponsible…" I argued, "That doesn't make her a bad parent." I hated the way the words tasted the moment they left my lips.

"Wes quit the shop and took a job for your dad, making more money to support them. That meant leaving Ellie home with Kennedy." Bob shook his head. "One afternoon, Wes went home early and found Ellie screaming in her crib. Who knows when the last time she'd been fed or changed was and Kennedy was nowhere to be found. She stumbled in around 2am the next morning, drunk off her ass."

My jaw hit the floor. "You're kidding."

Miss Barrett shook her head. "After that, I modified my work schedule so I could help out, and Tatum started watching her when I couldn't."

My eyes snapped over to my best friend, "Why didn't you tell me?"

She laughed and shook her head, "Correct me if I'm wrong, but anything involving Wes was a forbidden topic…"

I cringed, embarrassed that I allowed my hurt feelings to negatively impact my niece, an innocent child. "I'm sorry. If I knew…"

"Don't," Lainey reached over and placed her hand on mine in support. "I may not have known you well back then, but the whole situation was hard." She looked around the table at each person who nodded their heads along with her. "I don't think anyone here blames you."

"I saw her with Ellie at the funeral, she seemed like she was okay with her."

Miss Barrett shook her head and placed her hand on my shoulder. "That little girl is so attention starved when it comes to her mom, she'll do anything."

"Okay, so why the sudden custody issue. They've been fine all this time, why'd he file for custody when he basically had her to himself anyway..."

Secret glances were shared across the table, and I knew exactly what they were going to say... "I need to talk to Wes, right?"

Miles nodded.

"Okay, so one more question... Why the hell have you all stopped talking to me?"

Tatum looked down, guilt written all over her face. Once again, Miles answered the question. "At first it was because we all knew what was coming and, at least for me, it was hard to not say anything. But Wes deserves to tell you everything. If I didn't talk to you, it wouldn't slip out..."

Tatum looked up, her eyes finally meeting mine. "Then, after he lost custody, we had to come up with a way to get her back."

"And that means not answering my calls? Why?"

"It's no secret that Kennedy despises you," Miss Barrett said, her voice full of sadness. "If she had any idea we were talking to you, that you knew..." she shook her head, cutting herself off.

"If she finds out we're talking to you, then she'll make extra sure we don't catch her being neglectful."

I rolled my eyes, "She won. She got the guy, and I left town. I don't even live here anymore..."

"But it's no secret that Wes still loves you," Brandon said, his voice full of conviction.

Hope once again swirled in my belly, but I had to push it down. I don't know that I could ever forgive him, but Ellie didn't deserve to lose him. "So what do we do? How can I help?"

Miles cocked his head to the side, "You want to help get Ellie back? Excuse my surprise, but why?"

Hurt sliced through me. *Was I really that bad?* I blew out an angry breath. "She's just a little girl! It's not her fault her parents are assholes."

Chapter Thirty-Nine

Linford

Present

Ember

I scratched my head; the wig Tatum bought me was itchy. "I don't know why I have to wear this stupid thing," I grumbled, smoothing down the long brown locks.

"You want to hide out the entire time you're here?" she asked, passing me a pair of sunglasses. "Besides, now we know - you look awful as a brunette."

"Rude," I laughed. "Do you think this is enough?"

She shrugged, "Probably not if someone you know gets close, but from a distance, yeah."

"Maybe I should just stay in." I adjusted the sunglasses, hating the way they made my face look. "Wes goes back to court in a couple of days and you still have nothing. What if I ruin any more chances?"

"I seriously doubt if you riding with me to pick up the boys is going to change anything."

We climbed into her car and I looked out my window the whole way to the library, wondering if anyone we passed could tell it was me. She parked and minutes later, the car was full of animated voices, talking about whatever book they were reading. Jadon pressed his face between our seats and crinkled his face. "Why do you look like that?"

I laughed, "It's a disguise."

"Like a secret agent?"

I nodded, "Something like that."

"Buckle up!" Tatum said, her voice brooking no argument.

She pulled out of the lot, but instead of taking a left to head home, she turned right. "Where we going?"

She sighed, "Kennedy left the house and Brandon doesn't think Ellie is with her. He's following her, but wants someone to check out the house."

I arched a brow at her, "Are you sure that's a good idea?"

She shrugged, "Yes and no. If Ellie's not there, then we can snoop around. Maybe we'll find something."

"We're going to Ellie's?" Jadon sounded so hopeful, I had to look at my friend.

Tatum met her son's eyes in the rearview window. "We're just going to stop by for a second, make sure she's okay." I gave her a curious look and she shook her head. "Kennedy won't let them play together," she whispered.

My heart broke for them both. To not be able to spend time with your best friend sounded like the worst kind of punishment.

We pulled up outside my childhood home. There were no cars in the driveway, or even on the street. "Park a couple houses down," I told her, putting my sunglasses back on.

"I won't be able to keep an eye on the boys…"

"You're staying in the car. I'm going to go in there and check it out."

"You sure?"

I nodded. "Yeah. I need to do this."

Tatum reluctantly parked a few houses down and I checked myself in the mirror. I still looked like me, but at a glance, I was a stranger.

With my head held high and my purse slung over my shoulder, I walked with more confidence than I felt. I knocked on the door, not expecting a response. Then I heard something. I pressed my ear to the door; it sounded like crying. I dug through my purse until my hand was wrapped around my keys. I always meant to throw out my old house key, but I could never bring myself to do it. Now I was thankful for it.

I stuck the key in the lock and turned it. "Hello?" I called out, pushing the door open. The crying stopped immediately. I closed the door quietly behind me and stepped softly down the hall. "Ellie? Is that you?"

I heard a noise coming from upstairs and turned to go up. The rest of the house seemed quiet, the thought of Ellie being here alone made my heart ache. "It's Ember!" I called out, hoping if it is her and she is alone, that she remembered me.

Just as I reached the top of the stairs, a little blonde head poked out of my old bedroom door. "I want my daddy!" she cried.

I rushed over to her and dropped to my knees. "Hey, there, sweet girl. Where's your mommy?" Tears pricked at the back of my eyes as I took her in. She was wearing a dirty nightgown, her hair a mess of tangles. *How long had she been like this?*

"I want my daddy!"

I reached out for her, and she took a step away, panic written all over her face. That's when I remembered I was wearing a stupid wig. "It's just me, aunt Ember," I said quietly, my fingers working on pulling the pins holding the wig in place from my hair.

"Ember?" She raised hopeful eyes to mine and my heart swelled.

"Hey, sweetheart. Are you here alone?"

She nodded, wiping her nose with the back of her hand. "I want my daddy."

"I know. And we're going to get him," I pulled her in for a hug, needing to offer her whatever comfort I could. "I have to make a phone call. Are you okay to wait here?"

She nodded, but wrapped her arms around my neck in a firm hold. I didn't want to let her go or to make the calls I needed to where she could hear me. Something told me it had been a while since she last ate, so I picked her up and carried her down the stairs. "You hungry?"

"Mmm hmm."

I set her in a chair at the table, but she still didn't let go. "I'm gonna get you something to eat, but to do that, I need you to let me go," I laughed. I kissed her cheek and she let go a second later.

"What do you like to eat?" I asked, pulling open the fridge. It was practically empty. I went to the cabinet, and it was just about the same. It didn't surprise me that Kennedy was this neglectful, but my dad lived here too...

When she didn't answer, I looked over my shoulder to find her crying quietly. Without any real options, I pulled down a jar of peanut butter and grabbed a spoon from the drawer. "Do you like peanut butter?"

She nodded. I twisted off the lid and scooped a big spoonful and passed it to her. "When I was little, this was one of my favorite snacks."

Her eyes got big as she took the spoon. "I like peanut butter crackers," she whispered. "My auntie helps me make them."

"She sounds like fun."

She nodded and took a hesitant bite of the peanut butter. It wasn't ideal, but it would hold her over for a few. I stepped out of the room and pulled out my phone. Tatum answered on the first ring. "What's going on, is everything okay?"

"She's here alone." I sighed, looking back into the kitchen, "She's dirty and it doesn't look like she's eaten in a while."

"Shit. What do we do?"

"*We* don't do anything. I'm going to call the police, and you're going to go home."

"But..."

"This is my family home. *Me* being here doesn't look weird. They might ask questions if you and the boys are here too."

"Em..."

"Plus, Kennedy doesn't know I'm in town, so she won't have the time or ability to spin it."

She groaned as I heard her engine roar to life. "You're right. I hate it, but you're right."

"Can you tell everyone? But they can't come over; just let them know that I think we have her?"

"Yeah."

The police arrived fifteen minutes later.

"Good afternoon, I'm officer Greer and this is my partner, officer Holloway."

I immediately recognized officer Greer. Back in school, he and Kennedy used to "hang out" In the back seat of his car, in the bathroom, even under the bleachers... I pulled my phone from my pocket and discreetly started recording; I didn't trust him.

"What's going on?" Greer asked.

"I just came home - well, to my family's home," I corrected when he gave me a look. "Things didn't go well the last time I saw my dad and I wanted to clear the air." I gestured for them to follow me to the kitchen. "Imagine my surprise when I unlocked the door and found my niece alone and crying."

"Where's Kennedy?" he asked, sounding like they were still *familiar* with one another. He made a show of walking around as though she was going to pop out from nowhere.

"I don't know. I've been here for about an hour or so and haven't seen anyone."

"What took you so long to call?" he arched his brow in suspicion.

"Well," a small hand tugged on the hem of my top and I looked down to see Ellie holding up an empty spoon. I took it, scooped up another dollop of peanut butter and passed it back to her. "My niece was crying and it took a little bit to calm her down. Then I had to look around and see if anyone was here. I called my dad and Kennedy - neither of whom answered their phones..." I didn't mention that neither knew my phone number and likely wouldn't have answered either way. "And Ellie was hungry. The fridge and cabinets are basically empty." I absently ran my hand over her tangled hair, feeling surprisingly protective of her.

"I'm sure there's a logical explanation for all of this," he started, but I cut him off.

"A logical explanation for leaving a six year old home alone for who knows how long? It's been at least an hour... who knows how long she was alone before I got here..."

While he tried making excuses, his partner was on his radio, calling child services and whoever else needed to be informed. "You don't need to do that," Greer told him. "I'm sure it's just some sort of misunderstanding."

I arched my brow at him, and turned to Holloway. "I'd really appreciate it if you'd continue that call." I held up my phone, showing them I was recording the whole thing.

I grinned as all the color drained from Greer's face, while Holloway just nodded and kept talking.

It took about an hour for Katie from child services to show up. Apparently she was the woman who did the home visits and interviews for their initial custody case. Pain was written all over her face as I led her to the living room where I had Ellie watching the Discovery Channel. She was quick to tell me it was her favorite, just like it used to be mine.

"How long has she been like this?" Katie asked.

"How do you mean, exactly?"

She sighed, "Dirty? Alone?"

"Hungry?" I added and she looked like she wanted to be sick.

"I recommended custody be given to Mr. Barrett." She frowned, wringing her hands while she spoke. "Something about Miss Davis just didn't feel right. When they awarded her custody, I prayed my gut was wrong."

I sat down next to Ellie and gestured for Katie to take a seat in the armchair next to us. "I don't want to speak poorly of my sister, but..." I shook my head. "Wes is a really good man, and a really good father," I was surprised by how genuine my words were; perhaps more so that I actually believed them.

"I gathered as much, but once I file my report, it's out of my hands."

"What do we do now?" I glanced at the TV and then to Ellie. She was fully engrossed in a documentary on dolphins, her eyes huge as she absorbed everything. I couldn't stop myself from wondering how my sister spawned such an amazing kid.

"Right now, we're trying to find her mother. I need to take a look around and talk to Ellie myself. Are you okay to stay for a little while?"

I nodded, "I'm not going anywhere until she's safe." I wrapped an arm around her shoulders and pulled her into my body. She relaxed into me instantly. "Should I call Wes?"

"Officer Holloway will make that call." She gave me a sad smile and excused herself to take a walk through the house.

I settled in and kicked my feet up on the coffee table. "What did I miss?" I whispered, running my fingers over her tangled hair.

"Dolphins use ec... ec..." she scrunched up her face and I grinned. "Ecocation," she finally managed, "to find stuff. It's like using sound to see."

I nodded, "Ah, you mean echolocation. That's super interesting. Did you know bats do the same thing?"

"They do?" She scooted to the edge of the couch and looked back at me. "Did you know some bats are like bears?"

The excitement in her voice was contagious and I found myself smiling my first genuine smile in what felt like months. "They are?"

She nodded fervently and hopped off the couch, "They sleep in the winter. I'll show you." She grabbed my hand and tried pulling me up.

"Sorry, sweet girl. We have to stay in here for now while the police look for your mommy."

She deflated and climbed back onto the couch. "I wish you were my mommy," she whispered and my heart ached for her.

I didn't know what to say to that, to this girl who stole the heart of the only man I ever loved. I had to change the topic before I let my mind wander to the "what ifs."

I pulled my purse onto my lap and started rummaging around in it until I found my brush. "Can I do something with your hair?" I asked.

Her little hands went to the top of her head, as though just realizing it was a mess. "My daddy always braids it so it's not so messy." She frowned, "Mommy doesn't know how."

"Lucky for you, I'm a pretty good braider."

She hopped up and settled on the floor in front of me. Her hair was such a mess of tangles, I didn't know where to start. It took a while, but I finally started to make progress when the front door flew open, slamming into the wall and making me jump and drop the brush.

"Ellie!" Wes' voice boomed through the house and Ellie was on her feet a second later.

"Daddy!"

She ran straight into his outstretched arms. The look of relief and pure love stung as I was reminded why I left in the first place. For so long, I blamed the baby - blamed Ellie. I blamed Wes for cheating. I hated Kennedy, but until now, I didn't really place any blame on her - after all, she was a child and that sort of behavior was in her blood.

The love pouring from him reminded me that he truly was a good man, and he'd never hurt me intentionally. He wouldn't outright cheat on me... so what did Kennedy do?

I picked up my brush and stuffed it back in my purse as I got to my feet. His eyes met mine as I walked past them and into the kitchen where Holloway was deep in conversation with Katie. "Do you need me? Wes is here, and I think I should go..."

Katie gave me a kind smile, and it made me wonder how much, if anything, did she know? Holloway pulled out a notepad and pen. "Can I get your number in case we have any followup questions?"

I rattled off my number and adjusted my purse higher up on my shoulder. As I walked out the front door, I pulled out my phone. "Can I get a ride?" I asked my brother as soon as he answered.

"Where are you? Where's Ellie? Tatum Called..."

"I'm at the house, but I can't stay here, it's…" I sighed, "Can you pick me up at Deja Brew?"

"They're closed. I can just swing by the house…"

"Wes is at the house with Ellie, and I just need to take a walk."

"I'll be there in ten."

CHAPTER FORTY

L'inford

PRESENT

Wes

I tugged at the constricting collar of my navy button down. Brandon's shirt fit the same way it had the first time I sat in this courtroom, but nerves had me feeling claustrophobic. Katie assured me everything would be fine, but I had a good feeling the last time I was here, and look how that turned out...

It's only been a couple of days, but Ellie still isn't sleeping in her own bed, too afraid I'm going to leave her. She doesn't understand that it wasn't my choice.

I stole a peek at the other table across the room. Kennedy sat sandwiched between two lawyers, her hands folded on the table in front of her. The corner of my lips tipped up as I zeroed in on her ink-stained fingers. I wish I had been there to see them load her in the back of the police car. I was informed that she didn't return home until sometime after midnight, and thankfully the police had someone watching the place.

Child neglect didn't sit well with officer Holloway...

I turned my head to see who all was in the room with me today. Miles and Lainey sat in the front row just behind me. I gave them a nod of appreciation. I couldn't have done any of this without them.

Penn and Jazz were a couple of rows back. It still surprised me that they flew out from Texas to be here for me. Angie sat just beside them, the three of their heads dipped close, quietly discussing something.

When my eyes made it to the back of the room, all the air escaped my lungs. Tatum, I expected. But not Ember. I still didn't fully understand why she came back to town, but I couldn't be more thankful to her. She saved my little girl, and if I get custody today, I'll owe it all to her. I swallowed past the lump in my throat when our eyes met. I didn't deserve her.

The bailiff's voice pulled me back to the front as he called out, "All rise!"

My stomach clenched as the same judge from last time took his seat. The doors opened in the back of the room and I quickly stole a peek. Katie from child services took a seat in the back of the room and gave me a warm, reassuring smile.

The judge didn't spend nearly as much time going through the papers this time, and when he looked up, his eyes met mine for just a moment before flicking over to Kennedy. "Miss Davis, I see here you were arrested two nights ago for child neglect. Would you like to clarify what happened?"

Her lawyer stood, smoothing down his tie. "My client has not yet had the opportunity to defend herself on this issue, and we would like to request a continuance until that matter is resolved."

"Considering the seriousness of these allegations, and the report I received from a Ms. Katie Jacobs, I think we can resolve this today. Request denied."

The judge turned his eyes back on me. "Mr. Barrett, where were you while the child was home unsupervised?"

Aaron stood before I could speak. "Your honor, my client was home, unaware of the circumstances involving his daughter. In the time since the temporary custody was ruled in favor of Ms. Davis, she has refused him any contact with his daughter. This includes any form of visitation or phone call."

The judge snapped his eyes to Kennedy, "Is this true?"

She nodded, but that wasn't enough for him. "Speak up," the judge commanded.

"Yes, sir," her voice was small and timid. She almost sounded like she was going to cry.

He settled back in his seat and pulled out a paper. "As you're aware, the child was questioned in the presence of Ms. Jacobs. I'd like to read what she said about her parents."

I sat up a little straighter. I knew Ellie was questioned, I approved it so long as Katie was present. Ellie was familiar with her and felt safe with her. Plus I trusted her to have Ellie's best interests at heart. I never thought to ask what sort of questions were asked or what she said... I was just glad to have my daughter back.

The judge cleared his throat, "Question: What types of things do you do when you're with your mom," he started. "The girl replied: I stay in my room with my books and toys." He looked at Kennedy, "Question: What does your mom do when you're together? The girl replied: I don't know."

It wasn't anything I didn't know, but having it said so bluntly in court hurt.

"Question: What types of things do you do when you're with your dad?" He turned his focus on me. "The girl replied: All sorts of things. We read books, or watch movies. Sometimes we play outside. On library days we go to the coffee place and he gets me my favorite muffin. Question: What does your dad do when you're together?" He shook his head, the corner of his lip tugging up as though he wanted to smile. "The girl replied: He reads with me and pushes me on the swings. Sometimes he lets me help him make lunch. One day we made grilled cheese, it was yum."

He took off his glasses and looked down at Kennedy. "Do you have anything you'd like to add?"

"Your honor…" Her lawyer started, but the judge cut him off.

"I'll take that as a no." The lawyer sat back down, looking like he'd just been scolded. "Mr. Barrett, can you explain to me why the girl would say these things?"

Aaron looked like he didn't know what to do as I stood up. "Your honor, I love that little girl, and I love spending time with her. She's the best part of my day, and even though she's only six, I feel like I learn something new from her every day."

"And you didn't coach her on what to say?" He arched an eyebrow, daring me to lie to him.

I shook my head. "One of the greatest things about kids is their honesty, and I encourage her to always speak her truth. Sometimes I don't like what she has to say, like when she told me my breath stinks in the morning, or when she decided country music was better than rock…" Quiet laughter filled the room. "It just means that I need to brush my teeth before I wake her up with kisses, and we have to compromise when we have dance parties."

The judge couldn't hide his smile this time. "Where is she right now?"

"She's spending the afternoon with her best friend, Jadon. He's the son of my good friends, Brandon and Tatum Williams." I turned around and nodded at Tatum. "Tatum is here today," I added.

"You may be seated," he said, shuffling through his papers again. "I received a couple of character statements, I'd like to read." He cleared his throat, "First, on the behalf of Ms. Davis: I have known Kennedy since we were children. She has a big heart and loves with everything she has. Her family comes first and she works hard to take care of them. When her mother was first diagnosed with cancer, she took a job outside the home to help pay the bills. This job kept her away more than she would have liked, but she always made sure everyone had what they needed. Kennedy is a good woman and a good mom. She deserves to prove herself fit. Sincerely Frank Greer."

I internally rolled my eyes. Leave it to her regular booty-call to provide a character witness statement.

"Can you provide proof of employment?"

Her lawyer stood, "Your honor, the work she provided was under the table, and therefore there is no record of it."

I grimaced as my mind ran through the types of "under the table" work Kennedy was qualified for.

He nodded and pulled out the next sheet of paper. "On behalf of Mr. Barrett, the author would like to remain anonymous." He cleared his throat, "Wesley Barret and I have a sordid past, and most would not consider us to be friends."

I frowned, trying to think of who all possibly wrote letters for me.

"Despite that, I can say with complete certainty that he is a man of honor and integrity. He has always worked hard to care of his family, for instance when he first came to Linford, it was solely to care for his aunt. She refused his help, being a stubborn woman, but he would not be deterred. When she was well enough to take care of herself again, he could have left, but he stayed. He found a job at an auto garage that had all but closed up. The shop owner could only pay him for part time work, but he spent every second of his spare time cleaning, fixing up, and even updating the computer system. He taught the shop owner about newer cars, and now that shop is once again thriving. When he found out he was going to be a dad, he gave up everything so he could be there for her. He cares for her like no father I have ever seen, not even my own. He listens to her, encourages her, and makes sure she always has everything she needs. This custody battle should have beaten him down - when he lost her, he also lost his job, but as I have learned, nothing can keep Wesley Barrett down. He had a new job the next day and spent every moment thereafter trying to find a way to see his girl - who was kept from him. He is the best man I know, and Ellie deserves to grow up being cared for like only he can."

By the time he set the letter down, I had lost the ability to see through the tears that welled up in my eyes. Only one person could have written that letter, and I'd give almost anything to prove to her that I was the man she wrote about. Aaron discreetly passed me a tissue and I dabbed the tears away, not even caring who saw. And based on the glare coming from the table across the room, someone saw. When I looked over, my eyes met Kennedy's, but I felt nothing.

"Based on everything presented here, I'm granting full custody of Eleanor Grace Barrett to Mr. Barrett. Ms. Davis, if you'd like visitation, I'm going to ask that you file a separate request, after your other case is resolved."

Part of me felt bad that I was taking her daughter away from her, but that feeling quickly dissipated when she showed no reaction to losing. "Mr. Barrett, will you be seeking child support?"

I looked at Aaron, we hadn't discussed this, but I didn't want anything from Kennedy. I shook my head and he stood and answered for me. "No, your honor."

The judge nodded. "One last thing. Mr. Barrett, I'd highly recommend you formally adopt your daughter."

CHAPTER FORTY-ONE

Linford

PRESENT

Ember

The judges' words played on repeat in my head. "I'd highly recommend you formally adopt your daughter." What did that even mean?

I was so distracted I didn't even realize when Tatum pulled into a spot at the grocery store. "I'm going to run in and grab some ice cream, you know those little cups with the wooden spoons? Ellie and Jadon love them..."

"What?"

She arched her brow. "We're celebrating. Miles already grabbed a bunch of burgers and hot dogs just in case. But now that we know for sure, I'm getting ice cream."

"Hey, what did the judge mean?"

She paused with her door pushed open. "What?"

"He said Wes should adopt Ellie. Why would he say that?"

"He said that?"

I rolled my eyes. "Don't play dumb. We both know you're not. Now tell me."

She got out of the car and slung her purse over her shoulder. "Let's get that ice cream. Oh, and cookies. We definitely need cookies."

I got out and practically had to jog to keep up with her. "Tatum!" I snapped.

She spun on her heel. "I can't, Em. I promised."

"Promised who?"

Her shoulders slumped, "Don't ask me," her eyes pleaded. "I don't want to lie to you."

I threw my hands up. "Then who do I ask?" I groaned, "Talk to Wes, right?"

She nodded and turned toward the bakery. "Cookies and ice cream. Anything else?"

It almost shocked me at how easily she deflected and changed the subject. She was good at it before, but something told me being a parent made her even better.

There were already several cars parked outside of Miles' house when we arrived; a plume of smoke drifted steadily up from the back yard. No sooner had I set foot in the house than I had little arms wrapped around me. "It's the princess!" Ellie shouted, looking up at me with the biggest smile, a stark contrast from the last time I saw her.

"She's no princess, she's a spy!" Jadon shouted from across the room.

"No way! My daddy said she's his princess!"

"Hey, there Ellie," Wes appeared as if out of nowhere. "Why don't you guys go play out back?"

"Okay!" they both shouted in unison, and then they were gone.

I suddenly felt awkward and out of place, holding a bag of cookies in the middle of the living room. Wes didn't look any more comfortable with his eyes turned down, his hand rubbing the back of his neck. "Hey," I managed.

"Ember, I..." His eyes met mine and he blew out a heavy breath, like he didn't know what to say.

"What did the judge mean?" I asked.

He cocked his head to the side, "The judge?"

"He said you should adopt her. What does that mean?"

His body tensed and his Adams apple bobbed when he swallowed. "We, uh..." He gestured to the living room. "Can we talk?"

I dropped the bag of cookies on the coffee table and sat on one side of the couch while he took the other, careful to keep space between us. "What don't I know, Wes?"

His knee bobbed at a steady pace and he raked his hand through his hair, "I've thought about how I'd start this conversation a million times, and now that you're here..." he shook his head. "I don't even know where to begin."

"How about with what the judge said?"

He took a deep breath and quickly looked away when our eyes met. "Ellie's not mine."

The words hit like a punch to the gut. "What?" I barely managed.

He leaned forward, his arms resting on his knees with his head hung low. "She's not mine, Ember. I..."

"She's not yours? But..." I shook my head. "I don't understand."

He sat up and started to reach for me, then pulled his hand back. "Fuck, Ember, I wanted to call you, to tell you, but..."

"I blocked you then changed my number," I said mechanically, my brain still not registering his words. *Ellie's not his. He never cheated on me.* I inhaled sharply, tears stinging my eyes as the last seven years caught up to me. "How long have you known?"

"I don't know... I guess since the beginning. I knew in my heart that I never would have cheated on you, *especially* with her, but... she got in my head, and then you ran."

It would be so easy to forgive him, but things didn't quite add up. "What about Kansas City? I saw her leaving your room, Wes. She had a picture..."

"I can't tell you how many times I ran that night through my mind, trying to make sense of it all. The last thing I remember was carrying you back to your room and putting you to bed before returning to mine. I finished that damn bottle and passed out."

"So you don't remember getting into bed with my sister?" I scoffed.

He shook his head and rubbed his hands down his thighs. "I wish I could say that never happened, but I'll never lie to you. I didn't... I mean..." He groaned and raked his hands through his hair. "You've gotta believe me, I didn't know."

I shook my head and moved to get up and he reached out to stop me. "Just... Wait, don't go."

My heart hammered in my chest. "Why? I'm not doing this right now. I shouldn't be here, I don't belong."

"Please, Ember. I'm begging you, just let me explain. I'm not good at this," his voice wavered.

I studied his face, his wide eyes, and the hard set of his jaw. "Explain. But no bullshit, Wes. I mean it."

He nodded, "Yeah, okay." His knee started bouncing again, "So, that night... You don't know this about me, but I'm a heavy sleeper, just ask Ang. She once had to dump a glass of water on me to wake me up when shaking me didn't work. Add alcohol to that, and I'm not sure even the water would have worked," he laughed with a shake of his head. "Like I said, after I got you to bed, I finished the bottle. The next thing I remember was waking up, face down, with no covers."

"So when did you invite Kennedy in?" I arched a brow at him, daring him to lie to me.

"I didn't know about the picture. I didn't even know Kennedy was in my room until the day of your mom's funeral when she told me everything. She showed me the picture," he grimaced. "I'm so sorry, Em, I know why you ran away, and I don't blame you. I would have done the same, or worse..."

"So how'd she get the picture then?"

"You were right when you said Kennedy was possessed by Satan. She has a sick vendetta against you, and she used that opportunity to strike. Sometime after I put you to bed, she took off and hooked up with some guy. She said the condom broke and he freaked out and bought her a Plan B and dropped her off. Except, when she went back to the room, she realized she grabbed my room key by mistake."

"So that guy... He's..." I gestured toward the back of the house where Ellie was playing, "the dad?"

Wes nodded. "Yeah. Kennedy said she came into my room, I don't know why exactly, but she decided to climb into bed with me and take that stupid picture."

"And your arm around her?"

He leaned forward, his hands folded together in his lap. "I had no idea, I was passed out, I never felt anything. I wasn't even facing her..."

"Why didn't you fight for me?" It was irrational; I didn't give him much opportunity.

"I wanted to. I tried to find you. I had a plan, I was going to demand a paternity test, we just had to wait a couple more months..."

A tear slipped down my cheek and he was beside me a second later, swiping it away with the pad of his thumb.

"You were gone, and I didn't know how to find you. Kennedy was so far in my head I didn't even know what was real. And then I saw her, Em. This beautiful baby girl and I fell in love. She was so small and helpless... I couldn't leave her; not with Kennedy."

"Why didn't you tell me sooner?" I looked up into the depths of his gunmetal blue eyes.

"I didn't know how to find you. When I found out Miles knew where you were, I tried to get him to tell me, but he wouldn't."

"Even though..."

He shook his head, "He didn't know. I... I had an official paternity test taken, but I only told Bob and Ang. They didn't think it was a good idea to tell anyone; we were so afraid of Kennedy taking her away... I only told him a couple months ago."

I nodded, everything started to make a little more sense. "That's why he kept pushing me to talk to you."

"He was?" His calloused hands cupped my cheeks, his thumbs pushing away tears that wouldn't stop falling.

I closed my eyes, unable to look at the love and care on his face. I nodded as a sob broke free. "I'm so sorry."

He pulled me into his body, his strong arms holding me while I cried on his shoulder. Tears streamed down my face, soaking his shirt while my body shook with the force of my pain.

"Shhh," he whispered, his hand stroking up and down my back. "Don't cry, baby. Don't cry."

"I ruined us."

He pressed a kiss to my temple, the gentle touch reminding me of all the things I lost. "You didn't ruin anything."

I buried my face in the crook of his neck, his familiar woodsy, spicy scent calming my tears. I pulled back enough to look into his eyes and sucked in a ragged breath. "I still love you, Wes. I never stopped."

Relief washed over his face just before his mouth crashed into mine. His lips were soft, but firm, and when I parted my lips it was like no time had passed. He still felt like my Wes, *tasted* like my Wes.

I wrapped my arms around his neck as I crawled onto his lap; his hands settled on my waist, holding me tight to his body. He broke the kiss, his lips trailing across my jaw and down my neck and I threw my head back, giving him more access.

"I love you," he whispered just before bringing his lips back to mine. "I love you so fucking much."

I gripped his shirt, needing to hold onto something, afraid he would disappear and this would all have been a dream. Kissing Wes was like coming home and I never wanted to leave.

A gasp sounded behind me and I froze. Wes chuckled, tilting his head slightly so he could see our audience. I cringed the second I heard Ellie's voice. "Daddy?"

"Hey, baby girl. I thought you were outside playing?"

"Yeah, but... What are you doing?" I buried my face in his chest, mortified at being caught by his daughter.

"They're kissing. My mom and dad do that *all* the time." I couldn't help the laugh that bubbled out at the disgust in Jadon's voice.

"Why don't you two go back outside so I can finish talking to Ember, and I'll come find you in a couple of minutes." His arms gripped me tighter, his hands tracing up and down my spine in a soothing motion.

"Can we have bubbles?" Ellie asked.

"You sure can."

Giggles and thundering footsteps disappeared down the hall while Wes' chest vibrated with laughter.

I pinched his side, "It's not funny!"

He kissed my forehead, the action so natural. "It's kind of funny."

The interruption was a stark reminder that we weren't those people anymore. We were both adults, living very different lives. I lived in Colorado, and he lived here with his daughter. He was a single dad, with family and friends. I was just... me. The loser girl who never finished high school and still hadn't gotten her GED. Who still scraped by working in a diner and spent her free time talking to a cat named Mr. Jangles. I groaned, "Wes, what are we doing?"

"What we should have been doing all along," he pressed his head to mine, "I never should have let you go, and now that I've found you, I'm holding on."

"This is crazy!" I pulled away from him, awkwardly getting off his lap, wincing the moment I saw the bulge in his pants... "We don't even know each other anymore."

"Don't do this," he pushed his hair back away from his face; my fingers itched to run through it, but I had to restrain myself. Nothing good could come from this. Wes wasn't mine, despite how much we still wanted each other. It would be so easy to fall back into the way things were, except we weren't those people anymore.

"What am I doing?"

He dropped his head into his hands. "You're shutting me out, running away before we even have a chance."

I crossed my arms over my chest. "No, I'm not," I lied. "It's for the best," I whispered, but I don't know who I was trying to convince - him or me.

He shook his head as he glared at me. "I can't do this right now." His muscles tensed as he got up and stormed from the room.

I stared unseeing at the floor, jumping when the slamming of the back door echoed through the room. I blew out a shaky breath and when I looked around, I was alone. If I listened carefully, I could hear muffled voices and laughter, another reminder that I didn't belong.

I picked up my purse and slung it over my shoulder as I walked to the back door. I stood off to the side, out of sight, and peeked outside. Tatum and Brandon were sitting at a table in the yard with Angie and Wes' friends, Jazz and Penn. The kids were running around, holding up sticks like they were magic wands.

Over by the grill, Miles had one arm wrapped around Lainey and a beer in his other hand. He was talking animatedly with Wes, who popped the lid on his own bottle of beer and tapped it against my brother's. Miles must have said something funny because a moment later, Wes' head was thrown back in laughter.

It didn't take him long to get over our argument, if you could even call it that.

I backed away quietly and slipped down the hall to the room I've been staying in. "It's better this way," I whispered to myself as I dropped down heavily onto the bed.

I gathered some clothes and made my way to the guest bathroom, where I turned on the shower as hot as I could get it. I stared at myself in the mirror as I waited for the water to heat. It was weird being back here, surrounded by people I used to know, who *knew* me. Now we were all older and they seemed closer than ever. They didn't need me.

I stood under the hot spray, my mind flooded with memories of happier days. Days I always told myself were long gone. Days that could have continued if I hadn't been such a coward; if I had just trusted him. If I had just confronted him...

I was a fool, and it seemed running was what I did best.

I stepped out of the shower when the water ran cold and quickly toweled off. I dressed in an oversized t-shirt and shorts and gathered all my things. Back in my room, I laid my suitcase out on the bed. Right there on top was Wes' hoodie. I pulled it out and brought it to my nose, disappointed once again that it no longer smelled like him.

I set it aside along with clothes I would wear tomorrow, then began to meticulously pack everything away. The sooner I got on the road, the sooner I could start picking up the pieces of my life.

The sun was still shining when I crawled under the covers, though clouds were starting to roll in. It sent a cool breeze through the cracked window, and when I inhaled, I realized that it didn't smell like home. Home was 500 miles away. "You're doing the right thing," I whispered to myself, over and over again, until my eyelids were too heavy to keep open.

CHAPTER FORTY-TWO

Linford

PRESENT

Ember

I squinted my eyes against the sun; its warm rays baking me through the black cap and gown we all wore. I looked out over my peers and smiled. "Isn't it funny, that when we were young, school was exciting, and if you were anything like me, you couldn't wait to go. Weekends were too long, and the weeks too short. Then as we got older, it all changed. Our weeks were too long and weekends too short. We counted the days until summer break, and then pushed all thoughts of school aside until it was time to do it all over again.

"For some of us, this is the end of the line, heading off into the real world; taking jobs or joining the military. Then there's those of us who have decided to start the whole process over again, heading to college. I *don't know about you, but I'm excited and can't wait until school starts in the fall," I laughed along with my classmates.*

"The thing some of us forget though, is that school has always been about more than learning English, math, history, and science. It's also been a place of discovery. Do I like playing sports or singing in the choir? Am I really cut out for politics? Does that top really go with those shoes?" I grinned as laughter filled the air.

"As your valedictorian, I just have one more thing to say. In the famous words of Panic At The Disco, 'Hey Look Ma, I Made It."

Cheers and applause erupted all around me and my chest swelled with pride. I looked out beyond my classmates to the seats filled with friends and family. I smiled as soon as my eyes locked on Wes. I stepped down from the podium, careful not to trip over my gown. I looked back up to get another eyeful of my man as I made my way to my seat and came up empty. He was gone.

Instead of returning to my seat, I kept walking, scanning the crowd for where he could have gone. Movement caught my eye and when I looked, Wes was there, hurt lining his features. He turned his back to me, walking away from me, moving deeper into the crowd. I grabbed a fist full of my gown and picked up my pace, running after him. "Wes! Wes, wait!"

I sat up as a flash of light shot through the room followed quickly by a clap of thunder. The curtains blew wildly, and I jumped out of bed, slamming the window shut. I stared out at the rain pelting the glass, the details of my dream slipping away. A stab of pain radiated from my chest and I rubbed at it with the heel of my hand. While the speech, the people, even the podium faded away, the look on Wes' face never did; anger, hurt, betrayal.

I ripped off my sleep clothes and pulled on jeans and Wes' hoodie. I slipped on my shoes, grabbed my keys, and hopped in my car.

The weather was bad and getting worse, the rain so heavy my wipers couldn't keep up. By the time I made it to Wes' house, the streets were flooded.

I got out of my car; I was soaked through before I even made it to the house. I rang the doorbell and waited. I rang it again, and then again, a second later. No one answered.

I pulled open the screen door and pounded on the wood door, "Wes! Wes! Please! I need to talk to you!" I shouted as loud as I could. I pounded until my hand ached, then pounded some more until I saw a light flick on. "Wes!"

CHAPTER FORTY-THREE

Linford

PRESENT

Wes

I turned the lock and pulled open the door. "Ember?" Rain fell in sheets, a river of water racing down the street, spilling up and over the sidewalk. "What are you doing here?"

"I-I needed to see you." Her teeth chattered as she huddled in on herself.

I opened the door a little wider and reached out for her, "Come on, you're soaked."

Her shoes squelched with every step as she followed me down the hall. I led her into my room. "Wait here." I hurried down the hall, first making sure Ellie's bedroom door was shut, and then grabbed a couple of towels from the linen closet. I stood outside my bedroom door and sucked in a lungful of air that wasn't contaminated with the smell of honeysuckle and oranges. I knew once I breathed in her sweet, sweet scent, my ability to remain level headed would fly out the window.

I wanted Ember, but I couldn't keep putting myself out there, only for her to run. I deserved more, and so did Ellie. If she didn't want me, *us*, that was fine. We had enough friends and family without her. At least that's what I told myself.

I quietly pushed the door open and found Ember standing right where I left her. She hadn't moved a muscle. I slowly took her in, from her soaked shoes, and damp jeans, the oversized hoodie, all the way to her sopping wet hair that clung to her face and neck before trailing down over her shoulders. She looked like a drowned rat, but was still the most beautiful woman I had ever seen. Her eyes appeared haunted following my every move.

A shiver ripped through her and I realized I was still holding the towel. "Here," I handed it to her and took a step back, putting necessary space between us.

Her hands trembled as she took it, whether from the cold or nerves, I didn't know. "Thank you," she whispered.

I took another step back, crossed my arms over my chest, and leaned against the closed door. I wanted to be mad at her. I *was* mad at her. Today was supposed to be a celebration. Instead it felt like I was trading one part of my heart for another, and I wouldn't give Ellie up for anything - not even her. "What do you want?" I asked again, the need to protect my heart outweighing pleasantries.

Her hands, still clutching the towel, dropped to her sides. Slowly, she brought her eyes up to meet mine. I looked away. "Wes..." Her voice was quiet, pained.

My fingers twitched to reach out for her, to comfort her like I had so many times before. I clenched my jaw and dug my fingers into my biceps to keep myself from doing something I'd regret.

"I... I'm sorry," she whispered, moving a step closer. "I-I don't want to run anymore."

My eyes snapped up to hers. She still held that haunted look, but there was something else there too. "What?"

She took another slow step toward me, "I don't want to run anymore."

Hope flared in my chest, sending a rush of heat all the way to my fingertips. When it came to her, all I did was hope; hope she'd come back, hope she'd forgive me, hope she'd realize that I was worth the effort. Then Miles helped me realize something. I don't need her forgiveness - I didn't do anything wrong. I just needed her to see beyond her fear and anger.

It would be so easy to close the space between us, wrap her in my arms, kiss her, and make promises for the future. If I learned anything over the past several years, it was that easy was rarely the right choice. I held a hand out to stop her from coming closer. "Don't."

She halted her movement. "Wes, please." She blew out a heavy breath and looked down at where her fingers clutched the towel. "I have spent the last seven years trying not to love you. I was so angry, so hurt that I never stopped to think about how you felt."

I swallowed around a lump in my throat as she brought her eyes back up to mine, looking up at me through dark lashes. "You've always been there for me, even when I didn't deserve it, and I repaid you by running, hiding, and painting you in a bad light."

While her words sought out the chinks in my armor, her eyes burned straight to my soul. My pain was reflected back at me from the depths of those cornflower blue eyes. "Em..."

"Watching you walk away from me today hurt more than when I thought you betrayed me."

Cool fingers brushed over the stubble on my jaw. I shuddered, exhaling a shaky breath. "Don't do this unless you mean it."

"I don't want to run anymore."

"Don't play with me," I whispered, covering her hand with my own.

She shook her head. "No more games, no more running."

I searched her eyes for any trace of a lie; my heart clenched when I found none.

"I love you," she whispered. The last of my armor chipped away and I crashed my mouth into hers.

The kiss was frantic, I couldn't get close enough to her. She tugged at my shirt and I ripped it off over my head while I gripped the hem of her sweatshirt and pulled the soggy material up and over her head, dropping it to the floor. A shock ran though my body when her frigid skin pressed into mine. I was a bumbling idiot when I reached around to unclasp her bra and met bare skin.

"No bra?" I grinned against her lips. I swear I could see her blush, even in the dark.

"Shh," her fingertips tugged at the waistband of my sweats, "Less talking, more kissing."

I fumbled with the button on her jeans; the material was so wet I had to drop to my knees and peel them down her legs. I pulled her shoes off, then was finally able to rid her of her pants.

I looked up the length of her body from where I knelt in front of her until I met her eyes. I slowly ran my hands up her thighs, pressing soft kisses along the way. "You're so beautiful," I gripped her waist and pressed a kiss to her belly. Her hands came down and smoothed through my hair as she held me against her smooth skin.

I rose to my feet, my fingers trailing over her ribs until they met the swell of her breasts. I flicked my finger over her hardened nipple, earning a moan, so I did it again.

She wrapped her arms around my neck and whispered in my ear, "I love you, Wes."

I gripped her under her ass and lifted, her legs automatically wrapped around my waist. I carried her to my bed and laid her down, her blonde hair, still damp from the rain, splayed over my pillow just like it had in so many memories. "I love you so much."

I settled between her legs, holding myself up with one arm on either side of her head. "Are you sure?"

She nodded and I pressed my forehead to hers. "There's no going back for me. If we do this, then that's it, you're mine."

"I want you, Wes. Forever."

I reached across the bed, needing to feel Ember's smooth skin beneath my fingers. Instead, I found nothing but the cold mattress where she had been just hours before, sated and happy. I sat up and looked around the room. There was no sign that she had ever been here; I was alone. I fell back into the comfort of my pillow and scrubbed a hand over my face. *Was it all just a dream?*

I blindly felt around the nightstand until my hand closed around my phone. I brought it to my face and grimaced. "Shit!" It was after ten, I should have been up hours ago with Ellie.

I hopped out of bed and it was not lost on me that I was completely naked. I grabbed my discarded sweats and tugged them on along with the first shirt I saw. As soon as I yanked my bedroom door open, I was hit with the smell of pancakes and bacon.

Quiet giggles filled the air as I stepped lightly down the hall. *Angie skipped work today,* I told myself, setting my expectations. If I allowed myself to hope and I was wrong, I would be devastated.

All the air was sucked out of the room as soon as I reached the kitchen. Ellie stood on a chair in front of the stove with a spatula in her hand, and Ember was right there with her, her hand over my daughters as they worked together to flip a pancake. As soon as she flipped it, Ellie bounced up and down with a squeal, "I did it!"

"You did!" Ember laughed, giving her a high-five.

They flipped a couple more, Ellie celebrating after each one. She bounced up and down, wiggled her butt, and then she danced in a little circle on her chair. "Daddy!" She squealed when she spotted me.

She jumped off her chair, knocking it over. I knelt down and caught her as she ran into me. "We're makin breakfast!"

"I can see that," I kissed her cheek, looking beyond her to the woman standing beside the stove. Ember's hair was pulled up into a messy bun on top of her head. She wore one of my t-shirts, her legs bare underneath. "You're still here."

Her teeth sunk into her bottom lip. She looked nervous, one arm hanging by her side while her other gripped it just above the elbow. Her chin dipped in a tiny nod, "I hope that's okay."

"I thought you left."

She shook her head. "Ellie came in early this morning and you looked so peaceful. I wanted to let you sleep."

"We made mouse pancakes! With chocolate chips!" Ellie wiggled out of my arms. "Come on!"

I couldn't take my eyes off her as I slowly rose to my feet. She got up early and took care of my daughter. Not only that, but the two of them made breakfast together. Emotion clogged my throat. "I…"

"I told you, I'm done running." She closed the space between us and took my hand. "I love you Wes, and I want to be with you." Slowly, her eyes lifted to mine, "If you'll have me."

"Do you mean it?" I managed.

She nodded and a second later I had her in my arms, right where she belonged. "I love you so much."

She hugged me back, her head resting against my chest, "I love you too."

"Daddy!" Ellie shouted.

We broke apart with a laugh, but I quickly took her hand, lacing my fingers with hers. I wasn't ready to stop touching her, afraid she would disappear.

We sat at the table where Ellie made up a plate for me complete with a mouse pancake, bacon, strawberries and whipped cream. "Today is the best day ever!" She shouted just before shoving a forkful of whipped cream covered pancake in her mouth.

"Yes, it really is," I grinned as I felt peace for the first time in seven years.

I grazed my fingertips lazily up and down Ember's back. She sighed against my sweat slicked skin, her warm breath sending a shiver through me. I would never get tired of this. "Sleepy?"

"Mmm hmm." She leaned up on her elbow and brought her hand to my cheek. "Wes?"

I took her hand and kissed her palm; her smile lit up the deepest caverns of my heart. "Yeah?"

"I have to go home tomorrow, but I don't want to leave you." She looked over her shoulder to my bedroom door. "Either of you."

I took a deep breath and blew it out slowly. "I know."

"What are we gonna do?"

I cupped the nape of her neck and pulled her lips to mine for a soft kiss. "You're gonna go home and start looking for a place for us to live. Something affordable with two bedrooms."

She pulled away, "But..." Her forehead creased in confusion.

"Frank called me a couple of weeks ago." I ran my finger from her smooth neck, down between her breasts. "One of his guys is leaving and he could use another mechanic."

"Frank? *My* Frank?"

I chuckled, "I didn't know you had a Frank."

She swatted at my chest, "You know what I mean."

I looked up into the depths of her cornflower blue eyes. "Yeah, your Frank." I slipped my hand into hers, lacing our fingers together before bringing her hand to my lips. "When I was up there trying to get you to talk to me, I looked for work. I figured if I wanted you, I had to be where you were."

"But..."

I brushed a strand of blonde hair away from her face. "I want to be wherever you are."

"Wes..."

"I love you, Ember, and I'm not letting you go this time."

She buried her face in my neck. "You didn't exactly let me go last time."

"No, but I like to think I'm older and wiser now."

"You really want to move?"

I thought a lot about what I would do if I ever got another chance, and the answer was easy. I'd go wherever she was. Nothing held me to Linford besides my aunt, and I could always visit. Besides, while this place held the memories of us falling in love, it also carried the memory of losing her and years of heartache. "A fresh start seems like a good idea."

"What about Ellie?"

I took a deep breath and blew it out slowly. I resumed stroking her back. "She'll be fine. She's young, and besides, the benefits outweigh the bad."

"How do you mean? What about her friends? School?"

I kissed the corner of her mouth, if I wasn't so in love with this woman, her care for my daughter would have me falling all over again. "For one, the school in Coyote Ridge is actually better than the school here. For two, she doesn't really have a lot of friends. You know how it is here, everyone knows everyone - and..." I moved to sit up, the sheets pooling at my waist.

"And what?"

"The moms aren't exactly fond of Kennedy, and that meant their kids weren't allowed to play with her."

"You're kidding."

I rubbed the back of my neck and laughed, though there was no humor in it. I'll never forget the first time I heard one of the moms tell her daughter that she needed to stay away from *trash*. I inhaled a shaky breath, "Jadon and Caleb are her only real friends, and I know she'll miss them, but..."

"But we're practically family so it's not like we'd be tearing them apart."

"Exactly."

Ember crawled onto my lap, her bare breasts pressing against me as she looped her arms around my neck. "You said benefits, as in plural, but I only heard one benefit. Are there more?"

I gripped her ass, moving her so she was straddling me. I brought my lips to hers in another soft kiss. "Just one more," I said against her mouth. "You."

"Me?"

I kissed her chin, her jaw, that spot behind her ear that drove her wild. "You're so good with her," I thought back to them in the kitchen, after breakfast. Ember showed her how to wash the dishes, then helped her get dressed and even braided her hair for her. Then they sat down and watched a nature documentary, and Ember never got tired of her endless questions. "Ellie needs a mother figure in her life, and I was hoping you'd be interested in the position."

She leaned back, her eyes searching mine. "I don't know, Wes. I'm not..."

"You're perfect." Before she could argue, I pressed my hips up into her, letting her feel just how much I wanted her. Her heart, her mind, her body.

Her head tipped back on a moan and I took the opportunity to flip us over. I settled between her legs, and when I slid inside, I knew I was home.

Epilogue

Coyote Ridge - One Month Later

Ember

The house was too big and too quiet, at least by the standards I was used to living. My apartment was only about 650 square feet, perfect for me and Mr. Jangles. But this place... 1,600 square feet of space. Quiet space.

Echoey space.

The thing about living in a small mountain town is that housing isn't easy to find, and when you do find it, you're gonna pay. Smaller was better, especially on a waitress' wages. Except small wasn't an option, not with Wes and Ellie coming to live with me.

It was pure dumb luck that got us this place. And our good luck was all due to the misfortune of another. The old man who owns the house fell and broke his hip and when his son insisted he move back east with him, he readily agreed, excited to be closer to his son and grandkids.

Brent called me as soon as the house was listed for sale.

One of my biggest fears about leaving Linford and returning home was Brent. It wouldn't have been so scary if it was just me, but I was basically bringing a "ready-made" family with me. A family I wouldn't trade for anything.

I shared my news and, as expected, Nancy squealed. Ned shook his head with a smile and told me he was happy for me. And Brent? He gave me a hug and asked if there was anything he could do to help. No animosity, no hard feelings. Sure, there was a spark of disappointment, but it was fleeting.

As much as I hated using him, I needed his help.

Brent was amazing. I don't know how he did it, but he convinced the old man and his son to rent the house to a young family for a reasonable price, instead of selling. When he explained who I was, they were more than happy to help. Apparently I had served his family at the diner the night they got to town to help pack him up; his kids liked the lady who brought them free ice cream.

It wasn't anything out of the ordinary for me. I always had a soft spot for kids, and these two looked like they could use a treat. Now I knew why.

The house was incredible. Three bedrooms, two bathrooms, and a stunning view. The only thing missing was the family.

Even though Wes and I spoke every day and facetimed every night, it still didn't feel real. What did feel real though was the ache in my heart every time we hung up and I woke up alone the next morning. I don't know how I went seven years without him.

Then there was Ellie. I kept looking for traces of Kennedy in her and I came up empty. I fell in love with her without even trying. And then Wes did things like explaining where her love for animals came from. She wanted to be like his princess; she wanted to be like *me*.

As soon as I got home from Linford, I collected my cat and sat outside, snapping photos of my regular visitors. Finding Deer in the yard behind my apartment wasn't at all uncommon.

Wes and I both agreed that Ellie was going to lose her mind when she got here. Not only because I have a cat - something she always wanted, but the wildlife was everywhere, even more so where we were going to be living, just outside of town with nothing but nature surrounding us on all sides. Deer, elk, coyotes, bobcats, and I even came face to face with a bear the first night I stayed here.

Today was the day.

I gave Mr. Jangles a scratch behind the ears then stepped out onto the wide porch and lifted my face to the sky. I closed my eyes against the sun that steamed through the giant trees. Wind whipped around me, carrying the scent of pine with it. It felt good to be home.

My ears perked at the sound of gravel crunching under tires. I didn't even have to look to know Wes and Ellie were coming up the long drive in their moving truck.

My heart thundered in my chest, drowning out the sound of rustling wind and chirping birds. I sucked in a deep breath and opened my eyes to my future. Wes jumped from the truck and jogged up the walk, pausing just inches in front of me. "Hi," he grinned.

"Hi."

His mouth crashed over mine as he wrapped his arms around me. I grabbed a handful of hair at the nape of his neck, pulling him closer, wanting, *needing*, more. The kiss was hot and frantic, and over far too soon. He leaned his forehead against mine as he fought for breath. "God, I missed you."

"I missed you too."

"How did we go this long without each other?" he whispered against my lips.

I grinned, pressing a small kiss to the corner of his mouth while my hands trailed down his hard chest, over his abs, and under the hem of his shirt, dipping just inside the waistband of his jeans. "I've been wondering the same thing."

His head tipped back with a groan, "I want you so bad, but first I've got to get this truck unloaded."

I reluctantly let him go and took a step back, tucking my hands into my pockets to keep from reaching for him. "Where's Ellie?"

"Sleeping." He rubbed the back of his neck, "I've been debating waking her up or leaving her in the truck."

"Why don't you bring her in the house and let her sleep. You can put her on the couch or in my bed."

"You sure?"

I arched an eyebrow at him. "Uh, yeah. If we're gonna do this, then I'm all in."

I still felt unsure about playing "mom" to Ellie, though Wes insisted it wasn't a big deal. I didn't have to be "mom," I could just be Ember, her dad's girlfriend.

We got everything moved in just before the sun dipped below the horizon. We were hot and tired, and to Ellie's delight, that meant ordering pizza for dinner. Wes and I curled up on my old couch while she danced circles around the living room and played with Mr. Jangles until she crashed and he had to carry her up to her room.

After a short makeout session, too exhausted to do anything more, Wes and I crashed too. I almost forgot how good it felt to fall asleep in his arms.

We fell into a bit of a routine over the next week. Ellie and I made breakfast before I went to work. While I was away, Wes and Ellie learned everything they could about the town. They visited the library, found both of the playgrounds, and even started taking nature walks. Every night I came home to a new "present." Leaves, rocks, and even a couple pinecones.

Sunday came too soon and with it a change I don't think any of us were ready for. Ellie sat at the table, twirling her fork through her spaghetti, but not actually bringing it to her mouth. I glanced at Wes, who was also watching her carefully.

"Are you ready to start school tomorrow?" I asked her. School started a little later here than it did in Linford. Jadon grumbled to her about his new teacher and how none of the other kids are as much fun as she is on their nightly facetime calls.

She shrugged, looking from me to her dad. "I guess."

"What's wrong?" Wes asked, dropping his fork, his face screwed up with worry. This is what I was afraid of.

"I miss Jadon," she sighed, putting her elbow on the table and rested her head against her hand while she continued twirling her noodles.

"I know you do, sweetheart," Wes ducked his head low to look into her eyes. "We talked about this though."

"I know, it's just…"

"Just what?" I asked.

"I don't know anyone. What if they don't like me?"

I set my fork down and reached for her hand. "Are you kidding me? You are the coolest kid I know. I just hope *they're* cool enough to be your friend."

She stopped twirling her fork and looked up at me. "You think so?"

I nodded, "Oh yeah. Plus," I leaned closer and dropped my voice to a loud whisper. "I know some of the kids from the diner. I'd say you've got a pretty good shot at making some new friends."

"Really?" Her grin melted my heart.

Wes reached under the table and gave my knee a squeeze, mouthing the words "Thank you," when I looked up.

After dinner Ellie helped with the dishes, I rinsed and she loaded the dishwasher. It was just another part of our developing routine. Except tonight, she needed music.

"What do you want to listen to?" I asked, taking out my phone, already pulling up Wes' old playlist - because of course I could never bring myself to delete it.

"How about some Carrie?"

I looked to Wes, who stood leaning his shoulder against the doorway watching us. "Carrie?" I mouthed, and he just grinned.

I looked back at the little girl who looked too much like me and arched an eyebrow. "Any particular song?"

She tapped her chin with her finger as if deep in thought. "How about my daddy's song?"

Again, I looked to Wes for help, his grin getting even bigger. Butterflies fluttered in my stomach. "How's that one go?"

She bobbed her head to the beat of the music only she could hear as she started to sing in her sweet little voice, "He's wrapped 'round her finger, she's the center of his whole world!"

My heart melted, knowing exactly what song it was and why it was her daddy's. It took less than two seconds to find it and press play. A moment later, Wes was behind me, his arms wrapped around my waist and his chin on my shoulder. "Maybe one day we can try for that boy," he suggested, nipping at my ear.

Heat swirled in my belly, God, I wanted that. A little boy with his dark locks and my blue eyes... We put Ellie to bed early, and not just because it was a school night.

The next morning, we all loaded up in Wes' truck and took the fifteen minute drive to Coyote Ridge Elementary. I helped Ellie out and made sure she had her backpack and lunchbox, nervous excitement flowing through me. Wes stood on the sidewalk, hand stretched out to her like I'm sure he's done a hundred times, but she wasn't looking at him.

I squatted down in front of her and adjusted the straps on her backpack. "Today is going to be the best day ever. You hold your head high when you walk through those doors and remember that you're the coolest girl I've ever met."

"What about Tatum?" she whispered.

I kissed her cheek as I stood up. "Even cooler than Tatum. But don't tell her I said that."

She grinned and finally took Wes' outstretched hand. "Will you come with me?"

I looked to Wes, not wanting to overstep, but willing to do whatever this girl needed me to. He nodded and I took her other hand. We swung her between us, her giggles catching the attention of the other kids nearby. They all looked curious, and I found myself breathing easier when a few even waved.

It was a short walk down the hall to her classroom, and this time I took a step back while Wes gave her the pep talk she needed. "Remember what we talked about?"

She nodded.

"This is your chance to make a whole new group of friends, all you have to do is be yourself."

"Okay," she said, her voice small once again.

Her teacher met us in the hallway and squatted down beside Wes and held out her hand to Ellie. "Hi, I'm Mrs. Macy. What's your name?"

"Ellie."

Mrs. Macy cocked her head to the side, as though she were thinking. "That's a really pretty name, but I'm not sure I have an Ellie in my class..." Then she tapped her chin, "I do have an Eleanor in my class though."

Ellie's face lit up and she raised her hand. "That's me! I'm Eleanor!"

"It's very nice to meet you," she held out her hand. "You like to be called Ellie?"

Ellie took her hand and nodded excitedly. Mrs. Macy stood up, but kept her focus on Ellie. I heard parents talk about her, and not one of them had anything bad to say. She was loved, and if this is how she treated all her students, I could see why.

"Is this your mom and dad?"

"Yup!" Ellie grinned with a bounce in her step. She was back to her usual energetic self.

I opened my mouth, ready to correct her when Wes placed his hand on my shoulder and gave me a subtle shake of his head.

"Tell them you'll see them soon," Mrs. Macy said, already leading her into the classroom.

"Bye! See you soon!" Ellie waved over her shoulder.

I turned on Wes as soon as we were in his truck. "Why didn't you say something?"

He started the engine, clearly not taking this as seriously as I was. "What's there to say?"

"I'm not her mom, Wes! I don't want to lie!"

He pulled away from the school, a huge grin on his face. "Ellie asked me a while ago if you could be her mom. I thought I had time to talk to you about it, but..."

"She wants me to be her mom?"

He nodded without looking away from the road.

"What about Kennedy?"

"What about her? She was never a mom to Ellie. Part of me wonders if that had anything to do with the fact that Ellie looks more like you than her."

"Yeah, but..." I slumped down in my seat and leaned my head against the window. "Isn't this gonna confuse her?"

"How?" He pulled to a stop at a red light and gave me his full attention. "She sees Tatum and Brandon with Jadon and Caleb. They're a family with a mom and a dad."

I opened my mouth to argue and nothing came out. As much as I wanted to argue, I also wanted to be her mom. I *really* wanted to be her mom, and for her to be my Eleanor, the baby that was supposed to be his and mine, but is actually only his, and then not even his... I shook my head, "This is such a mess."

We made the rest of the drive in silence, and when he parked outside of our home, I got out, heading straight for the house.

"Ember, wait!"

I made it to the door before I stopped and turned around. I wasn't mad, I was just... confused?

Wes raked his hands through his hair, then took my hand as though he needed something to hold onto. He swallowed thickly, his Adam's apple bobbing with the motion. "If you don't want this, I need to know."

"I... Wes, come on."

"No, Em. I need to know. Do you want this? Her? Me? Us? Because we're a package deal, and I can't..."

I stared up into his beautiful face, his forehead creased with worry. I brushed my fingers over the lines, down his cheek and across the stubble of his jaw. "That's never been a question," I whispered, looking up into the smoky depths of those gunmetal blue eyes. "I want this. I want you."

He held my hand against his cheek. "Then marry me, Ember." He kissed my palm then put my hand back on his cheek. "Marry me and be her mom for real."

"Wes," I whispered, unable to form any other words.

"I wasn't planning on doing it like this. Ellie and I had a plan, but..." He pulled away and rubbed the back of his neck like he was nervous. He took both of my hands and looked into my eyes, "Without you, I was stumbling through the dark with nothing but a match to see by. I had given up hope of ever seeing the sun again, and then there you were. Your name may mean that your light is dim and burning low, but all it takes is one spark, and an Ember can become a raging fire. You're the fire that burns in my soul. I love you. I've always loved you."

His words knocked the air from my lungs, never had I heard such a beautiful declaration, not even in my favorite country songs. "I love you, Wes."

"Is that a yes?"

I nodded, "Yes."

Wes

Ellie had a grin on her face all through dinner. She knew what was coming, we'd been planning it for a while - ever since I told her we were moving to Colorado with Ember. The first thing out of her mouth was "Can she be my mom now?" I asked her if that's what she wanted, and she nodded emphatically.

That day we took a special trip to Wickett. I already had the ring, I'd had it for seven years, since before everything fell apart. We just needed a little something "extra."

When Ellie didn't look like she could be still a moment longer, I gave her a nod. She hopped up from her chair and came to stand beside me. Ember set her fork down and eyed us suspiciously.

"Now can we do it?" Ellie asked, her whisper not quiet at all.

"Yeah."

I pulled a black velvet box out of my pocket and handed it to my daughter. She cleared her throat and held the box out on her palm. "Ember?" she glanced at me nervously. I gave her an encouraging smile and nod. "Do you wanna be my mom?"

Ember's hands went to her heart, a soft smile on her face. "I would really love that," she nodded, holding out her arms for a hug.

Ellie handed her the box and climbed onto her lap. "You can open it," she said, bouncing with excitement.

Ember looked to me for permission and I nodded. She carefully opened it, her hand going straight to her mouth, tears forming instantly. She picked up the little charm that had just three letters on it. MOM.

"Do you like it?" Ellie asked. "I picked it out myself."

Ember nodded and when she looked up to me, her eyes held a mixture of elation and sadness. "Ellie, isn't there something else?" I prompted.

"Oh, yeah!" She hopped up, holding her hands out to me, and I passed her the little velvet pouch. She climbed back on Ember's lap and gave it to her.

Ember looked from Ellie, to me, and back before pulling the little bag open and emptying it onto her hand. "Wes?" She shook her head like she didn't understand what she was seeing. "But... how? I thought I lost it?"

The bracelet that I bought her all those years ago sat in the palm of her hand, just waiting for its newest charm. "I found it in your old room."

"And you held onto it?"

"I did."

She handed the bracelet to Ellie, "Will you hold this for me?" Ellie did as she asked, while Ember clipped her new charm to the bracelet, then secured it to her wrist. "Thank you, sweet girl." She hugged her tight and kissed her head.

She was busy admiring her bracelet when I slipped onto one knee in front of her. I pulled the ring out of my pocket. It wasn't expensive. It wasn't fancy. It was so simple that when I bought it, I didn't even get a velvet box.

"Ember?" The second our eyes met, her breath hitched. "I'll never forget the day we met. The moment our fingers first touched, I knew you were different, special. I knew I had to have you. When you said yes to that first date, I was on cloud nine, I didn't know anything could top that. But then we kissed and it was game over for me. No one has ever made me feel the way you do. I'm my best self when I'm with you." I cleared my throat and held the ring up between my thumb and forefinger. "I love you so much. Would you do me the honor of being my wife?"

"And my mommy?" Ellie added.

Ember nodded, tears streaming down her face. She kissed the top of Ellie's head and set her on the floor, and then her arms were around my neck, her lips pressed against mine.

I kissed her deep and long, until Ellie had had enough, and pushed her way in between us until we were an Ellie sandwich. "Don't forget about me!" She exclaimed.

A laugh burst from my chest, so happy and light. This was it; this is what my life was supposed to be like, with my two best girls. We may have taken a detour along the way, but ultimately we ended up exactly where we were meant to be.

Acknowledgements

Thank you so much for taking the time to read this book. I truly hope you enjoyed Ember and Wes' story as much as I enjoyed writing it.

This story came to me one afternoon, driving down Highway 36 into Boulder from Estes Park, on my way to see the first of Sam and Colby's "The Conjuring" videos in the theater. If you've ever made that drive, you know that it's a long one, down a mountain canyon, then through a valley surrounded by open space. It leaves the mind with no option but to wander, and that seems to be what my mind does best.

I was in love with Ember and Wes from the beginning, and as the story began to take shape, I knew I was going to break some hearts – including my own.

I want to thank everyone who has supported me, especially my daughter who has suffered me talking about my fictional "friends" to no end, and my son who has no problem reminding me what the real world looks like.

And finally, if you'd like to review Tarnished Memories, that would be greatly appreciated!

About the author

What happens when your inner child "forgets" to choose a career? Suddenly, the princess, doctor, lawyer, and mechanic all come looking for their piece. Without a cloning machine, what's a girl to do?

Write.

As a writer, I live vicariously through the characters I create and the stories they tell. Every day is an adventure to be had, and if I can't do it myself, I'm going to put my daydreams to work.